B LOOD
IN
THE SAND
ROBIN SAXON
AND ALEX KIDWELL

Dreamspinner Press

Published by
Dreamspinner Press
382 NE 191st Street #88329
Miami, FL 33179-3899, USA
http://www.dreamspinnerpress.com/

Blood in the Sand

Cover Art by Anne Cain   annecain.art@gmail.com
Cover Design by Mara McKennen

ISBN: 978-1-61372-574-0

Printed in the United States of America
First Edition
June 2012

eBook edition available
eBook ISBN: 978-1-61372-575-7

For my beloved R.
Anywhere I go you go, my dear;
and whatever is done by only me is your doing, my darling.
You are the wonder that's keeping the stars apart.
I carry your heart with me. I carry it in my heart.
A.

To Alex. And to Zach.
R.

PROLOGUE

Redford

"How's that feel?"

Redford touched the earpiece that Jed had put on him, making sure it was secure. "It's good," he confirmed. "No static this time. Did you upgrade?"

Jed had been talking about his new "toys" for the last week. Redford knew this, and he knew that Jed had bought new earpieces, but he asked nonetheless. Jed enjoyed any chance to enthusiastically show off the equipment he procured; Redford just liked listening to him talk.

Standing next to Redford, dressed entirely in black, Jed grinned at him. "Yep. Got them a few days ago. My contact sold me a few models up on the receivers. Cost a couple thousand more, but worth it." He was wearing a matching earpiece, which he carefully tucked away under the ski mask, tugging the thick knit cover down over his face. "Remember the plan?"

Redford nodded. He pulled a carefully folded blueprint out of his pocket, giving it a final glance before handing it over to Jed. "You need to follow the yellow line," he reminded. "It's the quickest and the safest."

"Following the yellow brick road, huh, Fido?" Jed smirked, studying the map briefly.

"No, it's a line marked in yellow highlighter. There's no brick flooring in the house." Redford frowned in confusion. "Actually, there's no yellow brick roads anywhere near here. What—"

"It's a movie reference, darlin'," Jed cut in gently, reaching out with a gloved hand to brush some of Redford's hair from his forehead. There was a fond smile touching the corners of his eyes, the only part of him visible under the mask. "We'll watch it tomorrow."

Redford still didn't get it, but he accepted the explanation. Jed made a lot of movie references, and some of them were very strange. "Okay. Well,

1

the yellow line is the one I've marked out. It goes through the back door, through some of the back hallways, and into the room where Mr. Mandic keeps the paintings. I made sure to avoid the rooms where the household staff will be at this time of night."

A smirk practically radiated from Jed, a quick laugh buried into a snort. Redford didn't even have to ask what he was laughing about. For some reason, Jed found Mandic's name to be quite funny. He also had expressed, over and over, his desire to make some reference to the butler doing it. Jed's sense of humor was... strange, sometimes. Redford did enjoy hearing him laugh, though.

"Got it, Toto." Jed nodded, tucking yet another gun away, this one hidden in his shoulder holster. "Yellow line all the way to the wizard." One hand was held up before Redford could form the question. "I know, I know. There's not actually a wizard. Jesus, sweetheart, we gotta get you some Garland, stat."

Redford moved closer to the gate they were standing next to. He only gave Jed a brief, mystified glance at his further references. Much more important was handing Jed a small leather case, unfolding it for him. "Lock picks," he prompted.

Deftly, Jed chose the medium-sized one and went to work, tapping away, twisting his wrist just so. In some of their quiet nights together, over pizza or whatever Redford had cooked for the evening, Jed would sit sprawled out in his lap and show him how to pick locks. It had looked so simple when Jed did it: tiny, graceful movements of his fingers coaxing the pins to release. Except when Redford had tried it, he hadn't been able to get the practice lock to cooperate at all. It seemed to rely on intuition— the kind he didn't have. Jed insisted, though, that he had the touch. So, with unwavering faith and a buoyant determination, Jed would bring out those practice locks, easy ones at first, and use his own hands to guide Redford's. The first time he'd managed to make one click open, Jed had grinned like it was his triumph too.

"Fucking shit in a goddamn motherfucking hole." Apparently, tonight was not going to be as easy as those lessons. Jed threw down the bent pick in a fit of pique before looking up at Redford, eyes sheepish.

Redford gave a sigh. "I'll put a new one on the list. It'll make us a little over budget."

"It's not my fault these new boots weren't on sale," Jed protested. "How else was I supposed to match tonight?"

2

Redford snorted quietly, pulling Jed's "backup plan" box out of his duffel bag. "I'll expense the broken one. But you get to explain to our customer why you needed it."

"Done." Gleefully, Jed took the box, handling it carefully, cradling it like a fussy newborn as he pulled out the low-grade explosives he'd made earlier. "This is much more fun, anyway." Pressing the compound to the hinges of the gate, Jed set the timer and grabbed Redford's elbow. They jogged away, Jed throwing them to the ground with urgency, plastering himself over Redford's body. Jed's breath was ragged on Redford's neck, the press of him heavy and solid. Redford braced himself, waiting for the fire and heat of the explosion, wishing that Jed hadn't felt the need to resort to such unsubtle methods.

Jed loved his explosions. He took any chance he could to blow something up, preferably as violently as possible. Many, many times Redford had witnessed the fire and shockwave of a well-constructed explosive. Redford still got nervous every time, and now he held his breath, waiting.

The compound detonated with a very quiet *pop*. The gate swung open, barely creaking at the slow movement.

"Oh. That was anticlimactic," Redford remarked.

"What?" Jed was grinning, Redford could feel it, and there was a very lewd grinding of his hips against Redford's ass. "Like I was going to miss an opportunity to grope you." Jumping up, Jed offered his hand to Redford, laughing behind the mask as he helped Redford up. Having his face covered didn't stop him from leaning in for a kiss, snorting at his mistake when the material got in the way. "Later," he demanded, backpedaling to the gate, still facing Redford. "I'm going to want that when I get back!"

Redford watched him go for a moment and then muttered into the earpiece, "You are so overdramatic. Good luck." He dusted off his pants and took a matching blueprint out of his pocket, opening it up. He rested his fingertip on the yellow line, following where Jed would be at that moment.

"Dorothy to Toto. Come in Toto." Jed's voice crackled in his ear, and Redford thought he could almost make out a dark figure against the faint, reflective moonlight on the windows of the house, approaching the back doorway.

3

The code names changed every time. At least this time it wasn't Sir Sexybutt. Jed was terrible at coming up with names. Redford smiled a little and answered, "Toto here. Are you just testing to see if I'd answer, or do you need something?"

Jed laughed into the mic, but he was otherwise silent. He must be approaching the door. Redford then heard a quiet click, near-silent footsteps—a benefit of the wolf side of him, he supposed. The average person probably couldn't have picked that up.

Waiting, unseen in the pitch-black shadows the gateway to the mansion created, Redford kept studying the blueprints he held, a map of the huge place, belonging to one Mr. Mandic. Their client, Leonard O'Malley, was paying them to break in and retrieve three highly valued paintings that Mr. Mandic had. Leonard insisted that the man had stolen them for a very unfair price at an auction he'd failed to be there to manage.

Redford thought Leonard shouldn't complain about something that was his own fault, but it was a job—one that he certainly hadn't ever imagined himself being involved in. Jed's line of work was entirely mercenary, though Redford would admit there was a certain thrill to it and a satisfaction that came from planning it just right. It was the kind of rush he would have never been able to experience in his old life.

Over the mic, he heard Jed mutter to himself. More footsteps, a door closing, a rustle that sounded like material being brushed aside. "Just the paintings, Jed," Redford warned lowly.

Jed grunted something that sounded like "first edition," but there was a reluctant sigh and the sound of leather scraping back into place. Being inside the mansion of a man who was reputed to be an avid collector was obviously proving a temptation. Redford just hoped Jed could resist. Whatever dubious morals allowed for the "reacquisition" of the paintings probably did not extend to rare books. Even Redford knew that having the police come after them for theft would not be a good outcome of this job.

He continued listening as Jed made his way through the mansion. Occasionally Redford could hear some quiet cursing, some grumbling, not loud enough for even him to make out the words. Following the yellow line on his own map, he could pinpoint when Jed had reached the paintings. The irritated growl gave it away too. There must be extra security on them.

Remaining silent so that he didn't distract Jed, Redford leaned against the gateway, looking up at the stars again. They were bright this far out in the country, and he could make out the occasional constellation. Around him were the scents of trees and grass, of raccoons and mice. The mansion itself was a miasma of overly expensive food and perfume that just smelled like harsh chemicals to his nose. It was almost relaxing here. Or it would be, if he wasn't busy being a little nervous about the possibility of Jed being caught.

Thankfully, that didn't seem fated to happen. Redford could smell him before he saw him, even wolf-sharpened eyes failing to pick out Jed's camouflaged form against the dark grass until he was closer. There was the creak of the gate, and then Jed was next to him, shoving the tubes, canvases rolled up inside, into Redford's hands and urging him toward the car.

"Is this like the explosion?" Redford asked, eyebrows hitching upward. "Because you pretty much already played that—"

A beautifully embossed leather book was waved in front of Redford's nose. A book Jed most certainly had not had before he went into the mansion. Redford sighed heavily and started jogging after Jed toward the car. What was it Jed always said?

At least life isn't boring when you're with me!

CHAPTER
1

Redford

"AND how does that make you feel?"

Redford stared upward, contemplating the question. The ceiling had exactly eighteen tiles, a pockmarked white plaster that wasn't all that interesting to look at. He wondered if it had been deliberately made that way to discourage idle study, to instead direct the room's inhabitants to concentrate on the more pressing matters. There certainly was something of greater importance he should be paying attention to. Unfortunately, it wasn't anything to do with interior decorating.

"It's...." Redford took a bracing breath. The ceiling wasn't offering any answers—that was the job of the man sitting on the couch opposite. Any hopeful looks sent his way, though, were met with an unerringly calm expression. Dr. Max Alona had come highly recommended by David. *Good at your sort of thing* was the exact phrase he'd used. Though Jed hadn't been all that thrilled, in the end, it couldn't *hurt* to talk to someone. "It makes me feel upset."

Max nodded, and Redford craned his neck to try to read what Max was writing down in his notepad. He had no such luck, unfortunately. "Definitely upset," Redford continued. "It just shouldn't be that way. There's an order to things. And when that order is broken, I get really nervous. Is that stupid?"

"It's not stupid to be nervous over what you perceive as chaos, Redford," Max said gently. "But perhaps we should go back to why you're here."

"But Jed really doesn't put things away," Redford protested, shifting nervously. "Especially not his clothes. Or the towel. He just leaves everything on the floor after he uses them. It makes the bedroom very difficult to walk through, and the towel starts to smell." The doctor—the *headshrinker*, Jed called him, although Redford thought Max's head was reasonably well proportioned—simply fixed him with a bland, expectant look.

Apparently he should talk about something other than Jed's tendency to leave piles of clothes and a wet towel lying around. Redford rubbed a hand over his face and avoided Max's gaze, fixing his own on the floor. Like the ceiling, the floor was also rather boring to look at. He had come here for a reason, but now that he was sitting in this office and being "shrunk," as Jed put it, he was beginning to feel not so great about this decision. Like he was squirming under a giant microscope with everyone just waiting to find his flaws.

Like he really might be crazy.

"David mentioned you were having dreams?" Max prompted, crossing his legs and leaning back. The doctor was dressed as bland as his office, tan slacks perfectly pressed, a navy sweater that looked like it should be on some department-store mannequin. But he had a friendly face, completely nonjudgmental, and he nodded encouragingly at Redford. The tip of his pen rested against his notepad as he asked, "When did they begin?"

"Um." Redford glanced up at the doctor, a quick look, then away again, his eyes settling instead on the brightly colored parrot perched on a corner of Max's desk. Max had introduced the parrot as Rufus. It stared back at him with black eyes, unconcerned about his silly personal issues. He thought it was nice that Max didn't keep the parrot in a cage, even if it was a bit odd that he took it to work with him. "The dreams aren't— they're not why I'm here. Really. I mean I've *had* dreams, but they're not as important as… the other things."

Damn it, why had he thought this would be a good idea? Now that he'd come here and sat on the couch, he couldn't think of a single thing to say that wouldn't sound absolutely crazy. The kind of crazy that would get him locked up and sedated for the rest of his life.

"I'm hearing voices," Redford ended up blurting out. Saying the words aloud was not the relief he'd thought it might be. A sick, twisting fear churned in his stomach instead.

For a beat, there was only silence. Max's pen scratched lightly across the paper before he set the notepad aside with a sigh. It certainly wasn't the look of disgust that Redford had been expecting. He took off his

7

glasses and rubbed his eyes, smiling faintly when the parrot hopped over and nudged its bright red head against his fingers. "Okay," Max finally said, fixing pale-blue eyes on Redford. "Now we're getting somewhere. Tell me about the voices."

THE sky was very blue outside. Redford squinted as he looked up at it, his eyes still adjusting from the low light of the psychiatrist's office. He felt wrung out, exhausted—like he'd just taken his mind, shaken it upside down, and held out all the contents for Dr. Alona to examine. But for all of that, he did feel better. Calmer, somewhat. Nothing had been solved, but perhaps it was a start.

Not that the loud shriek of tires and the engine revving helped his almost-Zen state. Shielding his eyes against the sun with his hand, Redford looked out across the parking lot to the road beyond. A motorcycle tore through a red light amidst honks of horns and the cursing of angry drivers. The figure on the bike cheerily flipped off his fans before coming to a screeching halt in front of Redford.

"I'm not late!" Tugging off the helmet, a grin flashing infectiously as his face was revealed, Jed pointed a finger at Redford. "I am not late. You, mister, are early. Right?" Rolling up the sleeve of his leather coat, he peered down at his wrist, groaning theatrically. "Shit. I'm late. I'm so sorry, babe. Knievel wanted to come, and you know how she primps."

Under the grins and the teasing, Jed's eyes were worried. The man didn't trust psychiatrists, apparently, having been through his share after his discharge from the military. David had insisted that Max Alona was the best. Jed had threatened to rip David a new one if that didn't prove to be true, though Redford had missed the part of the conversation where Jed described exactly *what* would be torn. He was still wondering about it— how did one rip a new *anything*?

"You're a little late, but it's okay." Redford smiled, leaning forward to press a light kiss to the corner of Jed's lips. "The doctor was... helpful. I think."

A faint frown flickered across Jed's face, but he hooked Redford in, one hand buried in the hair at the nape of Redford's neck. This kiss wasn't light, and it definitely wasn't appropriate for a public street. But at the end of it, when they pulled away, the tiniest fraction of that pinched concern had faded from Jed's eyes. "So maybe you won't wake up snarling at me or go chasing shiny things?" he teased, holding out a second helmet for Redford. "I gotta tell you, I don't mind the growling one bit. It's the fear I have that you're gonna piddle in the corner next time you feel like marking territory."

"I don't—no. I'm not going to do that." Redford frowned, though he was more embarrassed than annoyed at the teasing.

Tapping the top of a modified hard-plastic carrier on the back of the box, Jed smirked. "Ready, 'Nievel?" There was a happy chirping meow in response, and Redford could see Knievel curled up tight, staring out at him with luminescent hazel eyes. Jed had insisted that the cat loved going for rides, and it had been with great pride that he'd brought home a cat carrier designed to fit on the back of his bike. It had slats wide enough for Knievel to see through, and Redford had to admit, she did seem to enjoy her outings. Though it probably had more to do with Jed liking to take the cat out than anything else, as much as he'd protest otherwise.

It was a strange sight. Jed, a man's man, decked out in leather that was hiding half a dozen weapons, acting like an old cat lady. Jed was an odd dichotomy of a man sometimes. "How about you, darlin'?" Jed drawled, swinging his leg over the seat and holding out a hand for Redford. "You ready to go?"

The smile came back to Redford's lips again as he grasped Jed's hand, taking a seat behind him on the motorcycle. He put his helmet on, wrapped his arms around Jed's waist, getting himself secure. Riding on the motorcycle no longer terrified him, probably because he had been rigorously trained in getting used to Jed's way of driving. Jed seemed to feel the roads were a war zone, and every single car was an enemy that must be overtaken, swerved around, or cursed at. Sometimes all three at once.

"Ready," Redford confirmed. He reached out and smoothed a hand over Knievel's carrier, making sure she was secure too. Before Jed revved the engine back to life, Redford lifted his visor briefly to press his lips to the back of Jed's neck. It was a silly routine, perhaps, started on a whim. Now Redford couldn't imagine going anywhere without the little touch. He couldn't see Jed smile, but he could feel it in the relaxing of the muscles in his shoulders, the way the worried burnt-wood edges of his scent lessened. The engine roared, and they took off toward home.

A voice in the back of his head rustled and whispered, *No Wolf-Journey-Jed happy?*

Redford gritted his teeth and tried to ignore it, but he couldn't help muttering into the back of Jed's jacket, "Don't call him Journey." Thankfully for his perceived sanity, the wind rushing past their ears meant Jed didn't hear that. He probably would have agreed, however. "Journey Walker" was, apparently, a hippie name and not suitable for a man who thought fried bologna sandwiches were a national treasure and explosions were a perfectly acceptable way to end a dispute. Redford sometimes wondered what kind of parents would give a name like that, or if Jed's hatred of it came from more than aesthetics. Conversations like that weren't really Jed's strong point. Redford wasn't even sure if Jed's parents were alive, dead, or simply gone.

Four months ago, he and Jed had stumbled their way home from the hospital after killing Filtiarn, the Lord of Wolves, the twisted man that had tried to take Redford and make him into something new. A real wolf, Fil had said, one able to change at will, not just a half-breed werewolf. He had injected Redford with his blood, but the ritual had not been finished. Though Redford had soon discovered he could then shift to wolf at any time, he hadn't thought much about any further consequences of that failed ritual.

Then, on the next full moon, the voices had started.

They'd been whispers at first, things that Redford ignored, thinking they were just his own mind taking unexpected turns in thought. But they'd grown stronger. Then he'd started waking up not quite himself. Yesterday morning, barely squinting through that hazy, half-asleep state, he had bolted out of bed and sprinted through the door to chase down a squirrel he had seen from the window. Jed had not been happy, since half of the bedsheets had still been tangled up in Redford's legs and, consequently, were dragged down the hall and out into the street. Redford had been even less thrilled about his excursion once he had come to his senses, half-dressed and finding himself barking up a tree on a street corner. Their neighbors had not reacted positively.

One of the voices—the squirrel-chasing one—seemed mostly benign. It happily called Jed its own odd nickname and was content to get distracted by moving objects. The other was less so. The other was the reason Redford had been waking up snarling, had felt a flash of much more than jealousy when men had gotten too close to Jed. It wasn't mere *jealousy* that had Redford biting back the urge to rip out throats.

Dr. Alona had told him that he thought the voices were a manifestation of the wolf side of him. He'd reassured Redford that he was not going crazy, but it sure felt like it. He still had no clue what to *do* about it, how to make them stop.

"You still in there, sweetheart?"

Redford blinked, dragging himself out of his thoughts to find Jed lightly tapping on the side of his helmet, worry scrunching up the corners of his eyes, a hopeful little smile attempting to be a smirk tugging up his lips. "Earth to Fido. We gonna sit here all day?" They were parked on the street in front of the apartment building, Jed twisted around to half face Redford, his helmet already tucked under his arm.

Tugging his helmet off, Redford rubbed a hand over his eyes, trying to get himself back to reality. Talking with Dr. Alona had just made him worry *more*, not less. It wasn't exactly the result that Redford had been hoping for.

"Sorry. My head was in the clouds," Redford offered apologetically. He got up off the bike and handed his helmet to Jed, freeing up his hands to take Knievel's carrier. She glowered at him, gifting him with an annoyed-sounding meow. "I know. I'm sorry, ride's over." Redford gave Jed an amused glance as he picked the carrier up, being careful not to jostle the cat too much.

A clank sounded from within the carrier. Redford frowned in confusion, holding it up to peer through the slats. "Jed, you can't keep a knife in the cat carrier," he exclaimed, appalled.

"Says you," Jed returned easily. The helmets were stowed, and Jed stole the carrier away from Redford with a kiss to his cheek, his arm wrapping around Redford's waist as they walked upstairs. "Knievel likes a little security, don't you, baby? Besides, it's in a buttoned sheath, all nice and childproof."

The cat's purring seemed loud enough to validate that statement. Redford just huffed quietly, amused despite himself. "So Knievel likes security, but the knife is sheathed? She has paws, Jed. Not thumbs."

"You'd better watch out, Fido." Jed was grinning at him devilishly, eyebrows waggling as he unlocked the door to the apartment. "You'll hurt her feelings, insulting her capabilities like that. And I will not be

11

responsible when she shivs you." Handing the carrier back, Jed slipped the gun out from the small of his back, quickly and handily doing a sweep of the place before he nodded for Redford to come in. No matter what was going on, how long they'd been gone, or the fact that he had more locks than door, Jed always checked the place. Redford had to wonder when that habit had started—or if Jed would ever feel safe enough to just walk into his home like a normal person.

Shaking herself off as she was released from the carrier, Knievel wound her way around both of their legs before hopping onto the counter and meowing plaintively. Despite the full food bowl, it was clear the cat was starving to death, right that very minute, and the only way to fix it was to have some of the real meat she knew they kept in the fridge. Then again, Jed was giving Redford the same look, so perhaps it was catching.

"You feed your demanding cat. I want to go collapse on the couch for a bit." Redford sighed, making his way over to the couch. It was hard to breathe as he flopped face-first into the cushions, but the darkness it provided for his vision was somewhat relaxing. "I'll cook in a while," he continued, voice muffled into the couch cushion.

There was the distinct noise of the fridge opening and closing, of Jed moving around in the kitchen. A can was opened, there was the rustle of water, and then a cool rag was pressed to the back of Redford's neck. "How about we order in," Jed suggested quietly, running his free hand through Redford's hair. "And you just relax. I gave her royal highness some tuna, so she's living the good life. Maybe tonight you don't worry about us, okay?"

"I always worry about you," Redford mumbled. The cool cloth was doing wonders for the tension headache that had been starting to creep up the back of his neck. He was thinking too hard, he knew that was the problem, but he couldn't seem to stop doing it. "Dr. Alona says I might not be crazy after all."

A loud snort sounded, and Redford sensed Jed settling in, sitting on the floor next to the couch. His fingertips were making light circles against Redford's scalp, a bit awkwardly, as if Jed was making it all up as they went along. "'Course you're not crazy," he said stubbornly, voice hard, almost like he could convey through tone that if Jed Walker said so, then it must be true. "It's that bastard, King Psychopants McFurlord and whatever he shot into you." A low growl then, Jed's whole body tightening. "Fucker. If I could kill him again, I would."

Redford smiled against the couch cushions. He rolled onto his side and, finding that not comfortable either, shifted to sit cross-legged. "King Psychopants McFurlord? I thought his name was Filtiarn," he said lightly.

Jed had never, not once, thought he was crazy. About this, at least. Yes, okay, Jed might have thought a crazy ward was warranted when Redford had first told him about being a werewolf, but then Jed had seen the evidence with his own eyes. Even before, though, he hadn't thrown Redford out, hadn't done anything but bullheadedly stick by Redford, no matter what. That hadn't changed with the emergence of the voices and Redford's sudden proclivity for acting a little weird at times.

Redford was more grateful than words could convey. It meant everything to him that Jed was willing to stay around and be with him, even if Redford didn't think he was exactly the picture of sanity right now.

"I'll have to thank David for the recommendation," Redford added. He moved a hand to Jed's shoulder, fingers digging lightly into the muscles there. "How was your day?"

Jed snorted lightly, but his whole body shifted back into Redford's hands. "I didn't shoot anyone," he offered with a smirk, tipping his head back to look up at Redford. "And I missed you. So all in all, I'm glad it's over."

This would be the right moment to say the rest of it. To talk about the session, his fears about what the failed ritual had done to him. Or he could lean forward and catch that smirk with a kiss, smiling himself at the way Jed just melted back into him. This was better, just like this, to forget that there were rooms with pockmarked white ceilings where Redford had talked about voices in his head he didn't understand. It was easier not to stutter and stammer his way through a hesitant explanation, to remind Jed that Redford might just be too broken to fix.

"No shooting people? Sounds like an uneventful day," Redford murmured.

"You have no idea." Jed's lips trailed down Redford's jaw, teeth catching gently at his throat. "I almost died of boredom. It was a sorry sight to see."

Redford laughed quietly and sank down to sit on the floor next to Jed, wrapping an arm about his back. He leaned his cheek against Jed's shoulder, letting his eyes fall closed as he relaxed further. It was difficult to get the psychiatrist visit out of his mind, but it was easier with Jed by his side—Jed was a very good distraction.

His life before Jed had been silent and solitary. Redford had lived with one foot permanently in the basement cage where he changed into a mindless, violent creature every full moon, his entire life revolving around it. He'd thought of nothing else, *lived* nothing else. Now his days were full of warm light and Jed's rumbling voice, windows where he could see the world passing by, and the kind of companionship he'd never dared to hope he would have. Jed had saved him, in more ways than one.

"So, Chinese?" he asked, nudging his chin against Jed's shoulder. "We should order in. Where's the phone?"

"Oh, no, baby." Jed smirked, kissing the top of his head and wiggling a bit to shimmy his cell phone out of his back pocket. He really did have pants that were tighter than strictly normal. Redford wondered sometimes if that was helpful to him in his work, but he wouldn't deny that he liked the sight that Jed presented. "I'm taking care of you tonight, remember? Just you watch me work my magic."

Unsurprisingly, Jed had all of his favorite carryout places on speed dial. He flipped through to the right number and dialed, shifting a little so he could loop his arm around Redford in return. Jed's fingers played up under Redford's shirt, painting circles against the warm skin at the small of his back, and he grinned into the phone. "Hey, Jimmy. It's your favorite customer. You guys ready for this? I'm starving." Six main dishes and an assortment of sides an entire army might find difficult finishing off later, and Jed tossed the phone aside and turned so he could get both arms around Redford, hauling him up into Jed's lap. "Thirty minutes or less. So beats cooking."

Gladly settling in on Jed's legs, Redford pressed his forehead to Jed's and placed a light kiss on the bridge of his nose. "Sounds good," he murmured. "No dishes either." Jed was terrible at doing dishes, as well as doing laundry. Or cleaning of any sort. But that was another way that Redford thought they fit, right then—Redford quite liked cleaning. Even if their one towel did sometimes get a bit musty on the floor. "Does that mean in thirty minutes I'm going to have to move?"

"Not if I have anything to say about it." Jed had been thoroughly absorbed in a case for the past week, spending several sleepless nights poring over his maps, talking to contacts on the phone, hauling home mysterious crates filled with weapons, the kind that Redford had only seen in the explosion-filled action movies that Jed was overly fond of. It felt like it had been a very long time since they'd just sat together without Jed looking at a map over his shoulder or peppering the conversation with idle musings about how much dynamite it would take to blow up a thirty-story building.

Jed was incredibly dedicated to his work. At first, what had seemed like a complete mystery to Redford was now something he was beginning to understand. Jed had been teaching him things: how to use a gun properly, how to track people through paperwork, how to read maps. Redford had, very recently, even taken over the administrative duties. Jed, it turned out, was absolutely useless when it came to tracking profits and expenses. He just kept talking about making enough to take a fishing vacation, as if that was the benchmark for how much he should charge. The first case Redford had helped with, Jed had been thrilled at the thought of charging the customer for all the C4 he'd ordered. And had promptly doubled the order. They were still working out the kinks.

They worked in insurance fraud, item recovery, with the occasional kidnapping recovery thrown in if Jed felt like the pay was enough. Redford wasn't too happy that Jed still killed people for money—there were some who deserved it, in his mind, others that definitely did not, but he hadn't brought that topic of discussion up with Jed yet.

Maybe someday he would. When he wasn't still half-scared that raising his opinion to Jed, or to *anybody*, would make them leave him.

"So, I finished that job today," Jed brought up casually. He'd been absorbed in trailing fingertips along Redford's shoulder, down the slope of his arm, smiling slightly at the goose bumps left in the wake of his touch. "We've got some cash in the bank, thanks to my brilliant new partner." Here Jed leaned up to kiss Redford slowly, lips curved up into a smile that Redford found impossible not to mirror. "I think we should finally get that trip in. Come on, what do you say? Change of scenery, maybe a nice cabin by a lake somewhere? We could fish, lay out in the sun, and drink beer. Knievel would be in heaven."

Redford muffled his laugh against Jed's shoulder. "You'd take Knievel on a fishing trip? I'm beginning to think you've got the soul of an old cat lady."

Jed pulled back, an overexaggerated, wounded expression on his face. "What are you even talking about? Of *course* we'd take 'Nievel. Do you have any idea how much she'd bitch at us if we went on a trip without her?" His eyes narrowed and he leaned forward, fingers slipping upward to tickle along Redford's ribs at the same time as his teeth caught the slope of Redford's neck, just hard enough to make the skin flush. "And why don't you say that again, Mr. Cooked Extra Turkey For The Cat?"

Trying to look a little shifty was difficult when a grin was threatening to emerge, but Redford attempted nonetheless. Jed's fingers were alarmingly close to the extremely ticklish part of his ribs, but he held firm. "You," he said deliberately, "are an old cat lady. Cooking extra turkey is nothing, compared."

His world shifted, and Redford found himself on the couch after Jed hauled him up and threw him there, fingers digging mercilessly into his ribs. The sound that Redford made was, in his own opinion, a horribly embarrassing shriek of laughter, louder than he'd ever laughed before. "Jed! Don't—don't you dare, stop tickling me—" There was no mercy to be found from Jed, however. He was laughing too, expression lit up in a grin of fiendish amusement.

"Oh, no, Fido," he crowed triumphantly, straddling Redford's hips so he could get a better tickling angle. "I warned you! There are no cat ladies here!"

Struggling was little help, but Redford tried nonetheless, trying to get his own hand up to Jed's waist. There was a spot just above his hip that Redford wanted to exploit, but it was difficult to get any kind of coordination when he was laughing so hard that his stomach was beginning to hurt. "Jed! You evil—" He broke off into laughter again, so distracted that he didn't notice the rustle at the back of his mind, something stretching out and baring its fangs.

A bestial snarl ripped its way from Redford's throat, and a growl of "Journey has not proved himself yet!" He lunged, clamping one of Jed's wandering hands between his teeth, biting down. It wasn't the soft throat that the Other wanted, but he shook his head nonetheless, tugging, drawing blood, another rumbling growl sounding in the back of his throat.

There was a loud curse, Jed yelping in surprised pain, the laughter dying from the air. A struggle then, Jed trying to get free, an almost panicked "Red?" lost in another startled sound of agony. There was the tang of blood in Redford's mouth, skin tearing, and then Jed fell away, holding his hand to his chest. In the air, the scent of fear was strong and bitter.

Jed was scared of him.

The red haze of fury lifted itself from Redford's vision, his thoughts clearing. The other presence faded, but the growling remained. He lifted his eyes to look at Jed. Vivid red bloomed across his shirt, dripping from his palm down to the floor. Ragged breaths panted from Jed, and he stared at Redford, wide-eyed. For a long few moments, Redford couldn't quite comprehend what had just happened, like his memory had been blurred and scattered.

"Red?" Jed's voice again, worry peaking the sound of his name, something Jed had said a thousand times, a thousand different ways. It'd never sounded quite like that, though. There was pain there, under the words, as well as the fear that still hung, acrid, in the air. "Red, come on, baby. Are you okay? Please, talk to me."

Redford used that voice like an anchor, blinking slowly, trying to sort out his muddled thoughts. "Jed, what... what did I do?" The blood caught his attention again, and horror made for a sour taste at the back of his throat. "Oh, God, Jed—I'm so sorry. I didn't—that wasn't me." He scrambled up off the couch, grabbing a nearby discarded shirt, one of Jed's, to wrap around Jed's hand, trying to staunch the flow of blood. "Is it bad? Do you need stitches?"

"Hey," Jed said, catching Redford's chin to force the man's eyes up away from the mangled mess of his palm. The pain had faded, and now the cool green depths stared calmly at Redford, assessing him, studying his face intently. "I'm fine. It's just a bite. I'll clean it out and it'll be fine. Stop for a minute, babe." Gently, Jed tugged Redford to sit. Redford went with him numbly, shocked, only vaguely feeling the fingers on Jed's uninjured hand trailing along his jaw before he hooked a strand of Redford's hair behind his ear. "Are you okay?" he asked again, insistent. "For a minute there...."

Trailing off, Jed laughed shortly. The sound wasn't like the laughter of before; there was no joy or mirth in it at all. "I thought I lost you." The admission didn't appear to come easily for Jed, and he leaned forward, nudging his forehead against Redford's. "You got really wolfy there." Redford didn't understand how Jed could be so calm and helpful after he'd just *bitten* Jed. The only good thing he could think of was that David had confirmed, a few months ago, that werewolf bites were only contagious on the full moon.

17

That was *one* positive thing. One thing, amongst a whole mess of very bad things that had just happened.

"I'll help you clean your hand," Redford mumbled, getting up off the couch again. He could taste Jed's blood on his teeth, and it made him feel sick. The presence, the Other, had enjoyed it. Taking Jed's other hand, Redford pulled lightly. "Bathroom?"

A faint frown flickered over Jed's expression, and for a moment, Redford was certain he was going to push to do the whole *talking* thing. But in the end, he simply stood and followed behind him, grumbling under his breath about how fine he was. The bite was deep, though, as they discovered once Redford started washing it out under the tap. Jed turned an odd green-tinged pale when pressure was put on it.

"Get me my whiskey bottle," Jed said, sagging to sit on the edge of the bathtub, his hand still held over the sink. Blood was making a Rorschach blot test on the white porcelain. "And the first-aid kit under the couch."

Redford nodded shakily as he left the bathroom. The whiskey was easily found—easier to find than the first-aid kit—but he had to stop for a moment in the dim light of the kitchen, one hand gripping the neck of the bottle, trying to take deep breaths. Every breath carried with it the scent of Jed's blood, strong and still bleeding, and the smell of it made nausea roll in Redford's stomach. He'd done that. Something had fractured in his mind, and he'd bitten Jed so hard that he was still bleeding.

Dr. Alona was wrong. He *was* crazy. This wasn't normal.

"Red?" Jed's voice cut through his thoughts, the man leaning over to peer out at him through the bathroom doorway. "Stop it. I can hear you thinking from here. So don't even go there, okay? Just bring me that damn kit."

Jed's cell phone rang, loud and harsh in the quiet of their apartment. Redford jumped, his heart skipping a beat at the sudden intrusion.

"And my phone! The kit and my phone, Red! And the *goddamn whiskey!*"

CHAPTER
2

Redford

"IT'S too goddamn early to be doing this shit," Jed was bitching, dark glasses covering red-rimmed eyes, striding into the pub and scowling at the room at large. Typically, Jed didn't seem to care if there were other patrons, or that someone might look at him a bit oddly, dressed in leather and one hand tucked into Redford's back pocket. Jed had a way of ignoring things that didn't fit into his world-view. Redford wasn't sure yet if that was an admirable quality or simply another one of Jed's many quirks.

"It's an hour after sundown," Redford pointed out. "And you're still hungover. Maybe you shouldn't have gone through half a bottle of whiskey." As soon as the words were out there, though, he knew how stupid it was saying them. Trying to tell Jed to not drink or curse was like telling fish to stop swimming.

Jed smirked broadly and slung himself into the nearest stool, tapping two fingers on the wooden countertop to attract the bartender's attention. "Pain management, Fido," he drawled, taking the beer that was poured and sipping it with an appreciative sigh. The reminder made Redford shrink a little, hunching his shoulders as he sat down next to Jed. "Whiskey is better than pills. More fun to drink too."

The injured hand was out of sight. Jed had stitched it himself, after copious amounts of whiskey and with a cacophony of cursing. It was now wrapped up and hidden under Jed's fingerless gloves. The man claimed it didn't hurt much. Redford knew firsthand how many scars Jed had, how he seemed to accept pain like it was his due, but it was different when *he* was the cause. This scar would be because of Redford and not a bullet or Jed's recklessness.

19

There was a nudge at his foot. Redford looked up to see Jed staring at him. Jed didn't do genuine smiles that often—he smirked and he grinned, but there was a smile that seemed to be just for Redford, one that Jed was giving him now. It said everything that Jed wasn't saying out loud: forgiveness, acceptance, love. It was clear, then, that Jed wasn't really as hungover as he was acting. He just enjoyed giving David a hard time and would continue bitching about how terribly insensitive it was to be dragged from his drinking into the harsh, cruel world when David arrived. The two had an odd, antagonistic back and forth that was hard to understand, even up close.

As his guilt calmed into something less overwhelming, Redford noticed Jed sliding his beer across the bar, putting it closer to Redford in an unspoken offer to share it. Redford smiled, taking a sip. He still didn't like the taste all that much, but it was hard to refuse anything that Jed shared with him.

"Are you two lovebirds going to sit here all day and gross out the rest of the room?" A mellow, dryly amused voice floated over to them from the back corner of the room. Sitting in a booth, the one furthest from the door and the large windows that surrounded it, David was sipping his pint and watching them.

Jed's smile, and their moment, vanished. Now scowling, Jed jabbed his sunglasses further up on his nose and spun around, hollering back at David over the heads of the other patrons. "You are one creepy fucking bastard."

Redford winced, automatically scanning the room to make sure that Jed's outburst—and David's rather obvious outing of them—wasn't going to attract any attention. Luckily, it seemed everybody else was too deep in their drinks to care. The fact that Jed had a rather large gun strapped to his hip might also have had something to do with the rest of the bar's pointed inattention.

Taking his time to finish off his beer, Jed tossed some bills on the bar and nodded back toward the table. He pointedly took Redford's hand in his uninjured one, and Jed cheerfully stared down the one table that seemed most likely to say something. The two men turned back to the women they were with, muttering under their breaths but letting Redford and Jed pass in peace.

"David," Redford greeted, seating himself in the chair opposite David. "Thank you for recommending Dr. Alona." He still wasn't sure that the doctor was going to be able to *help* him, but it seemed to be worth the effort to try. The fact that David had been able to find a psychiatrist that would talk to a werewolf was something Redford was very grateful for.

A smile flashed across David's face, smooth and charming, and he leaned back and shrugged. "I'm glad you found him helpful. Alona is making a name for himself in certain circles for being willing to work with the—" Again that grin, crinkling up the corners of his eyes, amused and sardonic and, as always, just once removed from whatever it was David was talking about. "—shall we say, the more *unusual* cases."

With how the man smelled, it made sense, Redford figured, that David would have his ear to the ground for those kinds of things. Everybody had their own unique scent, of course, but humans all had one common marker. Jed had it. The people in this bar had it. David didn't.

"Oh my God, *please* tell me, sunshine, that you didn't drag my ass all the way over to meatheads anonymous' headquarters just to gab your fucking mouth about headshrinkers. Because I swear to the little virgin Jesus, David, I will rip off your balls." Slouching in his seat, sunglasses slipping down his nose so he could fix David with a heated glare, Jed only perked up when the bartender brought over a bottle of whiskey and three glasses. "You are a prince." Jed bestowed a wide, leering grin on the solid mass of a bartender, an expression which made the grizzled older gentleman's seemingly permanent scowl deepen substantially.

Not that Jed seemed to mind. He idly checked out the man's ass as he walked away. Redford, catching this look, frowned at the table, hiding it by pouring the whiskey into the glasses provided. "Too bad he's not ten years younger," Jed mused. "He might actually be worth being in this shithole for."

The growl that rumbled in Redford's throat wasn't something he could stop, and he covered it with a cough. "Sorry," he muttered. "Got something in my throat."

When he looked up, he found that David's normally bland expression had sharpened. The man's dark eyes were focused on Redford, piercing and knowing, and Redford suddenly felt very exposed. Like David could see through his pitiful attempts at covering all too well. "Yeah," David murmured slowly, long fingers tapping absently on the side of his glass. "I can see that."

Jed swung back around, completely clueless. "You okay, Fido?" he asked, concerned, thumping him helpfully on the back. "I can get you

21

some water." He went to do just that before anyone could stop him, bounding up to the bar, sweet-talking the bartender into washing up a fresh glass and getting some cold bottled water from the back room. Despite what had just happened, Redford couldn't help but appreciate, out of the corner of his eye, the far too tight jeans that Jed was wearing and the picture he made leaning over the bar.

Desperate to change the subject, Redford volunteered, "Did you see the doctor's parrot, Rufus? He was nice." It was obvious small talk, but Redford didn't know David too well, and he felt awkward around the man. David was effortlessly charming, handsome, everything that Redford considered himself not to be.

"Parrot?" David's eyebrows lifted and he tipped his chair back, cradling his drink carefully. "I heard he had a *dog* named Rufus. Maybe he is just overly fond of that name."

"Oh." Redford frowned faintly, confused. No, it had definitely been a parrot that he'd seen. "That's... odd."

"What's odd?" Jed was back, like a force of nature, setting the glass and water bottle down in front of Redford with the same care that an errant schoolboy might bring the teacher his slightly bruised apple. With an endearingly hopeful look, he rubbed Redford's back gently and sat again, fixing David with a glare. David, it seemed, had not yet earned any of Jed's good mood. "The fact that I still don't know what the fuck bugged up your ass and made you drag me down here? Or that Clive up there"—he jerked his thumb back toward the bar—"is out of onion rings? 'Cause both of those things are a goddamn travesty, if you ask me."

"My, Jed," David mused, running his fingertip around the rim of his glass. He still hadn't taken a drink. "In our times apart, I almost forget how poetic you are. And such class."

There was the bang of two chair legs hitting the floor. Jed had been tipping back, balancing on the back legs, almost casual, if you didn't know him. That wasn't lasting long. He leaned in, eyes flashing. "I'll show you *class*, Tinker Bell," he hissed. "Talk. I got lots better to do and clients that'll actually *pay*."

In an effort to calm Jed down a little—even though Redford was fairly sure that Jed was just acting irritated to annoy David—Redford put a hand on his arm, squeezing lightly. "I'm sure David is offering to pay us lots of money," he coaxed, simultaneously offering David a dry smile. Jed seemed to calm instantly, relaxing under his touch.

David rolled his eyes and pulled out a rather thick manila envelope. "Of course I'm going to pay, you giant goon. God forbid you do anything for less than mercenary motivations."

Jed snorted. The stillness in him now was more waiting, wound up but held back—not by the offer of money, Redford realized, but by him. He could feel it, under his hand, the way Jed's muscles twitched, the irritation behind the sardonic smirk. Jed wasn't a patient man, and David did like to push his buttons. But he was holding back because of Redford.

"Damn straight," Jed said, arching one eyebrow. "So talk."

The envelope was tossed to Redford, and David leaned back. "Half now," he said, "half when it's done."

One shoulder lifted in a shrug. "Works for me. What's the job?"

Clearing his throat, only now did David take a long drink of the whiskey. If Redford didn't know better, if he wasn't so sure the man was absolutely unflappable, he would have thought there were *nerves* in the way he was clutching the glass like a lifeline, knuckles standing white against olive skin. But he'd watched David saunter toward him in the wreckage of Fil's building, with everything burning around him, Jed bleeding and passed out over Redford's shoulder, and all the other man had done was offer him a ride. David surely couldn't be nervous over anything. Perhaps he was just as annoyed with Jed as Jed apparently was with him.

"Have you ever been to Cairo?" David finally asked lowly, staring down at his drink.

"I haven't. But I've heard it's beautiful," Redford piped up enthusiastically. He had a whole book about Egypt back at home, and in his childhood he'd enjoyed staring at the pictures, wondering what it would be like to visit. "I've always wanted to go and see the pyramids."

A faint smile touched the corner of David's mouth, and at once it was easy to see how put on the rest of his expressions were. This one was tired, longing, and proud all at once, was genuine where David was normally all charm and a cool exterior. "It is very beautiful," he agreed, running his hand through his artfully mussed dark curls. "You would appreciate it, I think."

"So you want me to, what, be your Egyptian knowledge lifeline on a fucking game show? What? A location is not a job, David." Jed didn't sound too happy about the proposed destination.

"You have all the patience of a grubby toddler," David snapped, eyes flashing for a moment, lip curling upward. But in the next moment, he had contained himself, visibly straining with the effort of backing down, and continued, voice smoothed out again, "There are a rash of disappearances in the city. Authorities haven't seen the connections yet, but they're there. I want you to find whoever is responsible and stop them. That's all."

"Why are *you* asking us to do this?" Redford replied curiously. "You're not involved with the police."

"I'm much, much worse than the police," David said darkly. "And I want this stopped. That's all you need to know." It wasn't a very informative answer. Redford would have pressed further, but the expression on David's face stopped him from doing so. In any case, it was clear that David knew more that he wasn't sharing.

Jed leaned back again as he watched David with a thoughtful look, balancing the chair again on two legs exactly as Redford's grandmother had always warned him not to. Apparently it was very easy to break one's neck that way, or to ruin good furniture and flooring. "I need everything you've got on the case," Jed finally answered, pointing at him. "And you're paying airfare for me and Fido. First class. *And* a hotel. A nice one." He paused before adding quickly, "With a bar and a *pool*." A beat later and that was amended to, "A *pool bar*. One that floats. And a *jet ski*."

"You want me to come with you?" Pleased, Redford smiled at Jed. He'd been involved in most of Jed's jobs lately, but this one sounded big.

For his part, Jed seemed baffled that the question even came up. "Well, yeah," he said, turning to look at Redford. "Where else would you be?" He spun quickly back to David, pointing at him. "*Two* jet skis!"

David rumbled a growl under his breath, arms folded. "I'm not buying you a blasted *jet ski*, you idiot. And don't pout at me. You know that doesn't work. But yes, I will provide transportation and accommodations. In fact, I'll be joining you. I know the city, so you won't have to worry about hiring a local once you're there."

"You know how much I hate having the client on the job," Jed pointed out. For once, though, he didn't seem to be simply trying to be argumentative.

"This isn't a normal job." David met his eyes steadily. When, after a long moment, Jed nodded in agreement to his terms, there was a visible relaxing in the tense lines of his shoulders. Redford mirrored the nod for his own agreement, containing an excited smile. It wasn't about the job.

Getting to go to Cairo was something he'd always dreamed about. Now he got to go with Jed, to explore the city with him, discover all the things he'd read about in books with Jed by his side. It was perfect.

Maybe he could make Jed excited about this too. Redford leaned close to him, nudged his chin against Jed's shoulder, and whispered, "If we can get him to give us a budget figure, we could slip in the jet skis under 'equipment repair'."

"I think that is the sexiest thing you've ever said to me," Jed murmured back, a slow grin working its way across his face. "My hot little bookkeeper is fucking awesome." Louder then, to David, he grandly waved his hand and said, "Done. We're in. My partner"—here he nudged Redford a little, playfully—"will be sending you over our budget requirements."

"No fucking jet skis, Journey," David grumbled, but he looked relieved.

Jed flashed a shit-eating grin, standing and hooking his arm around Redford's waist. "Don't call me Journey, you cocksucker." With that fond farewell, he sauntered out of the pub with Redford by his side, waving a two-fingered salute to the disgruntled patrons they passed.

The minute the pub door shut behind them, Jed eagerly opened the envelope as they walked back toward his motorcycle. Redford glanced over, but all he could tell was that the manila envelope seemed reasonably full and that Jed wasn't immediately bitching about being, as he called it, "stiffed." Redford assumed that was a good sign. "How much is there?" he asked, watching Jed scoop up the money and count it.

And count it again.

Then a third time, eyes round with disbelief. Without a word, Jed handed over the stack of bills for confirmation, and Redford took them, giving Jed a sideways glance as his fingers fumbled through the bills. Most of Jed's clients worked in cash, for obvious reasons, so Redford was getting better at counting it quickly. He took his time, though, because if Jed wanted to double check, maybe this count was especially tricky.

"Twenty-five thousand," he said when he reached the end, impressed. That was quite a bit for one job, especially one that Jed seemed to think would be half vacation. Still, although it was a lot, Jed had also dropped that amount of cash at a gun show for new "toys." At least now Redford was making him expense those as much as possible. Jed got so distracted so easily when weapons were involved. "And that's only half."

25

"Holy shit." Jed was grinning. He grabbed Redford around the waist and turned them in a fast circle with a whoop. "That's a lot of fishing!"

"Technically, your vacation plan would be very cheap, all things considered. The major cost would be the cabin you want," Redford felt the need to point out, even as he was being spun around. "And cash doesn't equal more fish." He considered this for a moment and wrinkled his nose in confusion. He didn't actually know how to fish at all. "Does it?"

"That is *fifty grand* of pure, uninterrupted, beers-on-the-beach *fish*, baby!" Jed was not bothered by Redford's logic. He spun them around again before kissing Redford dramatically and tucking the envelope of cash into Redford's front jacket pocket. "You keep that safe. Once we get done with this job, we are going someplace with sand and sun and a little cabin all to ourselves."

Laughing at Jed's exuberance, Redford tucked an arm around Jed's waist, keeping him close. He leaned over and placed a kiss at the corner of Jed's lips, nudging his forehead to Jed's temple for a moment. Jed's happiness was infectious. "It's a plan," he agreed softly.

"Damn straight. We've been working too fucking hard. I want my goddamn fishing trip."

Jed sauntered down the street, tucking his hand into Redford's back pocket, using that to pull him closer. If people were staring, he obviously did not care. Jed never did, even when those people in the grocery store had looked awfully upset at him bending Redford over the cabbages to kiss him last week. Redford was beginning to think that maybe he shouldn't care about other people's reactions either. Even if his grandmother wouldn't have approved.

"Come on." Jed had slung one leg over the bike and was holding out Redford's helmet to him. "We're going shopping on David's dime. What kind of gun would go best with Bermuda shorts?"

Redford just stared at Jed for a moment before climbing onto the back and settling in behind him. "I don't know. What are Bermuda shorts?"

Laughter tripped over the sound of the engine roaring to life. Jed leaned back into Redford's arms, warm and solid and filled with the kind of happiness Redford was beginning to suspect had something to do with the two of them. Jed never laughed this much with other people. "We'll get matching pairs," he said, a teasing tone in his voice. "With black socks and sandals. Trust me, sweetheart, we'll be hot as hell."

Before Jed started driving, Redford took another look in the envelope, pulling out a note that had been tucked off to the side of the money. It read: *Flights are on Tuesday. Don't be late.*

It looked like they were heading to Cairo.

CHAPTER
3

Redford

THE morning in question dawned cloudy and overcast, rain threatening along the edges of every gust of wind. Redford was standing outside of the airport, watching Jed curse and struggle with their luggage.

He'd insisted on handling it himself, even when Redford had offered multiple times to carry some of it. At a certain point, there was no hope of out-stubborning Jed, so Redford had just let him do it. When they were packing, they'd had a long talk about what exactly was allowed in carry-on luggage on airplanes. Redford had very carefully read the rules online, and Jed had sulked for an hour when it was discovered that he couldn't take so much as a switchblade onboard. When a man kept about three different weapons in reach of his bed, complying with the FAA regulations was apparently like cutting his arm off. At least, that was what one might think to hear Jed complain.

"Mr. Reed. I was wondering if you'd be here." So absorbed in watching Jed, Redford hadn't noticed Victor Rathbone approaching him. He jumped, startled, and forced himself to relax again. Victor gave him a dry smile. "Sorry. I didn't mean to scare you."

"It's fine, just—I'm a little distracted," Redford replied. Victor nodded but didn't ask anything more than that. Maybe he didn't like small talk either.

"Fucking professor is here?" Jed whined. He was not going to get over the lack of weaponry in easy reach anytime soon. "What the hell? Is this a school field trip or something?"

"Seeing as neither of you can speak Arabic, I thought it prudent that I come along." Victor directed an unamused look at Jed. "I wouldn't want you getting confused and blowing up the wrong building, after all."

"I speak it." Walking up to them, perfectly dressed in a dark linen suit and a fedora perched at an angle, David should have looked ridiculous and out of place. Somehow, though, he managed to fit in even with Jed's worn jeans and Redford's baggy hooded sweatshirt. David shook his sleeve away from his wrist to glance at his watch impatiently. "Just because you can translate fifteen ancient languages does not mean you needed to tag along, Vickie. I highly doubt hieroglyphs will even be necessary on this trip."

"Yeah," Jed shot at Victor gleefully. Redford wasn't entirely sure Jed knew what hieroglyphs were, but when the man was unhappy he tended to take joy in sharing that with others. "And blowing up the wrong building is *always* funny. So fuck you." That said, he grabbed Redford's arm and hauled the man away toward the check-in counter, cursing and stumbling over their bags. He wound up kicking one in front of him, which probably wasn't the best idea. In fact, it definitely wasn't, because two steps later he was tumbling end over end, right into a rotund woman pushing a luggage cart.

Sprawled on the ground, staring up at her and her squawking indignity, Jed just gave her a lopsided, charming grin. "Howdy, ma'am. Nice dress. Circus tents are back in style? I really have to pick up the latest *Vogue* and catch up."

Restraining a sigh, Redford didn't attempt to save Jed from the vicious beating he was now receiving from the woman wielding her sizable purse. "Goodness," Victor noted, also looking unconcerned and maybe a little bit amused at seeing Jed get whacked over the head. "He's not in a good mood today, is he?"

Victor and David were an odd couple. It struck Redford all over again as he looked at them now, watching them pick up their luggage and trade bags between them to carry. Whereas David was dressed in a way that Jed would term totally unfashionable—he apparently found it hard to understand why anybody outside of a bank or a cologne commercial would dress like that—he made it work. Victor, on the other hand, was a man in his late twenties dressed like he was sixty, complete with a tweed jacket and leather elbow patches. If there was something dangerous about David, there was nothing of that in Victor.

Although Victor didn't smell entirely human either. He also never, ever looked anybody in the eye. Jed had told Redford that he shouldn't

29

trust anybody who didn't look him in the eye. The second addition of Jed's philosophy had been never to trust anybody who wouldn't suck your cock in an elevator, but Redford didn't entirely understand that one.

"Oh my *God*, fine, whatever, you're practically an Olsen twin." Jed darted to hide behind Redford, glowering murderously at the woman who was puffing like an angry bull, staring him down. "Leave me the hell alone!"

"I'm terribly sorry." Victor stepped closer. "He's not taken his medication today." He offered the woman a sympathetic smile. "I do promise to force it down his throat shortly."

The woman seemed to decide that her point had been made, snorting at Victor but accepting the apology, and strode off, leaving Jed to mutter darkly under his breath, *"This* is why you should be able to pack weapons." The narrowed eyes turned to Victor, and Jed flipped him off. "Fucking professor runt."

Not insulted in the slightest, Victor just lifted an eyebrow at Jed, adjusted his glasses, and went back to fussing over his luggage. There was an impatient *hmm* from David, the man lifting Victor's bag with his own, a slight nudge of his hips against Rathbone's. "Children, please," he murmured mildly, sharing an amused glance with Victor. "You're embarrassing the puppy."

Redford stared down at the floor. It was impossible not to notice the people looking at them now, with the noise they were making and their commotion. He felt a flush rising in his cheeks. He glanced up at the flight board and double-checked quickly that their plane was on time, fidgeting with his sleeve, trying desperately to blend in to the crowd. Embarrassed might be the right word for it. People were *staring*. Like a giant spotlight was suddenly trained on him, all those eyes focused on his too-big clothes and shaggy hair. Redford still wasn't used to it, to the way it felt when the room went quiet and all at once he was at the center of attention. Jed never seemed to notice. Sometimes Redford almost thought he did things like that on purpose, to get that kind of focus.

"I do apologize, Redford." The crisp tones of Victor's accent reached his ears, forcing him to stop staring at the floor. Victor actually sounded kind, right then. He was normally somewhat removed and very dry. David said it was because Victor was English, and the English only showed affection through tea and scolding. Jed, however, insisted it was because

Victor had a giant stick shoved somewhere unpleasant. The reality, Redford thought, was possibly somewhere in between. "Jed and David antagonize each other something awful, don't they? It's like watching a circus." He put a hand on Redford's elbow and led him to the check-in counter.

"Stop apologizing," he heard Jed mutter behind them. "You sound like such a fucking doormat." But all at once Jed was right beside him, hip pressed against Redford's, arm tucked in under his. There was an apologetic tilt to his usual smirk, noticeable only if you knew Jed like Redford did, if you'd spent hours memorizing the curve of his lips and the way the planes of his face fell.

There was the soft brush of Jed's fingertips against Redford's palm, and just like that, just that easy, they were holding hands as they walked up to the counter. Victor gave Jed an unreadable look but fell back to join David instead.

"I've never been on a plane before," Redford told Jed. He was sure that fact would have been fairly obvious to Jed, but he said it nonetheless. "I don't think I've even seen one up close." The closer they got to the check-in counter, the more of a reality it became, and Redford was starting to get nervous about his first flight.

Jed squeezed Redford's hand as they stopped in the middle of the crowd, perfectly willing to take a moment to talk to Redford about it. Like they had all the time in the world. "Well, yeah," he said, tugging Redford in closer. "But now you get to take your first flight with me." A smirk grew across Jed's face, eyes lighting up wickedly. "If I recall, you liked the other *first flight* I gave you."

Redford had to take a moment to think about that one. "Oh," he said stupidly, flushing once more when he realized that Jed was talking about sex while they were in the middle of a crowd. "Um. Yes, I did. But I don't think... *that* is anything like traveling in an airplane. Is it?"

"Well, you get up in both." Jed was laughing now, quite enjoying himself. Fingertips brushed across Redford's cheek, chasing the flushed skin, and Jed hooked him in closer. "There's a lot of keeping it in the upright position and tight spaces. And if you're really, really good, you can sit back and enjoy the ride with some delicious salty nuts."

"Oh my God, Journey." David was rolling his eyes. His hand latched onto Jed's arm, and he hauled the man and, by extension, Redford, up

31

toward the counter. "Stop molesting each other in public. Also, that was a *horrible* pun. Seriously. You should be ashamed of yourself."

"He should be ashamed of himself in general," Victor noted, his voice bland. He hefted a bag over his shoulder and nodded toward a line near the check-in counter. "That's where we need to queue."

Redford went to grab one of his and Jed's bags, only to be thwarted at the last second by Jed grabbing it and giving him a sunny grin. As they made their way toward the line, Redford darted his gaze from person to person, overwhelmed at the sheer size of the crowd in the airport. Once they got themselves in the queue, they were sandwiched between the woman with the heavy handbag—who kept shooting murderous glares at Jed—and a family of seven.

"Hey, professor." Jed had plastered himself to Redford's back, chin resting on his shoulder, seemingly uncaring that it drew attention to be so intimate with someone in a public place. "Why don't you put that egghead to use. Tell me about the triangle building thingies and the guys with funny hats."

Two places ahead of them in the line, Victor turned back to face them, squinting his eyes in confusion. "The triangle build—oh, for goodness' sake, Jed." He sighed. "They're called *pyramids*. And I assume by 'guys with funny hats' you mean the ancient pharaohs." Once again, he somehow managed to look at them without meeting either of their eyes. His gaze seemed to be lined up somewhere around Jed's left eyebrow. "Well, you see...."

As Victor launched into a lecture about the cultural use of pyramids in the ancient Egyptian society, Redford daringly leaned back against Jed. Jed seemed to be completely uninterested in what Victor was saying, but he was smiling at Redford. It was clear, then, that Jed had only asked Victor that question for Redford's benefit.

"So, you have to realize that the ancient Egyptians weren't actually as obsessed with death as many academics think," Victor was saying, his whole demeanor lighting up at the chance to tell someone about what interested him. David had reached the counter in the meantime, checking all four of them in, and had Jed move forward to hand over their luggage. "Many academics assume that they were because of bad translations. It's terrible, really. What many people claim is *The Book of Death* is actually, in a more accurate translation, *The Chapters of Coming Forth By Day*. E. A. Wallis Budge, a remarkable man, I suppose, theorized...."

Victor, too absorbed in talking, clearly was not paying attention to anything else. David had put a hand on Victor's shoulder to steer him as they walked, guiding him out of harm's way with a long-suffering expression. There was a hint of fondness, though, as he easily helped Victor upright after he stumbled over a bag.

"And the name Bastet is actually an inaccurate translation too. It's simply *Bast*...."

Security took longer than it probably should. Jed grilled the TSA official on the proper way to pat someone down, even demonstrating where he could hide a weapon, if he was so inclined. There was a brief flurry of whispers behind the scenes, and it seemed, for a moment of panic on Redford's part, like he would be taken into custody.

"Nowadays, of course, Cairo does not practice the ancient Egyptian religion. I think it's a shame, such a wonderful belief system...."

But the military record attached to Jed's name, along with the fact that, thanks to Redford's meticulous packing, his bags were clean, allowed them to get through finally to the other side.

"They aren't very cheerful," Jed announced, mood somewhat restored.

"Yes, I wonder why," David replied dryly, guiding them toward the gate with the air of an overly vexed teacher escorting a group of wayward toddlers. "Couldn't be the people they have to deal with."

"I know!" Jed wrapped one arm around Redford's waist, always making sure they were in contact. It was like Jed knew, instinctively, when Redford needed to be grounded. "I'm a fucking treat, for one. And Redford's hot as hell, so they got some eye candy too! Must be sourpuss over there that set them off." He glanced over at Victor with a smirk. He was undeterred by Victor ignoring him, instead choosing to veer over toward a food stand set up by the side of the main walkway. "I'm buying supplies. David! I need snack money."

"For christsakes." David glowered, clearly losing patience. "You're going to make me regret asking you along every step of the way, aren't you?"

33

"Yup. I want a soda, and Red here is definitely gonna need something sweet. I'm thinking an extra-large number four with a cheesecake shake. With extra whipped cream."

"What on earth happened to the twenty-five thousand David gave you?" Victor, taking a break from his fount of information, took a moment to stare incredulously at Jed. Redford was sad at the lecture ending—he'd been thoroughly enjoying it, actually, even if Jed and David had seemed not to be interested at all. "You can't have spent that already, surely."

Jed gave him a shocked look. "That's *fish* money," he said, with no further explanation. Then again, his tone implied that none was needed. David had apparently decided not to argue, instead ordering the food and paying for it, though he refused to touch the greasy bag or the hideously over-sweet shake. Redford happily took the offered concoction, taking a sip. Jed had somehow managed to get him addicted to overly sweet things, perhaps because they'd been a rarity in his childhood.

"I am going to the gate," David announced. "Our flight boards in half an hour. Don't be late." He swanned off, Victor in tow, and Redford saw David's hand rest briefly at the small of Victor's back to guide him through a crowded area.

"They're kind of odd together," Redford remarked. One minute they were joining forces to tease Jed, and the next it was almost as if they were strangers. He watched them leave, disappearing into the crowd, and wondered what it was that David knew about this job that he hadn't chosen to share. "Thank you for the drink," he added, smiling at Jed. The sugar rush was helping nicely to take his mind off of their imminent flight.

Jed just gave him a crooked little smile in return, picking up the bag of food and walking up to a harried mother carting along a small kid. "Hey," Jed said to her, keeping a respectful distance, trying to look nonthreatening. "Sorry, my friend ordered the wrong food, and I don't have time to fight with these guys." He tipped his head back toward the busy food counter. The mother seemed a bit startled, keeping her son firmly beside her, but she didn't run away. "If you want to check with the red-haired kid working there, I totally didn't even open the bag. See? Still stapled shut. But, you know, if you or the kid is hungry, it's a cheeseburger and stuff." Handing over the food to the woman, Jed grinned at the kid and walked off, contentedly sucking down his soda.

"Can't stand airport food." He shrugged. "Just wanted to give David a hard time."

Right then, all of the disapproval in the world couldn't have kept Redford from pressing a kiss to Jed's cheek. Surprisingly, Jed actually flushed slightly, shoulders rounding a bit in what might actually have been embarrassment. Shocking, for the man who seemed to care so little about what people thought. That didn't stop him from sneaking an arm around Redford's waist, though, bumping hips with him lightly. "We've got half an hour until we have to board," Redford pointed out. "Do you want to go sit and watch the airplanes land?" Redford happily leaned into Jed's side, steering him toward the huge viewing window he'd seen off to the left.

Chuckling, Jed flopped down into one of the little plastic molded seats. "Sure thing, Fido." He smirked up at Redford. They laced their fingers together absently, and Jed slouched back, watching as a huge 747 touched down on the outside tarmac. "Sounds great."

REDFORD had never experienced anything quite so unique as the feeling of a plane taking off with him inside of it, and he had quickly determined that he would very much enjoy experiencing it again. There had been a rumbling as the plane taxied down the runway, a terrifying but exhilarating *lift* in his stomach as the plane's wings caught the air and took off into the sky. Even the popping in his ears was a new, interesting experience, even if it was slightly painful.

A very nice lady seated behind them, older and with round glasses that reminded Redford of his grandmother's, had offered him a hard candy to suck on, to help his ears pop. Jed had just snorted when she held out the bag to him in turn, hands gripping the seat handles so tightly his knuckles were white. He did, however, put up the shade on the window so Redford could see out as they took off.

A few months ago, Redford would have been terrified out of his mind. New experiences had never been a good thing in his life. Foreign sensations hadn't been something curious and interesting, they'd been things to avoid, to be terrified of, to hide himself away from. Now he was eagerly watching out the window, his gaze running over land and sea and fluffy white clouds as they broke above them.

"Jed, we're *above* the *clouds*," he exclaimed. David had gotten them seats in what Jed had called "the fancy fuckers section," so there was plenty of room for him to lean over Jed and stare out of the thick glass and into the sky below them. "Isn't that amazing?"

With a low huff of breath, Jed muttered, "Just peachy, sweetheart." He unbuckled and reached over to undo Redford's as well. "Come on, switch me spots. You should get a front row seat." The offer was taken eagerly— Redford clambered over Jed to get to the window seat, apologizing when knees and elbows collided. He landed heavily in the seat, taking a moment to appreciate the better view he was afforded.

A man in a uniform came by with a tray of drinks. Jed took two of the little bottles and quickly dumped them into a glass with ice. "Keep 'em coming, darlin'," he directed. "And my friend here will have a Shirley Temple, heavy on the cherries."

Redford didn't have the slightest clue what Jed had just ordered him, but a drink sounded nice. Taking a break from staring out the window, Redford sat up straighter in his seat to peer over the top of the next row. David and Victor were seated a row in front of them. David didn't look too happy, and Victor was inhaling from a strange device; it had a small metal tube that attached to some kind of hard plastic sleeve. He shook it several times and then put it to his mouth, breathing in deeply as he depressed the metal on the top. Redford turned to ask Jed about it, but he was busy with a small wall of glass bottles. He had sucked down the contents of the first two already and was pouring three more into his cup.

"Fuck," Jed grumbled, knocking back his second glass. "Fucking bottles are too small." The flight attendant returned with more, also setting a glass down in front of Redford. It was a cheery carbonated concoction with cherries, ice, and a straw.

"It's very... red," Redford remarked, pleased by the vivid color. He didn't normally like anything that fizzed, not after Jed had gotten him to try beer for the first time, but he thought the hue might make up for the strange bubbles that got up his nose. Jed just sighed and went to work, twisting open the tops of his own bottles.

"Can I get you two anything else?" The man flashed a big smile at Jed, then at Redford, though Redford caught his gaze going to the steadily growing pile of bottles. "Dinner will be in a few hours, but we have an assortment of snacks."

"More whiskey," Jed ordered tersely.

Redford wanted to protest. He even tried raising his eyes to the man and opening his mouth to say something, but he let the man go with Jed's order. Instead, he reached out and laid his hand over Jed's where it was clamped tight to the arm rest. "Do you not like flying?" he asked, curious, now picking up on the hints of nervousness in Jed's scent.

"Everything's better when I drink," was the only reply he got, but under his touch he could feel Jed's hand relax a little. Jed had told him stories about flying in his special ops days, about parachuting in close to enemy lines. They were the kind of stories that Jed only told while he had a few beers in him, his grin tense and his gestures overenthusiastic. They usually included death, Jed's eyes going distant as he recalled the names of the people he'd worked alongside who never made it to the ground, or getting dropped off into nothingness over the blooming violence of bombs and gunfire. None of them were happy stories, really, though Jed usually ended them by talking about an especially good fuck or the time he took out a target while sloppy drunk and with his pants on his head.

"It'll be okay," Redford murmured, feeling a little helpless. He wasn't sure if he was very good at being reassuring. "Is there... can I do something to help?"

"Yeah. Get into the bathroom and fuck me so hard I can't walk." Jed grinned at him, smile already a little loopy. His smirk only grew when Redford turned bright red. "You can join the mile high club."

Having no idea what the mile high club was, Redford struggled to come up with a response that wasn't stuttering. Had Jed actually just suggested that they have sex on the *plane*? Surrounded by hundreds of people? "I'm not sure that's a good idea," he eventually managed to say, although he couldn't help but wonder what it would be like.

Jed immediately pouted, reaching for his drink again. "Fine. Prude." A man walked down the aisle past them, his elbow bumping against Jed's shoulder. The whiskey sloshed in the glass, and Jed cursed loudly, immediately standing up and looking very much ready to take a swing. "Fucker!"

Redford tried to yank him back down, his hand tugging at Jed's sleeve. He had read that people were paranoid about planes these days, and anybody acting aggressive was not a good thing. The man stopped in his tracks, turning slowly to fix incredulous eyes on Jed. "Excuse me?"

Jed's anger seemed to immediately dissipate into the leer that curled his lips. "Hello," he all but purred, eyes dipping up and down the man. "You jostled my drink. Maybe you and I should talk about it?"

Startled, Redford twisted in his seat to watch. The man that Jed was talking to was broad shouldered, heavyset and stocky, with gray hair cut close to his scalp. He was exactly the kind of man that Jed's gaze often lingered on—like the man at the bar a few days ago, or the man last week in the supermarket who had been buying oranges. "Jed," he said lowly, tugging at Jed's sleeve again.

"I was going to the bathroom," the man was saying, expression somewhere between incredulous and interested. The latter hint in his face made Redford rather unhappy. "What, are you offering to help me piss?"

Without thinking, Redford stood, putting himself between Jed and the older man. "No, he's not offering," Redford replied, feeling his lip curl back over his teeth in a silent snarl. "Keep walking."

Immediately Jed smoothly pulled Redford back, smiling at the guy, saying something about sending back the flight attendant with another drink. David had turned around and was giving Jed a look, but he didn't step in. The gray-haired man walked away, and Jed sat back down heavily, eyebrow arched. "What was that, Red?" he asked quietly, shifting a bit in his seat. "You know I like the growling just as much as the next guy, but—"

"But if both of you don't get it together we are going to have a very unpleasant welcoming committee," David hissed, glowering at them between the crack of the seats. "Jesus fuck, *behave*."

Redford shrank back into his seat, giving David an apologetic look. His previous anger had vanished, but there had been no prompting from the *other* thoughts in the back of his mind, nothing triggered by the strange impulses he'd been feeling lately. That had been all him. "I didn't like the way he was looking at you," he whispered to Jed.

A faint flicker of guilt crossed Jed's face and he sighed, shifting again uncomfortably. "Jesus, Fido," he murmured, glancing over at Redford. "It was just… you know."

No, Redford didn't know, but he held his tongue. Instead, he just shook his head and clasped Jed's hand in his own again, squeezing their fingers together. He gave Jed his drink back—he'd taken it from Jed's tray when he'd stood up, making sure that Jed didn't spill it everywhere—and examined his own beverage. It didn't smell alcoholic at all, thankfully.

Redford amused himself by fishing out the cherries, eating them one by one between sips of the sweet carbonated drink. He'd have to remember the name of it, as he found he quite liked it, even if Jed *had* smirked while ordering it.

The excitement of the flight seemed to fade the longer they were in the air, the rush of wind over the wings becoming a dull white noise that underscored everything. After a while of sitting, after he'd touched all the buttons and adjusted the air flow so that it wasn't blowing directly into his face, there wasn't much else to do. The plane started feeling *smaller*, somehow. Redford glanced up at the other passengers, noting that there were people walking around. That meant he must be able to walk too. "I'm just going to stretch my legs," he told Jed lowly, squeezing his fingers again. Redford handed his drink over to Jed and managed to get out into the aisle. The ceiling didn't feel any higher, and the air didn't smell any fresher, but it was a little better.

He got up for a walk every hour after that. It helped, somewhat.

Jed had passed out soon after Redford's first jaunt around the cabin, and Redford had gently shifted him back into the window seat so he wouldn't have to climb over Jed every time he wanted out. Three hours in, three walks around the cabin, and a dinner cart was pushed around. Jed just snorted in irritation when he attempted to wake him, so Redford ate his chicken and steamed vegetables in silence. David ignored the offered food; Victor poked at the tray a few times and ordered another cup of tea. Redford didn't know why they were turning it down. He thought the meal was quite good, especially since it'd been prepared midair. That seemed very impressive to him.

Around his fourth walk, the lights had been dimmed. David was passed out as Redford ambled past, a gray satin eye mask hiding half his face, and Victor was still awake, wide-eyed and staring out the window with a fixed, constant look of mute horror on his face. Redford assumed that he was not very good with flying either.

Leaving Jed to nap, Redford idly played around with the television screen in front of him but lost interest fairly quickly. Left in vague boredom, he huffed a sigh and leaned back against his seat, just in time to catch Jed listing over in his sleep, winding up pressed against Redford's side. There was a faint rumble of a snore at the end of Jed's every exhalation, and Redford had to carefully move Jed's hand away from where it had been creeping up his thigh. Apparently even passed out, Jed would not miss an opportunity. Redford tipped his head to the side, cheek pressed against the soft spikes of Jed's hair, and smiled to himself, looking out the window again.

There was nothing much to see on the other side of the glass now, the world blanketed in darkness, but Redford could still catch the occasional wisp of cloud. They had a layover in London, David had said, and he wasn't looking forward to even more security checks and masses of people. Even Victor looked to be nodding off. With Jed snuggling in closer to his side, Redford couldn't help but relax into him. The soft slur of the engine noises outside the window lulled him, finally, into sleep.

CHAPTER
4

Jed

"FUCKING son of a fuck." There were birds perched around the sun-baked half walls leading out of the airport. Jed's loud cursing startled them away, and they wheeled up into a sky already clear and blazing even only shortly after sunrise. No *normal* human being should be expected to function when it was so goddamn *bright* out. Shoving the sunglasses further up on his nose, Jed squinted and tried to ignore the mariachi band attacking his head. Goddamn hangover.

David refused to even leave the airport. His queen prissiness had insisted on them getting a cab and pulling up to the door first. He also was completely covered, head to foot, in a long duster and a wide-brimmed hat and *gloves*, for fuck's sake. Jed had too many jabs about that shit. He hadn't been able to pick just one.

Leaning on Redford, Jed waved his hand ineffectively at the taxis. "Fuck," he mumbled again miserably, resting his forehead on Redford's shoulder. "Why is it so goddamn *sunny*? I hate desert countries. They're all bright, and shit."

"We're in *Cairo*, Jed," Redford said, awed, craning his neck to look around. "It's beautiful. It smells so different here."

Jed huffed out a sigh. He just pressed himself further into Redford and muttered, "Smells like camel shit." Perhaps that tenth mini-bottle of whiskey hadn't been the best idea in the world. Or maybe he should have just kept drinking. He'd been in a much better mood before he sobered up.

Finally a taxi stopped in front of them. Jed tossed their bags into the trunk, finding a small amount of vicious glee at putting David's on the bottom of the pile. They got in, Victor first, followed by Redford, and Jed sprawled out half on Red's lap, groaning and bitching the whole time. After picking up David, they were driven to the hotel, Redford's face pressed against the taxi window to stare outward the whole time. Thankfully, Victor seemed too tired to prattle on about legends or population sizes or whatever the fuck he liked to babble about.

The hotel was huge, built of blindingly white stone, fountains in the courtyard and a soft breeze from the nearby Nile to the east cooling everything down significantly. Redford, seemingly having gotten over his jet lag in his sheer excitement, leaped out of the taxi to grab their bags. Victor climbed out at a much slower pace, wincing, holding a hand above his eyes, and David was scowling as he remained in the taxi.

"You want me to carry you in, princess?" Jed sneered, hauling his worn-out duffel bag over one shoulder, peering into the taxi at David. "Sorry, I'm fuck out of red carpet for your special shit toes."

He saw Redford cast him an amused little smile over the roof of the taxi. David, however, gave him no such favors. "Move your fat ass, Journey," the other man bit out, eyes gleaming in the dark of the car interior. "The sight of you is making me queasy."

"Wait, we need to pay first," Redford said, ducking down to the window to look at the driver. Jed could see him draw up his courage for talking to a stranger. "Thank you for the ride. How much do we owe you?"

"Red, c'mon," Jed protested, tugging at Redford's sleeve. The reply the driver gave was in a mix of Arabic and English, and as hungover as he was, he had not a fucking clue what the total was. All of the euros David had handed him to use were too brightly colored to deal with without either a lot more or a lot less whiskey in his system. "Just pay the fucker," he demanded, shoving what looked like possibly enough into Redford's hand. "Get change back. Make him do the fucking math."

Inside the car, the man seemed to pause as he took the handful of cash and then nodded, a wide grin splitting his face. "Is enough, yes, thank you very much."

Okay, that hadn't gone as well as Jed could have hoped. "Wait, hang on. How much was that?"

"Just enough perfectly, thank you." The driver was still nodding, quite happy with his annoying bastard Cheshire-cat grin, and Jed, head throbbing, was pretty sure he'd just gotten the less than fun kind of fucked with his pants on.

"Please don't handle the money, Jed," David muttered, reaching over to pluck the crumpled bills from the driver's hand. Ignoring the flow of protests, he peeled off a much smaller stack and handed it back. "They have their hands full fleecing tourists who don't bother to learn the language or the monetary system. I really did think you'd be better at this."

"Now aren't you glad you have fluent speakers with you?" Victor sighed. "Or people who can handle basic arithmetic." He nodded toward the hotel entrance and started walking, Redford following closely behind. Caught up in their wake, in the wide-eyed astonishment of Redford's exclamations over the palm trees lining the walk and the bright, dusty tents of the market across the square, Jed decided to drop the issue of taxi drivers and gleeful exploitation of tourists. Instead he looped his arm around Redford's waist, tucking himself into the curve of the man's side. Even with his head pounding and the fun whirligig of nausea, Jed had to admit, Redford discovering new things was still a favorite sight.

If only he could have that sight while lying down in a dark room.

David joined them inside, stripping off his gloves and hat and handing them off to a bellhop. Waving his hand, he gestured for the young man to take their bags as well, striding up to the desk to check them in. Jed amused himself by pacing around the courtyard lobby, squinting up at the arched windows above and wondering how many sniper perches could be hidden there.

A lot. Fucking open floor plans, they were a menace.

Redford was sitting by a fountain, watching as fat, brightly colored fish plopped up to the surface and flashed their lips at him. The man was caught in the sunlight, light-brown hair shining with golden streaks, face lit up with wonder. Redford would find a leaf in the wind fascinating, but there was something infectious about his innocent joy in the simplest of things. It was very hard to be cynical around someone like that.

Sitting on the marbled stone beside him, Jed watched him for a moment with a faint smile. "You're so beautiful," he said, grin growing at the startled look that flushed into pleasure, at the way Redford instinctively shifted closer to him. Reaching out, Jed tucked a stray strand of hair back behind Redford's ear. "How the fuck did I get so lucky?"

"Well," Redford said, voice low, almost teasing, smile transforming his expression into something heart-wrenchingly gorgeous. "You went on a job and did it very well."

"That I did," Jed agreed, leaning in to kiss Redford, so lightly it was barely even a touch. "Best job of my life." Glancing over at the counter where David and Victor were still checking in, Jed lowered his voice slightly. "Can you do me a favor?"

Redford followed his line of vision, then turned back to Jed and gave him a curious look. "What kind of favor?"

"Take one of those chairs," Jed said, voice low, almost sultry as he tipped his head closer, "and *bash my fucking skull in*." He stood up, glowering across the lobby. "Are you *building* the room for us? Jesus Christ!"

"Maybe if you hadn't consumed your body weight in whiskey on the plane you'd be able to exert even a drop of patience," David responded coolly. But he did come over, graceful and calm, dropping key cards into Redford and Jed's hands. "Come along, you giant baby. And take some fucking aspirin. I'm sick of hearing you complain."

Giving Jed a very concerned look, Redford shifted forward to nudge his shoulder under Jed's arm, clearly thinking he needed to help Jed stand upright. Which he did *not*, thank you very much. Even if the floor was doing a weird tilty swirly thing. Goddamn Egyptian flooring. "We'll get water and some pills when we get to the room," Redford assured, pitching his voice to a quieter volume. "And maybe you can nap? That always seems to help."

"This ain't my first hangover, Fido," Jed grumbled. And maybe, yes, he did lean against Redford just a little. Only to be polite. "I don't need to be babied. Besides, no time to nap. Got a meet and greet to attend and some errands to run."

"Are you going to purchase some personal hygiene items?" David asked, eyebrow arched, as they walked through the hallways toward their rooms. "I hear soap is all the rage now."

With a snort, Jed almost laughed before he remembered how much that fucking hurt. "You're pulling out 'you smell' insults? Goddamn, you're scraping the bottom of the barrel."

A flicker of a smile then, and David pushed open the door to their rooms. "Yes, well, it's been a long flight."

Victor, waiting off to the side with a long-suffering expression, heaved a sigh. "Good *God*. Why don't you just pull them out and measure them?"

Never one to let a challenge go, Jed dropped his bags, right in the middle of the hallway. "Oh, your wish is my command, Professor," he growled, fingers going to his belt. "I got a good four inches on His Royal Micropenis."

Redford's eyes went wide, and he shot out a hand to grab Jed's, stopping him from reaching his zipper. "Jed!" He pushed all of their bags into the room with his foot and hauled Jed inside as well. "That's not—people could *see*." Victor, on the other hand, clearly had no interest in the results of his proposed competition, wandering off to inspect his and David's room.

The suite was respectably large, a common area between two rooms. It had its own kitchen and a mini-fridge. A balcony overlooked the courtyard below, with Redford's fountain of fish plinking softly in the distance. Balmy and cool, white gauze lining the windows and linen everywhere, it looked like some interior decorator's wet dream. Jed plopped his bag down on one couch and collapsed, face first, onto the other one.

"Someone fucking shoot me," he grumbled, sunglasses squished against his nose. "Or get me an aspirin. Either or, I'm not picky."

He heard the shuffle of papers, and when Jed pried his face away from the cushion, his nose bumped into a pile of brochures that Redford had stacked on the couch next to his head. "I picked these up from the lobby," Redford said, a hopeful look in his eyes. "They're about tours."

Jed's gaze wandered past the brochures to the bottle of water that Redford had set on the table, and briefly considered if he could get it to float over to him through sheer willpower.

"Look, this one's about the Wadi El-Natroun monasteries," Redford continued, pointing out a paper he'd placed at the top of the pile. Its cover bore a picture of a white stone building with a domed roof, bright and smooth under a clear blue sky. Just looking at it made Jed's eyes hurt.

He squinted at it. "Waddle what?"

"Wadi El-Natroun," Redford repeated, tripping up slightly on the unfamiliar words. "It says the tour starts at a place called Deir al-Baramus. It's the oldest of the monasteries, Jed, and—"

"I've been on that tour." Victor's interjection sounded from the bedroom he and David were settling their luggage into. "Three times, actually. It's quite fascinating."

"We are *not* going on a tour that *Princess Tweed* finds interesting," Jed grouched, burying his face into the cushion again. "Seriously, anyone? Aspirin?"

A few seconds later, Redford was pressing the bottle of cold water he'd been trying to Obi-Wan over into his hands. "I'll find the pills in our luggage," he said. "It might take me a few minutes, okay?" He sounded

45

just as concerned as he had when, on the last job, Jed had been slashed across the chest with a knife. Like a hangover was just as bad as a knife wound.

Waving him off, Jed struggled to sit up. Half the water was drained in a few gulps, and he sagged back, shoving the glasses up on his head and rubbing his eyes. "Nah, don't worry about it," he decided. "I'll grab some unidentifiable meat on a stick when I go out. That'll take care of the worst of it." Meat and grease, after all, were nature's hangover cure. Meat, grease, and hair of the dog, but unfortunately he was on a job. Drinking and passing out on a random street in Egypt was fun once or twice, but he was getting too old for that shit. Besides, he still had nightmares about that damn camel.

Victor and David had disappeared into their room, giving him blissful peace for the moment. Redford had moved into their bedroom to start unpacking their bags, very carefully hanging their clothes in the wardrobe. Jed forced himself off the couch only to take the same spread-eagle sprawled position on their bed, kicking his boots off.

"Are you sure you're okay?" Redford's hand smoothed over Jed's hair. He sat down on the edge of the bed next to him, gently rubbing his fingers against Jed's temple. "I can go meet your contact, if you're not feeling well."

It was strange, the jump of fear that soured in his gut. It spread, ice through his veins, better than any hunk of street-cooked meat to sober him right the fuck up. Rolling over, his head pillowed against Redford's leg, he squinted up at him. Seriously, why did it have to be so bright? "I'm fine," he said, trying not to show how *scared* he'd just gotten. The idea of Redford, of the guy that marveled at flying above the clouds and grinned at fish splashing in a fountain, dirtying himself in Jed's world? Yeah, fucking scared him to death. Rolling around in the muck and the underbelly, that was for him. That was who he was. Redford was better than that.

"See?" He gave Redford an overly bright grin before reaching lazy fingers up to gently bop his nose. "Stop worrying so much, Fido. It's just a hangover." Redford gave him a doubtful look, but he didn't offer to go meet the contact again. Thank fucking God.

"Okay." Redford leaned down to brush a kiss across Jed's forehead. "Victor mentioned that he had books about Cairo. He offered to let me read them. So, um, I guess I'll do that while you're out?" He looked a little unsure.

"Sounds like a plan." Honestly, Jed was glad no one was asking *him* to make nice with the bookworm. He was sure Victor was a very nice guy, but just talking to him made Jed feel like he had all the intelligence of a caveman. Compared to Jed, Redford was way more suited to the smart shit. Jed just wanted to go do his thing, get this job over with, and go someplace he had no bad memories about with Redford.

He hadn't been in Egypt a lot, really. Not compared to some other places. And it wasn't like he'd ever gotten to wander around and take in the sights. At least he still remembered the best places to go for *shawarma* and information. Usually they were found at the same time. Even criminals liked spicy meat and bread.

First things first, however. Jed hauled Redford back into the bed when he started to stand, wrapping himself around him and kissing him slowly, tangling his fingers into Redford's hair. "Hey," Jed murmured, nuzzling his nose against Redford's. "We're in Egypt."

Yeah, okay, he'd been kind of a shit lately. And probably not the most fun traveling companion. Normally, Jed wouldn't care. Hell, if it'd just been him and David here, he probably would have gone out of his way to continue being an asshole, just for shits and giggles. But something about Redford made him want to give the man something better than cranky, hungover complaining. It was the guy's first time for, well, *everything* in a foreign country. Maybe Jed could help make that something good.

"We are," Redford confirmed, that happy little smile lighting up his features again. "Did you just realize that now?"

"Been kind of distracted. You know, being an enormous asshole. That shit takes concentration." It was an apology of sorts, Jed kissing Redford again, loving the way their lips molded together, how their tongues knew how to dance. His hand slipped down to the small of Redford's back, rolling them so that Red was on top. "You know what else takes concentration?" He waggled his eyebrows suggestively, teasing his mouth along Redford's jaw.

"I would say 'studying', but I think you mean sex," Redford replied with an amused smile, nudging his forehead against Jed's. Even a few months ago, Jed was pretty damn sure Redford never would have made that connection—he never would have teased him about a hangover either.

"Give the man a prize." Jed grinned, hands sliding up under Redford's shirt. Redford fit easily on top of him, the words half-lost in the scattered, messy kisses Jed kept pressing to his lips. "And by prize I mean get the lube out of the bag because you're going to fuck me so hard."

They rolled to the side, Redford's hands going to Jed's jeans, Jed's leg hooking over his, and the sudden movement sent the whole world crashing into sick, swirling dizziness. Jed sat up, looking a little green. Goddamn airplane whiskey. "Hold that thought," he managed, vaulting over the bed and stumbling into their bathroom, Redford's quiet laughter echoing behind him. Jed barely made it into the room before bad things began to stir. He was suddenly very glad that this fancy-ass room had a door on the bathroom.

"I'd say 'better out than in', but frankly, you're too pathetic for pithy wisdom." David was leaning against the wall when Jed dragged himself out, looking far too pressed and put together for someone who'd been traveling for a day. There was a kind of sallow tint to his skin, a sunken-in look, but Jed figured he just hadn't eaten yet. Fuck, he wished he could say the same. Goddamn last week of food had just vacated the premises.

"Fuck you," was Jed's response, collapsing back on the bed with a loud groan. His hand shot out, though, to catch the bottle David tossed at him. He really hated when he had to take medicine for something as dumb as a hangover—especially one he walked right into—and he *definitely* hated it when David was right about anything. But he had work to do, and he was in no shape right then. Hell, he'd just stopped sex from happening. It was like a goddamn sign of the apocalypse.

After going into the bathroom, Redford returned with a dampened cloth, gently laying it over Jed's forehead. "He'll be better in a few hours," he said to David. "I think he just needs some food."

"No food," Jed protested. He did manage to get upright again, though, dry swallowing a handful of pain pills and taking the bottled water Redford handed him. "And I'm fine now. Feel loads better."

It was slightly true, at least, and Jed was hardly going to hide inside from a goddamn hangover, of all things. Gulping down the water, he got his feet under him and toed on his boots. "Red, you play nice with the professor," he said, gently tugging a strand of Redford's hair. "I'll be back in a while."

Redford still looked concerned for him, but the worry dimmed slightly when he saw that Jed was managing to move around without swaying. "We'll find out what we can about the kidnappings," he assured Jed.

Saluting his goodbyes, Jed grabbed his sunglasses and the room key, ducking out into the hallway and leaving Redford and Victor to their books.

THE streets were loud and crowded, noisy, brightly colored awnings dotting the sides. His headache was the bass undertone to the sounds of chatter and the honk of horns, the jingle of a bicycle bell as the rider buzzed past him. Jed ducked into a shop, smiling pleasantly at the weather-lined old man who sat there, tending the wares. Brilliant fabric hung down from the ceiling like stripes of a rainbow left to dry, swinging in the slight breeze.

There was a wooden box with long rows of beads. Necklaces made out of smooth glass were lying next to matching bracelets. The colors of the fabrics were mirrored there, sunlight catching and scattering the beams across the walls.

Jed's eye caught on a simple leather piece. It was a three-strand bracelet of thick brown leather holding in the center a blue bug of some kind. Jed picked it up, transfixed by it, sliding his thumb along the cool stone of the insect.

"It brings protection."

Gaze jerking upward, Jed almost dropped the bracelet. He fumbled to catch it, staring back at the old man. He'd just come inside to see if anyone was following him, pretend to shop while he watched the crowd. Jed hadn't intended on browsing. Still, he didn't put the jewelry away. Holding it up, he arched a sardonic eyebrow and smirked. "This thing?"

A toothless grin and the man rocked back, laughing at Jed. "Stone," the man said in a thick, rolling accent, gesturing toward the bracelet, "is lapis lazuli. We buried with the dead. Brings protection." A finger, long and graceful, smooth even in age, reached out to touch the blue bug. "Brings truth. Not everyone can wear it."

Studying the bracelet, Jed pursed his lips in thought. He wasn't exactly a jewelry guy. Sure as fuck wasn't the *present*-giving type. And yet he found himself reaching for his wallet, even as he scowled, "Fuckers are

49

dead. Either that's the shittiest protection in the world, or it's just plain worthless."

The merchant snorted. "You want it or not? Ten American dollars."

"Eight," Jed returned, nodding up toward the ceiling. "And I want one of those scarf thingies."

Haggling done—the man had shrewdly countered with nine dollars, and Jed hadn't felt too much like arguing—and Jed was back out on the street, purchases tucked into his jacket pocket and eyes scanning the buildings. No one was following him. That or they were way fucking better than he was. Either way, he could sit in peace at a small metal table outside a cafe and order a cup of steaming-hot, strong coffee. It would only take a little time for word of his arrival to reach the right people, and then they'd be in business.

"HONEY!" Jed nudged open the door of the hotel suite, grinning carelessly. "I'm home!"

It looked like a bomb had gone off. Books were strewn everywhere, papers stacked haphazardly, a room-service cart with the remains of tea parked near the doorway. Jed paused, eyebrow tipped upward as he scanned the damage. "And Jesus's little possessed piggies, what the hell went on in here?"

"And *that* is a picture of Bes," Victor was pointing out to Redford, completely ignoring Jed's arrival. Redford lifted his head to grin at Jed and then went right back to studying the picture. "He's the dwarf god. The ancient Egyptians used to draw him on the wall above their beds to scare off nightmares."

"Looks like a short fuckin' man with a Tarzan loincloth," Jed grunted, peering over Redford at the book, head tilted to the side and eyes squinted down at it. His hands rested on Redford's shoulders, giving them a brief squeeze, a silent hello. "What the hell does he do to nightmares? Head-butt them in the dick?"

Victor gave him a withering glance over the top of his glasses and made a coughing noise that sounded suspiciously like *philistine*. "I realize it's not relevant to our case at present, but Redford was interested," he explained.

"Yeah, well, Fido's the brains of the operation." Jed pressed a kiss to the top of Redford's head, catching sight of the resulting happy smile that Redford gave, and picked his way carefully over to the couch to sprawl out. David was lying on the one opposite, laptop balanced on his stomach, wine glass in hand. He obviously had tuned out the geek spazzing a while back.

"Did you find anything?" David glanced over at Jed, eyes half-closed, looking somehow both interested and like a cat disturbed from a nap. It took Jed a handful of seconds to stop smiling stupidly back at Redford—there was something about the way the man would light up sometimes that made Jed feel all warm and overwhelmingly *full*.

"Yeah," he grunted, kicking off his boots and settling back. Goddamn, he'd kill for a beer. If memory served him right, there were some damn good Egyptian brews to be found. He'd have to get a bead on those; drinking on the job wasn't his style, but there was nothing like a cold one at the end of the day to wash the dust out of his throat. "Got passed a note about three hours and fifteen pots of coffee in. Thought I was going to float away. No good spot for a piss anywhere." David didn't look overly interested in the trials of his bladder.

"Charming," Victor cut in. Nor, apparently, was the professor. *Now* who was the phili-whatever?

"Anyone hungry?" Jed ignored David's exasperated look in favor of beaming a big grin at everyone. "I found us a nice little place, 'bout ten minutes' walk. You're gonna love it."

"*Jed.*" It was harder to ignore the pillow that beaned off his head or the way David was glaring at him.

Jed informed him, with a sigh and much clucking of his tongue, "You must learn patience, grasshopper. Everyone get cleaned up. Dinner in twenty."

Another overly cheery grin and Jed sauntered off to the bedroom, stripping off his clothes as he went. By God, in the sanctuary of a man's room, he got to get naked whenever the hell he wanted. Even if said room was a shared suite. He took a moment to be thankful for the westernized bathrooms—after a long day, all he wanted was a shower that was as familiar as home. That had not been his experience his last trip through Egypt. Then again, pitching tents in the desert was hardly a four star hotel.

Forgetting about the door to the bathroom entirely, Jed ran the tap hot enough that the mirror fogged up. He stood under the spray, head bowed, hand braced against the wall, and let the water sluice away the dust and the dirt, the hangover and the disgusting airplane smell. Goddamn, that felt good. Almost better than sex.

Well. Better than some sex he'd had, anyway.

"He's very… he does realize that he's not the leader here, yes?" Victor's voice came from the lounge area, muted and probably sure he wasn't being overheard. "Did we vote, and I just don't remember it?"

"It's Jed." Redford's voice was even quieter. "This is how he works. He doesn't like following anybody else's directions."

Victor gave an audible snort. "Well, at least nobody's expecting *me* to give orders. And I can't argue that Jed does get results, however much it pains me to say something nice about him."

Jed wasn't sure if it was a rumbling in the pipes from bad plumbing or some other noise making its way to his ears, but he was sure he heard a growl. "There's lots of good things about Jed." Redford didn't sound too pleased with Victor's opinion—not angry, but unhappy in a kind of apologetic, hesitant way, because Redford was still always so damn sure that nobody wanted to hear him speak.

Jed tuned the conversation out and focused on his shower again, letting the hot water pound into the tense muscles of his shoulders. Yes, he was well aware that he wasn't exactly Princess Friendship Magic Pudding or whatever the fuck, especially not when he was working a job. This one was weird, because usually the guy that hired him was content to bark orders over a cell or in a strongly worded e-mail. This time the client was right there, and Jed felt like he had to constantly be pushing back to make sure David knew that regardless of who had paid for the fancy hotel room, Jed was running the show.

Whatever. David and his snack's feelings could be hurt all they wanted. Jed knew how to get shit done, and that was exactly what he was doing.

The floor creaked, there was the sound of soft footsteps, and Redford shuffled his way into the bathroom, holding a bottle of beer. "Jed? I found a beer in the mini fridge. I know you like having them during showers for some reason—"

Without a word, Jed wrapped his fingers around Redford's wrist and hauled him into the shower. Yes, he was aware that Redford was fully dressed. In no way did that stop him. His arms slid snugly around Redford's waist, and Jed just smirked at Redford's startled yelp. His chin rested on Redford's shoulder, and Jed plucked the beer out of Redford's fingers, setting it on the rack up out of the water. "Hi."

Quickly getting soaked through, Redford stared at him incredulously for a moment. Then, slowly, a little smile tugged at the corner of his lips. "Hi," he replied.

"Thank you for the drink." Jed was grinning back at him, water sliding down their skin, their hair dripping into their eyes. He nudged forward, noses rubbing together, laughing into the breath between them. "You're getting all wet."

"You dragged me into the shower," Redford pointed out helpfully. "And I think Victor will kill me if I drip on his books."

"Well, clearly, we can't have that." Jed pursed his lips thoughtfully, a wicked gleam lighting up his eyes. "We'll have to do something." Very slowly, Jed tugged the bottom hem of Redford's shirt up, dragging the soaked fabric over his head and tossing it away as Redford divested himself of his shoes and socks. His hands smoothed down Redford's chest, taking his time, enjoying the feel of soft skin drenched in hot water. "Hi," Jed murmured again with a grin, leaning forward just far enough to barely slide his lips over Redford's. It wasn't even a kiss so much as a shared exhale, a quick breath of want.

"What do you suggest?" The gleam in Redford's eyes said that he knew exactly what Jed was thinking. "I guess I can't go back into the lounge now." He wrapped his fingers around the back of Jed's neck, trailing down to his shoulders to massage at the still-tense muscles there.

Like always, like every damn time since the first time Redford had touched him, Jed's whole body just *sagged* into the contact. It was as if he was on strings and Redford could cut them with one look, with one hand, with the hint of a kiss. All that tension and worry, all the ceaseless planning and exit strategies, they just stopped. The only thing that mattered was Redford and the fact that his very soaked jeans were standing in between Jed and the holy grail.

He deftly undid the button on Redford's pants, unzipping them and tugging them down, the wet fabric clinging to the other man's hips. There really was something so sexy about how Redford looked then, Jed thought, being undressed, Jed getting on his knees in front of him, the water cascading over Redford like some ancient god being worshipped.

Kissing Redford's stomach, the dip of his hips, tossing the sodden jeans away, Jed happily mouthed his way back up to his chest, standing with him. Redford's pulse was beating faster now. Jed pressed a kiss over his heart, hands sliding down his sides to curl around his hips. "You'll just have to stay here with me," he whispered, kisses trailing up Redford's shoulders, the soft curve of his neck, to bury himself there in the sweet spot just under Redford's ear. "Always."

Redford's fingers tangled into Jed's hair, smoothing over the wet strands, and Redford smiled at him—still a little shy, even after months of being together and falling into bed, or the shower, or whatever horizontal surface they could find. Sometimes vertical surfaces too. What could he say; Jed liked sex. A lot. "I think I'd be okay with that," Redford murmured, his fingertips trailing over Jed's jaw.

It felt like ages since they'd kissed. Since they'd come together with a crash, with a quiet murmur, with a whisper and a moan and everything between. Far, far too long between touches. Then again, wasn't it always? Jed turned his head, Redford tilted his jaw, and they met, perfectly, exquisitely, simply. A rush of heat built in Jed's gut, and he whimpered softly as Redford pushed him lightly back against the wall.

There really wasn't any moment when it wasn't amazing. Even after all these months with the same person, long after Jed would have thought he'd get bored, Redford was still exciting, was still something incredible, every single time. They'd had slow sex and fast fucks and the occasional moment when Jed fell out of bed or Redford got lube in his eye. It didn't matter. Redford was just the best goddamn thing Jed had ever gotten close to, and every time it was better.

"You said twenty minutes," Redford reminded him, soft lips sucking a light path down Jed's neck. "I hate it when we have time constraints."

Yeah, so did Jed. Though God knew twenty minutes was more than enough, as they'd proven many times over. Jed reached around behind Redford, eyes fluttering shut when the man found the sensitive dip of his collarbone, teeth raking over his skin. His fumbling fingers found the shampoo, and he dumped a healthy dollop into his palm, leaning back against the wall. Hands tangling into the silky strands of Redford's hair, Jed began to wash him gently, grinning when the soapsuds dripped down to Redford's nose. "You'll just have to hold onto this for me," he teased, patting Redford's cock. "For later."

"I really wish you'd not leave the door open," Victor bitched from the next room, but instead of being annoyed, Jed just smothered a laugh into Redford's shoulder, relaxing into the soothing motion of his fingers going through Redford's hair. Redford's eyelids had fallen half-closed, looking the very picture of contentment.

"He's just jealous," Redford said lowly, a smile pulling at his lips. His own hands lifted to smooth soap across Jed's back, palms sweeping across damp skin.

"Hell yeah, he is." Jed grinned, moving to wash Redford's shoulders, his chest, loving the way Redford's body felt under his touch. "I get to be in here with you. Half the world would be jealous of me, and the other half would just join in."

Redford looked faintly startled at that idea, but instead of protesting, he simply retrieved the bottle of beer and handed it to Jed. "Relax," he insisted. "Even though I have no idea why you like beer in the shower."

Snorting, Jed took the bottle and leaned against the wall. The water was cranked even hotter, and Jed pulled Redford in, his chest to Redford's back, cradling the man as the water cascaded over them. Jed took a long pull of the beer, closing his eyes as the cold liquid washed its way down, a blissful contrast to the way his skin was burning under the pounding spray. Then he lifted the bottle to Redford's lips, nuzzling kisses into the side of his neck as he swallowed. "See?" he murmured, biting at Redford's shoulder playfully. "Best thing in the world."

He knew Redford didn't like the taste of beer that much, even though in Jed's mind that possibly counted as a capital crime, so he was gratified to see a look of surprised pleasure on Redford's face. "That *is* good," Redford admitted. "Despite the bubbles. The bubbles are still weird." It was the cold and the heat that made it fantastic, Jed knew. That and the way the alcohol lit you up from the inside. Perfection, especially now, like this, with Redford leaning back against Jed's chest, wrapped in his arms, was pretty damn close.

"I, uh." Jed hesitated, rubbing his chin along Redford's shoulder. They really should get out. Prissy McBitchface would probably poke his nose back around the corner and yell some more if they didn't. Jed cleared his throat and mumbled, "I got you somethin'. From the market."

"Really?" Redford turned in his arms. Still, even now, the smallest thing could make Redford look so incredibly happy. "You didn't need to do that."

"Maybe not," Jed agreed in a rumble. "But I wanted to." He always wanted to. Shit, Redford had hooked in deep. Jed had lived most of his life barely thinking about anything other than himself and his spoiled cat. Now here was Redford, dominating his thoughts, demanding that Jed give him parts of himself that he'd thought were hidden but good. And the guy did it all without asking for a goddamn thing. Jed *wanted* to give him that, give him the moon and the stars and a stupid fucking bracelet he'd haggled off some old guy in a market. Jed wanted to give him everything, just for a chance at showing him how much he meant. That he mattered. That he was important.

"Thank you." Redford was still smiling at him, that shy, pleased little smile that he only seemed to wear for Jed. The one that made Jed want to get every weapon in the world just so he could surround Redford, so he could protect him and that smile, make sure nothing ever took it away again. Leaning against him, chest to chest, thigh to thigh, Redford caught Jed's lips in another kiss. "I love you," Redford murmured.

Still, that jolt in Jed's stomach. Redford made those words sound so easy, so perfectly normal. And they were, for him. For them. But every goddamn time Jed heard them, he felt like he'd wandered into lightning and was left tingling, head to toe. "Love you too, Fido," he muttered, a bit gruffly, but there was an infinite tenderness in the way his hand gentled down Redford's back, how he kissed him, slowly, ignoring everything else in the world.

Eventually they did make it out of the shower, clean and well kissed, still tangled around each other. Jed, laughing, grabbed all the towels and ran into the bedroom with them, forcing Redford to chase him. Naked and dripping water they darted around the bed before Redford finally tackled him and kissed him into submission, stealing back the towels to finish drying off.

Jed reached over the side of the bed and grabbed his jacket off the floor, pulling the bracelet out. It was wrapped in the silk scarf, a scarlet and gold that had made Jed think of Redford the moment he saw the color. "Here," he said awkwardly, grabbing a towel of his own from Redford's stack of victor's spoils and rolling off the bed to briskly rub himself dry. "Uh, if it's stupid or some shit, we can give it to David and tell him it's a magic Be Gone Broody Emo Hair amulet. He could use one."

Redford eagerly sat up on the bed to examine his gift. He smoothed his fingertips over the soft silk, eyes widening in delight at the vibrant color. He gently unwrapped the scarf and immediately slipped the bracelet onto his left wrist, holding it up to examine it. He promptly wrapped the scarf about his neck, seemingly completely forgetting that he was still naked, quite happily sitting cross-legged in just the silk, the bracelet, and the chain necklace he never took off, the one that held Jed's dog tags and the whistle Jed had given him, lying against his bare chest. Jed would admit a certain sense of possession the gleam of silver gave him. He'd never taken his tags off until he gave them to Redford, until he'd draped them around the man's neck in some unspoken need to bind them together. The fact that Redford always had them—the whistle that had led Jed to him in Fil's hellhole, the dog tags that bore his name—made Jed feel a little bit like maybe this was a *forever* kind of thing. That Redford wanted to belong just as desperately as Jed did.

"They're beautiful, Jed," Redford exclaimed, peering at the bracelet. "What stone is this? I've never seen it before. It's so *blue*."

God, Redford was beautiful. It struck Jed at odd moments, usually not when he'd expect it. Sitting on a bench, eating a hotdog and watching Redford drink in the sights and sounds of a park, or walking in to find him nose to nose with Knievel, Jed found that Redford had a habit of taking his breath away. This was no exception. Reaching out, Jed's fingers lightly brushed along the scarf, liking the way the vibrant red stood out against Redford's skin, how the flecks of gold brought out the brown in his hair, the smoky blue of his eyes. "It's called lapis lazuli," Jed said, faintly proud of the fact he managed to pronounce it correctly. "Apparently the ancient Egyptians buried it with people. It's supposed to mean protection or something."

Jed wasn't sure why he'd bought the damn thing, really. Maybe 'cause he liked the color—God knew he was like a magpie sometimes, always picking up shiny things. Then again, his shinys usually blew big holes in stuff too, which this one sadly could not. If he was being really honest, really bone-deep, scary-as-fuck truthful with himself, he'd have to admit that he was feeling a little helpless ever since Fil. Ever since Redford's nightmares had really started and the odd changes began. It was one thing to fall in love with a werewolf. Okay, freaky as shit, sure, and kind of hard to wrap his brain around even still, but fine, whatever. So Redford had a little fur problem. Everyone had issues, right?

This was more than that, though. This was Redford *changing* sometimes, going someplace Jed couldn't follow. For all his guns, all his weaponry, all his training and his goddamn *maps*, he couldn't protect Red from this. There was a thin white scar on Jed's hand, still flushed with healing, still sore sometimes, and Jed knew he hadn't a fucking clue how to fix that. Couldn't even begin to figure out how to make it all better.

So he bought a goddamn bracelet. Jed wasn't even sure what he thought that was going to do, but maybe he was just desperate enough for answers he was willing to try anything. Even if it didn't make sense to him.

Sitting up on his knees, Redford crawled his way over the bed to kneel on it in front of Jed, reaching up to cup his hand over Jed's jaw. "It's beautiful," he said solemnly. "It's the best gift that anybody has ever given me."

There was nothing of the "other" in Redford's eyes right then, that made him growl and snap and bite the shit out of Jed's hand. Nothing of the voices that urged him outside to chase after a squirrel like a dog with a sugar high. Just Redford, smiling softly as he brushed a kiss over Jed's lips, murmuring, "Thank you."

Palms flat against Redford's warm, still-damp skin, Jed slid his hands down to settle at the small of his back, just above the curve of that very sexy ass. "It's just a stupid ladybug bracelet," he mumbled, but he couldn't help but be pleased, the sensation of making Redford happy better than any drug in the world.

"Come on." He nipped lightly at Redford's lip, reluctantly pulling away. "We've got work to do, babe. And as much as I love your current outfit, the prudes out there will probably insist we put more clothes on."

Redford huffed a faint laugh and pulled away, moving toward the cupboard where he'd neatly stored their things. "I thought we were going to dinner," he said, half-muffled as he pulled a shirt over his head. "Not working."

Jed looked out into the common area as he tugged on a new pair of jeans. Not that he, personally, gave a fuck that the doors were open, but he'd half expected David to come start bitching at him when they'd been chasing each other around. However, no one was even out there, and the door to his and Victor's room was very decidedly closed. Possibly they weren't as restrained as he and Redford had been, which made Jed want to rip off his pants again and mess up the bed properly. Glancing at his watch, he scowled. Not enough time. Fuck. So not fair that David and the professor were getting some and he was forced to wait. Celibacy was not his style.

"Mmm-hmm," he murmured absently, avoiding an answer. Pulling on a T-shirt, Jed mourned the goddamn flying laws that prevented him from having his babies with him now. A man shouldn't be separated from his guns. It just wasn't right. He felt naked without them.

As he and Redford headed out to the middle of the suite, David's door opened. Victor stumbled out first, hastily buttoning his shirt up to the top button and looking like he had spent the last few *hours*—not merely fifteen minutes—having extremely vigorous sex. He pushed his glasses up his nose and gave Jed a preemptive glare, warning him not to say anything. Even in the sultry heat of the Egyptian late summer, the man looked pale. Paler even than he'd looked an hour ago, if that was possible. Pale and slightly clammy, like he was actually *losing* color in his skin. Jed made a mental note to lock the guy out on the balcony the next day. He could use a little sunbathing time.

"You two have fun?" he leered. Oh, yeah, right, like a little glare was going to stop him.

David sauntered out of the room, looking much better than he had earlier. That permanent tense edge was gone, the faint manic tightness, like he wasn't so much holding himself together with white knuckles at the moment. Sex was the great relaxer, apparently. "More than you could possibly imagine," he all but purred at Jed, his hand slipping around Victor's waist as he pulled the other man in for a light kiss. "Now I suppose we have to all go out for this field trip instead of you simply *telling* me what you found?" He rolled his eyes at Jed's shit-eating grin. "You do love your little rules, Journey. Fine. We'll play the game."

"The game of a *madman*," Victor muttered, resting his head on David's shoulder. "Whichever restaurant we're going to had better be clean."

Jed took Redford's hand and just nudged Victor playfully as they passed him. "Nope. Eating on the ground, with all the bugs. In fact, you catch your own meal there, just grab the scuttling things right up and pop them over the fire. It's gourmet eatin'."

Victor's spluttered protests were underscored by Jed's laughter as the four poured out onto the street. Taking the lead, Jed walked hand in hand with Redford, jostling his way through the crowd. He glanced back at David and Victor as David dropped his own hand away from the other man, barely appearing to even make a movement. It was a pretty damn decisive separation, though, made as they headed away from the tourist-laden areas and into the darker, twisted streets of Cairo's marketplace. Not really hard to understand, though. Egypt wasn't exactly flashing a rainbow flag or anything. Still, Jed tightened his grip on Redford, pulling him in closer, almost in defiance. Let someone try to say shit to him. They weren't bothering anybody, and it wasn't like they were locals, subject to whatever the morality police decided to care about at the moment. He wasn't going to keep his distance from Redford for a *good* reason, much less some leftover narrow-mindedness.

"You're going to like this place," he murmured into Redford's ear, kissing his temple as they sidestepped around a camel. Goddamn things spit. "Lots of things to smell. And most of them are good!"

They found their way to the place, Jed checking their twenty the whole time, watching for a tail. It seemed that his presence hadn't attracted the wrong kind of attention. Not yet, anyway, and hopefully not at all. David, interestingly enough, was doing the same thing, though his gaze always seemed to be drawn to the deepest shadows, to the darkened windows and side alleys they passed. Jed let it go without comment—for now.

Seated at a table, a perfectly clean one with napkins and forks and plates and not a bug in sight, Jed poured Redford water out of the carafe and glanced through the menu. Which was entirely in Arabic. Well, he knew enough to say *hello, goodbye, where is the toilet, this thing will kill your ass*—though that one was a slightly wonky translation, apparently— and *come back to my place*. Oh, and he could count to seven. Jed usually managed to get by in restaurants by pointing and smiling and eating whatever was brought to him, but he kind of wished he'd paid closer attention in his language training.

David and Victor, however, seemed to be reading through the food choices with no problem, discussing between themselves what looked good. With a stray glance, Victor noticed Jed and Redford staring, mystified, at the restaurant's offerings, and sighed slightly, leaning over the table to point to Jed's menu. "I'll translate," he offered, somehow managing to also say *see, aren't you glad you brought a prissy-ass know-it-all professor of linguistics with you* with just his tone.

While Victor read out the menu to them—including little side lectures on the context of a certain word—David's keen gaze was roving over the restaurant's patrons. He inhaled deeply, deliberately, in a move that was somewhat similar to Redford's tendency to sniff the room to pick up scents. Jed took the opportunity to have his own look around, briefly tuning out Victor's babble.

He'd strategically seated them in the booth furthest away from the door, sitting so that he was facing the entrance of the restaurant. The crowd was beginning to pick up, more people coming to eat as the hour grew further into evening, a nice mix of younger locals and tourists willing to get off the beaten trail. Together they provided enough of a background noise that nobody really paid attention to what anybody else was saying. Helpful, because Jed didn't want to have to convince anybody that the four of them were here just to pose next to the pyramids and buy cheap souvenirs.

Turning his eyes back to the table, he barely caught the end of Victor's order. Something about beans, maybe? Fuck, it'd been too long. Unless Victor was ordering a side of sex, Jed was pretty sure his limited vocabulary was going to fail him. In any case, Jed just leaned back, arm slung around the back of Redford's chair, hitching an eyebrow up as he looked at David. "See anything interesting?"

Feigning innocence, David took a sip of his water. "What, you're the only one that can watch our back? You hardly invented the art of reconnaissance, and I am not new to this."

"Technically, the earliest form of reconnaissance is credited to ancient forms of cavalry," Victor pointed out idly. He looked like he wanted to say more, but after taking in each of their expressions, just went back to intensely studying his glass of water.

"Now, I'm getting a little bored of this." David filled the silence with a glower, both elbows thumping onto the table as he fixed his glare on Jed. "I didn't bring you here for a tour. Talk."

Jed huffed out a sigh as he rolled his shoulders back, fingertips drumming absently on Redford's chair back as he let his gaze slowly go around the room again. "I made contact," he finally said. "An old army acquaintance, now she works private security here in Cairo. Very careful, very much into the whole spy game thing. She got me word that she might have some info on your missing people."

A slow loosening of David's frame and the man visibly relaxed. He dragged his hand across his face and looked around again, almost unconsciously checking to see if they were being overheard. "And?"

"Walker. What the fuck are you doing in my city?"

61

The voice was sultry, suited for the desert. At least, that was what Jed had always told her. She'd called it empty flattery, 'cause it was, but hell, it was true. Tipping his chair back on two legs, Jed grinned widely up at the woman towering over their table. Nikki's hair was cut short, dark red cropped close to her skull, body very nicely displayed in a tight shirt and jeans. She never had problems with people looking, as Jed recalled, and knew what to do with the ones that did. Sadly, she wasn't his type, nor he hers, but they'd had fun trolling for those who were. "Nik," he greeted. "So nice of you to join me."

"And your little friends," Nikki replied dryly, pulling up a chair and slinging one leg across the seat, arms folded across the back as she fixed each member of the table with an intense stare by turn. "You know how much I hate surprises."

"Me too." David definitely didn't sound happy. Jed just smiled at them both, though his eyes flicked down to the tell-tale bulge at Nik's waist. She was carrying, which wasn't much of a shock. Still, with Redford around, Jed tended to be more wary.

"David, Nikki. Nikki, this is our benefactor for the evening. Order whatever you want. He's buying."

A knife appeared out of nowhere, sharp and fast and quivering in the table between Jed's fingers. Nikki hadn't even looked before she'd plunged it in, missing skin by barely enough to count. "Stop fucking around, Walker," she hissed. "Why are you here?"

Redford had immediately gone to staring at the table and the knife, a shy flush creeping over his face. "Hello," he managed, trying to introduce himself. "I'm—my—Jed is—"

One finger was held out, Nikki shushing him mid-sentence. "Don't care." She was definitely as single-minded as Jed remembered. Redford looked crestfallen but otherwise slightly relieved that he didn't have to continue to try to talk.

"I sent you a note," Jed sighed. Normally he'd try to encourage Redford. He knew how hard it still was for the guy to do the whole "people" thing. But this wasn't really a holding hands, sharing-and-caring type thing. Maybe it'd been a bad idea to bring Redford along. "Made one of those stupid sideways hearts and everything. I'm hurt, Nik."

"You seriously came halfway around the world for some kidnappings?" After holding his gaze for a beat, trying to search out a lie,

Nikki snorted and sat back. The tension dropped palpably. Even the knife disappeared again. Nikki shrugged, stealing Victor's water with a wink. "Well, that's easy. The mummies got them."

After a moment of stunned silence, Nikki laughed right into Jed's face. His brows were twisted in confusion, and he glanced over at David before snorting loudly. "The... *mummies*," Jed repeated in a disbelieving drawl, arm laid carelessly along the back of Redford's chair.

Nikki shrugged. "Sure. Why not? It's as good an explanation as any."

"Nik, come on, you said you had info." Eyes narrowed, Jed stifled back the surge of impatience. Goddamn it, he *hated* when leads turned out to be rabbit trails. This whole thing smelled funny. There were news reports about the missing people, but not enough to show any connection. One person three months ago, one again a month later, and then three during the three weeks before they'd arrived. That was it. Different backgrounds, different areas of the city—no reason at all to connect them.

Except David had. And Jed was getting pretty damn curious as to why.

"That's my info, Walker." Their food had arrived, bowls and bowls of brightly colored vegetables and sauces and rice. Nikki stood, kicking the chair back to its rightful table, shrugging. "People disappear. It happens everywhere. You know that. They vanish, like ghosts. Maybe they leave town, maybe they run away, maybe they die out in the desert. Who knows? So we say the mummies get them, they wander into the wrong tomb, they get a curse, an old god smites them, whatever. They belong to Osiris now, in the afterlife. There's nothing here, Jed." Another laugh, ruffling Jed's hair, pinching Victor's cheek, and she sauntered away.

Nothing here. Jed was beginning to think she was right.

"*That* was your contact?" Victor was looking a little flushed from the attention, which made sense. He was about as straight as a rainbow-shitting unicorn. Still, he managed to get that hoity-toity imperious look on his face pretty damn quick, pouring some tea and huffing out a derisive breath. "What a fantastic waste of time."

Restraining the urge to smack him, Jed just growled lowly and sulked back in his chair, arms folded. While the others dished up food, he sat in thought, brow furrowed. There was something he was missing. Jed had figured this easy—if David had seen a pattern or a connection in the disappearances from thousands of miles away, surely someone with an ear to the ground in the city would know more. Except Nikki had *laughed* at him. Jed hated being laughed at. She thought he was chasing ghosts. Which meant that either she knew a hell of a lot and was holding out completely, which, while completely possible, was something Jed liked to think he'd have picked up on. Or, and this was looking like the winner, David was leaving out the crucial play. He knew something, something *big*, and he wasn't sharing.

"Talk." He broke into the gentle clink of dishes and the conversation that had stirred up while he'd been brooding. His eyes fixed on David, who was pushing some roasted vegetables around on his plate. "Come on, David, you can't tell me to do a job and then send me in blind. This isn't something anyone else in town has picked up on. Nikki has a knack for knowing everyone's dirty little secrets. So what gives? Why the fuck are we here?"

David put his fork down, his lips pressed tightly together. "You're here to figure out who has been taking people," David said slowly. He'd been on edge since they sat down, that relaxation Jed had noticed back at the hotel fading in the chaos of people. Thinking back, Jed wasn't sure he'd ever seen David *out* for anything other than making contact or gathering intel, not that they were best friends forever and braided each other's hair and giggled over the phone every night. Still, it was weird, to see someone who was normally as controlled as David visibly uncomfortable. Maybe the guy just didn't like crowds. Or maybe the food didn't agree with him. Jed had yet to see him taste anything but the water.

"You're leaving something out," Jed pressed, irritated. "I can't do my job if you don't give me the info, David. Come on! You know that. You've worked with me before for shit-heel clients who withhold stuff, and you know that's how it all goes really wrong, really fast."

The strong line of David's jaw clenched, and he glanced quickly over at Victor. "The police probably don't see a connection," he finally said, waving his hand and leaning back in his chair. "Or anyone else. Because there isn't one, per se. The victims, they'll appear... meaningless. Taken slowly enough that no one sees the pattern, over enough time that people forget. But someone saw something. They just don't know it yet."

"How do you know that?" Jed's intense gaze studied David, like he could pick through the layers of secrecy and figure out exactly what the hell was being left unsaid.

"Because I've seen it happen. Many times before." Draining his glass of water, David's fingers wrapped around it so tightly his knuckles paled.

Eyes narrowing, Jed pointed a finger at him. "You already know who's doing this? Son of a bitch, David—"

The other man cut him off with an impatient wave of his hand. "I know the *type* of man who does this. You're here to get me proof."

A jug appeared on their table, carried over by a waiter. It looked like some kind of juice, redder than Jed would have expected, considering most beverages seemed to be tea or water. The glass container was tinted blue, so it was hard to tell. The stopper in the top was ornately carved, silver and beautiful and old. "From the gentleman in the corner," the waiter started to say, in very good English, his accent making the ends of words lilt musically. "They say—"

"Send it back." David's nostrils had flared, and Redford had shifted a little beside him. Confused, Jed looked around. He was clearly missing something. It was not a good feeling. "Send it back now, please." David's voice was thin and strained, but he forced a slight, sickly polite smile at the waiter. "We're not interested."

Jed sure as hell was, but before he could grab the jug it was gone, whisked away again to the mysterious benefactor.

"That was weird, right?" With a too-bright smile, Jed fixed a look on David, Victor, and Redford in turn. "Anyone want to start talking?"

"It's—" Redford started.

"Nothing," Victor cut him off, smiling blandly. "Absolutely nothing for you to worry about, Mr. Walker."

Jed wasn't buying that. Craning his neck, he peered over into the corner, trying to see who had sent them the fancy juice mug. The furthest table from the door was dimly lit. Jed could barely make out a figure sitting there, though the hairs on the back of his neck stood up but good. Somehow, he figured he had the bastard's attention.

"Let's just see about that." Standing, Jed strode over to the back, a manic smile fixed on his face. There was the scrape of chair legs against the floor, and then David was beside him, walking quickly, expression inscrutable.

Up close, Jed was surprised to see the fucknut in a *suit*. In this weather. Somehow, in the middle of the bar that was rapidly warming up with the press of people, the man in the corner was sitting pretty in a perfectly tailored three-piece suit, watching their approach with a vaguely amused smile. Before he could get out a greeting, David put himself in front of Jed, slippery as an eel.

They started talking in a rapid-fire bullet hail of words, and neither of them was speaking English. Goddamn it. "Hey," Jed cut in, sharing a glower between the two. "Dumb it down for the non-locals. What the fuck is going on?"

"I'm simply delivering a message," the guy in the suit said smoothly, seemingly unconcerned even though Jed was pretty sure he'd busted out his very best *I know how to kill you* look. Seriously, he practiced in a mirror. "It's not what you think, Davie. Go home."

David's frown was even scarier than Jed's, and he turned on his heel and stalked away, shoulders a straight, angry line. Redford sidled up behind Jed just in time to watch the asshole in the suit move away too, vanishing into the crowd. "It was blood," Redford said quietly. "In the jug that he sent."

"You sure, Fido?" Jed murmured, still watching where the guy had disappeared. Feeling Redford's nod, he snorted out a little disbelieving laugh. "Holy fuck. What is that shit, a horse head in the bed? What the fuck."

He and Redford returned to the table, where David was sitting ramrod straight, jaw so tight Jed thought he might actually shit diamonds. Victor was sitting close, concern creasing his features, and he was leaning against David, speaking to him in what sounded like Spanish. Fucking multi-lingual bastards. He could pick up a word or two, but since no one was threatening, fucking, or ordering tacos, he wasn't much use.

David didn't seem to be relaxing much, and Victor ended up grasping his hand. Jed was sure he picked up the word *dancing* in what he said next, and that was purely because Jed knew how to speak in strip clubs. He just hoped that David and Victor weren't about to do *that* kind of dancing. His eyes might actually melt away in protest. Victor tugged David out of the booth, and they moved toward the open area near the front of the restaurant where a band was playing, and couples were beginning to dance to the quick-paced music. Men and women and every combination of both were moving together, talking, eating, laughing in a messy crowd of nationalities. The food was good enough that adventurous travelers seemed to have taken over the spot, mixing with young locals in an explosion of traditions and varying cultures.

"Jed, I think there's something you need to know about David," Redford said lowly, watching them. They moved together with surprising grace, considering Jed had seen Victor trip over absolutely nothing on more than one occasion. It was more than that, though. David's shoulders were beginning to ease, his head bowed forward to catch what Victor was telling him. They were close, and David's hand dropped to rest on the small of Victor's back, and for the first time, Jed looked at them and saw a couple. Most of the time, it was a mystery and a half how they even could stand each other. But just then, moving in the crowd of other dancers, Victor's fingers lightly playing with the hair at the nape of David's neck, they almost looked like they might fit.

"Yeah, I know." Tipping back in his chair, Jed smirked a little at Redford, reaching out to gently tug on his earlobe. "I've known for a while. David's been my contact for a couple'a years now, babe. What, you think I'm that thick?"

"You do?" Redford looked shocked, which was more than a little insulting. Jed might not be fucking *Sherlock* or anything, but he liked to think he was pretty good at putting pieces together.

"Yeah. He's Egyptian. I mean, come on." Jed reached over to steal a bite off of Redford's plate. "It's kind of obvious, don't you think? That's why he's so into this job. Probably from Cairo, back before he decided to start wearing those stupid fucking hats and wander around the States."

"That's... not...." Redford's shoulders slumped as he looked out into the crowd. It looked like he was going to say more, but Jed grabbed his hand and pulled him up with a laugh.

"Don't worry about it." He grinned, leading Redford onto the dance floor. "I've been doing this a while. You'll get one before me someday." With a quick turn he tugged Redford into his arms, cheek to cheek, moving them easily around the floor.

Though Redford looked stiff and unsure, clearly not knowing where to put his feet, he wrapped his arms around Jed's shoulders and attempted to follow him. When Redford *did* end up stomping one of Jed's toes, Jed just grinned at him and pulled him closer. "I've never danced before," Redford mumbled apologetically.

"I never liked it before," Jed said quietly, nudging his forehead against Redford's. Jed's idea of *dancing* was far more like swaying, occasionally turning them around the dance floor, not caring about the other couples or the speed of the music. It was just an excuse for him and Redford to move together, to exist for a little bit just inside each other's arms. And it made Redford smile when he was twirled around, laughing freely, dizzy and collapsing back against Jed. That was worth everything in the world. Jed would burn it down, would haul the moon in and raze every damn thing that stood in his way, if he could keep that look on Redford's face. If they could always be like this, easy and together and moving around the dance floor.

ALCOHOL was not easy to come by in Egypt, but for once Jed didn't seem to mind that he was ending his evening without a drink in him. Jed wrapped his arm around Redford, and they walked home, long past midnight, the streets still bright and vibrant and filled with people, with the scents of food and spices. David and Victor had left a little while before them, but Jed hadn't wanted to stop dancing. It was stupid that he'd felt so warm, so utterly content, doing something so trite. He wasn't a dancer. Hell, he didn't even like shit like that. But it'd felt so good, swaying to the music, talking lowly with Redford about absolutely anything and nothing at all.

Now they had spilled out onto the street with the rest of the evening crowd. It was like another dance, the crush of people, the brilliant fabrics, the lights strung along the stall awnings. Fireflies caught in silk, under a sky that stretched further than Jed had thought possible. The new moon was barely a sliver in the black velvet above them, and Jed hitched Redford in closer, wondering at the bloom of warmth in his chest. Redford was staring in awe at everything they passed.

"Back to the hotel?" Jed asked.

Redford smiled at him, nudging his cheek against Jed's shoulder. "Good idea," he replied. "It's been kind of an eventful night."

Jed's hand found its way into Redford's back pocket. God only knew why he loved walking like that, but he did. That, and the faint flush that Redford wore, every single time he did it. Funny, how something like watching a blush curl its way down Redford's neck, disappearing under his shirt collar, made Jed remember what they'd interrupted before dinner. Like he'd just put it on hold, that same arousal came trickling back in, coiling heat in his gut.

"You look so damn sexy tonight," he murmured, kissing the curve of Redford's ear. "Did I tell you that already?" It was true. It was always true. How someone could be at once so goddamn *innocent* and so unbelievably alluring was a mystery of the ages.

As always, whenever he said that, Redford got that same slightly confused look and glanced down at what he was wearing, taking in the old faded shirt and baggy jeans. It was like no matter how often Jed insisted that he found Redford attractive, Redford still got a little baffled. But he smiled then, tightening his arm around Jed's waist. "You did tell me that. But I like hearing it. And I liked dancing with you too."

A grin flashed across Jed's face, and he couldn't help but let his kisses trail down Redford's cheek to his jaw, nudging in closer. Walking was a bit hard like this, but he figured Redford would look out for things they might run into. He was far more interested in sucking soft little pinked marks along the slope of Redford's neck. "Me too. And you are. Sexy. Really, really sexy."

Thankfully, Redford seemed aware enough to guide them to their hotel, although by several of the stumbling steps he took, Jed was doing his distraction job well. Some people gave them second glances as they walked, a few scowls were shot in their direction, but Jed ignored the reactions. Soon they were inside, away from the Judgy McJudgersons, and Jed forgot about them completely. The second the elevator doors slid shut, Jed was pushing Redford against the wall, catching his lips in a slow, hungry kiss. He didn't want to wait any more. Hell, he hadn't wanted to wait during the walk home, though he did figure that if kisses had been unacceptable, throwing Redford down and having his way with him in the middle of the street might be more than frowned upon by the general public.

Pity. Jed was sure they could have put on one hell of a show.

"This elevator needs to go faster," Redford mumbled against his lips, grabbing Jed's hips, his arms, whatever he could reach. Deciding he didn't give a fuck, Jed pulled his T-shirt off, tossing it aside and tangling his fingers into Redford's hair. Redford's shirt soon followed. Rocking against Redford, Jed wondered if they had cameras in these things. Probably. Damn it, if this thing didn't hurry up, he really would stop caring.

When the ding of doors signaled they had arrived, he and Redford stumbled out, refusing to break apart. Jed abandoned his shirt, much more

69

interested in the slide and tangle of their tongues together, the heat of Redford's body, the way that he was *consumed* by him. "Fuck me," he begged when they broke apart for a breath. "Right now. God, I need you."

At least one of them—and it sure as hell wasn't Jed—had the presence of mind to gather their shirts and very quickly guide them toward their room. They slammed the door shut behind them, their roommates forgotten in their stumble toward the bedroom. That door was firmly kicked shut too, and Redford crowded Jed up against it. Heat bottomed out in Jed's stomach, and he moaned softly, hooking his fingers into Redford's belt loops. Fuck, he loved it when Redford got pushy.

"I've been thinking about this all during dinner," Redford confessed, fumbling to drag Jed's zipper down, fingers shaking slightly in need. "Ever since our shower."

"Me too," Jed assured him thickly, shimmying out of his jeans and kicking them away. "Red—" His words were lost in a kiss, Redford surging forward, meeting him with a fire that threatened to overwhelm him. How Redford could take him from zero to *fuck me now* in no time at all was baffling, but Jed wasn't complaining. No one had ever turned him on like Redford.

Their hands were everywhere—sliding along skin, grasping and pulling—and their hips rocked greedily against each other's. Jed jerked Redford's pants off, hooking one leg up around his waist and giving himself up to him like there wasn't anything else he was made for. Redford had to spend a fumbling moment digging in Jed's pants pocket, which had been discarded to the floor, to find the lube he carried everywhere. When it took him longer than a second to get back to the fun part, Jed looked down to find him rifling around in the pocket with a frown creasing his features.

"What is it, babe?" Jed was panting, arousal mixing with the humid air coming in their open window.

"I can't find them." Redford was turning out both pockets, shaking Jed's jeans, and Jed had to admit he was a bit too occupied with running his hands along those beautifully bared shoulders to really focus on what he was saying. "Where'd you put the condoms?"

Oh. Right. "Didn't bring any." Jed shrugged. "We got tested. It's not like we need them for anyone else. Figured we could do without. Unless you want to blow up some party balloons." He paused, realizing that maybe, possibly, he should have talked about that with Red beforehand. "Uh. That okay?"

Redford, apparently deciding to take advantage of his new position, grinned up at Jed, kneeling up to rake his teeth over Jed's hip. "More than okay," he murmured. A choked little whimper worked its way out of Jed's throat, and he sagged back against the door. Redford seemed to like biting more, these days. Whatever the cause, Jed sure as fuck wouldn't complain. He'd woken up on more than one occasion with marks on his throat and inner thighs—marks that Jed definitely enjoyed wearing and feeling for the rest of the day.

Nuzzling against the crease of Jed's thigh, Redford kissed the base of Jed's cock, looking up at him. Redford, Jed had learned, had really come to enjoy foreplay. He went about it with a single-minded precision, always watching Jed closely. "You smell really good when you're turned on," Redford mumbled, trailing his tongue up the underside of Jed's cock, a teasing, light little motion. "Did I ever tell you that?"

Any reply Jed might have given was cut off by a strangled groan as Redford decided to get down to business, wrapping his lips around Jed and taking him in. His fingers clenched into Redford's shoulders, and his head hit the door with a loud thump. "Fuck, Red," he murmured restlessly, legs spreading, toes digging into the carpet. Trying to stay still was helped by Redford fitting his hands over Jed's hips, pushing him back against the door.

Watching his cock disappear between those gorgeous lips, already bee-stung and red from their kisses, was almost more than he could take. Unsteady fingers ran through Redford's hair, and Jed watched him, biting his lower lip, transfixed. Redford pulled away, and Jed would swear that he was almost *smirking*. That might be because of the strangled, protesting whimper that escaped Jed's throat. Redford stood again, hands still fitted over Jed's hips, kissing him eagerly.

"Bed?" Redford started to suggest before he paused and grinned again, leaning against Jed. "Although I kind of like right here."

"Yeah." Jed's head bobbed up and down, eyes dark with need. "Here. There. Fucking anywhere, Red, Jesus." Grasping at him, Jed pulled him in again, arching into the hands that Redford smoothed over his ass, kissing him with a hunger that threatened to consume him. Against the door was *great*. Turning in Redford's arms, grinding his ass against that gorgeous, thick cock, Jed groaned, "Lube. Now."

71

Redford laughed lowly against his ear, nuzzling against it. He put on a good show of being patient, but the hands that grabbed for the lube again were fumbling slightly, and he was panting against Jed's shoulder, teeth raking over the skin there. "I can't think when you get all demanding," Redford said faintly. There was the quiet click of the tube cap, slick fingers rubbing gently against Jed's hole before one pressed in, just a fraction.

"Maybe you should make some demands, then," Jed murmured, turning his head to bite Redford's jawline, the curve of his ear. "What do you want from me?"

"Everything." Redford bit again at Jed's shoulder. He inched his finger further in, still fucking *teasing* and trying to drive Jed absolutely nuts. "And right now I want to fuck you." There was a rumble of possessiveness in Redford's voice. A shiver worked its way down Jed's spine at the low, commanding tone. At that moment, he'd have done *anything* just to hear that again.

He whimpered once more, the noise teasing out into a low groan, rocking back against Redford's finger, desperate for more. "Everything," he promised, hands splayed against the door, Redford, tight and hot and hard, pressed against his back. "Oh, *God*, Red, *please*." His begging had Redford smiling against his shoulder, going *way* too slowly in introducing another finger, but it was worth the wait when those long, perfect digits crooked upward, seeking out his prostate.

"You're so beautiful," Redford murmured, finger fucking him in earnest now, holding him up when Jed sagged backward in trembling, boneless pleasure. Jed was pretty sure that time blurred, hanging on a precipice where nothing mattered except the low rumble of Redford's voice in his ear and the need running through his veins. He barely noticed when another finger was added, too busy desperately shoving back against Redford's hand.

The words *please* and *love* and *more* were a constant litany past Jed's lips, lost and tangled up and hidden in the groans and panting breaths. Every push felt like he was falling harder. Every thrust back made him shake and plead for more. His protesting moan was even louder than the others when Redford pulled back, putting a hand to Jed's hips to gently guide him to turn around, facing Redford again. Both of Redford's hands smoothed to wrap around the backs of Jed's thighs. "Can you...?" Redford gave him a questioning look, flushing a little.

Dazed, it took Jed far too long to figure things out. All he knew was that he felt empty, and that was not how he wanted to be. Grumbling, Jed pouted, busy running his hands down Redford's chest, his stomach, teasing his thumb along the head of his cock. "Can I what?"

Redford blushed harder, and his fingers clenched tighter on his thighs, getting a better grip. Jed breathed out a startled "Oh!" His expression fell into a wicked leer. "Fuck, yeah." Redford lifted him up, Jed's legs wrapping around his waist, leaning against the door. Completely supported now by Redford's arms, Jed had to admit, this was hot. He liked how strong Redford was, how in control, how Jed was at his mercy. Flipped all the right buttons. "God," Jed breathed, hauling Redford in for a kiss, fingers getting lost in those gorgeous, messy strands of hair.

"I like seeing your face," Redford whispered against his lips, the muscles in his arms flexing and straining to hold up Jed's weight. Hey, maybe there was one good thing about the new and improved werewolf stuff.

"Yours ain't so bad either." Jed smiled a little, hips rolling down against Redford's cock, greedy. "Sure you're okay?" Being held up and fucked against a wall was sexy. Being dropped would probably not be. But Redford just hitched him closer, bracing Jed against the solid wood of the door.

"I won't drop you." Somehow, even in the middle of sex, Redford managed to do his earnest face. It wasn't something that Jed could concentrate on for very long, though, considering Redford was shifting him in his arms slightly, bringing him down onto his cock. "You can trust me," Redford panted.

"I know." Arching his back, Jed gasped as Redford slid inside of him, as he was filled and stretched. "Already do." It was perfect. It was always perfect. Redford was big, just long enough for that delicious *ache*, more addictive than anything Jed had known before. He craved this, always. Because it felt so damn good, because Redford's cock was gorgeous and being fucked with it was like seeing God, but mostly because it was *Redford*. It was *them*.

The moment that Redford started to move was like something *better* than seeing God, whatever the fuck that might be—Jed would think about it later. Though Redford usually favored a slow buildup, he was just as caught up in the need as Jed was, short, sharp thrusts thumping Jed's hips back against the door. It didn't matter that their position didn't allow for much movement, not with Redford clenching his hands under Jed's thighs and lifting him up a few inches, pulling him back down. Crying out loudly, Jed rode him as best he could, clinging tight to Redford's shoulders, hungry for him deeper, harder, for more of everything. Who the fuck cared that they were shaking the door? Restraint was so far gone it might as well be on a plane back to the States. All that mattered were the shock waves of pleasure ricocheting through him, making every panting breath a moan.

Each thrust in, tight and full, hit just the right spot. Jed was seeing stars, eyes glazed with pleasure, staring into Redford's. And every time Red pulled out it was like dying, like he was losing part of himself, so much so that Jed was consumed with taking him back in deeper than before, like he could somehow meld them so he never had to lose this feeling. So he'd never be without. "Babe," he whispered hoarsely, biting his lip so hard he tasted copper. "Fuck, Red."

It didn't seem possible, but somehow Redford picked up the pace, his tongue swiping over Jed's lower lip. The door was slamming, thumping against the frame with every thrust, and Jed had a delirious moment of hoping desperately that they didn't manage to break it down. Although he figured adding that to David's bill might be worth the damage. There was a low growl, Redford pulled Jed's legs higher, and Jed hissed at the change in angle, losing himself in a shout and a rush of pleasure.

It was the way Redford was fucking him, the desperate way he was taking and being taken, the look in Redford's eyes, like he'd never wanted anything more. Just one more thrust, one more low, stomach-rumbling growl, and Jed couldn't hold back any longer. Redford's name was on his lips, a tumultuous cry, and he lost himself in a blaze of heat. Two, three more thrusts and Redford was following him over the edge, teeth digging again into Jed's shoulder, muffling his moans of Jed's name.

When reality faded back in, when the overwhelming crash of pleasure faded into a low hum, Jed found himself still held aloft against the door. Redford's arms were trembling with the strain, but he didn't seem to want to let go just yet. His face was tucked in against Jed's neck, chest heaving as he struggled to return to regular breathing. "God," Redford mumbled.

Squeezing his legs briefly around Redford's waist, Jed rumbled out an exhausted, giddy laugh. "Yeah," he managed, panting shallow breaths, still half stupefied by the aftershocks of orgasm rippling under his skin. "Hell, yeah."

74

Redford slowly let him down, shaking out his arms a little and echoing Jed's laugh. "Bed now?" He sagged against Jed to kiss him lazily, content.

"I don't think I can move." Jed smirked, holding Redford close, arms circled around him, legs barely keeping him upright. "That was seriously incredible." Kissing Redford's shoulders, his arms, Jed smiled against his skin, biting lightly at one bicep. "My man is so goddamn strong," he teased. He went gladly when Redford tugged his arm, tumbling them onto the bed that was, thankfully, close by. Any more than three feet away and Jed would have declared the walk to be too much effort.

Redford drew the blanket up over them, making sure that it was tucked securely around Jed's waist. It was humid, and they were still overheated from the exertion, but Redford played the caregiver anyway, fussing just because he could. He settled down to lie on his side, facing Jed. Redford reached out to touch his fingertip against Jed's lower lip, eyebrows creasing in concern at the patch of skin he'd bitten raw.

"I wasn't too rough, was I?" Redford worried, his fingers then smoothing over the bite mark he'd dented into Jed's shoulder.

Jed's own hand lifted, finding the bruised skin, a smile flickering lazily across his lips. "Nope," he murmured, stretching, feeling utterly content. That nice burn was settled into his gut, legs still weak from exertion, and there was no question at all that he'd been very thoroughly fucked. Redford still worried about every bruise and bump, a remnant of the days of being overly careful about full moons. "I like it, Red." He lifted his head just enough to catch Redford's lips in a slow, languid kiss. "If I could get you to cover me in the damn things, I'd be thrilled." Everyone would know then, from the marks on his neck, the love bites that would cover his skin, and Jed would be damn proud to show them off.

Redford looked reassured that he hadn't caused Jed any serious pain, gladly returning the kiss. His eyes were beginning to slip closed, and Redford nudged his forehead against Jed's shoulder, looping an arm over his waist, curling around him. "I'll remember that for next time," he mumbled. "I like people knowing that you're mine."

"Course I'm yours," Jed murmured fondly, shoving his way in closer to Redford. A huge sigh lifted his chest, rumbling down to his toes, and he nuzzled in against the other man. This was the best thing ever, falling asleep in Redford's arms. Before, he'd be lucky to get his eyes to shut without help from his good friends Jim, Jack, and José. Now all it took was that sleepy little smile, those gorgeous eyes sliding shut, and Jed was right there with him. Yawning so hugely his jaw cracked, Jed mumbled, "'Night, sweetheart."

The reply that Redford gave was little more than a mumble of a string of vowels, a noise that was *probably* meant to be a word, which was lost to falling asleep. His arm tightened around Jed's waist and he dozed off, a small smile still curling at the corner of his lips. For a few moments Jed watched him sleep, the strange feeling of contentment still settled around him. He wasn't used to being this happy, this perfectly satisfied. But he definitely could get used to it.

His eyes slipped shut, the last sight before sleep that of Redford's face. Yeah. Getting used to this was no problem at all.

CHAPTER
5

Jed

IT WAS like an internal alarm clock. Maybe he could thank years of military training, or a mother who'd insisted they keep their school schedule even in the summer, or just some fucking wire crossed in his brain, but Jed had never had any trouble waking up when he had to. He loved to sleep, that was definitely true, but if he told himself to get up at a certain time, there he'd be. And this was a day he didn't want to sleep in.

For a little while he just lay there, Redford slumbering contentedly beside him, going over everything in his brain. The disappearances. David's shifty behavior. The carafe of blood. The message.

There was something still missing. He could almost *taste* it, it was so close, but he hadn't quite figured it out. Like when you saw something out of the corner of your eye, there and gone before you could register what it was. Jed hadn't gotten all the pieces yet. But he knew who did.

Well, no time like the present!

Sauntering into David and Victor's room, hand over his eyes in case there were unmentionables on display, Jed announced stridently, "Wakey, wakey!" Jerking open the shades, he let the sunlight flood the room. "Rise and shine!"

With a loud hiss that reminded him of the one time he'd accidentally stepped on Knievel's tail, David flung himself out of bed so fast the top sheet flew off with him. He crouched in the far dark corner. Yellow eyes flared for a moment, a trick of the light, and David gave him a dark look. "What the *fuck* are you doing?"

Victor took significantly longer to wake up and, once realizing the sheet had been whipped off, stuttered in distress and grabbed the blankets again to cover himself up, even though he was wearing pajamas that would look more at home on a sixty-year-old. "Jed, for God's sake."

77

Victor scowled, and the scowl only grew deeper when he noticed David hiding in the corner. He got out of bed and whipped the curtains shut, then went to find his glasses. "David, are you all right?"

Jed had been about to point and laugh or something. Because, seriously, who jumped out of bed like it was on fire like that? "What's the matter, Nosferatu?" He smirked, leaning against the wall, arms folded. "You—"

David was burned. He was standing up, now that the room was dim again, scowling down at his arm. It was red and covered in blisters. Exactly like he'd stuck his arm into a furnace.

"What the fuck?" Jed breathed, eyes wide, moving forward. His gaze was locked on that burn. The one that hadn't been there last night, at least not as far as he'd noticed.

Redford's quiet footsteps announced his presence at the doorway. "I was trying to tell you last night," he said lowly. When Jed turned to glance at him, his confusion only grew—Redford did not look happy. At all. There was a yellow glint in his eyes, arms folded across his chest in a defensive posture, but the look on his face said that he had no idea *why* he was feeling threatened. "David's not human."

"The hell you say." Jed was now pretty sure this was a joke. Come on, of course it was. The burn was probably makeup or some shit. He bet Victor carted around loads of that stuff. Jed snorted and rolled his eyes, reaching out to the curtain again and yanking it open.

David reeled away with a loud curse, turning his back to the window. Where the sunlight hit, Jed watched the skin redden, like David had been sunbathing for hours without following the dermatologist's recommended sunscreen-protection plan. Victor once more snapped the curtains closed and, shockingly, walked over to Jed like he was about to impart some kind of violence. Which, if Jed had any mental capacity left, he might have found annoyingly adorable.

"He's a vampire, you utter moron," Victor seethed. "I know you have barely two brain cells to rub together, and I also know you seem to be willingly blind to most things in this world, but *try* not to deliberately injure my boyfriend further." He still didn't look very threatening in askew glasses, bedhead, and grandpa pajamas.

Jaw dropped, Jed stared between the three of them. David was trying to examine his own back, muttering under his breath, and yeah, his eyes were definitely yellow. And his teeth were… pointy.

"Oh my fucking God," Jed murmured. "You're a goddamn vampire."

"As always, you're right on top of things," David hissed, fangs bared. A low, rumbling growl came from Redford, who came forward to stand next to Jed.

"Let's not have this turn into a battle of the supernatural, shall we," Victor said dryly, gaze shifting to Redford before returning to David to examine the burns on his back. "Jed, you may as well be helpful and turn the light on."

Right. They were in the dark. Him, a werewolf, a vampire, and a prissy professor, just chilling in the dark. Jed bit back a slightly hysterical giggle, slapping on the light and moving closer to David. He'd first met the man in a bar, after getting the shit kicked out of him by some guy he'd tried to pick up. That had ended badly. David, however, had bought him a drink and proved to be useful at finding out things. For five years and some change, Jed had considered him a contact. An informant. Someone he could almost trust enough to turn his back on, which was saying a lot for Jed. And this whole goddamn time, he was... what? Dracula?

Fuck that shit. He was not Mina Harker.

Turning around, Jed stalked over to the suite's mini-fridge. After rifling around for a minute, he came back to the room and, dramatically, opened a box and threw the contents on David.

The slice of pizza clung to David's face for a moment before sadly flopping to the ground. Jed was met with twin exasperated stares. "What?" he said, baffled, examining David for signs of explosions. "We got extra garlic!"

Their leftover midnight snack was apparently not good vampire-fighting material. David's gaze narrowed. "You threw that at me, and you expected it to work? Seriously?"

"What? Movies say garlic kills vampires!"

"And you *threw it at me?*" David roared, moving forward with his fists clenched. Redford, who had been lurking in the background, yelped and skittered away, out of the room. "What if it'd worked?"

"I didn't think that far," Jed admitted, unaffected by David's temper.

Throwing up his hands, David announced, "I'm going to go take a shower. Someone please give this idiot a lesson in how not to kill me in the meantime. I'd like not to have to drain him like a chicken." The man slammed the bathroom door shut, and Jed was left staring at the lonely slice of non-lethal pizza.

"Red?" he called after a moment. "Baby?" Damn it.

Victor sighed heavily. He gave a glance at the door like he was considering joining David, but eventually moved out into the joint kitchen area, pulling a teapot out of the cupboard. "Werewolves and vampires aren't all that fond of each other," he explained mildly. "It works at an instinctual level. Somewhat like the dogs and cats of the supernatural world. Even if he's never met a vampire, Redford will be feeling that unease. Would you like some tea?"

"Never bothered him before." Jed, despite all evidence to the contrary, was still feeling skeptical. How the fuck was this even possible? He'd liked his world, before. His nice, ordered, *normal* world. Now there were werewolves and vampires and shit, and Jed honestly didn't know if he was equipped to deal with it. Redford was one thing. Hell, Redford could have been born on a giant flying saucer that spent time making weird squiggles in fields and Jed would have just learned how to pilot the damn thing for him. But this was... a lot.

"Perhaps not," Victor acknowledged. "A vampire baring his fangs is a sign of aggression. That could have triggered his unease. Or perhaps it's the stronger instincts he's experiencing now." Victor gave Jed a sidelong glance, stirring some milk into his tea. "Do I need to give you a list of vampire strengths and weaknesses?"

Officially the weirdest conversation of his life, and that included that time in Japan with the sumo-wrestling twins. Jed slowly shook his head, eyes still on his bedroom doorway. "I gotta check on Red," he mumbled, getting up, feeling a little dazed. "Um." Shuffling his feet, he looked back over at Victor, so calmly sipping his tea. "Thanks." Victor looked startled at the word but let it pass without comment, simply nodding.

Jed winced a bit as he knocked softly on the bedroom door, pitching his voice lower. "Fido? You okay?"

"I don't know," came the muffled reply. It sounded like Redford was leaning against the other side to prevent anybody from getting in. There was a shuffling sound, and Redford slowly opened the door, looking sheepish. "I'm sorry. I—" He cast a look toward the opposite bedroom, frowning. "I just had to leave."

Shit. Yeah, okay, big overwhelming moment, but Jed still felt guilty. Like he should have seen it coming or been able to keep the situation from going down like that. He hated it when Redford got that skittish look in his eyes. It reminded him, way too painfully, of how he'd found the guy, hiding away in a dead woman's prison.

"Yeah, apparently it's a whole thing," he said, eyes searching Redford's face carefully. Jed reached out to tug gently on a strand of Redford's hair. "Come on. Victor is just dying to give us a lecture, and he made tea and shit."

Nodding a little, Redford moved cautiously out of the bedroom. His eyes were still fixed on the opposite door, like he was expecting David to burst forth and get aggressive again. It was kind of weird, considering in the five years that Jed had known David, he'd always been pretty mellow. His hand slipped into Redford's, just like that, and he squeezed Redford's fingers lightly. His free hand went to tap very softly against where Jed knew his dog tags and whistle hung around Redford's neck, hidden by his shirt. It was a wordless reminder, a kind of *I'm here*. Redford had those things as a symbol, stupid maybe, but it meant he wasn't ever going to be lost again. Not so long as Jed had his guns and fingers to shoot with.

"Well, let's start at the beginning, shall we," Victor said cheerfully, settling the pot of tea down on the kitchen table. Four cups followed, and Jed's focus homed in on two perfectly round scars sitting at the base of Victor's throat, nearer to his left shoulder. "Vampires are not like you see in the movies. They—"

"Are those bite marks?" Redford asked quietly, sitting down in one of the chairs. Jed paced behind him, a little too freaked out to do much else. Bite marks. From a vampire. Somehow, all this supernatural shit was way harder to swallow when they weren't talking about Redford.

Victor, on the other hand, was still perfectly calm. "They are," he confirmed. "Vampires, as you have probably gleaned from the stories, need to drink blood to survive. Most vampires kill and drain humans. There are some, however, like David, that subsist on mostly animal blood. It's not satisfying for him, but it keeps him alive."

Jed cut him off. "Look, this is... well, I'm not going to lie. You sound fucking insane. But whatever, so David is a cocksucker *and* a bloodsucker. I don't really care. The jug yesterday, at the restaurant, that was meant for him. And it wasn't some Mafia scare tactic, was it?"

"No." Victor smiled thinly. He poured Redford some tea, slid the cup across the table to him, and set about pouring one for Jed. He was so fucking English. "David suspects that the kidnappings here may be related to vampires. Last night was not a confirmation, however. It simply proves there are vampires here in Cairo."

Fuck.

"Fuck." No reason not to share with the class. Jed leaned against the wall, pinching the bridge of his nose.

"That pretty much sums it up, yes." David was shirtless, the burns faded only slightly, toweling his hair off as he came into the living area.

"Hey, wait a minute." Jed frowned, pointed at him. "You're all wet."

Blinking, David glanced around like he was looking for the thread of conversation he'd just lost. "Yes, Journey, that's what happens in a shower."

"Don't call me that." The protest was almost automatic now. Jed was busy moving closer to David, face screwed up in thought. "You're all wet. From *water*."

"Again, yes. A shower. Look into it." David backed up a little, maintaining his personal space, but Jed circled him quickly. He reached out to nudge a finger against David's shoulder, slicking away some drops of moisture.

"So you're *not* a vampire!" Jed crowed triumphantly. "Vampires can't be in water." Hah. Mystery solved. "I *knew* you were all yankin' my chain."

David beat his head lightly against his palm. "Jed. That's *holy* water. Holy. As in blessed. As in definitely nothing that would ever be anywhere near you. Now stop acting like you've had some kind of head injury, and let's get back to work."

"Maybe you should just show him your fangs again," Victor said helpfully, and then added, "Jed, you're fairly sharp. I thought you would have figured this out sooner. Oh!" As if remembering something, he reached across the table to find his wallet and, with an annoyed look, pulled out two twenties, which were promptly put into David's hand.

"Never doubt how thick Journey Walker can be." David slipped the money in his back pocket, smirking at Jed. "Do you want to see the fangs again, Jed? Or can we move on now?"

Jed slumped down into a chair, sulking visibly. Yeah, he was the idiot because he hadn't thought *vampire*. 'Cause that was the conclusion normal people got to. "Whatever. I don't want to see anything you got, cowboy, so go put some goddamn clothes on. And what was the money thing?"

"Vickie bet me that you'd figure it out before we landed," David said over his shoulder, heading back into the bedroom to get dressed. "I said you'd literally have to see me rip someone's throat out. I guess we both lose, though I was way closer."

"I didn't figure it out either." Redford laid a consoling hand on Jed's arm. On anybody else it would have been insincere, but Redford just looked at him with those big cow eyes. "I knew he was something *else*, but I didn't know what. He smells different."

Jed rubbed his forehead, groaning a little. "And you tried to tell me. Shit. I'm sorry, sweetheart. I should have listened." Well, wasn't he just an idiot? "Look, fine, vampires are real, and I'm going to start checking under my seat for leprechauns and pixies. Why don't we get back to reality a bit? If we're dealing with, you know, freaks and shit, I'm gonna have to go about this way differently."

Victor, with an unamused glance at Jed, probably because *freak* wasn't PC or whatever, followed David into the bedroom. Redford watched him go for a moment and then said, very lowly, "He smells different too. Not like me or David, though."

Considering that, Jed shook his head. "One at a time, Fido."

Shit.

CHAPTER
6

David

THE storybooks were wrong about a lot of things. There was no princess in a tower, no knights in shining armor. No trolls waiting under a bridge or a wicked witch cackling in a dungeon. Werewolves weren't mindless beasts who ate without restraint, pixies didn't coat the world in dust and dew, and fairies definitely didn't come back to life just because a bunch of people clapped their hands. Out of everyone, though, out of all the supernatural creatures that still roamed the earth, David thought that vampires were the most misrepresented.

Then again, he was biased.

For one, he didn't sleep in a coffin. It was a gruesome idea. He had no clue where that particular rumor had gotten started, but it did have some staying power. No grave dust, no garlic, and running water only got him, well, wet, just like any other being. His skin wasn't pale, his eyes weren't red, and, thank God, his fangs didn't cause him to have a horrible fake accent or a lisp. People passed him on the street all the time without even the faintest hint of what he was. *Who* he was.

Rolling over in bed, David stared at the window, the heavy drapes keeping out even the faintest hint of sunlight. Thanks to feeding earlier, the burn marks from Jed's little demonstration were faded away, not even an ache to mark their memory. He could feel it, though. The sunset. The world growing cooler, darker, the shadows stretching and coming out to play. It was the time he felt most at ease, when the harsh light faded and gave him and his ilk leave to wander.

David gently eased away from Victor's slumbering form. The man was in stifling Egyptian heat, and he still had his plaid pajamas buttoned up to the neck. Frankly, David hadn't even been aware they'd sold sleeping clothes like that anymore. At least, not to anyone under the age of sixty. A fond expression touched David's face for a moment as he looked down at Victor, passed out with his face buried in the pillow, snoring lightly, though the man would hotly deny doing so.

His gaze then inevitably dropped to the two reddened marks on the soft curve of Victor's neck. They were healing quickly. By morning there'd be no sign of them, other than the smooth white scars that marked the bite. David would know, though. Of course he would. He put them there.

David turned away, his jaw clenched tightly, finding his clothes and tugging them on. There was no need to switch on a lamp. Bright light often had him squinting, everything a bit blurry and once removed. In the dark, he moved with grace and simple ease. A bonus, perhaps, of his turning. Or a curse. It really depended on how much one liked the sun.

The hotel disappeared quickly into the distance behind him as David set out after slipping quietly out of the room, eschewing the offered taxis in favor of walking. He used to know this city, what felt like lifetimes ago. While the facade had changed, had become more modern, clean and bright, and the infrastructure had definitely improved, the heart of Cairo still very much the same. The underbelly was seething still, as it would in all places, in all times. The ravenous dark never really let go of a place. It only found new ways to hide.

His nose guided him. A trustworthy thing, a vampire's nose, at least where blood was concerned. The city fairly pulsed with it, with the sweet highs and brassy, copper lows, like a symphony that crashed into him, overwhelmed him with promise and hunger and taste. He had to take a moment, standing in the middle of a street, people flowing around him. David closed his eyes and drank it all in, bathing in it, awake and *needy* and so, so at home. He'd belonged here too. It had been his city, his home, his blood as well.

Until it wasn't anymore. Until that lifetime had ended. Deep brown eyes snapped open, not a flicker of yellow betraying him, and David gathered his self-control around him again. It was a threadbare cloak, faded and worn down, but it was his own. He'd forged it again after it'd been ripped so completely away, and he held it close now, keeping himself together. *Not food*, he reminded himself sternly, ducking around a laughing, chatting group of women, their hands waving like conductors, their voices trailing after them like music. *None of them are food.*

Ducking into a side alley, David followed a tendril of a scent. It wasn't living blood, not any longer. That spice was gone, leaving it flat and quickly cooling. It was the scent of spilled blood, of the aftermath of feeding. He knew it far too well. Blocks passed quickly, David moving as a ghost among the crowds until even they trickled away, until all that was left was the aging night and the faint smell of death.

It was a young girl. It so often was. Her head was bent to the side, and her eyes stared up at him, accusing, milky and dull. David knelt beside her, smoothing a shaking hand over tight curls of hair that seemed more alive than the body that had been cast aside like so much garbage. The bite marks in her neck were savage, the lack of precision to them making it look like a wild animal had attacked her rather than a vampire. Her killer—or killers—hadn't been concerned about neatness. Gently, David closed her eyes and stood again, expression impassive as he brushed dirt from his pants. There was nothing else he could do for her. She'd been a snack, easily taken and just as easily discarded.

It also meant he was looking in the right place. Messy vampires, to leave trash at their door. David looked around, eyes narrowed in thought. Bracing himself, he jumped straight up, grabbing hold of an overhang and hoisting himself upward. This area of the city was run down, worn out, and not at all the kind of place he'd expected to wind up in while searching for the suspect. Even the metal fire escape creaked dangerously underneath his feet, rusted pipes groaning as they held his weight.

Keeping to the side of the window, David peered inside. The outside of the building might be close to crumbling, but the inside was a different story. Plush carpet lined the floor, opulent furnishings and tasteful decorations. Even the chairs had carved scrollwork arm rests. Paintings that looked like seventeenth-century originals hung on the walls.

The men and women that were lounging around fit very neatly into their surroundings: expensive suits and rich dresses, wine glasses held easily in their hands. Except they weren't sipping champagne. No wine gleamed so darkly and smelled so rich.

Oh, yes. He was definitely in the right spot.

Perhaps he'd been hanging around Journey too much, because David's next move, rather than walking in the front door like any civilized person, was to break the window with a well-aimed kick. He leaped down in a shower of glass, landing gracefully and straightening up, adjusting the sleeves of his shirt and running a hand through his hair.

"I believe you were expecting me?"

The present company, far from looking startled, just glanced over at him like he was a stray, ragged animal that had found its way in. Disdainful and vaguely annoyed, they hardly deigned to give David a passing glance. The man standing closest to him even grimaced and held his wine glass a little further away from David, as if afraid he'd spoil it or knock it over.

"Not so much 'expecting'," one of them answered. "More like 'hoping you'd go away'." The one who spoke was sprawled easily in a wingback chair. He was foppish in that way that David knew so well, strength lying under a carefully maintained mask of insolent uncaring. If he'd spoken, then he was the one David wanted.

Striding across the room, ignoring the sideways glances and the whispers, David grabbed the blond man from his posed relaxation, fingers wrapping around his neck. Slamming him carelessly against the wall, David arched an eyebrow. Stupid child. Did he really think David didn't already know every trick he could have learned?

"Where is he?" David asked, voice low, almost bland if not for the iron ribbon of threat running through it. The party still continuing in the room was barely interrupted, its revelers paying only the vaguest attention to him. "I can smell him all over you." Fingers tightening, David couldn't help the small, furious rumble in the back of his throat. "Tell me where he is. Now."

Far from being concerned about his current predicament, the vampire simply gave him a look that might have been inquisitive, were it not so bored. "May I inquire as to whom we're speaking about?" The overly correct speech was grating but not obviously forced. Meant the vampire had probably been turned about a hundred years ago.

David leaned in closer. Close enough that he could see the faint white scars standing out on the vampire's neck, close enough that he could feel the rush of stolen blood through his veins, the warmth he'd borrowed seeping into David as well. "Tell me where your sire is or I will rip your head from your body," he whispered almost lovingly. "You know your sire, don't you, little fangling? The one that gave you those?" David's eyes flicked down from the other vampire's to the bite marks and then back up again. "One last chance. Where is he hiding?"

"My sire doesn't *hide*," the vampire spat, anger turning his eyes into a flashing, muddy yellow. Behind him, David could hear the music's volume being lowered, conversation coming to a halt.

Everything stopped.

"You'd best stop talking about our sire." A distinct Texan twang came from his left shoulder, a brick wall of a man looking none too happy. David had to wonder when southern had gotten on the menu. Tastes had changed a bit in the time he'd been gone.

Far from worried, David simply flashed a slow smirk. "Your sire"—he spat out the word—"is a cowardly worm that would rather skulk around in low-rent warehouses than face me. You can tell him that Duha is in town, and if he doesn't want to wake up to a stake through the throat, he will leave. Tonight."

The flurry of violence that followed, perhaps, David should have seen coming. Or maybe he'd been looking for it, pushing right where he knew the whole genial facade of respectability would break. In any case, there was a fist heading for his head with a swiftness that would have shocked a human. Luckily, David was anything but. He ducked, rolled his shoulder forward, and caught the large, brutish vampire off balance. David slammed his opponent backward toward the wall, throwing a few punches of his own, feeling his fists strike against the vampire's stomach, feeling him sag inward in pain.

Accelerated healing or no, punches hurt. Vampires were notoriously averse to discomfort, if they could at all help it. Bloodletting and pain for pleasure was one thing. Broken bones tended to be far less fun. There was a crunch of cartilage as David swung back, connecting with the vampire's nose, and that one was down for the count. On the floor in a whimpering pile at David's feet, the massive vampire seemed to have the fight beaten right out of him by a few well-timed punches.

Feeling extraordinarily cocky—he certainly hadn't expected it to be *that* easy—David turned around with a smirk. "Who's next?"

From the sudden crack of agony along the back of his head, David would have to guess that *he* was. Staggering forward, he barely got a glimpse of the burly vampire, not so distraught and definitely a better faker than David would have guessed, lifting the chair for another blow. Five other vampires grabbed his arms, his legs, all eager to get their own hits in.

With a roar, David lashed out, struggling. The blond was leering at him, blood from his glass spilled all over his fashionable suit, lending a kind of frantic, savage air to his perfectly put-together appearance. "Cow eater," the vampire spat. "Did you really think you could walk in here half-starved and accomplish anything? My sire will be *so* happy to see you again."

Desperation licked at David's movements, and he kicked out, catching one vampire in the jaw, finally getting his foot free. Immediately, he twisted in his captor's arms, the toe of his boot gouging at another vamp's eye. There was a sickly *pop,* a loud wail, and David was standing on his own again. His teeth were bared, hair mussed, eyes brilliantly yellow in anger and, he'd admit, fear. This was not a good situation.

Hands reached out for him, the blond shoving David against the wall. Behind him, the other vampires lined up, fangs glinting, fairly shaking with barely restrained aggression. David snorted, trying to sound dismissive. "What is this, a dance off?" he sneered. "Sorry, twinkletoes, I forgot my tap shoes at home."

A fist connected with his jaw, and David saw stars. He spat blood to the floor, ignoring the laughter of the crowd, raising his head again. "Do you think you can get away with this?" David rasped. The blond punched him in the gut, smiling evilly as David bent over in pain. "People are noticing the disappearances. You're getting sloppy."

That laughter again, dismissive and jeering. David wasn't one for outbursts of anger. He'd learned a great many years ago that one got further by the cold steel of revenge than the hot flashes of fury. It was hard to take the mocking, though. Perhaps he shouldn't have punched the blond in the dick or used the opportunity of his choking agony to snap his neck. Then again, restraint only went so far.

The body fell heavily to the floor, and David stepped over it, eyes glittering coldly. It wouldn't kill the vampire, no, but it'd hurt like hell. Which was more than enough for him at the moment. "Do you hear me?" he said to the crowd, refusing to show fear, ignoring the aches and bruises they'd given him. "This is not your town. You can't take people and expect no one to notice."

"You really believe we're to blame?" The voice was smooth, oil over water, slick and calm. David turned to watch as a woman, stunningly beautiful in a simple black evening gown, rose from a couch. She'd remained lounging during all the commotion. Now she stalked forward,

89

eyes never leaving David's. "Such a rude boy," she chided, patting his cheek with just enough force to sting. "We were never introduced. The one that you so carelessly left on the floor is Kevin. I am Vanessa. And Johnny, the big lug"—she fondly patted the large southern vampire's shoulder—"you've met."

Scowling, David rubbed the back of his head. Yeah. He, *Johnny*, and the lump on his skull were just the best of friends.

"And you are *David*." The way Vanessa said his name made David's lips skim back up over his teeth, a low warning rumble in the back of his throat. "Such a pretty boy." Another smack on his cheek, condescending, before she grasped his face between her thumb and forefinger, yanking him forward like an errant child. "But dumb."

He was shoved backward again, regaining his balance after a brief stumble, half-crouched, fingers curled into fists. David watched Vanessa with wary eyes. Kevin's body was between them, sprawled out, elegant even now. She stepped over him, long skirt brushing over the unconscious vampire's chest, the rich fabric rippling like a lover's touch even as she barely cast a glance downward. Her gaze was bright, focused on David, devouring him with the full attention of her stare. "You're on the wrong trail, cow eater," she purred, one elegant finger pressing into his chest, pushing him backward with a surprising strength.

"You're honestly going to stand here, with a barely cold body outside your front door, and tell me you're, what? Having church meetings?" David sneered, leaning forward, refusing to be pushed around any longer. This was his world, or it had been. He'd lived in this space, in the sidelong glances, the subtle gestures that meant power and privilege and place. One cocky woman smelling of blood and strength was not going to make him cower.

The laugh that broke out of her was anything but musical. It was the dregs of sour notes, running up and down David's spine, ice and oil. "Really, David?" Moving forward, lightning fast, her hand was around his throat.

His had mirrored hers, though, just as quick. He might not feed and hunt as they did, but David was far from a blood bag to be toyed with. Fingers tightening, feeling the throb of her last feeding pulse through her, David didn't look away. Her eyes narrowed, yellow and far from lovely, not fitting with the coy beauty of the rest of her face. How young had she been when she'd been found? And now this life, this existence—was it what she'd wanted? Everything she'd been promised?

"You know him better than most." Vanessa's words pulled him from his thoughts, and David frowned. He didn't recognize her. He didn't know anyone in the room, actually, none of their faces pulling up memories he'd worked so hard to repress. Yet none of them struck him as newly turned. "And you still don't understand, do you?"

Her nails bit into the soft skin of his neck, drawing rose petal drops of blood. "I understand enough," David growled, shoving her away, ignoring the long scratches she left behind.

Another laugh, but she held up her hands and stepped out of his way. The rest of the clan followed suit, a path opening between him and the door. It was not a victory. They were letting him go, most turning back to their drinks and their conversations, dismissing him just that easily. Vanessa was obviously in charge, and she had sauntered away, Kevin's body carted behind her by two more vampires. They'd wait for him to revive and make sure there was a warm victim for him to feed from. Blood was the only way vampires could heal, after all.

David ruefully felt the lump on the back of his head, his bruised ribs, the black eye. Cow's blood, pig's blood, goat's blood—whatever substitute he managed to scrounge up in this country—it wouldn't do even a tenth of the good one decent feeding would. He'd be bearing these wounds for a day, at least. Unless….

No. He wasn't going to go to Victor for that, not again. He'd already fed, already taken the few sips he allowed himself. Damn it, he was not going to turn Victor into his own walking happy meal. He'd eat what he could find, and it would be enough.

David stiffly straightened his coat and walked out with as much dignity as he had left.

"WELL, don't you just look a right mess, princess."

The drawling voice greeted him as David softly closed the hotel door behind him, and he hid his cringe, gripping the handle tightly and briefly considering the delightful option of just leaving again. He really wasn't in the mood for Jed at the moment. The man might be good at what he did, he might be the perfect tool to use in this situation, but he did have a knack

91

for pushing David's buttons. Right then, all David wanted was a hot shower and the half a bag of blood he had left. Maybe then he could start getting his brain to wrap around all the pieces of the puzzle that didn't seem to fit.

Sadly, when he finally did turn to face the darkened room, Jed was still there. The man was lounging on one of the couches, maps spread out around him. Jed flicked on the lamp, cocked an eyebrow, and whistled softly. David grimaced as the light flared and narrowed his eyes as he edged toward his room, hoping Jed would take the hint.

No such luck. "Nice shiner, Davie."

"Do you always lurk in the dark?" David smoothed his hands down his shirt, as if making sure it wasn't wrinkled took precedence over everything else.

"Heard someone coming." Jed shrugged and stood, lumbering over to David to get a closer look at the bruises, the long scratches. "Didn't figure you'd be out wandering around by yourself." Cocking his head, smirking when David backed away, Jed spread his hands in a show of innocence and flopped back down on the couch. "Hell, I didn't even know your hair could be out of place, all that gel you use. You look even worse with the lights on."

"I'm fine," David muttered through a clenched jaw. "And I am going to bed. Try not to strain your brain too much with your little picture maps."

Jed might be fully human, but he moved much faster than David had been anticipating. Vaulting over the back of the couch, he blocked David's path, eyes narrowed. An edge of steel worked in under his mocking tone. "Nah, see, *I* think what's gonna happen is you and I are going to have ourselves a nice little chat."

"Sorry, Journey." David tried to feint around him, but Jed was like a brick wall, immovable and just as goddamn stubborn. "I'm fresh out of nail polish, and I don't know how to braid hair."

"Oh, hardy har har," Jed scoffed, a rigid, mocking smile splitting his lips. "You're a fucking riot, Davie, really. Now why don't you cut the shit and sit down, before I give in to the urge to present you with a matching set of shiners."

David had learned, many years ago, when to throw in the towel. Clearly he wasn't going to avoid this conversation, no matter how much he wished to. Waving his hand in dismissal, David turned and sprawled himself across the nearby armchair, hooking an eyebrow upward and shooting Jed a pointed, expectant look. "I'd tell you not to call me *Davie* again, but I suspect that will just make you more inclined to do it."

Flashing David a shit-eating grin, hard and brittle and more than a little annoying, Jed didn't sit. David had noticed that particular habit. When he felt like he was missing a part of the picture, Jed tended to pace. He did so now, fingers drumming along the sides of his thighs like he was trying to play an invisible piano. "Are we going to talk?" David prompted, expression carefully arranged into one of nonchalance. "Or did you just plan on irritating me to death?"

"Where'd you go?" Jed glanced over at David, eyes narrowed. "You look beat half to hell."

"Out." David realized that this was not going to end with both of them trotting off to their separate beds, Jed none the wiser. Somehow, though, he couldn't help the streak of obstinacy. These days he took a perverse pleasure in disobedience. Frankly, it was funny when Jed did that stupid little growl, lip curled up, like he was actually intimidating. Perhaps to some people. David just thought he looked slightly constipated.

"You hire me," Jed snapped, arms folded, eyes glittering in barely restrained anger. "Drag me and Red halfway around the fucking world on some wild goose chase. Okay, fine, you're paying. I've had weirder jobs. But goddamn it, David, you're sneaking out, not telling me shit, and you still expect me to do anything? Why the fuck am I even *here*?"

David neatly crossed his legs at the knee. "Why do you think that sack of fleas, Filtiarn, hired you? You're human, Jed. You can nose around in places where a supernatural would get caught in a moment. Kind of like how you don't notice the pigeons crapping on park statues."

Maybe that had been a little blunt. Jed's eyebrows winged up, his mouth opening and shutting like a beached fish as he searched for the right comeback. Which might take a while. David studied his nails, a careful look of boredom creasing his features.

"Fuck you!"

And there it was. Looking up, David arched one eyebrow. "We've been over this," he all but drawled, tapping his foot impatiently, the only sign in his languid posture that he was anything but utterly disinterested. "You're not my type. I like my men to wash now and again."

93

"Shut the hell up." Jed's ears were turning red. Not a good sign. His poor blood pressure. "Just… you dragged me out here, you got Red involved, and for what? I'm your goddamn *pigeon*?"

One shoulder lifted in an artful shrug. "Pretty much."

He saw the punch coming. Of course he did. Perhaps it'd been coming since he got back. But David let it land, wincing as the force of it knocked him backward. As promised, David suspected he'd now have a matching pair of black eyes. Picking himself up off the ground, his fingers lightly touching his already bruising cheek, David carefully brushed off the front of his pants and clucked his tongue. "Temper, Journey."

"Don't fuck with me, David. I don't care if you're straight outta a Rob Zombie flick, I will fucking rip your balls off if you've gotten Redford into some shit you can't handle." And there was the rub, David knew. It wasn't himself that Jed was all knotted up about. Hell, David suspected that if not for the werewolf, Jed would half enjoy the challenge. Ever since Redford had shown up, though, David had noticed a sense of *caution* seeping into Jed's work, a hesitance that hadn't been there before.

"Don't worry," David said, going to the mini-fridge and rifling around for some ice. Yes, he would heal, if he fed. But until he got a chance to drink and the cow's blood started working, he had no intention of walking around like a bar brawl victim. "Everything's under control."

"Yeah?" A hand towel was tossed at him, and David snatched it from the air before it could hit the back of his head. "Mind sharing with the class?"

David bundled up the ice and held the makeshift cold pack to one eye, glaring at Jed with the other. Finally, reluctantly, he leaned against the counter and shrugged. "I went to look for the man I think is responsible for the kidnappings. I found a clan of vampires, we had a discussion, I was outnumbered, and this is the result. They informed me that I was on the wrong trail."

Jed studied him, seeming to absorb all of this. He let out a quick breath, jerking his head in a nod, and settled in on one of the table chairs, sitting backward, arms folded across the back. "You believe them?"

David shook his head. "Not even a little."

There was no other option. In this city, these streets, there was only one monster that dared walk so much in the light. There was news coverage, for God's sake. Who else had balls like that? The vampires were covering for him. David fully intended to find out why.

Jed was staring at the ceiling, brow creased, thinking. Or perhaps trying to count to twenty, a dangerous task with his boots still on. "So you go wandering out and just *happen* to come across the bloodsuckers that work for the main bloodsucker," he said, eyebrows lifting. Maybe Jed wasn't as half-asleep as David had been hoping. "Goddamn, princess, gotta buy you a lotto ticket, your luck's that good."

"I knew where to look," David admitted in a murmur, rubbing a hand through his hair. "And there was another victim. Not a kidnapping this time, just a... a feeding."

David would give Jed this—for a guy who'd only known about the existence of vampires for twenty-four hours, it didn't take him more than a few seconds to catch all the unspoken meanings of that particular phrase. Confusion quickly melted to disgust and anger, all gone in a flash as Jed rubbed his hand across his face, muttering a curse. "Tell me you didn't—"

"I don't," David interrupted him quickly, corners of his lips creasing downward, eyes dropping. "Not like that. Not anymore."

"So what's Vickie, then?" Jed pressed, voice cold. "A late night snack?"

Grimacing faintly, David stood, rubbing his hand along the side of his neck. His fingers bumped over his own scars, faded and white against dusky skin. "That's different. Just... I don't feed off random people. These vamps, they got careless, left their mess for someone to find."

He glanced up to find Jed studying him, gaze unrelenting. "Didn't imagine vampires to be that stupid," Jed commented blandly before turning back to his maps.

"They...."

They weren't. At least, not those vampires, not the ones in that clan. Eyes narrowing slightly, David watched the way Jed was rolling his maps, the careful movements as he gathered up his notes and markers and brightly colored sticky notes. A weird observation to make, if it was random. It was very coincidental that the very vamps he'd been looking for had left a signpost shouting the way.

"*Fuck.*" David slammed his hand on the counter, face screwed up in anger. "Son of a *bitch.*" It'd all been a show. Every last goddamn fucking thing. That body had been left for him. The vampires had been *waiting*.

They'd known he was in town, they knew he'd come looking, and it had all been staged beautifully. And he'd walked right into it.

"Who is it?" Jed had turned back to him, and if David had been close enough he might have been tempted to bite the smug expression right off of his face. Fucking human. "You played into their hands like a sucker, so obviously whoever it is either knows you or knows how stupid you are. Though the two aren't mutually exclusive, I suppose."

"Christ, I hate you sometimes." Wearily, David rubbed a hand across his face, eyes falling closed.

"Just 'cause I'm so pretty." He heard Jed moving closer, and David held up a warning hand. Unsurprisingly, that didn't stop Jed. Fingers closed on his shoulder, and David started, back painfully hitting the corner of the counter. "Stop fucking with me. You're running around like an idiot, waving your cock around to whoever wants to take a look. Either tell me who the fuck we're hunting or I'm on the next flight home. I sure as hell don't need a front row seat to watch you get yourself killed." He paused, and David would swear he actually *heard* the smirk. "I would order the extended-edition DVD. Only if it has commentary, though."

David moved out of Jed's reach and gathered his distance again, his self-control. He crossed his arms tightly across his chest, as if that, somehow, would keep him all put together, then met Jed's eyes steadily. It was to the other man's credit that he didn't comment on the yellow blaze in David's. "Vampires aren't born." David didn't want to explain this. But Jed was like some idiot child that'd wandered into the grownup's party. If he didn't get a little background, he was liable to knock down a table and set his hair on fire. "They're made. That's why we're considered the purebloods, one of the very few races still fully undiluted with the taint of humanity."

There was a faint rustle from behind the bedroom door, and David looked up to see that Victor had emerged. Those silly pajamas were still done up to his throat, making him look so proper and yet so very vulnerable, standing there with his hair all sleep-tousled, his glasses ever so slightly crooked. The barest hint of a smile curved up one corner of David's mouth, more an okay for him to join in than anything else.

"Wait, what the fuck," Jed said, glancing over at Victor, glaring at everyone indiscriminately. "There's, like, a class system for freaks?"

"How very sensitive of you to put it that way," David responded dryly. "But yes, as crude as that was, it's accurate. There are some races that have become, shall we say, *less* over the years. They mingled with humans, and every generation saw a weakening of their particular skills or gifts. Or, in some extreme cases, they have disappeared entirely. But because vampires can't be born, can't breed, we are still pure."

"More importantly, why on earth are we talking about this at—" Victor checked his watch, blinking owlishly at them. "—four in the morning?" He took his glasses off to rub at his eyes, and when he put them on again, he stared at David and his double black eyes. "For God's sake, David. What were you doing?"

"Davie, here, apparently had a slight *disagreement* with some locals," Jed said, lips thin in annoyance. "And I don't care if it's the fucking high holy days, someone is giving me some concrete answers. As much as I appreciate the insight into the social standings of freak gene pools—"

Cutting himself off, Jed's mouth fell open slightly, realization dawning. David winced, glancing over at Victor. Christ, he hadn't wanted to do this with him. Sadly, no ground opened up to swallow him, no earth-shattering event chose that moment to take place, and Jed just could not resist showing off how goddamn smart he thought he was.

"It's your whatever you call it. The bloodsucker who made you. That's who you think is doing this?" Breathing out a quick, incredulous laugh, Jed rocked back on his heels. "You dragged us all the fucking way out here to camel country for your *daddy issues*?"

Growling, David turned on his heel, grabbing Jed's shoulder and shoving him toward his own room. "That's enough of sharing and caring time, Journey," he demanded, ignoring Jed's protests. "You know what I know now, so I'm going to bed. You can go bother someone who actually thinks the words coming out of your mouth are something other than a waste of air." Slamming the door shut in Jed's face, David sagged back, dragging his hand across his face, feeling every bump and bruise and scrape.

"Fuck."

"It's your sire?" Victor's voice was soft, but he didn't sound surprised. Of course he wasn't. He'd probably figured it out before David had even finished reading the first goddamn news story. Victor was a lot of things. He was insufferable and sexy and stuffy as hell. But he was also brilliant, in his own shut-in kind of way. Thinking he could hide anything from the guy, especially with what he could do, well, it was an exercise in futility.

David's favorite kind, apparently.

"I think so," David said, biting the words off, obviously not wanting to talk about it. "What are you doing up?"

"Oh, you know. The usual. Wondering if you were out getting yourself killed." Victor smiled wanly at him, reaching up to gently touch the bruised skin around David's left eye. "I didn't hear what you and Jed were talking about, but I assume you explained the situation to him."

"Do you really even have to ask?" Wincing, David reached up to curl his fingers around Victor's, holding them over his heart. "Enough, I guess. He's not interested in the whole 'the truth is out there' speech, but he has the gist." He wearily pushed away from the wall, heading for their room and the blood he had stored in their mini-fridge. All he wanted to do was eat and collapse.

Victor's voice took on a more amused tone as he crawled back into bed. "He's not interested in hearing details about who he's sharing a hotel room with?"

"It's Jed." David shrugged, grabbing the half-empty bag and pouring the remaining blood into a glass. "All he wants to know is what he has to shoot or blow up. Extra details never were his strong suit." Carefully turning his back to Victor, David took several long swallows of the blood. The rush, even from the cold, almost disgustingly cloying cow's blood they'd managed to find, was enough to cause David to grip the edge of the dresser, a quiet moan rumbling in his throat. He drained the glass far too quickly, chasing the last drops out with his tongue.

Fuck, he was hungry. And that was probably the last thing he'd get to eat for a few days. The religious majority in the area didn't allow for the blood of the animal to be saved for use in cooking, which meant finding it for his purposes was that much harder. David set the glass down with shaking fingers and tried to arrange his features into something other than pointed starvation.

Want rushed through him, even the cold blood warming him, curling under his skin and sending a flush across his cheeks. Gabriel had trained him very well. That bare mouthful, unsatisfying though it might have been, sent his senses into overdrive. He craved something more—

connection, intimacy, the thrust and heat that only came from feeding and sex. David hardly understood one without the other anymore.

Victor was watching him from the bed, curled under the covers, glasses awkwardly budged up against his face from the pillow. "That's not going to do much for your injuries," he pointed out unnecessarily.

"Yes, well." David unbuttoned his shirt, letting it slip from his shoulders to the floor. "It will do." He was not going to give in. This time, he would ignore the desire racing through him, he would disregard the jittery need pounding in his skull. His pants were next, kicked off and left behind as David padded over to the bed. Normally he'd hang his clothes up, but right then even the idea of bending over to pick them up seemed overly daunting. He would deal with the extra ironing the wrinkles would demand.

For now, he slipped into the cool sheets and attempted to relax. Huffing out an inscrutable sigh, Victor rubbed his palm over David's arm. He looked as if he was on the verge of suggesting something, but he shut his mouth again, slipping his glasses off instead. "How are you feeling?" He asked like he knew the question was completely useless and the answer would be the same.

"You know how I am," David muttered, staring at the ceiling. "But I'll survive."

Victor's expression was half-hidden in the pillow, but he shuffled closer and rested his hand on David's chest. A shiver worked through David, and he closed his eyes, biting back a quiet moan. That innocent little touch had him aching for more. His reaction, however small it had been, had Victor pressing into his side to brush a kiss against David's jaw.

And then promptly stuck his hand into David's boxers.

"Victor!" David squirmed, not away though, because God, he wanted a thousand touches just like that one right then. "What on Earth?"

Victor looked like he was half-asleep, eyes closed as he rested his head against David's shoulder. His movements were slow, lazy, and the smile he gave was much the same. "I would have thought it was obvious. Perhaps I need more practice if you're in doubt."

Biting back a low moan, David let his eyes drift shut, turning to bury his face in Victor's neck. "I know *what* you're doing, you evil man," he murmured, hips moving into the friction of Victor's hand.

"Good," Victor replied. "Then just relax and enjoy yourself." He tightened his grip, his movements languid as he stroked over David's cock.

"Vickie—" Cutting off, he turned his head, scattering kisses along Victor's jaw before he nipped very lightly at the curve of Victor's ear. All he needed was the faint taste of blood on his tongue, and he was coming, hard and fast, fingers clenching into Victor's back.

Victor gave a rather contented-sounding sigh and removed his hand from David's boxers. When he spoke, his voice was blurred with sleep, clearly a few minutes from dropping off entirely. "Better?"

David hated himself. In the afterglow, in the way his muscles just unwound, he despised everything about himself. He loathed how Gabriel's training still held onto him so much so that he couldn't even drink without needing that. He wanted to be better. David so desperately wanted to be *more* than what Gabriel had turned him into. He just hadn't been able to figure out how.

"Yes," he admitted hoarsely. "Thank you." After a beat he added more quietly, "I'm sorry."

The reply that Victor gave was nothing but an indistinct mumble before his breathing evened out into the rhythm of sleep.

Rolling over onto his back, David crossed his arms under his head and stared at the ceiling, willing himself to sleep. He could smell the dawn on the breeze trickling in their window, teasing him with its closeness, with the impossibilities it held. Victor was soon snoring softly again beside him, sprawled face down into the pillow, but David struggled to even force his eyes shut. Not until the sun was actually peeking through the edges of their curtains did he manage to slip into a restless, pained sleep.

HUNGER jerked him awake. It was a ruthless pang, a yawning, empty grumble that had David rolling over, reaching out for the warm, sweet scent next to him. *Christ*, he was starving, veins feeling like they were collapsing into dust, stomach begging for even a drop to sustain it. His injuries had barely begun to heal, bruises green and yellow mottled against his skin, cuts and scrapes still aching with every movement. David's grasping hands closed on heated skin, and he rumbled a needy growl, dragging the body closer, teeth ready—

"Fuck, Jesus, Victor." Shoving him away, David rolled out of bed with an ungraceful lurch toward the floor, face pressing against the carpet as he struggled to wake up enough to find that tentative control. He'd been five seconds away from tearing into Victor, hunger making it difficult to even *think* with so much blood so close, so *easy* to take. Shaking, David managed to force himself to maintain distance, eyes rimmed in yellow peering over the side of the bed at Victor, who was looking back at him, too groggy to really comprehend what was going on. "Maybe you should go get some tea," David said lowly, jaw tight with the effort this was taking. "I'll be out in a bit."

After he'd reminded himself that he was not a mindless monster. As much as, sometimes, he wished he could be.

The fridge was empty of blood. There was no easy source to get more. Which meant the hunger, that gnawing ache, was something he would have to live with for the moment. Not an ideal situation, no, but one he was familiar with. David gritted his teeth, heels dug into the floor, back pressed against the wall. He was not a slave to his desires, not any more. He was more than this. He had to be *more*.

There was a rustle of sheets, socked feet padding on the floor closer to him. Victor's eyes were still heavy-lidded with sleep, his movements clumsy because he hadn't put his glasses on yet. "You need to find another butcher, don't you?" Victor slipped his glasses on, frowning at the sight of David.

"I'll go out tonight." Trying for a reassuring smile, David patted Victor's shoulder before gently pushing him further away. God, he smelled so good. David could practically *feel* his pulse, beating slowly as his body climbed its way out of sleep, so sweet and vulnerable under the thin, pale skin. "Please, Victor, you... smell."

He smelled like food, like potential, like something David wanted to sink his teeth into. Not what he needed at the moment. His control wasn't strong enough to handle so much temptation so deliciously offered.

"Excuse me?" Victor momentarily looked insulted. "I *smell*—oh. Yes, of course." The insult faded into understanding, then consideration. "David, we already know how difficult it is to find blood here. You could...." He trailed off, one long-fingered hand lifting up to rub over the bite scars on his neck. "It would be better for you."

101

A low, shuddering keen made it past David's parted lips, and he found he was staring at the slide of those gorgeous fingers along the pale curve of Victor's skin. Oh yes, he absolutely could. He could a thousand times over, until he was buried into Victor's neck, until they were heaving and writhing together, until the last drops of blood flowed from Victor to him and he was finally *full*, finally at peace.

Gritting his teeth, David forced his hands down from where they'd started for Victor. "It wouldn't be better," he disagreed quietly, back teeth clenched together. "Especially not for you."

"*You're* the one that's going after your sire, he's—" David cut Victor off with a growl, a deep, rumbling warning. Victor paused and frowned. "Fine. But if you don't drink, you're going to be utterly intolerable. And weak. You can't afford to be weak, not here."

"I'm not weak," he muttered, shoving his way up to his feet. He wobbled once, but it was barely noticeable. His body had used up the few mouthfuls he'd drunk the night before in an effort to heal his wounds, leaving him with a throbbing emptiness that was making it hard to focus. Grimacing as he looked in the mirror, David shook his head. Well, at least the bruises weren't as dark as they'd been the night before. The split lip was mostly gone now. The rest he could live with. "Besides, you like it when I'm intolerable." He shot a quick smirk over his shoulder, one elegant eyebrow arched. "It's part of my charm."

Victor breathed out a laugh, moving closer. He stood just behind David, both of them studying the bruises in the mirror. "No, you're not weak," he amended. Victor carefully wrapped his arms around David's waist, chin resting on David's shoulder. "But I do worry for your safety here."

David snorted, though he nonetheless found his arms folding over Victor's, his head briefly leaning back to rest against Victor's temple. "Don't," he said, but the bite had faded from his voice. He just sounded tired now, a vulnerability David rarely allowed himself to show. "It will all be fine, Vickie. We're going to get the son of a bitch, and then we can go home."

And it'd all be over. Surely, this would mean it was all over. David could be free.

"Is overconfidence part of your charm too?" Victor's voice was wryly amused, and David wished the man hadn't started pressing his lips underneath David's ear. Whatever meager concentration he'd managed to hold onto was fading into the warm slide of Victor's tongue on his skin, the way the man knew just where to kiss his neck to make David's knees want to buckle.

"Victor," he murmured, warning him, trying not to let his eyes fall shut. "This is a bad idea."

Victor's arms tightened slightly around his waist, smiling against the skin he was kissing. "I know," he replied. "But I still can't keep my hands off you. Especially when I wake up being grabbed and shoved all over the bed."

Groaning faintly, David found his hips moving back against Victor, apparently having a mind of their own. Traitorous things, his hips. "Because I was trying to eat you, you damned fool." But his head was falling back; his lips had found the curve of Victor's ear. A tremor worked its way down his spine as his tongue tasted Victor's skin. "I don't want to hurt you." The words were said so quietly, almost begging, because David knew he didn't have the strength to pull away. He was too hungry; he needed this far too much. And he hated himself for that, just like he always did.

Victor simply moved, coming around to stand in front of him, his hands pressed to David's chest. "You have never hurt me," he said confidently, raising a hand to tangle through David's hair. "And I've never let you go too far. You *need* this." The unspoken *trust me* was there too, under the Professor Tone of Gentle Scolding.

He did need it. God help him—or whoever was out there that might listen—he did. David wished he could end that by saying he didn't *want* it, but that drive was almost more than the need itself. Taking in a deep inhale of Victor's scent, David buried his nose in behind Victor's ear. "I have hurt you," he whispered, his arms going around Victor, clinging tightly, desperately. "Every time. You just think I don't because that's what we do. You know that, Vickie. Why don't you stop me?"

Please, don't stop me. It was all he could think, with his lips so close to Victor's skin, with the smell of his blood filling every inch of him. David kissed his throat, so gently, worshiping him even as his words worked to convince him to leave.

103

Victor bowed his head, his lips brushing over David's ear as one of his hands came up to curl around the back of David's neck. "Because it's a two-way street," he murmured in reply. "I'm no martyr."

Their noses brushed, the breath from Victor's lips hot and heavy against David's cheek. Closing his eyes, *willing* himself to keep still, not to drift forward, *not* to let his hands curl into that goddamn neat and proper pajama top, a soft moan drifted from his throat. "God, isn't that the truth," he muttered, swallowing hard, his tongue a quick pink flicker against his lips. Evolution demanded that vampires find a way to make their victims crave the bite, rather than fight it. After all, how could they have survived as a race if every meal was a battle? Some people, though, certain people, people who enjoyed their pleasure tinged with pain, who liked the idea of domination and control even in the slight press of their partner's body holding them against the wall, in the sharp ache of teeth slicing through skin, they were the ones that really got off on the whole thing. Who desired it long after the bite had faded, long after the drink was done.

Victor's hands traced a path down David's arms, and he shivered in the wake, smooth, elegantly long fingers leaving a trail of goose bumps behind. "Victor," David whispered, voice rounded to a harsh noise of need. He *needed* this. And he'd used up all of his fight. Those hands guided David's head, pressing him in closer to Victor's neck, his lips brushing over the faintly raised bite scars.

"Take whatever you need." Victor's voice was low, rough with anticipation. The sound of it sent a thrill straight through David. "You know I'll stop you if you go too far."

He didn't know. Even if Victor had before, there was always a chance. David skirted that too-thin line every time they did this, every time they let passion and blood combine, and one of these days Victor wouldn't be enough to stop him. One of these days, David wouldn't listen. Or, worse, Victor wouldn't be aware enough to say anything at all.

But this time, Victor's skin was so warm under his lips. His pulse was racing, right under David's tongue, and there wasn't room in his brain for anything other than hunger. David dragged a kiss along the slope of his neck, tongue bumping over the scars, tasting Victor's shivering want. With a groan, David grasped Victor's arms, shoving him back against the doorway, fast and hard enough that they shook it in its frame, Victor's breathless laugh overshadowed by the thud of contact. Mouthing kisses pinked Victor's skin, and David ground against him, their hips meeting in a spark of arousal.

"Enough with the bloody foreplay," Victor urged, laughing again. David's fingers wound into Victor's hair, roughly tipping his head to the side. He should be more careful, more gentle. David knew that. There was that familiar sour twist of guilt even as his tongue swirled along Victor's skin, even as he was lowering his lips to suck hard enough to bring a flush of blood underneath the surface. Steadying himself, feet braced, whole body pressed against Victor's to hold him still, to keep them both upright, David paused.

"I shouldn't—"

But Victor's hand went up to cradle his head, to pull him down, and once his mouth was back on Victor's neck there was barely room for anything other than the pounding hunger, the sweet need. David's fangs sank into Victor's neck, cleanly sliding through the skin. With a shuddering pull, blood filled his mouth, dripping down his lips, and David grabbed Victor tighter, closer, desperate for more.

He swallowed hungrily, the warmth flooding through him, lighting him up. It was like he'd woken for the first time. It always was. Blood from a person, from another living being, it was like nothing else in the world. It electrified him, turned him on, pounding through his veins and flushing his skin. David gulped down great mouthfuls of Victor's blood, their bodies rocking together with every pull.

Too soon, far too soon, the hand that Victor had at the back of David's head turned grasping, pulling him away. "David," Victor murmured, tugging harder. A snarl rumbled in the back of David's throat as he sank his teeth in deeper, jealous and greedy of every last drop. It was hard for Victor to talk like this, but he made a noise, a little grunt that David knew from experience meant *don't bloody growl at me, David, enough.* Victor was eloquent, even in grunts.

Slowly, reality started to filter in. Through the blood haze, the high of feeding, David realized that Victor had sagged, his knees buckled, his body held up only by the tight press of David's, by the firm embrace of the door. Hands had grown heavy, the grip Victor had on his hair had weakened. It was all the signs of blood loss, the point which David couldn't pass. If he took more, if he took too much....

With a low keening noise, David ripped himself away, falling backward onto the bed. His chest ached, the rush of blood through him tingling in his fingertips, in every inch of him. He was hard and *aware*, awake like he had been created to be. This was what it meant to be a vampire. His bumps and bruises were fading away as his body stretched and filled and swelled with the borrowed blood.

And he wanted more. God help him, he *always* wanted more.

Out of the corner of his eye, he could see Victor slide down the door to sit in a messy sprawl on the floor. His eyes were half-closed with nearly the same rush that David was feeling. The two ragged tears in his neck were already closing, the blood little more than a trickle now. He knew that from first-hand experience—there really was nothing quite like being bitten. Rolling over, David reached out, grabbing Victor's arm and hauling him closer, tumbling off the bed on top of him and catching his lips in a hungry, demanding kiss. The flat of his tongue teased the last drops of blood away from Victor's throat, leaving nothing but pinked skin and the tell-tale marks of a vampire's attention. They were spread out on the floor, Victor's glasses lost somewhere, his pajamas most definitely not still neat and pressed. His eyes, still carefully not meeting David's, were blown wide like he was drugged.

A stupid smile tugged at the corner of Victor's lips. "That was good," he mumbled, hands roving over David's back. Victor got a lot less eloquent after being fed from. "Do say you're going to rip these clothes off now."

Less eloquent but a whole lot more fun. David flashed a grin, fangs bright in the dim light, eyes shining yellow. In response he ducked out of his shirt, kicking off his pants, his mouth devouring Victor in hungry kisses in between every movement. Those silly old man pajamas were the next victim, ripped off of Victor unceremoniously so that David could paint a wet trail down his chest, tongue circling his belly button, down to nip at his hips. "I could bite you all over," he murmured, palms flat against pale skin, running up and down Victor's legs. "You're positively lickable, especially when you're all buttoned up proper and tight. Makes me want to find a way to make you beg."

"I think you just have a tweed fetish," Victor teased lazily, all too happy to sprawl out on the floor, quite naked. "Or a professor fetish."

"Both," agreed David, licking tiny, teasing circles around the head of Victor's cock, smirking to himself when Victor arched up with a gasp.

"And now I'm going to get fucked by one." Feeding made David desperate for more contact, for skin sliding against skin, for the ache and burn of connection. It was how he'd been trained, maybe, or perhaps biting someone was just so intimate it demanded something more. Either way, David barely knew what it was like to feed without *this* afterward, or before, or even during, if his partner was willing. Unless he'd bled them dry. Unless there'd been nothing left but the dead eyes staring upward, but the hands curled in a last gasping grip.

Shaking his head slightly, David forced his thoughts away from the past. Much, much better to focus on his present, on Victor writhing underneath him, on the salty sweet of the cock he was sliding into his mouth. David took Victor deeper, tongue twisting around him, hands roaming over every inch of skin he could reach. Eyes still blazing yellow with feral need watched Victor's face, an inhumanely sharp need edging out David's expression.

Times like this were the only times that Victor wore his emotions on his sleeve. He looked utterly blissed out and very happy to be so, running his hand over David's shoulder in encouragement. "If you want to get fucked, you're going to have to stop," Victor managed, attempting a stern expression.

Such warnings only served to spur David on. Victor's cock was nice and thick, and David's lips stretched over the tight flesh as he swallowed more of him, as he feathered his tongue along the underside. There was a spot, just at the base, that when David gently raked his teeth against it made Victor moan, toes curling delightfully in pleasure. "Lube," David demanded when he finally pulled away, lips wet and shiny, pure need making it hard for him to think of anything else. "Where the fuck's our lube?"

The question was apparently much too difficult for Victor to process right then, desire-fogged eyes blinking heavily at him. "Lube? Oh, it's, er...." Victor waved a hand in a motion that probably didn't communicate anything as well as he would have liked to. "Your suitcase."

Growling, David glared over in its general direction. Their suitcase had the audacity to be all the way across the room, meaning David had to roll off of Victor and stalk over to it, looking for all the world like he'd like to bite someone just for the inconvenience. Grabbing the tube out of the front pocket, David made it back to Victor in two strides, sprawling back on top of him and kissing him desperately. The lube was pressed into

Victor's hand, and David rolled them over, spreading his legs and biting Victor's lip. Very gently, no fangs at all, but even that little gesture had him moaning. "Hurry," he urged. "Or I'm just going to ride you right here on the floor."

It wasn't much of a *threat*, as far as threats went. Victor just chuckled lowly, leaning down to kiss David again. "What a horrible fate that would be," he murmured, his hands sliding over David's thighs. There was a click as the tube cap went flying, and, dutifully hurrying, Victor eased the first finger inside David, moving it gently.

Their next kiss was deeper, Victor carefully raking his tongue over the sharp point of David's fang, drawing a few drops of blood. Shuddering with a long groan, David didn't know which was better—that long, beautiful finger fucking him slowly, or the cinnamon-spice bloom of blood in his mouth. Rocking his hips back against Victor's hand, begging in tiny sounds, in whimpers and a rumbling moan, for more, David sucked on Victor's tongue. Their lips clashed together again, Victor breathless, panting into the kiss, and David's fingers found their way into his hair, gripping tightly.

A second finger was introduced, and shortly after, a third, Victor's movements losing their gentleness as their need grew. David didn't care how loud he was, how their kisses had turned messy and hungry. All he knew was that Victor was finding all the right spots, that his eyes were rolling back in his head with how *good* it felt.

"Please," he heard himself whimper. "Oh, God, *please*, Vickie."

Victor's growls didn't sound nearly as threatening as his own—especially when they were tempered with a laugh—but he did his best, biting at David's shoulder. "You know I hate that nickname," he replied, but he was carefully hitching one of David's legs up, pressing a kiss to his jaw as he eased inside. Victor was panting, warm breath gusting over David's neck.

It was a feeling that David wasn't sure how he lived without. It started with an ache, a blaze of sensation that built into a burst of heat. This was how he felt alive. This and feeding were the only times David managed to grab hold of something *better*. Mouth dropped open, fingers scrambling for purchase against Victor's shoulders, David teased out a long, aching moan. He rocked back against Victor, trying to get the other man to move, to go deeper, to press harder—he was shortly given exactly that, Victor picking up the pace with long, deep thrusts.

Like an offering, Victor pushed his tongue against David's fang again, the movement messy and uncoordinated. They were little teasing drops of blood, what, many years ago, would have been nothing more than a taste. A prelude. Now he sucked them down eagerly, taking them like they were everything. Because they were. For him, now, in this reborn life away from who and what he'd been, those tiny drops represented all he could allow himself.

Victor murmured something against his neck, words that David didn't catch while he was far more preoccupied with better things. Things like Victor's thrusts turning sharp, fucking deeper, Victor's wandering hand that clasped around David's cock and stroked him. They were moving together, hard and fast, the rug rough under his back, Victor sweat-slicked and solid and perfect above.

The pressure of blunt teeth against his neck made David shudder, the innocent play of *what if* sending a thrill right down his spine. Victor could never bite him properly, but he liked to suggest it, hinting at it with the scrape of teeth. It never failed to send David into a writhing puddle of *want*, whimpering into their next kiss, tipping his head back to bare his throat. Victor's hand tightened around his cock, his hips snapping hard against David, low words murmured against his lips. "Let go. You can let go."

A moan got caught somewhere deep in his chest, and David shook his head, eyes screwing tightly shut. It wasn't that he didn't want to come, that the orgasm wasn't steadily building, *had been* ever since Victor had touched him. But to lose control like that was always a struggle. What if he couldn't get it back? What if this was the time he snapped? Before, this was the part where he would drain whatever evening meal his sire had brought in for them, in the absolute rush of ecstasy this would be where the monster would be set free. David couldn't go back to that. He wouldn't.

But Victor felt so good, so thick, and he was stroking all the right spots. Head arching back, biting his own lip to keep his fangs to himself, David let himself go. He came with almost no noise, with a shudder, a shake in muscles wound painfully tight. Legs clenched around Victor's waist, and David's whole body was a bow, strung out and trembling there in the throes of his pleasure. Victor raked his teeth over David's neck again, biting hard as he reached his own peak, significantly louder about it than David was. His movements turned erratic, then froze, warm, shivering skin pressed against David's own.

Victor collapsed in slow motion, sprawling heavily out over David's chest, panting harshly. His chin was resting on David's collarbone, face tucked in against his neck. For a moment they just existed there, in the space between the rolling tide of arousal and the real world. David let his hand, very briefly, smooth down Victor's back, a kiss barely pressed to the curve of Victor's ear.

Then, gently, he untangled himself, quickly getting that distance he so needed. Jaw tight, control rigidly held again, he went into the bathroom and locked himself in. He ran the shower as hot as he could stand it, and David stood under it until it turned cold. He wanted to go back in and take Victor in every way possible, to drink until he was sated, to fuck until they both screamed. But what he'd been given had to be enough, and the instincts that said it wasn't *had* to be controlled. So he washed the smell of them away, he found those ragged shards of his self-control, and he pulled them back around himself. Brief moments of letting go, that was all he could have now. It was better that way.

By the time he got out of the shower, he could hear voices coming from the joint lounge, the sound of a kettle and cups being clattered around as someone made tea, the low murmur of a television turned down.

Walking out of the bedroom, David was treated to the interesting and slightly disturbing sight of Victor, harried and scowling as Jed stood behind him and dry humped the air behind his ass, grinning widely. Jed's hands were even tucked behind his head. He was making lewd, overexaggerated moaning noises that more resembled a cow in heat than a person, and he appeared to be enjoying himself quite a bit.

Victor, however, was not. "Will you stop that," Victor snapped. "Some of us are mature adults, here."

"Oh, please, Professor Rug Burn," Jed smirked, giving one particularly lascivious thrust. "I think we just heard evidence to the contrary." His voice went high pitched, and he put on an absolutely horrible attempt at an English accent. "Oh, please, David," he crooned, batting his eyelashes at Victor with a wide, shit-eating grin, "do bugger my arse."

"Hilarious," David responded dryly, reaching over to take a mug, filling it up from the coffee pot. Jed had obviously been up first. Victor thought coffee was a four-letter word. "You should take that show on the road."

"Looks like you already rode the horse dry." Jed smacked Victor's ass and danced out of the way of the furious flailing that followed. Sauntering back over to the couch, Jed sprawled out and hauled a very confused-looking Redford down onto his lap, finding the remote and flicking the sound up on the television. "But seriously, folks, the walls? They are not soundproof. Keep that in mind next time, or Red and I might just take it as a challenge."

"What is a 'walk of shame'?" Redford piped up, clearly baffled. He looked between David and Victor, as if he could find the answers in their faces.

Victor muttered something rude under his breath before answering, "It's what happens when your boyfriend hogs the shower, and the only other option for personal hygiene requires you to walk through a den of iniquity and crass comments." Leveling a glare at Jed, Victor fussed over his tea, adding cream to David's coffee, and issued a long-suffering sigh. "Jed has been having *great* amusement at my expense."

Smirking, David sipped the coffee. He didn't often drink, though every so often he found he craved the faint taste that remained. Eating was right out, though. The texture simply didn't appeal to him, and chewing felt more than a little odd. "Yes, well, he's just jealous that he doesn't get a proper English fucking before breakfast." Leaning across the counter, David pressed a quick, dry kiss to Victor's lips before heading over to the couches.

Redford and Jed seemed to be deep in a conversation about what constituted "shameful" in a walk of shame. Jed had just declared, "Nothing about having sex with *me* leads to a walk of shame. Ain't nothing shameful about seeing me naked." He was leering at the room in general, which David ignored in favor of reaching for the remote and turning the television volume up.

The morning news was on, a bland-faced reporter presenting the latest happenings in Egypt. There were pictures of the front of a bookstore flashing by, a crude drawing of a man.

"It's all in Arabic. What the fuck's going on?" Jed spoke up, but there was a tightness to his expression even as he asked. Jed liked to play dumb;

it made people underestimate him. He'd obviously picked up something on the news, though.

"There's been another kidnapping." Victor's voice was as taut as Jed's expression. He had settled at the kitchen table, sipping at his tea while he watched the television. "An American student was taken from a bookstore last night."

Jed glanced over toward David, who was leaning against the wall, mug in hand. Impassive, he didn't move, even when Jed turned the volume up higher still, as if loudness would suddenly make him bilingual. The reporter went on, the next image on the screen a grainy shot of a bespectacled man who looked in his early twenties, all solemn eyes and messy brown hair. It was obviously a college ID picture of some sort—he had that deer in the headlights flash look—and David listened quietly as the reporter read off his stats again. American student, in Cairo on an exchange program, 178 centimeters high, last seen at a local bookstore— letting the words wash over him, David stared sightlessly ahead. He'd heard it all before. Different appearances, different stories, but all with the same ending.

"This our guy?" The rough gravel tone of Jed's voice broke into David's thoughts, and he looked up to find all three other men staring at him.

"Hmm?" David shrugged, trying for nonchalance as he put aside his mug of coffee. He'd just lost his taste for it. "Yes, I'd suppose so. It seems his type."

"I didn't think vampires would *kidnap* people," Redford said lowly. "Wouldn't they... um. Just kill them?"

A harsh laugh came from Jed. The man had pulled out his phone and was furiously typing with one finger, jabbing at the keys, tongue caught between his teeth in concentration. "That'd be too easy," he drawled, frowning at the screen. "Like old Fil. Can't just kill people, no sir, gotta ruin my day with all this planning to take over or inject people or build an army or whatever the fuck."

As inelegant as Jed usually was, and this time was no exception, he had caught the general gist of things fairly quickly. "No armies," David corrected. "Or injections." Pausing, a smirk tipped up the side of his mouth. "At least, not like you're thinking. But vampires, they don't jump straight to the kill. Not unless they're utterly savage or starving. There's no brutish wholesale slaughter like"—his eyes cut over to Redford, David's face carefully neutral—"other species. No, we like the buildup. If he's following his usual method, we have four weeks, five at the outside. That's more than enough time to tease all the possible pleasure out. Then they'll either be drained or turned."

Redford pulled a disgusted face. "You mean he's just playing with them."

Arching an eyebrow, David gave Redford a look. "Drinking blood requires more than sharp teeth, werewolf. And this vampire, he's an artist. Most will seduce their meal for an hour or two, maybe a day if they're really patient. Food isn't worth that much effort, especially if you just want a quick snack. But he...." Pausing, David bit his lip and shrugged. "He doesn't bond, but he enjoys the chase more than most. He takes his time."

The distaste didn't fade from Redford's face—instead, he just turned to look over Jed's shoulder, watching as the man continued to curse at his phone.

Victor snorted quietly. "Cats and dogs."

It was an analogy Victor had used before. Frankly, David didn't get it. He was hardly a *cat*, of all things. Glowering at Victor, David stalked over to the couch and draped himself over it, watching the news and ignoring the rest of the room. There was a clue there, in the disappearance. It was a message for him. An American taken? Someone was definitely trying to get his attention. Well, mission accomplished. He was more interested than ever.

"Wait." Redford was frowning, looking at the TV. He didn't seem to want to look at David, but he made himself do so, even if he did give the distinct impression of warily raised hackles. "This vampire. You talk about him like he's good at what he does. Why are there obvious kidnappings only in the last month or so? Why not all the time? Why...." If he'd looked vaguely disturbed before, Redford looked even more so now. David had been hoping to avoid this part, like a roach hopes to avoid a rock being turned over. Unpleasantness aside, it simply wasn't relevant, and people like Redford—like Jed—would get caught up in the details that were so much less important than the whole. "What about the people that were taken a few months ago?"

"Yeah, Davie." Jed's voice was clipped, brittle, as he moved back into the conversation. He'd tucked away his phone and was now sitting shoulder to shoulder with Redford, a dark scowl creasing his face. "What's up with the whole not telling us people are dead shit?"

Lips thinning out, David shrugged. "The first victim is most assuredly already dead or turned. The second likely is as well. Telling you that wouldn't have changed things, and it wouldn't have made them any less lost."

"You son of a bitch." Jed's expression was thunderous as he moved forward, hands curled into fists at his side. "You're a heartless bastard, you know that? Fucking sending us off running around to save people who are already six feet under is sick and twisted, even for you."

"Two are dead," David reminded him. "The others, including this latest, might be alive. You're a practical man, Jed. I thought you, of all people, would understand what we needed to focus on."

Individual lives didn't matter. Not in this case. It was sad, unfortunate, yes, but unless they stopped Gabriel, one life was hardly anything in the balance of what would come. Gabriel had destroyed so much. Worrying about two people in the light of that was like showing concern over a flower in the face of a hurricane.

Taking a slow breath, Jed briefly closed his eyes. "Fine," he grit out, movements jerky as he sat back down next to Redford, knitting his fingers together as if to stop himself from imparting violence. "Answer Redford's very good and very observant question. Why now? Three months ago the vampires suddenly, what, got super hungry? They're goddamn obvious. I mean, you're the only one crazy enough to see the connection, but they all were highly visible targets. That's some balls, Davie, and not the good kind."

Lips thinning out, David just shot Jed a glare and stalked over to the kitchen. "Maybe he got bored. Maybe he's getting sloppy. What am I, the fucking vampire whisperer?" It was him, it *had* to be him. Who else could it be?

"Just tell them who *he* is, David," Victor suggested. "They deserve to know."

In slamming the mug he'd been washing up on the edge of the sink, David sent pieces of ceramic flying. "*Damn it*, Victor," he growled, eyes blazing as he clenched his jaw, struggling against the urge to bare his fangs. "Keep your nose out of this, for once in your goddamn life."

Silence hit the room, awkward and heavy. Victor just looked right back at him, still calmly sipping at his tea. "You brought them here. They're fighting this fight with you. Tell them, or I will."

"Go right ahead." Furious, David kept his back carefully to them, shoulders tight under his shirt, arms tense as he held onto the edge of the sink, working to find his control again. Talking about this was not what he needed right then. There was someone else missing, some stupid kid who'd been in the wrong place at the wrong time and got taken so he'd pay attention. To *prove* something. To play some goddamn game that David had thought he'd walked away from.

"Tell us what?" Jed's lazy drawl was like nails on a chalkboard. "That we're all here for David's enormous father issues? Yeah, figured that out. This guy we're chasing down, it's his vampire leather daddy, isn't it?"

Victor made a rather inelegant snorting noise. "Leather daddy is perhaps the incorrect term," he said. "It's sire."

"Well that's just stupid sounding." There was the noise of Jed standing, the rustle of those stupid tight jeans he insisted on wearing. "Whatever, just give me a name and a description, and I'll blow his goddamn head off."

It was quiet again, for a long time. David could hear the slush of blood in Victor's veins, hard and tense, despite his outward calm. Jed's pulse was like a drum, steady and low, bass undertones that would taste like black cherry and beer. In the background was Redford, the flutter of his heartbeat filling the air with the stink of wolf.

"Gabriel." David said it like a sigh, like a release. "His name is Gabriel." Fishing out his wallet with shaking fingers, David dug through the cards and the cash and the receipts he kept meaning to throw out. Tucked away was a faded picture, taken in front of the pyramids what felt like a lifetime ago. A man, gorgeous and smiling, on the short side with a sleek build, was standing there with his arm around David. They looked like lovers, like a perfect set, with the same dark hair and dusky complexion, except for something off about David's posture, just a little too needy, just a little too strung out and desperate. David barely remembered that trip. He'd been blood high and horny for days, and, if his dim recollections had pieced things together correctly, that picture had documented the first time he'd worn clothes in months.

Reluctantly, he passed the picture to Jed. The other man barely appeared to glance at it before handing it back, but David had worked with him enough to know that Jed could now pick Gabriel out of a lineup in the dark, half-drunk and high as a kite. The man was insufferable, but he could do his job.

"That's an old photo," Redford said, hesitant and quiet. "How long ago did you live here?"

Jaw tight, David shook his head, frowning down at the image. His thumb rubbed along the edge of it and he could almost remember the weight of Gabriel's arm around his shoulders, the press of their bodies tight and warm. "This was one of the first photographs I'd ever seen," David murmured. "We were standing under this tent that Gabriel's lackeys set up for us, so that he could get the right lighting without us being burned. He kept this on his desk in a silver frame. To remind him, he said, of where we'd been. Where we belonged."

Pulling himself from the memories, David tucked the photo away with a faint scowl. "It's been a few years," he bit out. "Why?"

"Gabriel isn't an Egyptian name." Redford glanced nervously at Jed, as if asking permission to keep questioning David. "Neither is yours. I was just wondering."

Eyes darting over to Victor, David arched one elegant brow at the werewolf. "No, they aren't. My name was Duha. I changed it when we left Egypt for London."

"So Gabriel's was, what? Arabic for Fuckface?" Jed was leaning against the wall, arms folded, pinning David with a look.

"I called him Ib-Se-Kem," David said with a heavy roll of his eyes. "Though you have to understand, Gabriel is extremely old and always was strangely spiritual. He had many names and none of them were the one he'd consider his own. Giving away your chosen name was giving away your power."

"Did you have one of those?" Redford looked interested and David tried not to snap back in irritation. Just because all of this was something he'd rather forget didn't mean Redford was pulling up memories purposefully. It was curiosity and not cruelty that had him picking at scars David had thought long buried.

116

"No, I was born long after that sort of thing fell out of fashion. Though Usire—Osiris, by his more common name—is kind of a patron saint of sorts for Egyptian vampires, much like Hades is for those turned from the Greek culture. But Gabriel was my true religion. I never bothered to choose a spiritual name." A faint, bitter smile crossed David's face and he shrugged sharply. "What was the point? My god was beside me, not in a temple."

"Okay, kiddies," Jed announced with a too-broad grin. "Enough *It's A Fucked Up Life*. Daddy's going to go out and meet some grown-up friends. You all play nice and try not to burn down the house while I'm gone."

"Where are you going?" Redford gave a concerned frown. "Do you want me to come with you?"

Kissing Redford fondly on the forehead, Jed ruffled his hair. "Nah. It'll be boring. You stay here and bug Victor to tell you more smart people shit you can explain to me later." Instead of looking disappointed at not being able to go with Jed, Redford gave a happy smile at the prospect of getting to spend more time with Victor and his books. Tugging on his boots, Jed hopped around on one foot and searched for his jacket. David thought it was like watching a performing monkey, only without the little accordion and the charm. Taking pity on Jed, David threw him his coat and raised his eyebrows.

"It's Cairo, Jed. You're hardly going to be cold."

Tapping the side of his nose, Jed shrugged on the leather jacket and winked. "Patience, grasshopper. Soon you will understand all."

"Oh, Jed," Victor remarked, looking up from his book. "Wait a moment. If you're going out, I feel it would be prudent to inform you how to kill vampires, should you come across one and find yourself in danger. You see, what you have to do is—"

"And how many vampires have *you* killed, Princess?" Jed cut in, raising his eyebrows.

That gave Victor pause. "Er, well, none. But—"

"See, *I* got myself all manner of killing type education on Uncle Sam's dime. And then I went and took care of a big, bad wolf and several of his friends. So I'm thinkin' I'll just go with my heretofore undeniably effective record and *you* can go back to snobby bookville," Jed drawled.

He kissed Redford again, properly this time, and disappeared out the door. The hotel room felt somehow emptier without Jed to fill it to capacity.

David collapsed onto a chair, feeling wrung out. After a moment, he reached out to lightly touch his fingertips to Victor's. Opening and closing his mouth a few times, no words actually managed to be formed. Instead he just rolled his eyes and shrugged, as close to an apology as David knew how to get.

Victor shifted his hand an inch, briefly grasping David's, giving him a smile that said far too much for one simple expression. That done, he resumed drinking his tea. Redford had gone to gather up Victor's books again, eagerly turning the pages, peppering the man with questions. David tipped his head back, eyes falling shut. Mentally cursing the sun for keeping him imprisoned, David tried not to think of what sorts of things Gabriel could do with a young man and weeks to milk every drop from him.

CHAPTER
7

Jed

"LOOK, I don't *care* what normal operating bullshit procedures are, just *do it*." Jed was sitting up in bed, hair sticking up at all ends, scowling his very favorite scowl. It was very effective. Seriously, once he'd gotten into a very high-ranking official's personal bathroom just on the power of his glare and how good he looked in leather. Sadly, though, it seemed to lose some of its charm when used over the phone to disgruntled receptionists.

"Jed." Redford's voice was slightly muffled, probably because he'd buried his face under the pillows. He was just a lump under the blankets, grunting whenever Jed elbowed him back awake. "Tell me *why* we're up at two in the morning again?"

Jed covered the phone receiver with one hand. "Because," he explained, like it was the most obvious thing in the world, "the time difference means it's eight in the morning back home."

Back to the phone, he raised his voice. "No, *you* are a sack of shit, and if you don't fucking put the phone where I want it, I will personally— Yeah, you better run for your manager, you fucking pussysnatch."

"Okay." Redford was apparently unfazed by Jed's outburst. He'd rolled over just enough to peer out at Jed, eyes heavy with sleep. "But why does it have to be at eight? 'Cause it'll still be daytime back home if we did this at a normal hour."

Turning his attention back to Redford, Jed smirked at him, expression softening, running his hand through Redford's hair. "Yeah, but you know how she gets in the morning. 'Sides, I was *going to* do this yesterday, but I went out. And my contacts are very good at what they do, but I don't think this would have helped my credibility any."

There was a new voice over the phone, and Jed immediately started shouting. "Oh my God, whose cock do I have to fucking deep-throat over

119

there to get one fucking simple thing done, you fucking sack of fuck-faced—" In an instant, Jed's tone turned from murderous to crooning, and his whole face lit up. "Hi, baby. Who is being just the best kitty in the world? Hmm? How's my Knievel?"

There was a loud, disgruntled meow, and Jed could hear the rattling of the cage door. Probably their cat had just taken a swipe at the phone. "I know," he apologized, raising his voice to be heard over the meowing. "But it wasn't *my* idea to put you in a mean old animal hotel. That would be your other daddy. He is a very bad man."

Redford promptly thumped Jed on the leg, narrowing his eyes up at him from his cocoon of blankets. "Am not," he mumbled.

"Yes he is," Jed continued, voice a soothing singsong tone. "But don't worry, baby kitty, I will punish him. Now you be good, and I will be home to save you very soon. I just have to kill one little stupid man, and then we will all go fishing. Who likes fishes?" Delighted when he heard the loud carburetor purr and the distinctive sound of Knievel head butting the cage, he grinned. "That's right! You do! We will go get lots and lots of fishes."

The phone was thrust at Redford. "Say hello," Jed demanded.

"Hi, Knievel," Redford muttered dutifully. He'd never quite gotten into the habit of baby-talking animals. Jed didn't know why, but Redford claimed he just didn't understand the difference of speech pattern. Which was kind of amusing, considering when in wolf form he fell for it every time. That and ear scratching. "I'm sorry for suggesting a cat hotel. I hope you're not going to be mad at me when I get back and knead my face."

"Of course she won't." Jed kissed Redford's temple soothingly, taking the phone back. "Well. She'll knead your face regardless, but she's just a cat, Red, she won't remember."

Saying one last goodbye, Jed hung up, tossed his phone onto the nightstand, and sprawled back out into bed. He stretched, arms above his head, before collapsing back down and slinging an arm and a leg over Redford, hauling the man in close. "Sorry I got back so late, babe," he murmured, trailing kisses along Redford's jaw, sleepy and content. "We'll definitely go do dinner tomorrow, to make up for it. I just couldn't get away."

"'S okay," Redford slurred, seemingly already halfway back into sleep. He clumsily butted his head against Jed's shoulder. "Dinner later. Sleep now."

Even with how busy his mind was, even with the ever unfolding details of the current job, Jed had surprisingly little trouble dropping back to sleep. Ever since he'd met Redford, Jed had been struck with the most amazing luck with his sleeping habits. No matter how stressed out Jed was, no matter what nightmare fuel his day had been filled with, all he had to do was curl up around Redford and it faded away. Red was slumbering soundly in his arms, warm and solid and smelling like that sandalwood body lotion shit Jed liked so much. It was pretty damn close to heaven. Even if he did have to board his cat.

When the sun was just barely teasing across the horizon, Jed woke up, fumbling for his phone to check the time. While out the day before, he'd tracked down a couple of potential leads. Admittedly, unless this Gabriel bastard turned out to be goddamn Cher, one name wasn't going to help much. Who the fuck didn't have a last name? Well, other than David. Maybe it was a vampire thing. They sucked out blood, good taste, and the ability to have two names.

Whatever. He'd managed to find a few potentials just by throwing that name around. And if he was going to get the jump on things, he had to keep moving. Easing himself out from Redford's embrace, Jed padded to the bathroom and got ready as silently as he could. Where he was going, the people he'd have to talk to, it'd be dangerous. Not that something like that would ever stop Jed, but since getting with Redford he'd found a new sense of caution creeping into his decisions. It was okay for him to risk his neck on a hunch. God help the person who suggested he let Redford do the same.

No, much better to leave him. The guy looked so damn peaceful that Jed didn't even risk kissing him goodbye, out of fear of waking him. He instead tiptoed to the door and eased out of it, striking out into the barely waking city.

There was still dew clinging to the ground, his footsteps leaving a darkened path behind him as he trudged across the carefully manicured lawn of the hotel and set off down the street. Someone was frying something. Jed could tell because his stomach started growling noisily, demanding that he find out what. Fried *anything* was always a good way to start the morning.

People dotted the streets in twos and threes, not the busy, vibrant throngs he was used to back home. Not yet, anyway. Cairo was still stretching sleepily, and Jed watched as the city blinked its eyes and

121

greeted the sun. Stalls and stores were opening around him, and Jed followed his nose, winding up at a tiny hole in the wall that already had a line out the door.

A bright red awning flapped above him, like a ruby against the oncoming golden blue of the sky. Jed smiled at the woman serving breakfast, handing her the required coins in exchange for a big bowl of as-yet-unidentified something and some flat, fried bread. It turned out to be beans and rice with some kind of spicy sauce. Jed inhaled it eagerly after the first bite, scooping up the last drops with the bread. Strong tea was served as well. Not Jed's first choice, but the Egyptians didn't skimp on punch. It was better than the shit instant coffee they made do with back at the hotel, and he drank two cups before heading back onto the street, full and very satisfied.

He'd been in Egypt a couple'a three times. Never gotten to take in the local culture, though. Those were more in and out, covert missions. Last time, he'd been lucky enough to see the pyramids from a distance as they rode an open-topped Jeep out to some palace. And then he'd gotten shot at a lot. That had been less cool.

Now, though, Jed indulged himself. He wandered, studying everything, the layout, the streets, the people. When he'd been a kid, he'd had this giant atlas thing, with maps of everywhere. He'd lain in the den for hours, just studying it, imagining what kinds of people lived there. Were they like him? Did they go to school and try to avoid going home? Did they still resent Santa for not bringing them the kickass Atari system, and did they sometimes hate everything about where they were? Jed had always dreamed of trading places with someone else, until he'd gotten old enough to do just that. Well, to stop existing as *Journey Walker*, at least, to finally be a person he didn't always hate in a life he didn't always resent. And now he'd really stepped into one of his maps, into the throngs of people now filling the streets, into the waking morning of a foreign city.

Maybe it really did get better. Shit, who would have thought he'd have time to wander around a city without his team breathing down his neck to get the job done and get out?

Eventually, Jed made it to the cafe he'd heard rumblings about. He sipped yet another cup of tea, sitting at a corner table to watch the crowds pass. It wasn't an easy thing to pick up on, the pattern of one particular person, but that was what Jed did. He'd been a sniper. He had to be able to see things from a distance. This one kid, no more than ten or twelve, he was walking back and forth, about every ten minutes, and he'd go into a certain shop across the way. Go in, stay there for five minutes, come back out and walk deliberately across Jed's field of vision to disappear around the corner. Ten minutes later, he'd come back and go into the shop again.

So, a giant neon arrow pointing the way. Not the most elaborate sign he'd ever encountered, but it worked. Jed waited until the kid was gone from the shop before he made his move. He stood, left some money behind on the table for his drink, and ambled across the street. The shop looked run down and abandoned, crappy sign half-stuck in the dirty window, dust around the ledge. Jed opened the creaking door cautiously, eyes narrowed at the dank stink inside. Very carefully, he edged inside, back to the wall, jaw tight. "Well, Toto," he muttered, gaze flying around to the half-empty shelves, the baskets piled up in the middle of the floor. Dust covered everything in a vicious gray blanket. "Sure as shit ain't Kansas."

"No, but you did ask to speak to the Wizard." The voice came from the back room, strident and cocksure. Jed jumped about fifteen feet and immediately cursed both himself and the man, rubbing his head from where he'd smacked it on a shelf.

"Fucking cuntpunching donkey balls," he growled, shooting a murderous glare at the newcomer, all gussied up in a gold-edged flowing shirt and matching loose pants, looking cool and composed in the burgeoning Egyptian heat. "Don't *do* that. Jesus, you're lucky I didn't just shoot you."

"You don't even have a gun out," the man calmly pointed out to him. "Besides, I like making the great Jed Walker jump. It's amusing."

Immediately deciding he didn't like this guy, Jed just glowered, arms folded. "What makes you think that would have slowed me down? Asshole."

"It's actually Akil, but close enough." Akil held out his hand, which was soundly ignored. His grin didn't fade, though, and he just clapped Jed on the shoulder and urged him to follow him into the back room, with a, "Come, come. Can't have you sulking out here all day. I hear you're looking for someone?"

The hallway led them to a room that was as wildly different from the front as possible. Lush tapestries covered the walls, pillows strewn about for sitting, a low table covered with candles giving the windowless area a

123

sense of luminance. Jed was invited to sit, which he did reluctantly, glancing around and wondering what the hell he'd just wandered into.

"Sorry," Akil said, that damn smile never leaving. "I don't often have visitors to entertain. Very exciting. Very James Bond."

"Yeah, just a barrel of laughs," Jed grunted, eyes narrowed. "You're the know-it-all I was sent to?"

A laugh burst out of Akil, sounding like rolling rain on tin rooftops. The man flashed his teeth more than a bear at the zoo, grinning again, clapping Jed soundly on the shoulder like he'd shared a huge fucking joke. "Me? Oh, no, no, not at all. I'm just the go-between."

Fuck. Jed hated all the in-betweens and intrigue and fucking political bullshit that some contacts required. Why couldn't people just take his money and give him information without putting him through a three-ringed circus every damn time? It was like the second one of these puffed up idiots got the illusion of power, they decided to reenact a goddamn Ian Fleming novel. Grunting his displeasure, Jed stood and headed for the door. "Well, when your boss decides to play, tell him to give me a call. I don't do shit with errand boys."

That got the smile slipping off of Akil's face. The man hastened after Jed, stopping him with a light grip to his arm. "Please," he said urgently. "Listen. I have the information you seek. My master is simply unable to meet you himself. He sends his apologies, and me."

Huffing out a sigh, Jed turned and arched an eyebrow. "Fine. Go ahead. Wow me."

Akil clapped his hands happily, sitting back down. "Thank you. Excellent. My master will be most pleased."

"Well hunky-dory for him, sweetheart." Jed leaned against the wall, arms folded, and waved his hand impatiently. "What'll it cost?"

Looking almost insulted, Akil shook his head. "Oh, no, there's no cost. We simply want to make sure the correct information is given."

That was… not usual. At all. People weren't fucking Care Bears, they didn't just give away *anything*, much less information. Lips thinning out, Jed considered Akil for a moment. He looked pretty damn average, young and good looking enough to get noticed, sitting there like an eager puppy waiting for a treat. Kind of reminded him of David a little, in the eyes, something about the lips. Also, he was sort of annoying, so there was that.

"Great," Jed finally gritted out. In for a penny, in for a hell of a pounding. "What've you got?"

124

Akil sat forward on his heels, voice dropping into a low, intense tone. "You are looking for the wrong man. Tell David that he is chasing a ghost. Go to the bookstore where this last vanishing started and ask to speak to Ismail."

That was the same message the guy at the restaurant had given. The one who'd sent David a Bloody Mary, light on the Mary. Jed's expression was very carefully neutral, his trademark poker face, but inside he could practically hear his own brain churning. It was a wonder there wasn't smoke, sometimes.

It was awfully dark and stifling in here. What with the no windows and the candles and shit. Weird that Akil wasn't hot. Jed was hot. Fuck, he was sweating up a storm.

"Yeah, thanks for that." Something was tripping Jed's *oh, fuck* alarm, and he'd learned a long time ago not to ignore the hairs on the back of his neck standing up. "I'm going to be going now."

Akil just smiled at him again, perfectly calm, perfectly groomed, like goddamn Ken Doll Goes To Cairo. "I am pleased we could be of assistance. Peace go with you."

Yeah. That was gonna happen.

The air outside the shop wasn't nearly so oppressive, and Jed breathed deep, fanning his shirt away from his body. Sweat was outlining his arms, trickling down his back, and he was beginning to wonder why he always wore black. His wardrobe was not intended for heat, apparently.

It was late afternoon by the time he made it back to the hotel. After his weird-ass meeting, Jed had wandered around, taking in the sights. He'd also walked past the bookstore in question a few times. It would be stupid to go charging in, especially after an unknown entity told him to. And while sure, normally Jed wouldn't care—hell, he lived his life under the assumption that doing the stupid thing was a valid standard operating procedure—but for a reason that was back at the hotel, he was playing it safe. Instead, he got some unidentified meat on a stick from a street vendor, spent some time playing chess with a couple'a old dudes he didn't understand, and picked up a souvenir he thought Redford might like to start a collection with. Nothing said *class* like a shot glass with the pyramids on it. Memorable *and* practical!

Pushing open the door of the hotel room, juggling his bags and the fried spiced meat dough ball he had half-shoved in his mouth, Jed was immediately tackled by a blur of messy brown hair and wide, frantic blue-gray eyes. His bags went flying, and Redford landed heavily on top of him.

"Jed!" Redford grasped Jed's T-shirt in both hands, clutching the material tightly. "I thought—I woke up and you weren't there—I couldn't reach your cell phone—I didn't know—" He broke off, thumping Jed's chest with his fists, looking relieved. "You're not dead or kidnapped or drowned in the Nile."

Startled, sprawled on his back in the doorway with Redford sitting on his legs, Jed looked helplessly around the room. His eyes landed on David, who offered, sounding incredibly bored, "You didn't leave a note." The way he said it made Jed think this wasn't the first time those words were being said that day.

Oh. A note. Smoothing his hand down Redford's back, Jed struggled to sit up, propped up on his elbows. "I... my phone is off, Fido. I was working."

"I didn't know that," Redford said, a note of embarrassment entering his voice. He clambered off of Jed's legs, shuffling around to pick up the bags that had gone scattering from Jed's hands at the moment of impact. "I'm sorry, I should have assumed—" He aborted the sentence, shrugging awkwardly.

Jed got to his feet, bending to help Redford. Utter bafflement still creased his forehead, and he kept glancing over at Redford, trying to figure out what he'd done. "I said we'd go to dinner," he offered hopefully. Redford had that look on his face, what Jed had termed the *bad dog* expression. Fuck, Jed hated it when that happened. And, as usual, it was because he'd done something stupid, and now Redford was upset, and guilty *because* he was feeling upset. Thing was, this time Jed genuinely didn't have a clue why. "I, uh, I guess I forgot to check my phone for messages after my meeting." Was that it? Maybe? Fuck, he didn't know.

"It's not that," Redford said softly. He'd backed off a few feet to let Jed gather the bags and was now fidgeting with the chain of the whistle he wore around his neck. "You—you just left. And I didn't know where you were. And I couldn't call you. And people are getting kidnapped."

Blinking owlishly at him, Jed couldn't help it. He laughed, just a quick chuckle, but come *on*. "Fido." He grinned, going to the other man, hands on his shoulders. "It's me! What, you think I'm gonna get kidnapped? Everything's fine. I was just working."

David stood up suddenly, grabbing Victor's arm. "As fun as this is going to be to watch," he said with a low smirk, "I've had quite enough bonding togetherness time. Besides, seeing someone dig their own grave is just boring after the first six feet." He hauled Victor into their bedroom, despite the other man's indignant squawks as he got pulled away from his books, the door shutting behind them, leaving Jed and Redford alone. Now Jed was confused again. What the hell was going on here?

"You're not invincible." Redford was staring at the ground. "You could get kidnapped. Or killed. And I wouldn't be able to help you because I didn't know where you were."

"Red," Jed started but bit his tongue promptly. This wasn't Redford upset because he'd gotten the wrong kind of milk or forgotten to do the laundry for the third day in a row, even after he'd promised he would. "Look, what the hell was last full moon, then?" Oh, yes, starting a fight, that was going to help. Jed could see himself doing it, wanted to stop, but there was a tight, shameful heat in his throat he didn't know what to do with. It was like he had to shove it out at the nearest person, make him feel as bad as he did right then. "You wandering off to go sniff your ass in your grandma's cage ain't exactly what I'd call *together time*. It's okay for you to do it, but if I try to work, you get all... shit, however you're getting now?"

"I thought—" Redford looked startled, hand clenching tight around the whistle. It was a nervous habit he'd developed ever since Fil, ever since blowing on the goddamn thing had led Jed to him. Ever since whatever that bastard had done to him had started to take over. "I—oh." The surprise just turned right back into that *bad dog* look. "I thought you'd know."

"Know *what*?" Shit, now Jed felt worse. A hell of a lot worse, because keeping Redford from looking that scared, that lost, was pretty much all Jed wanted. Reaching out, hand cupping the back of Redford's head, he hauled the man into a tight embrace. Jed's chin hooked on Redford's shoulder, and he smoothed his hand up and down his back. "Talk to me, Fido, okay? Just... I don't know what you're thinking."

Redford relinquished his hold on the whistle to grasp Jed's sleeve instead. "I thought you'd know that I went there," he said, voice muffled against Jed's shoulder. "Because I mentioned it a few days earlier. And now I just got all weird at you for doing the same thing I did."

Huffing out a sigh, Jed shook his head, rough stubble from his too-lazy-to-shave shadow rubbing against Redford's jaw. "Difference is, I knew where you were. Just didn't like it." Redford wasn't hard to figure out, most of the time. He felt safe in two places in the world. One of them was their bed. The other, though, was still that goddamn basement, still all tied up and caged. If he wasn't at home, and it was that time of the month, Jed didn't have to wonder too much where he might have gone to. "Sat out in the car all night, watching the place, making sure you were okay. Longest night of my life, Red."

Redford looked like Jed had just handed him the sun, had done something impossibly sweet. "I know. I could smell you." He drew back to look Jed properly in the eye. "I could have figured out you were working today. I just... panicked."

Wincing, Jed reached out to comb his fingers through that messy brown hair, drawing Redford in closer so their foreheads could rest together. "I'm sorry," he said softly, meaning it. The bracelet he'd gotten Redford was still on the man's wrist, and Jed turned his head to kiss it lightly, the skin just above it, the palm of Redford's hand. "Maybe I should... leave notes from now on?" It was said hesitantly, Jed still feeling his way around, but he was hopeful it was the right thing. That this would make Redford realize how important he was. Jed obviously wasn't doing such a hot job of showing him so far.

Redford nodded against him, tilting his head up to press his lips to Jed's forehead. "I'd like that," he replied. "And maybe you can come with me on full moons... if you stay outside the cage."

A quick grin lifted Jed's lips. "Gotta be more comfortable than the car." He smirked, drawing Redford in to kiss him properly, long and sweet. "But not a chance. I like it when you get all growly at me until I show you who's boss. Besides, you're more in control now. No cages between us, Fido, not ever. That's not us."

"*Sometimes* more in control," Redford stressed. "It's kind of different on the full moon. Everything is—it's hyped up. Stronger. I can't think properly."

Meeting Redford's eyes, Jed was quiet for a moment. He could do quiet. Sometimes. Then, deliberately, he tipped his head back, exposing his throat. "I'm yours, Red," he murmured huskily. "Now, tomorrow, full moons, forever. No cages. I don't care."

He didn't miss the quick flash of yellow at the edge of Redford's eyes, the way he stared at the curve of Jed's unprotected throat. "Don't do that," Redford muttered, though he was smiling. He did, however, lean forward to press the lightest of kisses to the exposed skin. "You know it makes the instincts go all crazy."

"So let them go crazy," Jed said, smiling back slowly. "Maybe they need to. I can handle you, baby. All of you. And I am yours. So let them figure that out, so that *you* can figure it out."

Redford huffed a low laugh. He tangled his fingers in Jed's hair to tilt his face down again. "Maybe tonight. I…." A look of shame washed over his face. "I already had instinct stuff happen today. I may have woken up and…."

He muttered something that sounded suspiciously like *chewed the newspaper to shreds*.

Jed barked out a laugh and tipped forward to kiss Redford. "At least you didn't chase the mailman," he teased. Redford shared the laugh, although his was significantly more embarrassed. Redford took Jed's hand and tugged him over to the couches—there were maps spread out over the coffee table, bearing Redford's distinctive, neat marks. Immediately intrigued, Jed perched on the edge of one couch, studying them all intently.

"You do this all today?" he asked, sparing a glance up at Redford. He was always a little surprised how good Redford was at the technical stuff, at plotting and planning and figuring out patterns. Maybe Jed had just worked alone for too long, or maybe all the teams he'd been on before had been composed of wet job guys like him, following orders. It was surprisingly nice to have someone who was his equal on all this shit, who was smart and could fit into his day job.

"I had David tell me where vampires would prefer to hang out," Redford said. "And Victor told me all about where the less crowded areas of the city were. I also, um, called Dr. Alona. Not for map help, just my appointment."

The shrink. A look of displeasure crossed Jed's face before he carefully controlled it. "Yeah?" he asked, trying to keep his voice neutral. "How'd that go?"

Redford sank down to sit on one of the couches, picking up a pen and spinning it in his fingers. He was promptly hauled by Jed's hand grabbing his to sit in Jed's lap, Jed's arms circling his waist and his chin on his shoulder while he stared down at the maps. Redford gave an exhale that sounded relieved, leaning back against Jed. "It went okay." He stopped twirling the pen to look confused. "He has a *cat* named Rufus too. As well as the parrot, and the dog David said he had."

The government had sent Jed to a lot of headshrinkers after his discharge. Apparently he had anger problems. And an addiction to adrenaline. Also, a really big hard-on for explosions. Those things together worried Uncle Sam enough to mandate a couple of years of different kinds of therapy. Drugs, shock, group, one-on-one sessions so boring he'd contemplated shooting everyone just to get out of there, he'd had it all. Still just as fucking crazy as the day he'd joined up, though, so his opinion of such methods was decidedly dim. But Redford said he wanted to go, and Jed would have hauled the sun down with his bare hands if Red asked, so Jed was going to keep his own opinions to his damn self.

Well, except to say, "He's a shrink, Fido. Fucking crazy, the whole bunch of them. Probably has some story about how it represents his inner id or some shit."

Redford turned slightly to look at him. "How does naming three different animals Rufus represent his inner id?"

Lazily smirking up at him, Jed let his hand wander down to give Redford's ass a squeeze. "How the fuck should I know? I'm not a shrink." Kissing him soundly, Jed spent a very nice few minutes just exploring Redford's mouth, the curve and the shape of it, liking very much how Redford would rock his hips back if Jed bit his lip. This was much better than discussing boring psychologists.

"He doesn't *seem* weird," Redford murmured, suddenly a lot more distracted. "But it went okay. Dr. Alona said he thinks the whole, um, waking up chasing squirrels and growling thing is maybe because of Fil. And what happened. That maybe the instincts are going crazy because I'm... somewhere between a werewolf and a wolf like Fil, because the ritual wasn't completed." Redford looked like he was going to say more, but he shut his mouth and shrugged lightly. "Anyway. Look at the maps and see what you think."

Jed frowned briefly as he considered Redford. Clearly more had gone on in that conversation than he was letting on. After a moment, though, he just kissed Redford's shoulder and complied, turning back to the maps. When Redford was ready to talk, he would. Until then, Jed would just try for the supportive boyfriend role and hope he didn't fuck it up too much.

Studying the obsessively neat marks, color coded and labeled, Jed grunted lightly. "That's interesting." Tapping the map with one finger, he slid it down a road, turning the corner and finding himself at another mark, this one bright yellow to represent a kidnapping. A quick jaunt in the other direction had him finding the same thing. "Look at what's in the middle of all these."

The bookstore. The goddamn bookstore, where the American student was taken. Looked like his informant was more on the nose than he'd thought.

"Great work, Red." Jed kissed his nose and deposited him to the side as he stood and started to gather his things. "We've got a solid lead. This matches info I got today, which means I get to go sit in a hot rental car and do a stakeout."

"You promised me dinner," Redford pointed out, still smiling happily at the compliment. "Maybe we could both do the stakeout. And get takeout to eat in the car?"

The idea of Redford coming with him had honestly not even crossed Jed's mind. Which was maybe part of the problem of the whole fight in the first place. Standing there, strapping his belt on, he studied Redford. Messy hair had fallen across his face, highlighting the pale skin Jed had spent hours worshiping, the scars that he kissed every night before bed, a promise to himself that he wasn't going to let Redford get any more of those. This was the guy that Jed wanted to protect, so fiercely it took his breath away, and he was asking to go out on a stakeout to watch some place that could be a den of kidnapping vampires?

Yeah, not going to happen.

"Maybe a rain check on the dinner, Fido," he offered, holding out his hand to help Redford up. "Or I'll bring something back. We can have a picnic in bed."

"Jed," Redford protested. He took the hand up and stood in front of Jed, looking particularly stubborn. "I want to come with you. I'm not helpless. And my nose is way better than yours."

Jed met his gaze, eyes narrowed as he tried to figure out a way to go without him. Sadly, short of tying him up—and not in the fun way!—he couldn't think of anything. So he grumbled under his breath, pressing a kiss to said nose. "Fine. But you stay with me, and you do what I say. Got it?"

131

Redford looked so excited he actually bounced on his feet a little. "Of course." He did his best to appear solemn and attentive. "I'll do everything you say."

He couldn't help it. A broad leer crossed his face, and Jed backed Redford up against the wall. His hand went down to cup Redford's cock through the front of his pants. "Now that sounds like a fun afternoon," Jed murmured, mouthing kisses up Redford's ear. "Too bad we'll be working. I'd like to see just how good of a promise that is."

"I always keep my word." Redford still had that solemn expression, but there was a glint of mischief in his eyes. Apparently even the idea of sex couldn't stop Redford from being overwhelmingly excited about getting to go on a stakeout—he clearly didn't remember Jed bitching about how boring they were—and he happily broke away to go to their bedroom, collecting his bag.

Sighing heavily, looking down at his crotch, Jed muttered, "Down, boy."

It didn't take long to get their shit together and let David know what was up. Apparently the guy was still really hung up on the idea of this Gabriel guy, regardless of how many people told him he wasn't their man. Jed didn't really fucking care about David's issues. He had a lead, and he was going to follow it, regardless of what it turned up.

The hotel arranged for their rental, a nice, unobtrusive sedan, and they took off into the bustling streets of Cairo. Five seconds later Jed was cursing everyone on the street in as vivid language as he could come up with. There were no clear rules or directions or lights, just *people* and cabs and everyone going wherever the fuck they wanted. Jed had practically worn out the horn by the time they slid into a parking spot across the street from the bookstore. He'd never been so glad to turn off a car before.

Redford, on the other hand, looked like they'd just been driving through a particularly fascinating amusement park. "Cairo's *loud*," he observed, peering out the window to look at the bookstore. "Oh. I thought it would be... more dangerous looking."

Jed slid the seat back so he could get comfortable and shrugged. "Real dangerous shit doesn't come with cobwebs and a movie soundtrack, Fido. Just looks like everything else. That's what makes it so dangerous. Nobody believes they're going to run into something scary at a goddamn bookstore."

132

"Then all those horror movies you've been showing me have been completely wrong." Redford looked vaguely upset by this fact. He still hadn't quite figured out that movies presented things differently than real life. Unless it was dragons and giant robots. But everything else, Redford thought if it was on the television it was the gospel truth. Hell, Jed had even seen him getting all misty eyed over some romantic comedy where there was a proposal and swans and fucking rose petals. Everyone knew that shit was less real than the dragons.

"Well, if it makes you feel any better, I think this is just the first stop." Jed pulled out one of the maps, spreading it across their laps. "See, here we are." His finger poked at the street corner. "But look at the pattern. This might be the pickup, but it can't be the drop off point. See the cluster? The rest of the kidnappings happened further away at first, progressing closer and closer, until the last one. It doesn't make sense. You start out closer to home, get your feet wet, then you start getting cocky. You take more territory, until you're all spread out. So this guy, see, I think he's finding the victims here. But he stalks them a while, probably back toward whatever hideout he's keeping them in. Make sense?"

Redford was frowning as he absorbed the information, but he nodded slowly. "So if we stakeout here, we might be able to see someone suspicious and follow him back to the hideout?"

Jed shrugged. "That's plan A, yeah. Requires a lot more luck than I usually get, though. Other plan, if this turns up nothing, is to follow the pattern." He glanced over at Redford, who was staring intently down at the map, tip of his tongue caught in his teeth in an expression of absolute focus.

"I love you." It just came out. Just like that, said because the words *had* to be said. It hit him, sometimes, how goddamn lucky he was. How he really couldn't have expected this, someone to actually be by his side. "I mean...." Vaguely embarrassed, Jed rubbed the back of his head and cleared his throat. "Uh, take a look at that part of it. Tell me if you can see any probable starting point, 'cause I gotta admit, my eyes are going crossed just from staring at it so much."

Unfortunately, Redford had caught his little emotional moment. The man was smiling at him, looking like he'd forgotten the map and the car and the bookstore even existed. He reached across to take Jed's hand, tangling their fingers together briefly, squeezing them, before drawing back and looking at the map again.

"Well, their hideout has got to be somewhere around the kidnapping sites, right?" Redford traced a loose circle around the yellow markers. "There's all sorts of big buildings here. Lots of office space and developing apartment blocks, Victor said." He paused, finger tapping against the map. "*Are* there multiple vampires? David just talked about Gabriel."

Jed leaned back with a shrug, his fingers drumming on the steering wheel. "Fuck if I know. Davie's gotten kind of single-minded, if you haven't noticed." And it was going to get somebody killed if David couldn't get his head out of his ass. Jed just hoped it was him and not someone who actually mattered. "But yeah, I've gotta assume there's a crew. Shit like this, it takes more than one." Ticking off on his fingers, he chewed his lip as he thought it through. "These are all fully grown people, couple'a young guys, so you figure two to do the actual snatching. Then there's the lookout, because they're doing it right in the goddamn middle of everything, even if it is all nighttime shit. And I'd say a driver, just because I don't think they walked everyone nicely back to their lair." Holding up the four fingers to Redford, he arched an eyebrow. "That's a lot of people to keep locked up tight during the day. What you want to bet they're not as sneaky as they think?"

Redford nodded slowly, his expression turning worried as he watched out the car window. "Everybody makes mistakes," he said. It was something that Jed said often, one of his many mottos.

"Everybody except me," Jed responded, a cocky grin stretching across his face. It was fun to say, even if it wasn't true. And it might reassure Redford. Jed liked to act like he was invincible. He figured if he did it enough, if he believed it hard enough, maybe the universe wouldn't call his bluff. Redford certainly didn't call it, though he did shoot Jed an amused glance.

While Jed relaxed back in his seat, Redford was a lot more obvious about his watching of the bookstore—his face was practically pressed right up against the car door window, staring intently. He looked at Jed and seemed to remember the "be casual" rule, awkwardly trying to sit back in his seat and look like he *wasn't* keeping an eye on the bookstore.

"I don't think I do subtle very well." Redford sighed. He then started to try only watching the bookstore out of the corner of his eye. It could work, if he wasn't also making a terrible face and squinting severely.

Biting back a laugh, Jed reached out to take Redford's hand in both of his. "Relax, Fido," he urged softly. "It's not just about what we're looking at, okay? It's about seeing everything. Like, look straight ahead of us." He nodded out the car window, watching as Redford's eyes tracked to where he'd indicated. "See the woman in blue? She's been standing at that bus stop since we pulled up. Thing is, there's been three buses through here, and she hasn't gotten on one. Or, look, to our left. The two men at that cafe. Just sitting there, reading the paper, right? But they haven't ordered yet. Which could mean they want to be able to leave in a hurry."

His fingers were lightly massaging Redford's palm, thumbs digging into the curve and swell of it, feeling it loosen under his grip. "Learn to see everything," Jed said, almost under his breath. "Don't lose sight of the forest for the trees." First advice he'd been given, on his first sniper run. Well, after *don't jam that gun up your ass and spin, Walker, we need a hit.* That was less advice, though, and more a general rule of thumb.

Absorbing this information, Redford stopped scrunching his face up, his gaze carefully running once again over to the people Jed had pointed out. He took a deep breath in through his nose then, eyes narrowing as he concentrated.

"I can smell coffee," he eventually decided, shoulders slumping. "It's kind of overwhelming everything."

Jed didn't know much about werewolves or vampires or any of that shit. Quite frankly, he was operating under a "need to know" basis, so he didn't lose his mind over the idea that all that stuff from ghost stories was true. But he knew instincts. Hell, he practically lived off his gut. And he knew that, most of the time, Redford was scared spitless of his own. Which, hey, might be valid. What the hell did he know? But Jed had a sneaking suspicion that locking all those things up tight might be like stopping up a toilet—eventually, everyone was going to be stepping in your shit.

So he reached over and clapped his hand over Redford's eyes. Rolling down both windows, he bopped Redford on the nose, lightly, to stop his surprised squirming. "Concentrate," he urged, voice low, breath just barely more than a hot exhale along Red's neck. "Close out everything else. What do you smell?"

135

Redford was frowning, but he drew another deep breath. Then another, more slowly. "People," he said after a lengthy pause. "All of the shampoo and soap and perfume just smell like chemicals. And there's... animals everywhere."

He inhaled again, obviously trying to shut everything out. "And... old blood?"

A frown flickered across Jed's face, and he immediately scanned the crowd. But he kept his voice smooth, encouraging, trying to keep Redford in that zone. "Focus on that, babe. Tell me about that smell."

"Um." Redford turned his head slightly, though he kept Jed's hands over his eyes. "I hope nobody thinks you're trying to kidnap *me*, with you blinding me." He smiled quickly but continued, "The bookstore smells like David does, that kind of smell. Like dead blood. And like there was fresher blood a few days ago."

Smirking, Jed didn't even try to stop himself from pressing a kiss just in front of Redford's ear, a scrape of his teeth along the sensitive skin. "I *did* kidnap you," he reminded Redford with a chuckle. "And then you stole me right back." Jed squinted up at the sky, trying to figure how much more daylight they had.

Old blood in a city of millions didn't mean much. But if Redford thought it smelled like David, it was a lead worth following. Nothing major would be happening at the bookstore for at least two hours, when the sun got low enough that the vamps could come crawl around outside without extra-strength sunblock. So maybe they had time for a little side trip.

"Okay, Fido," he said with a wide, manic grin. "Buckle up and keep that sniffer working. We're following the blood." Peeling out of their parking spot, flashing a one-finger salute to the guy that honked at his exit, Jed turned down the street and started driving. "Tell me where to go."

Blissfully ignorant of the stereotypical image, Redford budged himself up against the door and put his head out of the window, the wind blowing his hair back as he squinted. "Keep going forward. I'll tell you when to turn."

Goddamn it, did Jed want to laugh. But there was something really cool about following Redford's nose, literally, so Jed swallowed the Lassie jokes and kept driving, one hand going out to gently fist in Redford's shirt, right at the small of his back. Okay, yeah, chances of Redford taking a nosedive out the window if Jed turned too fast were small, but it made him feel better to know he had a hold on him, just in case.

They kept driving straight until Redford called out to turn left. Then it was a right, Jed nearly running over a fruit vendor as he turned with a screech, and then another quick left before driving straight out of town, the buildings turning more and more run down. The main thoroughfare of the city was left behind, and the traffic had thinned out considerably. Obviously they were off the beaten path. "Kinda thinkin' we're out of tourist territory here, Red," Jed murmured, downshifting, slowing as they approached an intersection. "We getting close?"

"Really close," Redford confirmed. He put his head yet further out the window and pointed to a beaten-down building on the corner, rusted machines vaguely visible through the windows. "There. That's where the trail stops, and the dead blood smell is really strong."

He pulled himself back inside the car and beamed at Jed, looking proud of himself. "I think that's where the vampires are. Definitely more than one."

Parking the car in as inconspicuous a spot as he could find, Jed shoved his seat back and unbuckled so he could grab Redford's shirt and haul him in, kissing him soundly. "You are so goddamn hot when you go all bloodhound." He grinned against Redford's lips, kissing him again, quickly. "Great fucking work. Now we're getting somewhere."

And now they got to wait. Jed wanted to be damn sure they'd hit pay dirt before they made a move. With how fast word seemed to get around this town, he'd like to avoid any other interesting characters commenting on their investigation. At least not until he had some concrete leads on the kidnap victims. Settling in, arms behind his head, he watched the building, the street, getting ready for a long afternoon.

CHAPTER
8

Redford

TWO hours later, when they were driving back to the hotel, Redford tried to stop himself from rubbing at his nose too often. The dead blood smell felt like it had settled permanently into his senses, drenching him, overloading everything else.

Jed's leather jacket, tucked around his shoulders, was helping. The sun had started going down, draping the streets in orange light, and the chill of oncoming night was settling in. Without a word, Jed had put his jacket around Redford before he'd even had the chance to shiver. Slowly, Jed's scent was beginning to push away the lingering dead blood, filling his nose with pine and gunpowder.

They parked on the street outside the hotel, yellow pools of light from the streetlamps above them marking their passage. Redford's hand slipped into Jed's and he got a squeeze in return, the faintest upturn of Jed's lips as they walked inside. He did his best to smile at the people behind the hotel desk, the bellhop standing around in the lobby. Tired, Redford budged up against Jed's side in the elevator, thankful when no one tried to make small talk with them. After a whole day of concentrating on smells, on staring wide-eyed at the streets and buildings and trying to *see everything*, he was happy to be able to focus just on Jed, just on them, and let his brain have a rest.

Inside their room, Victor had taken over the kitchen table with books, precariously piled atop one another. He looked up as Jed slammed the door open, eyebrows arched in expectation. Even David stopped his uneasy pacing.

"We think we found them," Redford told them, though he looked at Jed a second later, uncertain about said announcement. Maybe, he thought, he should leave the information telling to Jed instead.

Jed had no such reservations, apparently, because he just kissed Redford on the cheek before slapping his ass lightly. "Fido's gonna tell you all about it. I've got to get some stuff ready." He headed into the bedroom, leaving Redford with the responsibility of bringing everyone up to speed.

David and Victor were still staring at him expectantly. Redford took a few seconds to fidget with the sleeve of Jed's leather jacket.

He was going to say something terrible and stupid, he just knew it.

"We—um, we followed a scent," he ventured. "Dead blood, like how David smells." The look that Redford flicked over to David was half-apologetic, half-challenging. "It led to what looks like an old factory. There's more than one vampire in there."

David's gaze got suddenly intense, pinning Redford in place. Victor twisted about in his seat, looking at Redford with the same interest. "Did you see them?" Victor asked.

Redford shook his head. "No, we couldn't see them. I just know there's at least five."

"What about the humans?" David's fingers curled into the arms of his chair, like he was physically holding himself back from running out the door. "Any sign of them?"

"I think they'd... fed off people there." Redford wrinkled his nose. He still wasn't sure how to describe the act of a vampire draining blood. It didn't seem *right* to him. "One in the bookstore. And there were some people in the factory." He'd wanted to go in as soon as he'd smelled them, but Jed had said that it wouldn't be a wise decision.

Well, Jed had actually said *you're not going in there half-cocked, Fido, unless you wanna get ripped several new holes by bloodsuckers,* but the point was made.

David glanced toward the drape-covered window. Even as he crossed his legs casually, as he leaned back in his chair with a cultivated air of nonchalance, Redford could practically *smell* the impatience on him. The stress and the effort David was making to keep still was palpable. "It's like a miracle," he commented dryly. "Journey advocating caution. Perhaps the apocalypse is nigh."

"Nah." Jed was strutting back into the room with a dark piece of fabric rolled up under his arm. "Just decided to use my head instead of my ass for once. Couldn't have Red's pretty face in with all those goddamn

139

bloodsuckers." Sitting, legs spread so that he could scoot closer to the coffee table, Jed cocked an eyebrow at them. "Gentlemen, I think it's high time we went hunting."

Jed did enjoy his flair for the dramatic. With a flick of his wrist, he let the fabric unroll onto the table, revealing a small arsenal of weapons. There were handguns, what appeared to be a few low-end grenades, and a small collection of knives, all glinting silver.

Redford just stared in shock. As did Victor. David still looked like he wasn't surprised by anything Jed did.

"Where on earth did you get those?" Victor adjusted his glasses, leaning closer to study the weapons. "I thought you didn't bring anything with you on the flight."

Jed lovingly let his fingertips slide over the weapons, one by one, a hello caress. "What'd you think I was out there doing the other day, princess? Getting lap dances?"

"I take it you smuggled them in in that hideous leather jacket of yours?" David asked, peering over at the assortment before resuming his lounge back in the chair. "How very secret agent of you."

"I know, right?" Jed was grinning happily, hefting up one gun to check the sight. "These aren't as good as I normally look for, but beggars and choosers can all get off if the dildo's fat enough, right?"

Victor was studying one of the guns, poking at it, lifting it awkwardly by the barrel to frown at it. His unpracticed grip even made Redford nervous, and he still didn't consider himself all that good with guns. He quickly took it out of Victor's grasp and set it back on the cloth. "We should probably let Jed handle these," he said hesitantly.

"Hmm." Victor leaned back, considering the weapons with a look of vague distaste. "You're right. I have no wish to carry one of those things around."

"Bad princess." Jed glowered at Victor, looking for all the world like he wanted to smack Victor's nose with a rolled up newspaper. "No touching the toys. These aren't for you." He stood, squirreling away most of the arsenal with deft hands, tucking a gun into each hidden holster, one at the small of his back, and the knives following suit.

The last one, a smaller gun with a nicely polished wooden handle, was presented to Redford. "This one's yours," Jed told him with that shy little hopeful grin he got sometimes. "I'm calling her Shebang."

"Shebang?" Though the name was questionable, Redford gladly took the gun. He held the gun loosely in his grip, barrel carefully pointed at the ground. "I want to name it Anubis." Victor had been telling him a lot of ancient Egyptian stories lately, and the legend of Anubis was one that Redford quite liked.

"Shebangs Anubis?" Jed smirked, gathering up the cloth and heading back toward their room. "Sounds like a stripper." He disappeared for a moment, coming back out with the soft leather shoulder holster he'd surprised Redford with after their first shooting lesson. Helping Redford into it, Jed took the opportunity to smooth his hands down Redford's chest with a familiar glint in his eye. "You know how good you look in this thing?" he murmured, lowly, just for Redford's ears. "I could get on all fours and beg right now."

Personally, Redford was sure he looked somewhat stupid with his holster. It fit perfectly—Jed never bought anything but the best available to him—but he didn't think he looked as good as Jed. Still, he smiled, bumping his shoulder against Jed's. Jed was wearing a leer that meant his mind had gone off the rails and straight into the gutter.

"So I assume we're going to pay these vampires a visit, yes?" Victor's voice cut in. Redford almost didn't hear him over the sight of Jed moving in close, the sharp pine smell that so easily overwhelmed everything else.

Jed was human, Redford knew this, yet he was still wondering how Jed managed to look so *predatory* when he started leering and got an idea in his head.

"Um." Redford made himself look away from Jed. Victor and David started talking lowly to each other, possibly discussing plans. "We should. There are people in there, and we need to save them." He glanced back at Jed, putting his best stern face on. "Jed. I know you're horny, and I know you're possibly entertaining thoughts of me in nothing but a holster doing extremely kinky things. We can do that later. Right now there are lives on the line."

He heard Victor fall silent, felt the man's incredulous stare. "Good Lord. The wolf can actually say something that isn't *um* and *maybe*."

But Jed was grinning at him, that blindingly wide smile, and he hauled Redford in for a slow kiss. "You're such a taskmaster," he grumbled, nipping Redford's lip. "I like it." When he pulled back to talk to David and

Victor, his arm remained around Redford's waist, hand tucked in his back pocket.

"Okay, guru of all things gross and bitey," Jed went on, arching an eyebrow at David. "What's our best plan of attack? Won't all the little vamps be out doing their vampy things right about now?"

Rubbing his mouth with his thumb while he thought, David's eyes went to Victor for a brief moment before his gaze returned to Jed. He shrugged. "More than likely, yes. If they have a victim in there they might stay in, but one human for five vampires isn't very good odds. Even if more of the victims are still alive, they won't be draining them, which means probably the lower-tier vampires will have to go out to eat."

Snorting, Jed muttered under his breath, "Yeah, I'm sure they're just picking up some late-night tacos."

David, for his part, ignored him altogether. "We go close to dawn. The whole clan will be in. We'll have the best chance of finding the victim without getting in the middle of a feeding frenzy."

It was starting to get very difficult to think when Jed's hand, still in Redford's back pocket, was very eagerly groping his ass. "Okay," Redford said, attempting to make his voice steady. "Then we should go… there?" His voice stuttered out at a particularly enthusiastic grasp by Jed's hand.

"I hate to go into such rudimentary terms," Victor sighed. "But *ew*, Walker. Stop it."

Quite innocently, Jed looked over at Victor, eyes wide. His hand had also moved from just in Redford's pocket to slip under his waistband, fingers teasing along the curve of Redford's ass. At the very obvious motion, Victor looked vaguely nauseous. "What? We're just trying to make plans."

"I think we should go now, so that I am spared the eye-searing sight of Jed attempting foreplay," Victor commented. "Walker has the worst timing in the world. Go do that behind closed doors, for God's sake."

Victor's appalled face was starting to be funny even to Redford. Jed had buried his face against Redford's shoulder, laughing lowly. "Oh, sweetcheeks—" Jed smirked broadly. "—if you think *this* is foreplay, then I am so sorry for you. This is just a little hello." With that he gave Redford's ass one more fond stroke before moving to the door. "Come on, I'm fucking starving. We'll get some food on the way. David, you can eat the waitress."

The growl that elicited from David practically rumbled the floor. "I'm not going to *eat* anyone, Journey." The vampire glared at Jed furiously, but that didn't seem to dampen the other man's wide grin.

"Fine. You can *bite* the waitress. Sorry, I'm not up on my bloodsucking politically correct terms. Then again, I'm pretty sure nobody wants your fangs in their neck, so maybe you just keep it all tucked in tight."

"Thank God," Victor was muttering as he stood, moving toward his and David's room to gather his things. "If I see Jed trying to be an exhibitionist one more time, I may puke."

Redford smiled to himself, following Jed—his gait slightly awkward, perhaps, because Jed's touch was something he always responded embarrassingly fast to, no matter what the situation or the company. As soon as he got close enough, Jed's arm was around his waist again. Thankfully, though, his hand stayed in a slightly more chaste embrace, resting on his side.

"Prude," Jed hollered back over his shoulder, pressing the button for the elevator as soon as they got out into the hallway. "Hurry up and primp. We'll meet you downstairs."

There was no response—Victor and David were possibly commiserating over Jed's antics—and as soon as the elevator doors closed, Redford found himself shoved lightly against the mirrored wall, getting kissed rather thoroughly. The surprise only lasted for a second before Redford responded eagerly, though he did bite Jed's lips in retaliation for the groping. "You are so evil," he murmured.

Redford was starting to wonder if elevators just made Jed horny, because it felt like they had not yet had a ride in this hotel without Jed kissing him, groping him, or otherwise attempting to tear his pants off despite the thirty-second duration.

"Please tell me you're going to punish me." Jed laughed breathlessly, mouthing his way down Redford's neck, movements quickening as the floors dinged past, every one bringing them closer to the lobby. "You're bad for my concentration, Red. I swear I haven't been able to focus on anything but you since you strapped that goddamn holster on."

Or maybe Jed just had a thing for weapon accessories. *And* elevators.

"I can take it off if it's really not good for the job," Redford offered, suddenly a little concerned. What if Jed needed to concentrate on something and found himself unable to? His protests were lost in Jed's kiss, though, buried in Jed's sigh, the noise echoing through both of them, longing and deep.

"Shut up, Fido," Jed commanded, the words softened by the way he looked at him, breaking apart just as the doors slid open. "You're the best part of the job."

The lobby was rather crowded. Redford didn't even have it in him to be embarrassed about his rather obvious "just been kissed thoroughly" state. Jed had told him that looking rumpled was something to be proud of—he put it more like *it means you're getting some, and those sad fuckers that aren't are just jealous*—so Redford held his head high, brushing his shoulder against Jed's as they walked. It felt a lot better than trying to hide, than being ashamed of being seen in public.

It felt like *confidence*. It was a good feeling.

The air had cooled considerably, even since sunset. Tightening the leather jacket Redford still wore around his shoulders, Jed rubbed his hands up and down Redford's arms, smiling gently. "You look good, Fido," he murmured quietly. They leaned against a pillar outside, watching the people in the lobby, brightly colored, silent, and once removed through the wide glass windows. It was the late after-dinner crowd, the last stragglers flitting about like butterflies before the nightfall. Soon they'd go up to their rooms, last drinks in hand, and it would be silent. Just them on the streets, just the things that knocked around in the dark.

"I feel good too," Redford replied, leaning against Jed. With Jed by his side, with the gun holster strapped over his shoulder, he felt *strong*. It was an unusual feeling, certainly not one that he'd ever thought he'd experience. Not when, even a year ago, he would have never considered his life could take this turn.

Victor and David emerged from the elevator; he and Jed watched them walk across the lobby. From this distance, it was so easy to see the facade David wore cracking. Up close, he still seemed so calm, so composed and in control. But now Redford noticed his shoulders, tight and held rigidly, the way his gait was less smooth, how he didn't quite *see* anyone. He was stuck, trembling and tense, a wounded animal screwing up his courage for one last bite.

It scared Redford. He knew what that felt like, the tenuous control exerted over instincts. He recognized the look on David's face. It was the same expression he wore when he was trying to shove down the voices.

What would happen if David broke? If he lost control?

Redford didn't want to think about it, because he didn't want to think about what would happen to *him* if the same thing happened.

"Sorry, I couldn't find my wallet," Victor apologized. "Right. Are we ready then?"

And David smiled and Jed led the way to the car and no one else seemed to notice how very close David was to breaking. How he stared intently at Jed for a moment. No, not at *Jed*. At his throat, at the steady throb of his pulse under thin sun-spattered skin. Redford tensed as they got into the vehicle, carefully keeping an eye on David. He didn't relax as Jed flipped through radio stations, as Rathbone rolled down the window and commented on the constellations that sparkled against the outline of the city before them. David met his gaze for a long moment, an unspoken acknowledgement between them, two predators warily keeping distance. Tires slushed over the pavement; the scent of meat cooking, of spices and sand, filled Redford's senses. But still he watched David, and David never quite sat comfortably, never quite stepped back from that trembling, shaking precipice of becoming undone, no matter how much he pretended to be absorbed with the view.

The drive went faster, now that most of the evening's traffic had cleared the roads. An hour later, Jed pulled the car into a shadowed side street and nodded toward the building he and Redford had found. "That's it," he murmured, twisting around in the driver's seat, arm slung over the back. "What do you think?"

Redford, sitting in the front seat, glanced in the rearview mirror. He'd thought the drive would give David time to collect himself, but it seemed to have had the opposite effect. However much his instincts were screaming at him to hate vampires, he found himself feeling sorry for David, sympathizing with his struggle.

If David went for Jed's neck, though, that sympathy wouldn't save him from Redford's retaliation.

"It certainly looks squalid enough for vampires," Victor mentioned, patting David on the shoulder. "No offense. Most vampires do tend to favor the run-down and grotty."

"Gabriel doesn't," David said absently. His gaze was fixed on the building, as if he could see through brick and concrete and metal if he just tried hard enough. "Outsides are deceiving, Vickie. After all, I look rather nice, don't I? You wouldn't guess what lurked underneath." Redford bit down a reactionary growl at the seemingly offhand comment.

David cracked his window, closing his eyes as he deliberately pulled in a long inhale, tasting the air. "Old blood," he agreed. "And humans, at least three, but I don't know if any are there now. There's a lot of blood, and most of it isn't fresh."

"They're still there," Redford offered quietly, hesitant. "At least two of them are, anyway. I think my nose is better than yours."

"Wishing for happy endings means about as much as Jed's retirement plans," David cut in, a frown etching his handsome features into something darker. "If they're still there, death will be the kindest thing you can offer them."

"Well aren't you just full of fucking sunshine and goddamn light," Jed drawled, cutting Redford a glance, checking in with him before he went back to flashing David an amused look. "Didn't think you had it in you, Davie. Why don't we stop counting chickens before we've got stones in hand? This is the place, we go in, and if anyone's there we haul their asses out. Agreed?"

"I think it would be better if I stayed in the car," Victor said, his mouth twisting in a wry smile. "In a fight I'm nothing but a liability."

"Well, holy shit." Jed grinned at him, not very nicely. "We actually agree on something. Sound the fucking trumpets." Clambering out, he tossed Victor the keys. "Keep her runnin', princess. And try not to impale yourself on the driveshaft. I know you've never seen anything that big before, but remember, she's not purring for you."

Redford stayed in the passenger seat for a moment, reaching out the window to tug at Jed's sleeve. "Maybe I should shift?" he volunteered. "If there's going to be a fight, I'll be much more useful that way."

It was obvious Jed was considering the proposal. His eyes narrowed as he looked over toward the warehouse. There was a look shared with David, briefly, before Jed smirked. "Aw, come on, Fido, no fair. You know I'm gonna vote for that just because it means I get to take your clothes off first."

Redford was laughing as he got out of the car. He nodded toward a nearby alley, Jed following him as they walked there. He hadn't wanted to undress in the car, so a dark, deserted alley would have to do.

The holster and gun came off first, carefully handed to Jed, who folded it neatly in his hands. The gun was quickly tucked into Jed's waistband. Redford went for his shirt next, unbuttoning it with shaking fingers.

Ever since Filtiarn's failed ritual, Redford could shift whenever he wanted. The full moons still forced him to change, but he kept his mind now, mostly. He'd seen the other wolves in Filtiarn's pack shift quickly, easily, without pain—not him, though. He and Dr. Alona suspected it and the voices had something to do with the fact that Filtiarn hadn't given him the final two doses of blood. His shifts still hurt, immensely, and it was never pleasant.

At times like this, though, it was necessary.

A hand on his arm stopped him for a moment. All the mocking smirks, the confident grins, they were gone from Jed's face now. "You don't have to do this," he reminded Redford quietly, roughened fingers gently, so surprisingly gently, sweeping along Redford's skin. "You're more than enough without it. That's why I got you the gun. I just…." Huffing out an apologetic breath, Jed tried for a smile. "I hate seeing you hurt."

"It's okay." Redford smiled faintly, undoing the rest of his shirt buttons. "I'm not that great of a shot, anyway. I want to be able to back you up properly."

He slipped his shirt and jacket off, handing them to Jed as well, rolling his shoulders to loosen his muscles. Tensing up before the shift always made it worse, somehow. He gave a careful look to both sides of the alley, checking that they were alone, before moving his hands to his zipper.

"Can you… um, keep a lookout?" Redford could feel his cheeks turning red, heat flushing over his skin. "I really don't want anybody to see me naked. Or turning."

Instead, though, Jed's fingers were right there, the familiar tangle of their hands as he moved to unzip his jeans. "Or I could stay right here," Jed offered with a crooked tilt to his lips. "I seem to remember you having a thing for alleys. Also, getting your cock down my throat might just be the thing you need to relax beforehand."

"Jed," Redford protested, his face flushing hotter. "There's people in there that we need to save." He could smell that nothing was stirring for

147

now, though. The street was silent, not even passing traffic to disturb the blanket of night. David had said the vampires would be sleepy and full this close to dawn, whatever brutality they'd inflicted already over for the evening. More than any of that, he could smell Jed's awakening arousal, the way his scent shifted more to pine, to an earthy green that was utterly addictive.

Damn it, he needed to focus.

Dropping to his knees in front of him, Jed murmured, "Five minutes isn't going to change anything. Five more minutes and David will still be a bitch and those bloodsuckers will still be at home." Jed did have the strangest ability to completely shift focus, to have his mind on ten things at once. Right then, all Redford seemed to be able to think about was the drag of Jed's lips across the bare flesh of his stomach. Goosebumps chased the kiss, and Jed worked his jeans down lower, mouth trailing along the dents of his hips.

Suddenly, Redford didn't want to protest anymore. He was still feeling a little wound up from the hotel, the anticipation of the upcoming danger itching in his veins. He did, however, wrap his hands around Jed's shoulders and haul him up to kiss him. "If you're going to distract me, I want to be able to touch you too," he murmured, fingers clenching tight around Jed's hips. Redford grinned then, nudging his forehead against Jed's. "Touching you is a nice way to relax."

Immediately, Jed began looking around for an appropriate area. Redford had no doubt in his mind that if he found even a slightly usable flat surface, one of them was going to be on his back faster than he could blink. But before Jed could move, David's voice trailed down the alleyway, irritation and impatience clipping every vowel tight.

"Would you two idiots hurry the fuck up? This is not Captain Yohoho-bag's Pleasure Palace. Get your asses in gear."

Redford couldn't help it—as much as most of his mind was circling around *must touch Jed now*, he started laughing loudly. He tried to muffle the sound, clasping a hand over his mouth. He pressed a quick, apologetic kiss to Jed's lips and moved backward to yank his pants off, toeing off his shoes. He gave them to Jed to hold. "Later," he promised. "Later we're spending the whole night in bed together."

Jed gave a frustrated little noise, glowering dangerously in the direction they'd left David to wait. "I hate that man," he said, voice rough, obviously working to get his hormones back in control. "Like, more than I hate Bieb-whatever his floppy haired face is, I hate that horrible, blue-balling man."

"Who's—" Redford cut himself off before he asked the question. He had the feeling that he probably didn't want to know.

Dragging himself away from his fury long enough to kiss Redford gently, Jed shook his head. "It's a very long story. You need to get your ass furry before you're flashing it to everyone when David hauls us out of here."

At the very least, Redford felt a lot more relaxed now. He still was a little awkward when he bent—now completely naked—to remove his socks, a shudder from the chill of the air ripping through him. Jed opened his mouth to say something, looking like he wanted to give Redford his clothes back, but a shake of Redford's head cut him off.

Choosing to shift was like flexing a muscle, triggering some unknown chemical shift inside his body that started the transformation. It always happened differently in some random order that left Redford wishing he could predict what would happen or that it would all be over within a split second. But the body needed time to change, time to make all of those shifts without completely overloading his blood pressure or his metabolism. It could only change as fast as he had energy to sustain. If Redford was exhausted and hungry, he was sure he wouldn't be able to shift at all. The shock and strain would likely kill him.

Tonight, it started with his legs. Redford hated when it started with his legs.

His joints buckled, cracked, shifting direction, and Redford barely saved himself from smacking his face into the pavement. Jed was there, kneeling next to him, supporting his weight. Redford wished that Jed didn't have to watch. It was ugly, brutal, and violent. Even he didn't want to see his own body shift like this.

He forced the pain to the back of his mind, biting down on his tongue, silent. The shifting of internal organs and bones was horrifically loud in the still night. One by one, the sound of his ribs shifting and shrinking sounded. His skull stretched to form a muzzle, starting with his jaw, gums itching as his teeth lengthened to form fangs and a powerful bite.

Fur swept over his skin, tickling as hair turned thicker, denser, and covered every inch of him. Fingers shortened, claws emerging, turning into heavy paws. His mind wandered, running away from the agony to retreat to a much more peaceful place.

His senses were the last things to kick in. Redford never quite got used to sensation as his vision dropped into much paler colors. The first time it had happened, when he'd been all of four years old, Redford had thought the world had gotten bleached out, or his curse was making him blind. What he'd realized—and what his grandmother's worn encyclopedias had taught him—was that though colors were less vivid, a wolf's vision was that of a predator, designed to focus on movement more than detail. As Jed had pointed out one night, it wasn't like a wolf gave a fuck what color the rabbit's fur was. He just wanted to catch it.

Then, scent. Jed thought his nose was good when he was human—it was nothing compared to now. His hearing sharpened, turning the alley from a silent refuge to a noisy highway of sounds: insects, wind, mice.

All in all, the whole transformation took about thirty seconds, Redford figured. It felt so much longer.

The pain faded away. Redford blinked himself back to reality, awkwardly half-draped over Jed's knees and arms. "You okay, there, Red?" Jed was running a gentle hand over his ears, rubbing the way someone would pat a domestic dog. It still felt nice, so Redford wouldn't complain.

Redford nodded, getting his paws under him to stand properly, budging his nose against Jed's cheek. Carefully, Jed reached around his neck and pulled Redford's necklace off, the whistle and dog tags clinking against each other. Redford huffed, an embarrassed noise, and lifted his paw to help Jed take off the scarab bracelet too.

"You always forget to take off your jewelry, Fido." Jed was smirking at him. His green eyes were soft and dark in the predawn morning, concern touching the edges of them. "Well, come on. Let's go gatecrash some bloodsuckers."

With Jed's hand tangled in the thick fur at the scruff of his neck, Redford trotted back to the car. He felt *good* in this form these days, strong and fast. He'd gotten to keep his mind while shifted, but the instincts were amplified even further when he was human. He wasn't sure if he liked the trade-off yet, but it did have its advantages.

"Goodness." Victor sounded startled. He was leaning out of the car window, peering with interest at Redford. "Are you quite sure you have control of your mind?" In response, Redford lifted up, front paws braced against the car door, to nod solemnly at Victor. "Fascinating. You say that you weren't in control of your mind and transformations before Filtiarn came along? I'd say you're actually closer to a true wolf now, a—"

"Nerd time later, ass-kicking time now," Jed interrupted. "Everybody got their weapons?"

Victor just rolled his eyes, settling back into the car seat. Redford helpfully snapped his jaws a few times, and David gave Jed a vaguely irritated look. "I don't use guns."

Jed started frowning, the expression dangerously close to a sulk. "You don't use guns? What the fuck is wrong with you?"

"Guns are a *human's* weapon." David sniffed, regarding the guns with distaste. He started forward toward the building. Redford trotted to catch up with him, shoving his body against David's legs to stop him. "What do you want?"

The gleam of David's eyes in the dim light, brown verging on yellow, made Redford want to shrink back, but he stood his ground. He tossed his head to gesture at Jed, knowing that the man would understand. "Fido says you should let him take point, Davie," Jed said, his voice seemingly lazy and relaxed. Redford knew better. Jed was on high alert, his senses honed as much as a human's could be. "Better nose. He's smaller too, less chance of getting seen on first glance if anybody's awake in there."

David gave a growl so low only lupine ears could pick it up. "Fine. Just tell him not to get killed."

Jed's eyebrows creased in confused amusement. "He *can* hear you, idiot." Redford flicked an ear in agreement and, with one final glance at Jed, silently padded his way down the street.

The building itself smelled like rusted metal and old oil, the wind whistling over broken windows, creaking past warped doors. The vampires had obviously been arrogant in their security measures—Redford easily slipped in through an open door, taking a few seconds to let his eyes adjust to the even dimmer light inside. His nose led him to a room at the back of the building first, through a doorway that was lacking a door.

There were two of them. A man and a woman, tied up with rope and heavy chains, thick gags shoved into their mouths. The man was asleep, dozing fitfully, but the woman saw him. Her eyes widened in fear, she shrank back against the wall, and Redford carefully backed out of the room.

No matter how much he wanted to free them, he knew he had to find the vampires first and make sure they were taken care of. It tore at him to leave the obviously terrified and wounded victims in the room, but Redford made himself walk through the building again, to another room deep in the bowels of the machinery. He passed rooms that appeared to have been offices, silently moving toward the main factory area.

It was grotesque in the low light, the hooks of old machines reaching out like gnarled arms, the deeper shadows hiding unnatural shapes. Dust was heavy in the air, the smell of blood lingering. Old faded signs in bold Arabic hung crookedly on the walls. The cracked concrete floor was cold against his paws.

The vampires were in an adjacent room. Redford could smell them and hated that he couldn't *hear* them. There were no heartbeats, no sounds of breathing. They were like ghosts to his senses, even more unnatural than the eerie shapes of the rusted machinery. Carefully, silently, Redford backed out of the room and went back toward the front entrance.

Jed and David were waiting, tense, Jed's fingers tight around one of his guns. "Did you find them?" Jed asked, his gaze flitting quickly over Redford, checking that he wasn't hurt.

Redford nodded, shaking himself to get the dust off of his coat. He scraped a paw twice over the street. "Two non-bloodsuckers in there?" Nodding again at Jed's question, Redford nudged his nose against the back of David's knee, spurring him forward.

With David and Jed close behind, Redford once again made his way through the building. It was a quicker journey this time, having walked the path once already. Jed's footsteps were quiet, carefully avoiding stepping on anything that would make noise—somehow, David was even quieter, near-silent, his steps surer in the darkness. This time, they stepped into the machinery room, walking closer to the vampires in the nearby room.

Redford could see them now. Five of them sleeping at various points around the large room, still silent to his ears. Beside him, David froze, eyes narrowing as he looked around. He moved as though it was daylight, stepping quietly into the room, avoiding scattered tools and boards to take a closer look. After a brief moment he turned back, grabbing Jed's arm and hauling him back around the corner, Redford following close at their heels. "Let's just get the people and get out," he murmured, glancing back toward the room. "If we're quick and quiet, they won't even know we were here."

Jed's forehead beetled up in confusion. "Well, yeah," he said slowly, "but then the bloodsuckers are still alive and we'll be right back here tomorrow. If you don't shoot the rat, Davie, it just keeps gnawing the goddamn cheese."

"They aren't rats." Eyes flaring yellow, David restrained himself with obvious effort. His fingers were curled tightly into fists, and Redford could smell how close he was to breaking, could practically taste the hunger on every word. He was just thankful that the other vampires were apparently very deep sleepers. Even the hushed tones of the two men sounded overly loud to his wolf senses. "And Gabriel isn't in there, so let's just grab the humans and get out of here."

It was a solid plan. If Redford could avoid confrontation, he would, so he took a few steps in the other direction. Only when he looked back, Jed wasn't following him. Still standing at the junction that would lead him back to the sleeping vampires' room, Jed was pulling out his guns. Redford recognized that look on Jed's face. It usually came out when he was refusing to clean out the fridge, or when he was insisting that three beers and a day old piece of pizza hit all of the food groups. Whatever the situation, it meant Jed was digging in his heels deep.

"You brought me in to do a job," he was saying quietly, double-checking both guns in his hands for ammunition before clicking off the safety. The noise seemed to echo around them, making Redford flinch. Jed's expression was hard. He was in that scary, remote mindset that Redford had termed *work mode*. "And I'm going to do it. Go pussyfoot around if that's what gets your panties wet. I'll be over there, killing some goddamn bloodsuckers."

Redford went back to Jed's side, pushing his head against Jed's knee to show his support. Even though the idea of killing the vampires while they were asleep seemed wrong to him, he agreed with Jed. The vampires *had* to be taken care of, and giving them a stern talking to wasn't going to help anything.

David, however, obviously didn't. Luckily, though, he didn't push the issue. Just turned on a heel and stalked off, movements liquid smooth and utterly silent. He disappeared in the dark of the corridor, leaving Redford and Jed alone. Jed's hand dropped to ruffle in the fur at the back of

153

Redford's neck, but when he looked up at him, the man was barely even paying attention. Every inch of Jed was tense, focused on the room they'd just left.

"Stick close," Jed muttered under his breath. "Stay behind me." They moved carefully forward, Jed taking the lead, gun held in a steady hand. The vampire closest to the door was sprawled out on his back, blood from the day's feeding still staining his shirt.

Without flinching, expression blank, Jed put three bullets straight into the vampire's heart.

The silencer on the gun turned what Redford knew was an earsplitting bang into more muffled *thwaps*, still loud but not nearly so deafening. Turning away, Jed moved to the next one, obviously wanting to move quickly. It had taken less than ten seconds from first aiming to last shot. If Jed kept moving, he could have all the vampires dead before any of them had a chance to react.

The first vampire, the one with three holes in his chest, blinked and sat up, peering down at his shirt. "Mother*fucker*," he exclaimed.

The vampire rose to his feet, hands pressed to his bloody chest. "What the hell?" Hungry yellow eyes rose, focusing on Jed and Redford. The shock turned to a slow, predatory grin. "Well, look at this. Dinner and a show."

The other vampires had woken up. Five of them, obviously not deterred by the bullets, were sliding to their feet, movements almost like a dance. It'd be strangely fascinating, if they all didn't look so very hungry.

"That's it?" Jed was smirking, that cocky expression Redford knew he wore when he was trying like hell to figure out what to do next. Still half behind Jed's legs, Redford tensed up, baring his teeth. "That's the great vampire wit? Jesus, it's like I'm stuck in a goddamn eighties movie." Raising the gun again, he emptied the clip into another vampire's head. There was blood and gore, and for a moment they were down to only four things to worry about.

Slowly, the corpse that wasn't really a corpse staggered to its feet, bullets only seeming to make it angry.

Redford shoved his head against Jed's leg urgently. "Yeah, I know, I know," Jed replied in a mutter, glancing around for inspiration. "Plan B. On it."

154

Redford wasn't sure what Jed's Plan B was. The vampires seemed to be hanging back, discussing something, clearly confident that their food wasn't going anywhere. Redford actually turned to listen instead of focusing on his adrenaline.

"Aww, look at the puppy," one of them was crooning, lips splitting in a twisted, rictus grin. "Let's keep him. I got some chains out back. He can be our guard doggy and eat the scraps." The other vampires were laughing, starting to move in, gazes focusing on Jed. Obviously dismissing Redford, they seemed to have come to the conclusion that dinner was served.

Redford jumped. He wasn't thinking, wasn't planning. He leaped at the vampire who was missing half his head, snarling loudly, powerful jaws clamping around his arm and sinking in. Even the startled yelp the vampire gave sounded half-mocking. "Fuck! Get it off me, it's probably got rabies." The vampire laughed, trying to shake his arm free of Redford.

The shovel that hit the vampire's head with a resounding *clang* shut the laughter right up. Jed was grinning, eyes alight, watching as the vamp's eyes rolled back and he collapsed. "I love a good joke," he enthused, swinging the shovel again, catching the second vamp right in the teeth. "Have you heard the one about the motherfucking pig cunts who decided to open a kidnapping shop? Oh how they *laughed* when they found out they were all going to get ground up into goat turds for that."

The third and fourth vampires were moving forward. Redford tackled them, using his weight to bear them to the ground. He kept one pinned with a large paw to the chest. Normally, he would have hesitated, would have been second guessing or cowering around the corner.

He didn't hesitate now. The taste of old blood was foul, disgusting as Redford clamped his jaws around the vampire's throat and bit in, jerking his head back, clotted blood oozing onto the ground. The vampire was screaming. The sound cut off as his vocal cords were severed. Beside him, Jed was swinging his shovel, again and again, the spray of blood off the tip painting the walls and ceiling.

But there were still two vampires, and the ones under Redford's teeth, under Jed's assault, they weren't dying. Even injured, even bloodied and broken, their hands were still reaching out to grab and tear and maul. Jed was shooting again, trying to give them some distance, shouting, "Why won't you fucking *die*?"

155

Suddenly the scruff of Redford's neck was grabbed. He turned to snap and snarl, only barely stopping himself when he realized it was Jed. Hauling Redford away from the vampires, laying down a steady line of bullets from his second gun, Jed threw them toward the door. It was heavy and old and rusty, but Jed seemed to be filled with a desperate kind of strength. Throwing his body against it, toes digging into the dust-soaked ground, Jed creaked it closed with a resounding clang.

There was the noise, the thump, of bodies hitting it from the other side. Then the handle was turned and Jed yelped, barely getting his fingers around it in return, stopping it from opening.

Redford threw himself against the door too, snarling, claws scrabbling at the door. He needed to get beyond it, needed to rip and tear into the vampires until they were dead.

That growling voice in the back of his mind was loud. *Enemies, kill them, rip them, enemies of wolves, blood-leeches*, it was howling. His vision was soaked in red, from either rage or the blood dripping from his fur.

Jed was shouting. Redford ignored him. He shoved against the door again, his own voice lifted in a howl to match the whirlwind in his mind.

There were hands grabbing his head. He tried to shake them off, but they were firm, unyielding, tugging his head up to look at Jed. The man's lips were moving, but Redford couldn't hear his words. Not yet. Slowly, coherence began to filter back in, the rage dimming.

"Redford!" Jed was shouting, his eyes wide, wild. "Babe, come on, give me a sign. You with me?"

Redford glanced at the door, seeing the handle twisting. Jed was bodily bracing the door, his feet moving forward a few inches every time the vampires shoved against it. Redford leaned up, grasping the handle in his jaws, stopping it from moving, and flicked his eyes toward Jed. He was with him. He hoped.

That was all Jed needed, apparently. Scuffing his hand over Redford's head, Jed dug into his pocket and pulled out one of the grenades. The pin was yanked out with Jed's teeth, and he jumped away from the door, pulling it open just wide enough to throw it inside before slamming it shut again. Using the seconds-long lull the surprise of that had apparently bought him, Jed dragged a heavy box from the side of the hallway over, grunting as he used his whole body weight to shove it into place in front of the door. Then, with a quick, "Move it, Fido," he was sprinting down the hallway toward where David had disappeared.

Paws skidding on the dirty cement, Redford almost got blasted off-kilter as the explosion nipped at their heels. Jed didn't slow down to admire his work, though. Redford could smell the flames, could hear the rocking noise of smaller bursts behind them. Jed kept them both going, legs churning, bursting into the room where the victims were, chest heaving for breath.

"Gas, oil, whatever, whole place is a fuse, we gotta—"

David had untied the victims. One was lying on the ground, moaning softly, awake but not moving. The other, the woman, was sprawled against David's chest. He'd obviously been moving her when her head had lolled back weakly, her bloodied neck offered up to him.

The gleam of David's needle-sharp fangs was incredibly white in the darkness. His eyes were burning yellow, and the howling in Redford's mind grew to a crescendo again.

Leaping forward, he shoved David away from the woman and stood between them. The snarl from David was matched by Redford's own growl, and the two of them tensed, one heartbeat away from attacking. Jed was suddenly there, though, smacking Redford's nose with light fingers, David's with a slightly more solid thump. "So do not have time for this shit!" Jed exclaimed, incredulous. "Burning. Building. We are in. Any of this ringing bells? Get outside, and then we will all whip them out for measuring. Now *move*." Barking the order, Jed wrapped his arms around both the man and the woman, hauling them to their feet, propelling them forward.

Shaking his head, looking vaguely disconnected and a little confused, David followed. Redford did the same, nipping at the back of David's ankle to hurry him along. Once David was running, he matched his pace, sprinting through the dusty hallways as the explosions built in speed, feeding off one another, fire seeking out more fuel.

It was just breaking dawn as they tumbled out of the building. Jed hauled the people toward the car, somehow faster than any of them. Though he did all but collapse when he got close, sagging down, letting both victims down gently before he sprawled out on the dirt next to the road.

Redford's ears and nose picked up the impending explosion seconds before it hit. Panicked, he threw himself at David, crashing them to the ground, covering the vampire with his body as best he could as the shock wave ripped through the air, the bone-shattering *boom* following close behind.

Dazed, Redford watched as Jed rolled up off the ground. Exhaustion didn't seem to matter. He was running faster than before, right back to Redford, frantically hauling him off of David. His hands ran over Redford's body as he repeated, over and over, voice tinny to Redford's ringing hearing, "Please be okay, *please* be okay."

Nodding quickly to confirm that he was fine, just stunned, Redford twisted his head to grab David's arm, dragging him up. He knew from experience now that an explosion of that size would have the authorities coming running, and they needed to move.

David, however, snarled at him, wrenching his arm out of Redford's grasp. He even raised his arm, as if to strike back, but Jed's hand caught it in an iron grip, holding it away from Redford. David looked strung out, pupils blown wide, mouth open as if he wanted to gasp in air his body had no way of processing. Jed, though, didn't appear to care. His expression was dangerous as he hauled David to his feet and rounded out the movement with a solid punch to David's jaw.

"Fucking even *think* about that again, you sorry sack of cow piss, I will end you," Jed said very quietly.

Then he turned and grinned manically at the two dazed people, at Victor, who was hiding behind the car, and Redford. "No worries, folks. I figured out how to kill vampires!"

Victor emerged, rushing toward David. Redford could pinpoint the moment his eyes dragged past the victims, seeing the bite marks on their necks, swinging over to the blood on David's shirt. He only paused momentarily, face paling, before continuing to David, kneeling beside him where the vampire was sitting, dazed, on the curb.

Redford turned back toward Jed, helping him get the victims into the backseat of the vehicle, nudging his nose against their legs. He didn't think that he was of much use, but he had to do *something*. The man was still unconscious, and the woman now seemed to be too. Which might be for the best. Jed's grin had slipped again, a grim kind of anger settling in, lining his face. He glanced around, head cocked as he listened, probably for sirens. Satisfied that they had at least a little more time, he sauntered over to where David was baring his teeth at Victor, shoving him backward.

David looked like he was barely holding on. His hands were shaking, dusky skin now grayed out and stretched thin. His fangs were showing, and he stared at the blood on his palms, on the front of his shirt, with a glazed expression. "Get away from me," he was demanding of Victor. "Fuck, why can't you just *leave*?"

"David," Victor replied, trying to keep his voice measured, though it was shaking as much as David's hands. "Calm down. You need to get yourself under control again, I know you can. Just take a few deep breaths, and—"

He went sprawling on the ground, sent there by a second shove from David. Victor's glasses were knocked askew, and although he looked startled at the violence, he didn't give up. "David, for God's sake, just—"

David towered over them all as he stood, so much taller than Jed. Funny, how Redford hadn't really noticed that before until every inch of David's normally languid frame was trembling with hunger and rage. The sight had Redford's hackles rising. "Just *breathe*? For fuck's sake, you stupid little man, do you have any idea—"

A gun was pressed into the space between David's eyes. Jed was staring calmly at him, expression blank. "I have no idea at all, actually, but I really don't need one. You're hungry. You almost chomped in on some helpless, nubile flesh, and that makes you a big goddamn predator. Until you get yourself calmed the fuck down, don't come back. I don't care what you have to do, but if you come to that hotel with blood on your hands, it sure as fuck better have come from a hamburger."

There was a moment when it seemed like David was going to spring forward. Redford tensed too, growling lowly at Jed's heels. But with almost palpable effort, David managed to pull himself back, lips tightly shut, and he jerked a nod before he turned and stalked away. Jed didn't move, watching him go before he turned back to Victor and held out his hand to help him up. "Talk fast, Vickie," Jed rumbled, "or you can take off after him for all I care. What the fuck just happened?"

The building was burning in the background, the flames sending sparks showering down on them. Their faces reflected in the orange and red flickers. Normally, Redford knew, Jed would be sprinting for the car.

He seemed reluctant to let Victor in, though, standing protectively close to Redford, shoulders bristled in irritation.

"He's lost his control," Victor said quickly. Victor was not normally a man of few words, and he'd lost his usual composure, face ashen and fingers trembling. "He's been fighting to stay in control the whole time we've been here, but it's hard for him. *Incredibly* hard. And the thought of his sire being behind all of this is only making it worse."

Victor glanced in the direction that David had vanished to. Redford just focused on trying to shake out his fur, the blood drying in it making his senses swim with the same howling that had taken over his mind. He felt like everything was lagging, Victor's words barely comprehensible.

"He can regain control." Victor corrected his crooked glasses, hands clenching tight to stop the shaking. "I'll go after him. Keep your phone on, Walker, we'll need to contact you. You just focus on getting those people to the hospital."

Grabbing Victor's collar, Jed hauled him back, starting them all moving toward the car. "Just how often do vamps need to eat, professor?" he asked quietly, unlocking the doors and holding the passenger side open for Redford to jump in. There was the brush of Jed's hand across Redford's back, a physical anchor, before he was inside the car, watching Victor and Jed silhouetted against the flames. Redford curled up on the seat, tucking himself into as small a shape as he could manage, tail draped over his nose.

"It depends on how sane they want to remain," Victor said wryly, his eyes still trained on where David had gone. He looked sad, Redford noticed. "Once a day. Three or four times a week to remain in control. David feeds once a week, Jed, and that's mostly animal blood, which is like eating sand when you're craving a steak. He's been eating more here, but it's mouthfuls, not enough to make a difference."

Jed just nodded, a tiny jerk of his head. "So he's starving. He's starving and he's scared and he's ready to snap." He didn't need to look to see Victor's affirmation. "Which means you're coming back with us. David will deal or he won't, but nobody's dying tonight. Not anyone who wasn't already there, at least."

He reached into the car, shoving against Redford's side gently. "Budge over, babe. You're riding with Victor until we drop those two off at the hospital."

It was the first time that Jed had actually used Victor's name—it was apparently startling enough for Victor to obey without question, silently getting into the passenger door as Jed climbed in behind the wheel. After a bit of awkward moving around, Redford wound up mostly sprawled over Victor and Jed's legs, his head cushioned on Victor's knee. Despite the instincts still roaring in his mind, he looked up at Victor, a bit embarrassed at the position.

"I won't tell anybody about this, if you won't," Victor assured him. He hesitantly rubbed a hand over Redford's ears, and Redford pretended not to notice when Victor grimaced as his fingers came away coated with flecks of dry blood.

Jed drove. There were other cars on the road now, dawn's light breaking over the horizon. After a moment, Victor reached into the back of the car to find a blanket, draping it over Redford to hide him. Jed drove as placidly as he could, trying not to look like they'd just blown up a building and killed a bunch of vampires.

Redford and Victor stayed in the car when Jed took the victims into the hospital. He got his arms around them again, tugging them over to the entrance of the building. Redford watched him from under the edge of the blanket as Jed was speaking, looking concerned, and then slowly began slinking away as the paramedics became more focused on the victims.

As soon as he got an opening, Jed sprinted back to the car, slamming the door after he got in. The tires squealed as he tore off. Redford had to brace himself against the passenger door to stop from hurtling into it.

Glancing over at Victor, his knuckles white as he steered them through early morning traffic, Jed cleared his throat and awkwardly spoke up. "David's a smart guy. Sunlight, instincts, whatever, he'll manage. I'm sure he'll be back tonight, and I can punch him one more time for luck."

"I should hope that he *does* come back," Victor said thinly.

Jed looked like he wanted to say more. Surprisingly, though, he kept his mouth shut, going the rest of the way to the hotel in silence. While Victor got out of the car, walking stiffly into the building, leaving them behind, Jed rifled around in the backseat for the pile of Redford's clothes.

"Sorry, no alleys this time," Jed said with a smile intended to hide the worry lines at the corners of his eyes, the way his whole body was bent over Redford, protective and tense. "But unfortunately I didn't pay the four-legged friends fee, so you'll have to change back before we can go up to the room. You okay to do it here?"

Redford had no doubt that if he indicated a negative to that, Jed would build him a changing room out of random items found in the car or bully the front desk into letting a bloody wolf upstairs. Redford just nodded, climbing into the back seat.

The smell of blood was even stronger there, the stench of vampire lingering. Sitting awkwardly, Redford closed his eyes and focused on the shift. Since getting into the car, his instincts had mostly quieted down, thankfully leaving him able to think.

Until now. *Not changing back, not going back to weak skin*, the voice was howling, throwing itself against his mind like it was a cage. *Weak skin, don't go weak skin. Wolf strong, not weak, rip tear kill better as wolf.*

Redford gritted his teeth, clamping down, trying to ignore the growling voice. Slowly, too slowly for his liking, he forced the change, doing his best to ignore the pain and the horrible noises of his bones shifting around.

When it ended, when he was human again, he found himself curled on his side on the back seat, panting through the pain as it faded. His skin felt sticky with blood, and Redford didn't want to imagine what he looked like. He could *taste* it on his teeth, in the back of his throat.

"Okay," he said shakily, sitting up, pulling his clothes on with trembling hands. "Um, maybe I'll put the blanket over my head or something. I'm kind of…." He waved a hand at the blood covering his mouth, chin, and throat.

But Jed clambered into the backseat, pulling a bottle of water and a spare T-shirt out of his ever present bag. Jed never went anywhere without some kind of supply kit, Redford knew, tucked away and barely remembered until he needed it. Now, excruciatingly gentle, Jed dribbled water onto the soft fabric and began to dab at the dried blood on Redford's face. "I'll run you a hot shower once we get upstairs," Jed whispered. He caught his tongue between his teeth, frowning absently as he concentrated on his work. "But this will do for walking through the lobby."

Pausing, he shrugged off his jacket and tucked that around Redford's shoulders. "Here, that'll help too. Just turn up the collar; no one will even notice." With infinite care, he washed Redford clean, tossing the bloodied rag away when he was done and giving Redford a faint smile, running his hand through Redford's hair. "Look at that. Gorgeous as always."

Retrieving the rag again, Redford did the same for Jed, wiping away the blood spattered over his left temple. His clothes were bloody, but they couldn't do anything about that until they got to the room. At least Jed was wearing all black; it hid the blood well. He tried to smile back at Jed, failed when the action brought the taste of blood to his tongue again, and settled for getting out of the car.

Thankfully, there were few people in the lobby, and they weren't particularly concerned with looking at them. Jed and Redford passed unseen into the elevator, the ride silent as they got back to their floor.

They were standing side by side, facing the doors, watching the floors go past. Redford, slowly, wound up resting his head against Jed's shoulder, trying to breathe through his mouth to avoid the lingering scent of blood. The back of Jed's hand brushed lightly against Redford's, the barest breath of a touch. Both men exited the elevator when their floor finally arrived and made it to their hotel suite without encountering anyone else. Dawn was waking, the faintest hint of rose-colored light streaming in under the drapes in the common area. Victor's door was firmly shut. Redford could smell him there, still awake, pacing anxiously, but the man made no move to come out and greet them.

With the lightest of touches on the small of Redford's back, Jed guided him toward their room and into the bathroom. No words were spoken between them. Jed's face was creased in worry, in something more than that. Sour guilt hung heavy on him, making his hands less than graceful, making his footsteps falter. He frowned at the buttons of Redford's shirt, laboriously undoing each one before he carefully removed the garment, hanging it up on the back of the door. Kneeling, Jed focused on Redford's jeans next, his boots, his socks, each item of clothing meticulously folded or hung, until Redford was naked in front of him.

There were no leers. No suggestive winks or swagger. Jed's touch was achingly gentle as he smoothed calloused fingertips over Redford's skin. Knowing that Jed was going to run the shower, Redford made his way to the sink first, finding the cheap hotel toothbrush and toothpaste. Exhaustion made his movements slow, but he needed to get the taste of blood out of his mouth before he did anything else.

His gaze accidentally catching on his reflection in the mirror, Redford stared for a moment. He wished he hadn't looked. It was better not to know.

His eyes were still yellow. Redford blinked, screwed his eyes shut, but the color didn't budge. He looked paler than he had ever been, even back when he hadn't seen the sunlight, living in his grandmother's home. He wasn't even going to dwell on the blood still streaked around his throat and chin, despite Jed's best efforts to clean it off. He dropped his head, trying to shake the image of his own face out of his mind. Redford brushed his teeth, spitting pinked foam out into the sink until the water ran clear.

When the shower steamed hot and strong, Jed helped Redford inside. Clothes abandoned, Jed joined him, but again, there was no suggestion of anything more. The beat of the hot water over his chest and shoulders felt incredible, cleansing, almost managing to silence the growling in the back of his mind. It was still there, still strong in his thoughts.

Lathering up his hands, Jed started on Redford's hair. Strong fingers worked their way through Redford's tangled locks, washing out grime and sweat and dried blood, sending the stink of the evening down the drain. Long fingers cupped over Redford's eyes as Jed guided his head back into the spray, rinsing him clean. Redford gratefully leaned into every touch, his hands settled solidly on Jed's hips.

Soap out, Jed began at Redford's throat. Every inch he cleaned was marked with a kiss, so feather light it was almost imperceptible. There, where blood had left a gash across his neck, and there on his shoulder where there'd been mud and bruises. There, on his chest, where the specks of blood had dripped, and there, on his stomach, a foot-shaped mark Redford didn't even remember, a kick he'd been too blinded by rage to feel. Jed was on his knees again, but there was only caring in his touch, in the single-minded focus of his work.

"Thank you," Redford murmured, smoothing his hands over Jed's shoulders. A smile nearly tugged at his lips as he felt Jed wash careful hands over his feet, those powerful fingers so accustomed to violence being so gentle with him. Jed's touch trailed up his calves and thighs as Jed stood, looking strangely vulnerable with his hair wet and sticking out at all ends, his eyes hooded and dark.

"Don't." Jed stopped him, shaking his head. Reaching behind Redford, Jed twisted off the taps. He grabbed a huge, fluffy towel and set about drying Redford off, careful of every bruise and bump and scrape. "This was my fault. I shouldn't have let you—" Biting off his words, Jed sighed and rubbed a hand through his own hair, towel wrapped around Redford's shoulders. "I'm so sorry, Red. I got you into that."

Taking a second towel, Redford carefully rubbed it over Jed's hair. "Don't apologize," he replied. "It was my choice. I'm glad I made it."

A quick frown creased down the full flush of Jed's lips, and he reached out to haul Redford in close. Jed hugged him tightly, face pressed into Redford's neck, and let out a slow breath. It seemed like Jed might have been holding that in since Redford had decided to shift. "I'm so goddamn proud of you," Jed mumbled, words almost lost with how desperately Jed was holding on. "You kicked so much ass tonight. I'm just sorry you had to go through that."

"It felt... good," Redford realized, pulling back to look at Jed properly, wondering if his eyes were still that burning yellow. "I—some of it I don't really remember. Like after you shut the door." He hesitated, struggling to bring the memories up. It was all anger and fear, a red wash across the images in his mind. "The instincts were... really strong. The aggressive one kept talking."

He just wished that didn't make him sound utterly crazy.

But Jed wasn't looking at him like he was nuts, or reaching for a straitjacket. A slow chuckle eased out of Jed, and he rubbed his thumb lightly along the curve of Redford's cheek. "Now you sound like me," he teased softly. When a shiver of cold worked its way across Redford's shoulders, Jed drew him into the bedroom and rifled around in their bags for a clean pair of pajama pants and an old, faded T-shirt. It was Jed's, technically, but one night when the nightmares had gotten particularly bad, Jed had held him, chest to back, all night long. In spite of the work strewn around him, the piles of maps and the half-cleaned guns, Jed had dropped everything to crawl into bed, fully clothed, murmuring reassurances and offering comforting silence until the sun had peered above the horizon. He'd been wearing that shirt. In the morning, Jed had showered and dressed and gone out for coffee. When he'd come back he'd found Redford still asleep, curled up with the shirt Jed'd left behind, the scent of the both of them and the softness of the fabric soothing Redford even with Jed gone. Jed had insisted Redford keep the shirt as his own afterward, and Redford found it was one of his comforts, one of the things that always seemed to bring him back to himself. A touchstone, of sorts, in the form of a faded cotton T-shirt.

"Here," Jed said, pressing the clothes into Redford's hand. "Get dressed before you get all sneezy."

Redford laughed a little, a faint breath of air, and dutifully tugged the clothes on. They were old and worn, soft against his skin, and once again the scent of both of them, entwined, helped ease his mind. He gratefully climbed into bed, tugging the blankets over him. "Are you coming to bed?" He blinked sleepily at Jed, smiling at the man when he slid under the covers.

Jed nearly always slept naked. At first, Redford had been very embarrassed about it, having never done the same himself. But now he loved it, loved the way he could curl into Jed and run his palm over the smooth skin of his chest. Jed was like a human heating pad, constantly radiating warmth. Sometimes, on hot days, it became unbearable—now, though, in the chill of the Cairo morning, it was comforting to be able to wind his limbs with Jed's and steal some of his heat.

Jed was already half-asleep. He had an ability to drop off anywhere, at any time, and while it constantly baffled Redford, he was slightly jealous of it too. When he'd asked Jed about it, Jed had said that catching sleep when you could was a lifesaver when you worked for special ops. Redford had seen the man fall asleep during commercials, only to wake up forty seconds later, bright-eyed and aware. Any sleep longer than a nap, though, Redford knew Jed had struggled with. Redford wasn't the only one with nightmares.

"Night," Redford said lowly. He carefully lay his head on his pillow, watching Jed slip into sleep. There was a murmur of sound, presumably Jed's response.

Redford closed his eyes, hand still resting over Jed's heart, using the steady rhythm to calm himself into sleep as well.

HE WOKE up with his teeth gently closed over Jed's throat. Jed was looking at him with cool green eyes, waiting.

Journey has proved himself now, the aggressive voice whispered. *Killed blood-leeches. Strong hunter.*

"Mornin' sunshine," came the rumble of Jed's voice, very carefully soft. The gaze from under half-opened lids was sharp, Jed trying to decide what was going on. "Bad dreams?"

If there had been bad dreams, Redford didn't remember them. It wasn't important. All that was important was the soft, vulnerable skin of Jed's throat under his teeth. Jed had at least three different weapons close by, but he wasn't reaching for them. Jed trusted him.

Strong. Trusting, the voice approved. Its presence was less a howl now, and more of an all-encompassing earthquake rumble, taking over his mind.

Redford bit down gently and pulled back to see the bloom of blood under thin skin, darkening into a mark that would stay there. It was satisfying to see. It must have stung, but Jed was still baring his throat, still so trusting.

Jed made the slightest movement. It was only a twitch of his shoulder, maybe even an involuntary shiver, and the snarl that Redford gave was sharp. "Still," he barked. To drive his point home, he bit at Jed's shoulder. "Trust."

Eyes going wider, Jed immediately went completely motionless. Except his head, which tipped back even further, exposing the entire curve of his throat, already reddened from Redford's first bite. "I'm still," Jed said, tone dipping down lower, gravel and hoarse. "And baby, you know I trust. I'm yours. See? All yours."

Redford pushed his nose into Jed's throat, inhaling deeply. The lingering scent of the violence last night was still there, but it was faded now, overtaken by gunpowder, pine, and the earthier scent of Jed's arousal. Surrounding himself in the scent was intoxicating, something that Redford wanted to commit the rest of his life to.

"Good." He raked his teeth over the curve of Jed's throat again, the smooth slope between neck and shoulder. Normally, Jed was very much an active participant in things like this. Normally, Jed would be touching him right back, hands grasping, pulling him down for kisses, his voice rumbling as he spoke of exactly what he wanted to do.

Jed was silent now, watching him closely. The difference in his demeanor made Redford pull back slightly, unearthing himself from the confusing whirlwind of instincts, blinking at Jed as he looked at him. But the *need* was still there, the want to take and claim and mark. And there was that light in Jed's eyes, the familiar spark of returning hunger, even as the man did exactly as he'd been told, lying perfectly still, breathing hitched up in shallow little intakes of desire.

167

It scared Redford, the claiming instinct that was drowning his thoughts, but the utter *lack* of fear in Jed's eyes was reassuring. There was nothing there other than want.

His own need spurred him to move down to Jed's chest, biting at the soft skin under his nipple, raking teeth over Jed's ribs. A moan caught in Jed's throat, but he bit it back, doing his best not to make a sound. Redford frowned at that, reaching up a hand to trail over Jed's throat, pressing down slightly. "Still, but don't hide," he encouraged.

He resumed his path, lips wandering over Jed's ribs, wanting to claim every inch of him. If Redford wasn't feeling so impatient, he'd probably make Jed roll over so that he could do the same to his back, his arms, but all thoughts of that fled once he reached Jed's cock. Pressing his lips to the base of it, Redford inhaled again, nosing over the smooth skin above it. Jed was making noise now, unhindered in showing exactly how much he was liking this.

Reaching up, Redford curled his fingers around Jed's wrists, holding his hands still by his sides. Briefly, Jed's fingers twisted, grasping at Redford's, before he gave in to Redford's control. His whole body was tight with the effort to not move, to not reach out and touch. Redford gave an approving rumble, though he wasn't sure if it came from him or from the voice in his thoughts.

Then again, he wasn't sure if there was a difference at this point.

With Jed's hands pinned, he happily went back, nipping lightly at Jed's thigh, smiling at the reactionary twitch of muscle and the hissed moan Jed gave. Jed's scent was stronger here, and Redford couldn't help rubbing his cheek over Jed's thigh, even if he did hear the man huff out a low laugh at the action. He tightened his fingers around Jed's wrists, moving sideways to run his tongue over Jed's cock, exploring from the base to the head, testing Jed's reactions.

He glanced up at Jed. The man was biting his lip, flushed, eyes dark in arousal. The sight sent a thrill through Redford's spine. He raised Jed's hand to cup his cheek, leaning briefly against Jed's palm. He wanted, for a moment, to ask what color his eyes were. To figure out how deep into the miasma of instincts he was sinking, because he couldn't figure it out for himself.

He didn't care for much longer, though, not when Jed was looking at him like that. All Redford could think about was kneeling between Jed's legs, using his knees to budge them further apart as he wrapped his lips around Jed's cock. The shock of sudden contact had Jed arching up, groaning. Redford kept his hold on Jed's wrists and pushed his knuckles against Jed's hips, holding those down too.

"Sorry," Jed immediately moaned. His heels dug into the mattress, and he was trembling, but he stayed still. "You feel so damn good."

Want. Claim, the voice was rumbling. Then the other, the voice that wasn't aggressive, whispered, *make NoWolf-Jed-Journey happy. Make pack.* Redford obeyed both, rubbing his tongue over Jed's cock and taking him as much as he could. It wasn't gentle or slow. Not now. Right now, Redford wanted to show Jed exactly who he belonged to, to claim him, to make Jed remember that *he* was the only one for him.

Under Redford's grip, Jed twisted a little, an involuntary arch of his hips upward. He gasped loudly before biting his lip again, whole chest rumbling in a groan. "God, babe," Jed muttered restlessly. His scent seemed to grow stronger with the movement, and Redford took another moment to inhale, growling again at the lingering scent of vampire. The soap and its chemical smell hadn't washed it away as well as Redford would have hoped.

The thought triggered a deeper rumble in Redford's chest, protective, angry at the vampires who had dared touch him. He shoved Jed's hips down again, sucking him hard, taking his cock as deep as he could. It was a marking of sorts, a claiming. When Jed cried out hoarsely, Redford didn't let up. Each whimper and moan from Jed's lips only encouraged him, making him tighten his hold around Jed's wrists.

Even when Jed's fingers started trembling finely, the signal of his approaching orgasm, Redford didn't slow down. He knew every one of those signals—the way his left leg would start twitching slightly, the way the flush in his cheeks would spread to his throat. He noticed, vaguely, that the growling seemed to have some sort of effect, driving Jed higher, making every groan louder, every begging sound so much *more*.

Jed's orgasm came like the explosions he loved so much: sudden, loud, and passionate. Redford swallowed around him, driving him further, prolonging his pleasure. Jed was whimpering his name, pleading, head thrown back and whole body shaking. Slowly drawing back, Redford let go of Jed's wrists, palms smoothing over the red marks his knuckles had made on Jed's hips.

Then, he quite happily flopped down on Jed, cheek resting on his stomach, arm thrown over his hips. The scent of the vampires was gone now, taken over with Jed's natural scent and both he and Jed mingled together. The howling in his mind quieted to a content rumble.

"Love you," he mumbled into Jed's stomach, still rubbing his palm over Jed's hip.

Sounding dazed, Jed replied, "Please tell me I can touch you now." Redford twisted his neck to look up at him. He was aroused, but it was more like a slow burn, nothing that he needed to deal with right away. He'd just been happy to make Jed the center of his world.

"You don't have to," Redford murmured, brushing a kiss against Jed's stomach. "That was about you."

The molasses slow smile in Jed's voice was easy to hear. "Oh, Jesus, Red, trust me, I figured that one out. That was...." Hesitantly, oddly submissive, Jed's fingers turned so that he could barely brush Redford's wrist, the touch almost an inquiry, asking permission. "That was incredible. I just want to show you how much."

His mind blessedly silent now, Redford got an arm underneath him to push up, shifting to lie on his side next to Jed. His eyes fell on the marks standing out starkly on Jed's neck, and despite his contentment that Jed had enjoyed that, his lips twisted in a worried frown. He wasn't sure if he liked this hesitant, permission-seeking Jed. It was just so different than how he normally was, and Redford started wondering if he'd frightened Jed somehow.

"I didn't scare you, did I?" Redford raised his eyes to look at Jed, placing his hand over Jed's heart. "I don't—my instincts kind of went... um. Haywire."

Immediately, Jed's hand went up to cover Redford's, Jed struggling to sit up on his elbows. "Hey," he whispered, bumping his forehead lightly against Redford's. "I can handle it. I've told you that since the day I met you. I can handle all of it, whatever you've got. And, shit, Fido." Cracking a little sheepish grin, Jed shrugged. "I liked it. A *lot*. Do you get that?"

Trying to process that, Redford watched Jed carefully. He wasn't wincing when he moved. He clearly wasn't in any kind of real pain. Jed had talked, previously, about how he *liked* to ache a little after good sex, how he liked the twinge of a reminder the next day. Jed was smiling, looking utterly satisfied.

170

Redford would confess, he couldn't understand the kink for submission that Jed had. It frightened him. It made him think he had scared Jed into acting meek and hesitant, or that he'd hurt him so much that Jed didn't want to reach out for him.

Maybe he was wrong about Jed's reactions.

"Here." Jed's voice was soft, hands gentle as he took Redford's shoulders and laid him back. "Let me show you. I want to make you feel good." Brilliant green eyes stared down at him, crinkling a little at the corners. "Trust me?"

Redford stretched out on his back, still watching Jed. "I always trust you," he whispered. He might not understand the dominance and submission thing—he knew he *wasn't* dominant, not in the way that Jed would like, not like the men Jed usually flirted with. But that voice in the back of his mind seemed to have a possessive streak. Or maybe just a bossy nature.

Licking his lips, Jed sat back on his heels. He took his time to let his gaze sweep over Redford, his palm running flat from Redford's chest to his hips, groaning appreciatively. "God, you're beautiful." His fingertips pushed under Redford's pajama pants to trace a little constellation of freckles hidden in the dip just under Redford's belly button. "I could stare at you all day."

Compliments always made Redford flush a little, and now was no exception. "Still nothing compared to you," Redford replied, smiling, reaching out to run his own hand over Jed's arm. He wasn't sure what Jed was planning, so he resisted the urge to sit up so he could touch Jed properly.

With a quick grin, Jed laid his finger on Redford's lips, quieting him. "No," he murmured. "We're just talking about you now. Let me get all soppy; you know I'm shit at it, so I'm practicing." Redford laughed lowly in response, kissing Jed's fingertip. Jed's hand grasped Redford's, lifting it for a kiss before placing it back down on the bed. "And no moving."

A little startled by that, Redford's eyes went wide, but he nodded quickly. What was Jed doing? Suddenly Redford was a little nervous about what Jed had meant by *showing*.

Although no further orders seemed to be immediately forthcoming. Jed rocked back a little, biting his lip, clearly thinking. "Um… okay! Undress." Leering, Jed leaned back. "Slowly."

Amused at Jed's obviously hesitant tone, Redford stripped off his T-shirt. Halfway through, he remembered the *slowly* part and wondered how on earth he could turn this into something sexy when he was kind of tangled up in his shirt. He settled for tugging it off the rest of the way and taking his pants off slowly instead. He hooked his fingers into the waistband, drawing them down inch by inch, keeping his eyes locked with Jed's.

He'd barely gotten the pants kicked to the floor when he was tackled back onto the bed. Jed was laughing into the kiss, nipping his lip, settling into the slow press of their lips with a shuddering groan. "You're amazingly sexy," Jed murmured. "And I am *shit* at being dominant. I'm sorry, please, just tell me what I can do. I want to watch you come."

Reaching to bring Jed in for another kiss, Redford hooked his legs around Jed's hips, his own muffled laughter matching Jed's. "You gave *one* order," he pointed out.

That cocky smirk was buried in their kisses, in the increasingly hard push and pull between them. "I got impatient," Jed mumbled, rolling them over so Redford was on top, rocking his hips upward. "You're too tempting."

Redford found the bite mark he'd made earlier, gently brushing his lips over it. "I like it when you get impatient," he replied lowly, kissing Jed again. It made him feel like Jed, normally so in control of things, needed him so much that he was willing to toss that all aside. It made him feel *good*.

That, and he would never, ever complain about anything that got Jed naked and in bed with him.

"Well, here I am." Jed chuckled, nudging his nose in under Redford's ear, teeth closing playfully on his neck. "What do you want? Anything, sweetheart, I'll do *anything* to make you feel good. I want to make you fly."

The indecision made Redford pause. There were *so many* things he could say, so many different things Jed had shown him that all made him feel amazing. Did he have to pick a favorite? He wasn't sure he could do that. Settling his chin on Jed's chest, Redford thought hard about this. Jed's thumb smoothed at the wrinkles that'd appeared between his eyebrows.

"Earth to Red," Jed teased. "Come on, babe, what's the first thing that popped into that big old brain of yours?"

"Is 'everything' a valid answer?" Redford grinned a little, pressing his cheek to Jed's collarbone. "Everything we do feels good." Although, there had been *one* thing that had immediately come to mind. "Um. Back at home, a week ago? When we were in the kitchen and you, um. Did that thing."

If possible, Jed's grin got even wider. Without missing a beat, he settled in, hooking his hands behind Redford's hips and tugging him up. In less time than it took Redford to make a noise of confusion, he was crouched over Jed's head, all but sitting on him. "What—" he tried to yelp.

And then there was a quick swipe of Jed's tongue over his hole, the barest flicker of the tip of it pressing in. All bafflement instantly fled from Redford's mind, leaving him clutching the headboard. "Oh my God, Jed," he managed. "You remembered what I was talking about?"

"I'd do this every damn day if you let me," was Jed's muffled reply. His touches were teasing still, wet and warm and the rub of his thumb along the curve of Redford's ass that made heat lick across his skin. "Course I remember. Now hang on, sugar. I'm gonna make you shout."

If forced to pick a favorite, Redford figured this would probably be his. He didn't know why, and he definitely remembered being incredibly startled the first time Jed had introduced him to it, flailing so hard that he'd accidentally kneed Jed in the face. Fortunately, after a lot of apologizing on his part, Jed had taken the risk to continue. Rimming—still an odd word for it, in Redford's opinion.

Settling onto his knees, Redford curled his fingers around the headboard, hissing in a breath when Jed decided he wasn't going to waste any more time. The wet warmth of his tongue was rubbing over Redford's hole, pressing in as deep as Jed could get it, reducing Redford to incoherent moans in an embarrassingly short time. He'd been ignoring his own arousal, too focused on Jed to think about himself. He could hear Jed laugh lowly, pleased, that smug tone to his voice that he got whenever he knew he was doing something amazing.

Rocking up into him, Jed seemed determined to drive him to the brink with slow, deep strokes inside of him. Jed's tongue would slip in first, teasing and wet and warm, and then his finger would follow, to find that spot that sent bursts of heat along Redford's skin. Redford pressed his cheek to the top of the headboard, needing something to balance on, hoping he wasn't putting too much weight on Jed's shoulders. If he was, Jed obviously didn't mind.

Jed's name was on the tip of his tongue, trying to be said but coming out as moans instead. Redford tried not to shove down too hard, his thighs tense, shaking with the strain. Jed had a gift in making him come *way* too fast. He said he liked it, liked seeing the way Redford's skin would flush, the shake in his legs, how he'd lose all ability to speak. It was like all that single-minded focus Jed had for his jobs or his toys or whatever else would, in that moment, zero in on Redford. Like now.

As it always did when Jed got so devoted to this, Redford's orgasm slammed into him like a tidal wave, too soon and too fast but all the more amazing because of it. He was left curled over Jed, gasping loudly, his knuckles white where he was gripping the headboard. For what felt like a very long time, Redford stayed there, knowing he should move—but Jed was smirking, still teasing with his tongue, and it felt far too good to do anything but enjoy it, the shudders of the afterglow rippling through him.

Eventually, he managed it, shifting with a groan to flop down next to Jed. The smile he wore was warm, happy, completely forgetting the previous violence of the night. Jed's hands were smoothing over his body, worshiping him, soft kisses scattered like rain across his skin. "Love you, Fido," Jed rumbled, nosing into his neck.

Redford caught a glance at the clock. It was only a few hours after they'd gotten into bed, which meant they had much more time to sleep. Stretching out with a happy noise, he draped himself over Jed's side, kissing his jaw. "That was the best end to a busy day," he whispered. "The best end to *any* day, actually." Getting comfortable, his arm looped over Jed's chest, Redford tugged his pillow back and forth a few times before settling down.

Laughing softly, Jed kissed the tip of his nose. "Yeah, but now I'm thirsty." He wiggled out of Redford's embrace, lips catching any patch of skin he could in a quick kiss, soothing away Redford's pout. Finally Jed managed to hop out of bed, grinning widely at Redford. "You want anything, babe? I'm just going to get some water, and I'll be right back, I promise."

"You'd better be," Redford grumbled, his eyelids falling closed, the embrace of sleep quickly catching up to him. "I get cold without you in bed."

174

"I'll have to think of a way to warm you up, then." Jed leered impishly, swaggering out into the common room. He hadn't bothered to put any pants on, and Redford could hear the sound of the television, faintly, through the opened door.

Though Jed would only take a few minutes, Redford found himself slipping into sleep, exhausted and content. It *had* been a busy day, but they'd done some good too. Vampire killing aside, they'd helped two people.

Hopefully, the rest of the kidnapped people would be just as easy to find.

175

CHAPTER
9

Victor

IT HAD been four hours since David had walked off into the darkness of the surrounding streets, and Victor was starting to get worried.

Technically, he'd been worried ever since their car had pulled up to the old factory. Victor had never been the kind of man who handled stress well, so he'd sat behind the wheel, gaze fixed on the door, waiting and hoping that all of them would come out alive. At one point, he'd taken a short walk up to the door itself, wondering if he could hear *anything* that would give him a clue if they were succeeding or not.

He'd found a pair of glasses, cracked and bent, the thick frames bent out of shape. Glasses that, if Victor recalled correctly, he'd seen on the photo of the latest kidnap victim.

Now he was sitting in front of the TV, slowly turning those glasses over in his hands as he watched the news. The quick-paced Arabic of the presenter was something of a welcome distraction, allowing him to focus on the beautiful puzzle of the language, the way it fit together so neatly and logically, helping Victor take his mind off of David. The picture of the latest victim—Randall Lewis—was flashing across the screen again, thick-framed glasses perched on his nose. Victor glanced at the glasses he held once again.

There was no doubt. They were Lewis' glasses.

Hearing nearly silent footsteps approach, Victor turned his head, heart leaping in his throat. It was Jed, though, not David. Disappointment twisted his lips into a frown, which only deepened when he saw that Jed was completely naked.

"For God's sake, Journey," Victor muttered, turning his gaze back to the television. "Would it kill you to put some pants on?"

It wasn't that Jed was unattractive. *Far* from it. Jed was exactly the kind of man that Victor otherwise might have tried dating, but he was... Jed. Victor didn't hate him either. That would require a lot of emotional investment in Jed, and Victor was not that invested. No, Victor had come to think of Jed as more like the annoying little cousin one saw at family gatherings that just sat around and picked his nose. Vaguely irritating, but not enough to get worked up over.

Unless Jed was doing something *spectacularly* frustrating, like his previous adventures in dry-humping.

"It might," Jed replied in an overly innocent drawl. The facade didn't fool Victor, though. Jed claimed not to know any of the language, but his eyes were fixed on the television, a particularly intent look on his face as he leaned back against the counter and watched. Most likely Jed had picked up bits and pieces of the language, either here or on previous trips.

Stunningly, Jed was an amazingly fast learner. He hid it very well.

"Well, it might kill *me* if I have to get an eyeful." Victor sighed. "Have you heard anything from David? Has he called you?"

A quick look flicked over at Victor, Jed's face caught somewhere between a smirk and an incredulous little frown. "Oh, yeah," he said with a snort. "We just had a long conversation about our feelings and emotions and how much he thinks you're just the *swellest* fella ever." With a stiff little shrug of his shoulders, Jed stalked over to the fridge and rifled through it, cursing under his breath at the lack of alcohol. Bottled water in hand, he collapsed onto the couch, eyes once again focused on the news report. "He'll come back when the sun's down again. And if he hasn't turned into the type of bloodsucker we're hunting, I might even reconsider kicking his pert little ass."

There were a lot of things that Victor could say to that, but in the end he held his tongue, cautious. Jed might be annoying, but he was the de facto leader of this strange little mission. It would be unwise for Victor to anger him more than was necessary.

Instead, he handed over the glasses for Jed's perusal. "I found these outside the building's door. I assume they'll look familiar to you."

Jed took them and immediately put them on, as bent and as twisted as they were, grinning goofily over at Victor. "Not exactly my style, professor, but I appreciate the thought." Shaking them off, he held the earpiece between two fingers, letting the glasses turn. "You know what they say about assuming. You can stare at my ass all you want, but me's still got no fucking clue what your point is."

Victor gave a sigh. If Jed was hiding his ability to be smart about things right now, he was doing so *extremely* well. "They're the same make as the latest kidnapped person was wearing in the photos on the news," he replied. "Seeing as I found them outside a vampire lair, where there were two of the same victims, I extrapolated from there."

"Jeez," Jed said, giving Victor a look of concern. "In *public*? You're lucky you don't go blind." Tossing the glasses back to Victor, Jed leaned back, arms behind his head, staring up at the ceiling. "Okay, so we have two out of four we're hoping are still breathing. The last one was definitely there, but they moved him. Why?"

"A moving target is much harder to find and kill than a target that stays still." Victor cradled the glasses carefully in his hands. "Most vampires, if their clan is powerful enough, will set up a base of sorts. They're strong enough not to care who finds them. These specific vampires, on the other hand, seem lacking in coordination and numbers."

Huffing out a soft noise, Jed looked over at him. Fox-bright eyes, green and sharp, caught his face, and Jed arched an eyebrow. "Now does that sound like this guy that's got David so scared?"

"No," Victor replied softly. Honestly, he wasn't sure *what* to think about this situation. Gabriel—David's sire—kept sending David messages indicating that he was not the driving force behind these kidnappings. But David seemed so convinced that he was. "It doesn't. From what I know of Gabriel, he is… nothing like those vampires you encountered tonight."

"Yeah." Jed dragged his hand across his face and, for a moment, he looked tired. *Old.*

Human.

"Well, I've got a werewolf to go warm up." Just that quickly, the leer was back in place and Jed was standing, swinging *everything* around just because, Victor was sure, he knew how it bothered people. No matter how honestly impressive it was. "You should sleep, princess. We'll have work to do tonight."

Victor shook his head briefly. "I'm staying up. I want to be awake when David comes back." He smiled thinly. "Besides, whatever work you have planned, I'm sure I'm not an integral part of it."

Tapping the side of his nose, Jed smirked. "Figured that one out, did you?" But his hand dropped to briefly clasp Victor's shoulder before he

178

strutted back to his room. "Just sleep. You're no good to anyone half dead."

With that final piece of advice, the door closed behind Jed. Victor wished, once again, that the walls were soundproofed. Or even just a little bit thicker. He could do without knowing some details. Not all knowledge was a blessing, after all.

He didn't sleep. He couldn't. Every time he thought about closing his eyes, he saw David, alone and slowly going crazy, succumbing to his own instincts. The image was enough to keep Victor awake for another few hours, sightlessly staring at the television.

Eventually, exhaustion had his head drooping, his body listing to the side to fall gracelessly to the couch cushions, settling into an uneasy sleep. The brief snatches of dreams that he had weren't any better than what he'd been previously imagining. Victor woke several times at a particularly loud noise on the television, or too-loud footsteps from an upstairs room.

He didn't know how much later it was when he jerked awake at yet another noise, though this particular sound was a lot more promising. It was the sound of a key turning in the door, prompting Victor to sit up, glasses askew, staring hopefully toward the entrance. After a moment of fumbling, David came staggering in, looking disheveled, normally perfect hair sticking out all ends, skin streaked with dirt and old, dried blood.

Victor was up in a flash, moving toward David, grasping his arms to help him balance. "You look frightful," he remarked, intending for a blandly toned comment. The shake in his voice ruined any chance of sounding calm.

"Yeah, well." David's hand rubbed over his chin, and he pulled away so he could collapse onto the couch, sprawled messily on his back. "It's been a long day."

Following him, Victor sat carefully on the same couch, perched next to David's legs. He went to reach out, hesitated, his hand hovering over David's chest. Then, more decisively, he laid his hand on David's knee. "You seem...." Calmer, somewhat. "Are you all right? Is there anything I can get you?"

Grimacing, David struggled to sit up. "Fine," he said, biting the word off sharply. After a beat his expression softened. David's eyes flicked over to Victor a few times before he managed, "Are *you* okay? What happened... I didn't mean...."

179

Victor gave a shaky-sounding laugh. The faint bruising he'd received from David's desperate attempt to shove him away after the explosions had been something he'd utterly forgotten about. He'd been too focused on worrying about David. "I've been up all night fretting," he said wryly, rubbing his thumb over David's knee. "I had to see Jed naked. Again. But other than that, I'm fine."

David actually snorted out a faint laugh, leaning back and closing his eyes. His fingertips lightly brushed against the back of Victor's hand. "Now that sounds truly traumatizing." Cracking open one eye, he frowned. "I hurt you. Didn't I?"

"Not particularly," Victor dismissed. Slowly, he twisted his hand, palm up, to grasp David's. "I should have followed you. I could have helped somehow."

He knew the words were a lie before they even came out of his mouth. With the state that David had been in, it wouldn't have taken long before he'd been unable to tell friend from foe. Boyfriend from blood bag. Had he gone after David, Victor realized he'd likely be either dead or very close to it. That knowledge didn't stop him from feeling guilty.

"You're smarter than that, Vickie," David murmured, fixing him with a look. "Today, I hid in an old building and fed off of rats. If you'd followed me, I would have eaten you." He gently pulled his hand away from Victor's, and David stood, walking away. "I hurt you. Stop making excuses for my lack of control. It's unbecoming."

"Oh, well, I wouldn't want to be *unbecoming*. How terrible of me," Victor replied dryly, trying to make light of the situation. They hardly ever talked like this, about serious things, things that actually mattered.

The smack of David's hand hitting the door frame seemed overly loud somehow, like a foreboding crash instead of what it was. David was standing there, in the doorway of their bedroom, back to him. Victor could feel the tension radiating off him. "*Damn it*, Victor. I swear to God, some days I don't know if you react to anything but fucking or goddamn books with something approaching actual *emotion*."

The words, rather than the noise, made Victor flinch. Guilt flushed hotly over his cheeks, shoulders curling in on themselves. "I—" He went to protest, went to point out that such emotional conversations were a rare occurrence in their lives, but he stopped himself from saying such a thing. David wasn't in a terribly rational state right now.

"I'm sorry," Victor wound up murmuring. He stood, crossing the room to David. Cautiously, he put his hand on the back of David's shoulder, wishing the man would look at him.

"You shouldn't be," was David's reply, so quiet it was barely even a noise. "You should be pissed, Vickie. You should have chopped off my fucking head the second I walked in the door." Almost imperceptibly, there was a hitch in David's chest, a choked-back sound lost deep in his throat. "Goddamn it, why won't you hate me?"

Gently, as if he were approaching an animal that could bolt and run— or maul him—at any second, Victor stepped closer, winding his arms around David's waist. "Because I like you far too much to hate you," he replied simply.

It wasn't love, what he and David had. It wasn't butterflies in the stomach, craving every moment with each other. It wasn't breakfast in bed on romantic weekends and long, emotional talks about the future. It wasn't *nothing* either, though; it wasn't merely a relationship of convenience.

Most days, Victor wasn't sure what to call it. If there was a word in any known language for what they had, Victor didn't know it. He had no clue what to call a relationship that had started with meeting in a supermarket, of all places, started by David saying *you're coming home with me* as Victor, startled out of testing the fruit for bruises, had stuttered and flushed and flailed a bit.

He had gone home with David, though. And that was how it had started.

"You smell like rat," Victor said bluntly. "You should shower. And stop worrying about whether or not you hurt me. I'm not a delicate flower, despite popular opinion."

Snorting quietly, David finally turned his head toward Victor. "I always worry," he admitted. "I felt like I was stuck in a nightmare. Like I still am. I shouldn't have brought you here. Any of you."

Victor pressed his cheek to David's shoulder, holding him tighter. "We can handle it. We can help *you* handle it. That's why you brought Jed and Redford along, because you know they're not useless."

"Well. Not *entirely* useless." It was only a faint flicker of a smile, but it was there. David pulled away, but his fingertips trailed lightly along Victor's arm as he did so. "I'd, uh, I'd better shower. Don't want you to have to put up with the rat stench."

"It's quite horrifying," Victor said, but he still brushed a kiss over David's cheek, careful to avoid a streak of blood. "Go shower. I'll be here when you're done."

David made his way to the bathroom, gathering up fresh clothes. Just before he shut the door, he said, very quietly, "Victor?" David's expression was haunted and taut, eyes rimmed in dark circles. "I would have fed from them. The two we found. I think that's why they were left there. It was for me. Because Gabe knows…." Fidgeting with the shirt in his hands, an extremely uncharacteristic gesture, David's eyes flicked away. "He knows I'm breaking."

The door shut between them, and Victor was left alone. There was the sound of the shower turning on, the faint hiss of water, but otherwise the room was silent.

Victor was almost glad he didn't have to come up with an answer for that. He knew now that Jed didn't think Gabriel was behind any of this. Victor was beginning to wonder the same, which meant that those two people hadn't been for David at all. They'd just been left there. Worse, it meant that none of the mind games, none of the mental torture that David was cracking under was real. He was doing it to himself, by himself.

He sank down to sit on the edge of the bed, looking out the window. Of course, Gabriel *could* still be responsible, even if none of the evidence was there.

This was starting to get confusing.

Victor took his glasses off to rub at his eyes, trying to get rid of the gritty feeling of a terrible night of sleep. David was back and seemed relatively in control for now. Unfortunately, given that it was nearing seven in the evening, Jed would likely be up and about, barking out orders and expecting them all to make themselves useful.

That was fine. He'd gone without decent sleep for longer periods of time before, and over much more trivial things.

The shower shut off some time later. Victor supposed he probably should have used the time to get something to eat, or do *something* useful, but all he'd done was sit, watch out the window, and hope desperately that David could get through this. He wished he was better at holding David together somehow, that he could find some magic way to pull David back from the edge.

It didn't work like that, though. The only person who could do that was David. It was called *self*-control for a reason.

While he waited for David to emerge again, Victor stood, groaning faintly at the ache in his back. That was what he got for sleeping awkwardly on a couch. Slowly, he adjusted his clothing, studying himself in the mirror to make sure he was presentable. He was still wearing the same clothes from last night—slacks, a shirt and waistcoat, a jacket despite the heat—but the idea of getting changed into new ones seemed too much effort right now.

Besides, it wasn't as if he had a high chance of needing to go outside the hotel.

Jed was standing right outside the bedroom door when Victor opened it. Startled enough to take a quick step back, Victor glowered at him. "Eavesdropping, Mr. Walker?"

"Just trying to figure out if your boyfriend's still on the one-way train to crazy-town." Jed peered over Victor's shoulder, back toward the bathroom door. "He eat any small children today?"

"You sound so concerned," Victor replied dryly. The acidic tone to his voice vanished then, along with his shoulders slumping. "No, he didn't hurt anybody. But he wasn't in the best shape when he returned."

"He's a big boy." Jed seemed a little more relaxed. At least he wasn't brandishing weapons or cursing like some foulmouthed sailor. He was also wearing clothes, thank God. "I'm sure he's fine."

"I'm sure too." David's quiet voice interrupted them. Looking over his shoulder, Victor found David had emerged from the bathroom and was toweling off his hair, with some inscrutable look on his face. His skin was still damp from the shower, a pair of dress slacks slung low on his hips, and no shirt to speak of. "We have work to do, Journey."

"Fine by me," Jed returned. "So long as you don't lose your shit again." Turning on his heel, Jed stalked back to his room, and Victor heard him loudly exclaim before he shut the door behind him, "Don't worry, Fido. Big, bad, and fangy is all muzzled up again."

Victor sighed faintly. As always, when Jed and David managed to converse, it closely resembled a pair of alpha males circling each other, tensely waiting for one or the other to snap. Victor was mildly surprised, every time, when they didn't just drop their pants and measure them.

He knew who would win that one, though.

"I do so enjoy our chats with Mr. Walker," Victor commented. "He's so charming. His deftness with the spoken word is simply inspiring."

Smirking faintly, David tossed the towel aside. "He certainly has a way with people."

Victor *was* going to go out into the main room to see if there were any new developments in the kidnappings, but he found himself caught half in the doorway, staring at David. How he, a relatively average-looking linguistics professor, had managed to get the attention of a man like David, he simply had no clue.

"You're looking particularly stunning this morning," Victor noted. Turning in the doorway, he leaned against the frame, giving himself a moment to simply stare. David had the kind of looks that meant he should be modeling, or acting, or *something* other than eating rats in an abandoned building. Even more so now, with his skin damp and gleaming from the shower, his dark hair pushed back from his face, curling loosely around his ears.

David looked down at himself with a faint laugh, wiggling his bare toes against the carpet. "Comparatively speaking?" But there was a flash of something in his eyes, and he moved closer to Victor, hesitating a little before he reached out, running his fingertips along Victor's lips. "You look beautiful when you're all rumpled. It's nice to see you less than perfect."

"Balderdash and piffle," Victor dismissed, making David smile. David looked so different when he smiled. It was almost an awkward expression on him, spreading to his eyes, the corner of his lips pulling outward almost too far, but it was utterly endearing. He usually looked so composed, so serious. "I look a right mess when I'm less than properly dressed. You should know. You've seen me on occasion first thing in the morning."

But he returned David's smile, leaning up to press a light kiss to David's cheek. "I'm glad you're okay," Victor murmured. Under his touch, he felt David's shoulders tighten, the line of his jaw clench. But the other man simply nodded and returned the kiss, dry lips brushing over Victor's cheek before he pulled back.

"I should get ready." David turned to the closet, pulling out a tie and looping it loosely around his neck. "Was there anything on the news today?"

Appreciating the sight of David's back muscles as he found a shirt, Victor glanced back into the main room. The news had moved onto something else. "Nothing new." David buttoned his shirt, pulling his tie out, knotting it around his neck with deft, practiced movements. "I

184

actually, er—" Victor hesitated, wondering if bringing up any topic about last night was a good idea. David should know, though. "I found glasses outside the building. They appear to be the same make as the latest kidnap victim, Lewis, is wearing in the picture they're showing of him."

Frowning faintly, David sat on the edge of the bed to pull on socks and shoes. The disheveled, hungry look was once again hidden behind a perfectly pressed shirt, by a neat tie and gelled hair. David looked every inch the wealthy businessman he portrayed. Except for that glimmer in his eyes, the way his movements were just a bit too sudden, just a little too harsh. "They moved him?"

"That's what Jed and I assume, yes." Victor took a few seconds to reflect on the strangeness of that sentence. "Jed and he" assuming anything, even talking civilly, was odd. "Jed...." He trailed off, hesitating again. "Jed doesn't think this is the work of Gabriel, David."

"That's because Jed is an idiot human who doesn't know his asshole from a hole in the ground. Can you hand me my watch?" David ran a hand through his hair as he stood. "I think we should go back to the warehouse from last night. If there's any trail to where they took the American, it will start there."

"Agreed." Victor toyed with the edge of his jacket sleeve. "David?" He glanced up at the man. "What I meant to say was, *I'm* beginning to think that this isn't the work of Gabriel either."

David's head had been bent, fingers working to fasten the band of his watch. He froze, unmoving for what felt like forever, before he shrugged. "You don't know him like I do. Of course it's Gabriel."

It was on the tip of Victor's tongue to point out that everything they'd seen and heard said differently. The ragged presentation of the vampires, the abandoned hideouts, the two messages supposedly from Gabriel. Instead, he drew a breath and said, "Let me look into your eyes. It may give us a clue, or at least some kind of direction."

"No, Victor." One long, elegant finger went up in protest, and David shook his head firmly. "Absolutely not. You *know* what happened last time."

"Exactly," Victor argued. "I know. There's nothing I don't know about your past. Nothing I don't know about your present. Seeing everything else... it may help us. It *will* help us."

Wincing, David kept his head down. Thinking about it, that was clear, from the way his fingers were toying with the tip of his tie. Finally he ground his teeth and nodded. "Fine."

David reached out to take Victor's hand, drawing him in close. He turned them so that Victor's knees were against the edge of the bed. Gentle fingers dragged through Victor's hair, and David shook his head. "Stubborn man," he murmured, sounding fond, before slowly tipping Victor's chin upward. Victor removed his glasses, tucking them into the breast pocket of David's shirt.

Fear began to hammer inside his chest, but he kept it from showing on his expression. It felt like every second spent staring at David's shoulder took a lifetime, before he slowly dragged his gaze up to squarely meet David's.

David had wonderful eyes. Dark brown, so dark they were nearly black in this light, framed at the outer edge by flecks of hazel. Victor, in the few seconds of calm afforded to him, raised his hand to cup David's jaw. "You have such beautiful eyes," he murmured.

The sound of the television, of his own breathing, of Redford and Jed puttering around in the main room, it all rose to an unbearable volume and then quieted. Then silenced completely. White began to creep in at the edges of Victor's vision.

There was David, standing at the edge of a grand stage, voice lifted in clear tones to recite lines meant to draw tears, to incite both laughter and deep sorrow. The crowd was huge, noisy, well dressed. The air was warm, almost stifling in humidity, and David's costume was getting drenched with sweat. Air was difficult to draw into his lungs, but the show must go on.

Victor blinked. David was watching him closely, a line of concern between his eyebrows. The white washed over him again, and Victor didn't feel his muscles jerking. The images were more important.

David meeting Gabriel for the first time, nervous and excited. David's eighteenth birthday, spent wandering the edge of the Nile with his benefactor, deep discussion driving out thoughts of the surrounding crowd. David, shrinking back in fear as Gabriel bared his fangs for the first time. As he felt that first bite, the first surge of panic fading into false bliss.

Memories, too many of them, swamped Victor's mind. He'd seen all of these already and was now struggling to force past them, ignoring them.

186

David's first kill, fangs sinking into the young man's neck, the ecstasy of life filling his mouth. That first month of his life as a vampire, a blur of memories, blood and sex and debauchery. Gabriel, watching over him the entire time, twisting him, driving him to kill when David hesitated, coaxing him into drinking until David couldn't think about what he was doing anymore.

After that, countless years of doing exactly the same thing. Feeding, fucking, reveling in it, Gabriel a guide the entire time. Countless days spent in Gabriel's bed, countless nights spent hunting by his side, sharing the kill.

Then—

David, wandering into a supermarket to see if he could withstand the crush of people, the scents and the blood and the heartbeats. Spotting a young man dressed in tweed, glasses, short hair a shade somewhere between red and blond. The resulting night spent in bed, delighting in slowly stripping away the inhibitions of the professor—himself, Victor vaguely realized—*falling into a relationship because it was just so different than anything else David had experienced with Gabriel.*

Yesterday. David hiding in an old building, his every cell screaming for blood. Wishing there was something there to sink his fangs into, and then there was. It wasn't ideal, it wasn't much, but it would still be blood. Even if it was a rat.

Here. Now.

And after that—

Possibilities. So many of them, like threads arcing off in the dark distance, some ending shortly, some going for so long that even Victor couldn't see the end of them.

David going to see Gabriel a few days from now, his control breaking, going back to his sire—

David giving up on the kidnap victims, they were just blood bags, giving up and leaving them in Cairo to go after the vampires himself—

—the victims, dead when they arrived, a young woman lying with her neck torn open, a man who was something more than just a man being chained and laughed at—

—Gabriel's laughing face, David at his side—

—David—

Darkness.

VICTOR struggled his way to consciousness. The very act of doing so felt like clawing his way upward from the bottom of a swamp.

"—just happened?" Redford's voice, lifted in nervousness. "Was he having a seizure?"

"He's fine. Back up, please." David's voice was utterly calm. His hand lay briefly on Victor's head before he moved away, toward the sound of Redford's voice. "We'll be out in a moment."

"Like fuck." Ah, and there were the dulcet tones of Journey Walker. Victor tried to give an annoyed groan but found himself making no noise. "What the hell kind of freaky shit is going on in here?"

The pain in his head was incredible, but the relief was stronger. Victor, once he realized that he was thinking coherently, forced his eyes open, though he almost immediately shut them with a groan that actually made a sound this time. "Shit that I'll explain momentarily," he whispered hoarsely. "Please go away now."

The commotion of David physically pushing the other two men out of the door was replaced by the sound of running water. A cool rag was laid over Victor's forehead, and David pushed two pills into his hand. "Take your medication," David told him, voice barely more than a whisper. "I'll go hold off the dogs."

Victor gratefully swallowed the pills dry, reaching up with a shaking hand to press the cold cloth harder against his forehead, pulling it down to cover his eyes too. "I wish I could have seen you on stage," he slurred, not quite in his right mind just yet. "You looked very talented."

The hands that were fussing with his pillow went utterly still for a moment before David muttered, "I didn't think you'd see all that again. We already went through this once."

"Sorry. Sorry," Victor managed, rolling over to press his face into the mattress. "Yes, we did. My apologies. I'll—er, yes. My mind isn't quite with it yet." He realized that the cloth would likely be getting the blankets wet and decided he didn't care. "Give me a moment to gather my thoughts about what I saw."

It seemed David couldn't leave the room fast enough. He'd reacted the same way the first time Victor had looked into his eyes. Perhaps for good reason, at least to David's mind. He didn't often talk about his past. And he certainly had aspects of it that he wouldn't want anyone else to know. Victor's ability let him have a front row seat for all of it. David tended not to know how to react to reminders of that. At least he'd left the lights off, and with the door shut the murmur of voices was almost inconsequential.

Still, Victor really did wish he'd seen David on stage when he'd been human. He'd looked like he'd enjoyed it very much.

Rolling over on to his back with a heartfelt groan, Victor waited until the throbbing behind his eyes had at least died down to a somewhat more bearable level. His migraine medication—although not strictly curing a *migraine*—worked wonders. Sound still lanced at his temples, making them ache, but he forced himself to his feet with an unsteady sway, catching himself against the wall.

Left foot first, then right foot. That was the trick.

By the time he managed to make it out into the main room, clumsily shoving his glasses on, Jed, David, and Redford were gathered on the couches. Jed was fiddling with one of his guns, elbows resting on his knees, fixing David with an entirely suspicious glare. "So what you're saying is, you *didn't* do some jacked-up bloodsucker shit to make the professor go all limp and weird like?"

"What I'm saying, Jed, is that you are an idiot," was David's response. He stood quickly and turned to Victor, giving the man his seat. "Now try not to let your tiny brain get in the way of your talking again." Victor sat gratefully, feeling as old as the manner in which he dressed.

"If you had paid any attention to my talking about the supernatural world, Jed, you might have figured out what I am much earlier," Victor said wearily, dropping his head to rest in his hands.

Frustrated confusion was evident in Jed's voice. Apparently the man didn't enjoy being called stupid. "Look, all this freak shit, it's kind of not in the manual. So why don't you stop acting all high and mighty mysterious and just give me a goddamn straight answer for once."

Victor found the energy to smirk briefly. Jed had never particularly been interested in anything supernatural—he only wanted to know what he *needed* to know. Redford turned on the full moons. David had to drink blood to survive. Those things were necessary. Victor's state of being was not. Though he supposed he did have to sympathize with Jed. All of this—werewolves, vampires, and more—had to be very strange and confusing at first.

He opened his mouth to reply, winced, and clutched at his temple. "David, would you please talk for me?"

Eyebrow arching, David looked between Victor and Jed. "Victor comes from a bloodline that is very diluted. If he looks into your eyes he sees all of your past, your present, and whatever possible futures you are heading toward. He gets all that information at once, and it gives him a headache." Reaching out, David grabbed the changer and flipped on the television. "Satisfied?"

Victor took his hands away from his face long enough to gauge reactions. Redford was staring at him with wide eyes, looking fascinated. "I *thought* you smelled not human," Redford announced.

"Yes, I'm not, quite." Victor massaged his temples. Jed probably didn't care to know much more than that, but Redford looked interested. And it *had* been a while since he'd been so honest with anybody other than David. "Are you aware of the Medusa myth? When she looked into people's eyes, she turned them to stone. The legend got it a bit wrong, though. There were actually multiple medusas, and while they did turn people to stone, it was because they took everything from the person they were looking at. Their memories, their future, their life."

He paused to gather the cold cloth again—now slightly warmer—and pressed it to his forehead. "These days, descendants of that line don't turn people to stone. The blood is too diluted for that. But most of them do kill or otherwise render their victim without memory. Thankfully, I don't."

"He also hasn't cracked or gone crazy," David added. He appeared to be absorbed in watching the television, but Victor could see his attention darting over to where Jed was sitting, uncharacteristically quiet. "It's a fairly rare bloodline, if only because, most of the time, humans can't handle the gift. They break apart under the strain."

Well, that was certainly depressing to hear out loud. "I'm a half blood, Jed," he clarified, lifting his gaze to look at the man. "I'm not the only kind, either. Even I don't know how many types of us are out there, but I've heard of everything from pixie to minotaur."

The gun had gone still in Jed's hands. He wasn't cleaning it anymore. Just holding it, staring down at the weapon and his fingers wrapped around it. After a few long, slow breaths he stood and shrugged. "Whatever. So your mom fucked a snake. I don't give a shit. If you have something useful to contribute, keep flapping your mouth, otherwise shut up."

190

"Technically, one of my ancestors would have 'fucked a snake'," Victor felt the need to point out. "And medusas weren't snakes. They were—" He cut himself off, seeing the seriously displeased expression that was growing on Jed's face. "Er. Yes. I'll contribute something useful once I get my thoughts together."

He sagged back into the couch. Redford had moved closer to Jed, looking at him in concern. David was watching the television. Victor wound up staring blankly at the opposite wall, slowly sorting through the images he'd seen.

None of them had been very good.

None of them had actually been very helpful, either.

His ability, as volatile as it was, didn't allow him to see *everything* about possible futures, just the potential futures of one person if they continued on the path they were currently on. Victor once again wished the ability was a little more broad spectrum, and not so narrowly confined. He would be so much more useful that way.

"I didn't get a definite answer on who exactly is behind these kidnappings," Victor eventually said, disappointed. "If I did, it was... lost in the tsunami of everything else. What I can say, however, is not good." He looked at David out of the corner of his eye. "The most likely path, considering the one you're walking right now, ends with you at Gabriel's side again."

It didn't appear that David had moved. He was still sitting there, watching the blasted television, expression blank. But the next moment had the sharp crack of the remote breaking in David's clenched fist, and he looked grayed out, terrified behind the impassive facade. Guilt rose bitterly at the back of Victor's throat, but he'd had to say it.

"So, let's just... not do that," Jed offered. "Change it or whatever. That's how it works, right?"

"I wish *I* knew exactly how changing it worked," Victor replied with a wry smile. His hand settled on David's back, just a light touch. "It's safe to say, though, yes, we'll need to do things differently. Perhaps for the next few days you and Redford take the lead on this case. You do things your way." Under no other circumstance would Victor *ever* encourage Jed to do things *his* way. That path tended to end with explosions, but it was better than the one he'd just seen.

"Well, shucks, sweetheart." Jed smirked, slinging his arm around Redford's shoulders. "It's about damn time." Nodding at David, Jed almost looked concerned. It was odd, seeing him appear *serious*. "Look, Davie, we've got some good leads. We'll figure this one out. Trust me, okay? That's why you hired me."

It was a scary thing, to place his trust in Jed. Victor wasn't sure if he wanted to do it, but for David's sake, he *had* to. David didn't look entirely sure about trusting Jed either, but he gave a quick nod, silent, lips pulled thin.

"Excuse me for a moment," Victor murmured, unsteadily getting off of the couch to shuffle his way back to the bedroom. The bathroom lights, when switched on, were bright. Not unbearably so, now.

He dropped the now warm cloth to the side of the sink, glasses set down beside it, leaning down to splash some water from the tap onto his face. It wasn't as cold as he would have liked it to be, but it served its purpose. Victor tiredly raised his head to study himself in the mirror, droplets dripping off his chin.

He was worried about David's future, yes, but for now the main emotion he felt was relief. David had glossed over the typical fate of medusa half bloods in explaining it to Jed. It was a cruel irony that most of the half bloods of his kind simply weren't built to handle what they saw when they met another's eyes. Their minds were human, and vulnerable to overload. Seeing one person so wholly, seeing everything about them, was simply too much.

Eventually, all of them succumbed to madness. Death in extreme cases. Vegetative states. Psychological damage closely resembling schizophrenia or severe autism.

Victor exhaled slowly, staring at his reflection. Every time he looked into someone else's eyes, he ran the risk of snapping. When it happened, it would happen suddenly, without warning, and the rest of his life would be spent in confusion and fear, unable to comprehend the world around him.

Not today, though.

Today he was still fine.

And seeing David's future—seeing how he could prevent him returning to Gabriel—had been worth the risk.

"Victor?" David's voice was lowered, footsteps almost silent as he came around the corner. "Jed wants to go out and do some recon. Alone." The way the vampire said the last word, with a twist of his lips, a barely contained bite of frustration, made his emotions on the subject all too clear. "He and Redford are now discussing the meaning of the word *alone,*

192

and I frankly don't wish to be around that much domesticity this early in the evening." He paused, hip resting against the door frame. "Are you all right?"

"Yes. Yes, I'm fine," Victor said, picking up a towel to pat over his face, drying the last of the water. Looking at David's reflection in the mirror, Victor smiled. "It was worth it."

David shook his head. "No, it wasn't," he corrected. "But I've long since stopped trying to argue with you." Reaching out, David gently ran his fingertips along the nape of Victor's neck, a faint curve appearing at the corners of his lips at the goose bumps he left behind. He was silent while Victor continued to dry himself off, to fuss over folding the towel just so, fixing the now damp strands of hair that always seemed to wind up in his face.

"I'm afraid." The admission came in a whisper, David looking at Victor in the mirror. "I don't want you to be right, Victor."

Victor turned, leaning against the sink to face David. "I don't want to be right either," he replied softly, reaching out to tug gently at David's tie. "I think rather fondly of you, you know."

There was almost a hint of a smile on David's lips, buried in the frown that chased down from the creases on his forehead. "We're so close. If I can just be strong for a little longer, this will all be over." The words weren't meant for him, Victor knew. It was the mantra David was using to keep himself sane, a variation on the one he used every minute of every day. As if by telling himself that he was fine, that it was only a little while longer, that the hunger was controllable, it would be so.

"Yes, it will be," Victor agreed. He'd seen David's memories. He could take a decent guess at the mix of emotions that would come if Gabriel was killed. Overwhelmingly, though, it had to be good for him. It would mean that person who taught David to be who he had been for so many decades was gone.

And then maybe David could start to let go.

Maybe.

"I can only guess at what steps we must take to prevent you from ending up at Gabriel's side again." Victor passed a hand over his temples, feeling the throb of his headache still fading. "Other than that, perhaps we should focus on the kidnapped victims first." David was starting to get a look on his face—a tense, thin look that meant he was at the end of his capacity for dealing with emotional things for the day.

193

That was fine. Victor was nearly at the end of his own quota too. There was only so much sharing and caring either of them could indulge in before it got to be too much.

"We should order in for food." A topic change, Victor felt, was prudent. "Well, *I* should order in for food. I'm feeling spectacularly lazy. Still, it's been years since I've been in Cairo, and I'm almost tempted to make you take me out to see the pyramids once more." They moved back into the bedroom while Victor fussed with his glasses, pushing them further up the bridge of his nose.

Giving him a look, David sprawled out onto the bed with a groan. "I haven't slept in two days," he reminded Victor. "But if you eat during my nap, I might be more inclined to brave the tourists and see the pyramids in the moonlight." There wasn't a flicker of emotion on his face, nothing that gave away anything but vague boredom. Victor knew, though, as well as David did, about the last time David had seen the pyramids. More importantly, who he'd been with. Still, making new memories might be the best way to help him begin to move on, and a nighttime tour of the desert did sound like more fun than holing up in the hotel again.

"You *might be inclined?*" Victor teased, dropping down to sit on the edge of the bed. "How very romantic."

Even with his eyes closed, David could give perfectly good amused looks. "Yes, because we so often do romantic things."

Victor didn't bother to restrain the laugh he gave, leaning down to rest his head against David's chest. No, neither of them were particularly romantic people, by any stretch of the imagination. "Just the other day, we spent many hours frolicking through fields of flowers in the sunlight," he agreed dryly, moving up to press a kiss to David's jaw. "Of course, I'm allergic to multiple species of flowers, and you would burn to a crisp, but our romantic spirit kept us safe."

Underneath him, he felt the odd sensation of David's chest rising and falling in a brief laugh. "This isn't a romance, Vickie," he murmured, running his hand through Victor's hair. "Someday, you'll have one. But at least you'll have stories to tell about the time you dared to put your head in the lion's mouth." David waggled his eyebrows at him, a fond look on his face, before letting his eyes fall back shut.

Despite the amused tone of David's words, Victor felt a sadness tighten his chest briefly. "Yes, and you'll have humorous tales about the stuffy linguistics professor you turned into a raging sexual pervert," he replied, thumping his chin on David's chest. "Honestly, David. I used to be so vanilla."

"Oh, no," David said, so quietly Victor barely heard the words. "No romances for me, I'm afraid." His thumb traced around the curve of Victor's ear. David's eyes never opened, and for that Victor was glad. For once, he didn't have any desire at all to know what they looked like, not at this moment. Not so soon after seeing *everything*.

Then it was gone, that aching sorrow, hidden away again. David smirked. "You were always a pervert, Vickie. I just provided an opportunity."

Victor's snort was not a particularly refined sound. "I beg to differ. I used to have sex with the lights off, under the sheets. And then you came along, and I very nearly had sex in a supermarket parking lot."

He couldn't complain much, though. While his and David's relationship might not be romantic, or based on passionate feelings in any way, he *was* fond of the man. David had come into his life at a point where Victor had been utterly sick of everything around him: his studies, his dry academic peers who were always several decades older than him. David had been so utterly *different*.

And they did have incredible sex. That was another thing that Victor would never, ever complain about.

"Again, I plead innocence," David protested, voice coiling into that smooth, deep tone, sunlight over water. "You were a deviant in a neat little tweed package, Vickie. Just because you dated boring men doesn't change the fact you had your hand down my pants five minutes after we said hello."

Blowing out a put-on long-suffering sigh, Victor conceded the point. "Yes, all right. You simply awakened the pervert within me." He did smile, though, quickly, at the reminder of that first time.

He shifted up to lie alongside David on the bed, on his back, hands folded neatly over his stomach. Their shoulders were pushed together in a silent gesture of companionship. The remnants of his headache were beginning to ebb away, thankfully, leaving Victor's mind clear once again.

"We're leaving!" Jed's strident voice hollered, but the man thankfully didn't feel the need to prove his announcement by coming in. "Red's with me. Don't leave, don't burn the place down, and don't eat anyone. Not even the professor. Red's got his cell on vibrate, and he likes it when it goes off, so if you get really bored you can show him a good time."

"I do *not*—" Redford's protest cut off as Jed closed the door behind them.

Victor laughed quietly, rolling over, pushing his forehead against David's shoulder. He was being awfully clingy right now, and he wondered if he should apologize for it.

"Blessed silence," he remarked. "I'd almost forgotten what it sounds like."

"If I ever wondered what it was like to have children…." David agreed with a smirk. Very subtly, he rolled away from Victor, moving to sit on the edge of the bed and toe his shoes off. "I think I'll try to get some sleep. I'm sure Journey will get himself into some kind of trouble, and I will probably need to be awake for it." Unbuttoning his shirt, he glanced over his shoulder at Victor. "My credit card's in my wallet." Which was promptly pulled out and handed over. "Use it to order your dinner."

Victor managed to get up off the bed, brushing a kiss over David's forehead as he went. "Sleep well," he murmured.

The only response was a grunt as David slid out of his pants and sprawled across the bed, greedily taking over the whole thing. Face first in a pillow, his shoulders finally relaxed, just barely, as he sank into the mattress. With an amused sigh, Victor gently un-knotted David's tie, slipping it off of him, his fingertips trailing over David's shoulder as he left the room.

Victor quietly closed the door behind him, turning down the volume on the television as he passed it. He absently cleaned the main room. Jed apparently tended to spread his belongings everywhere he felt was his, and the common area, it seemed, had been claimed as Jed's too. Victor didn't dare look at, or touch, the pile of clothing near Jed's bedroom door.

He ordered food and watched the television for a while, eventually winding up back at the kitchen table and his pile of books. Strictly speaking, vampire mythology wasn't going to help much with their case—it wasn't even going to help his own knowledge, given the first-hand account memories inside his mind, courtesy of David—but it was interesting nonetheless, and a pleasant diversion from the unanimously bad news the television was broadcasting.

He intended to let David sleep as long as he needed to. When even his reading began to grow boring, Victor quietly slipped out of the hotel, intent on finding the nearest butcher. Such a mission was a bit troublesome to accomplish in Cairo, especially when Victor, during his last trip here, hadn't been interested in the city so much as exploring the ancient ruins.

Due to religious majority, actually finding animal blood to buy was difficult in Cairo. It didn't help that Victor was still feeling somewhat out of it after looking into David's eyes, half-immersed in memory instead of paying attention to reality.

There, the street corner where a bright yellow awning flapped in the wind, brought a flash of an image to Victor's mind, an old memory of David's. The vivid color was very similar to a gift Gabriel once gave him, a golden necklace the vampire had found. He'd plucked it from the hand of a vendor, all smiles and grace, wrapping it around the dusky olive skin of David's neck with the air of a man claiming a great prize.

The roll and tumble of voices mixing in the air, a memory of a gathering, Gabriel's clan coming together, sharing blood and beds, ending the night in a graceful sprawl, David's head resting against Gabriel's chest.

Spiced meat from a vendor like the night Gabriel turned him, the last food he'd eaten as a man before he'd become something else.

Halfway down the street from the hotel, Victor paused in his walk to rub a hand over his eyes, squeezing them shut as he attempted to focus. Those weren't his memories. If he continued to dwell in them, he might very well wander into the desert and never be found again. He wasn't entirely sure if Jed would muster up the energy to come find him once he realized they were one person short.

Victor had to stop to ask a few people where he could find the nearest butcher that sold animal blood. Some gave him disgusted looks, one woman ignored him entirely. Eventually, though, Victor managed to get a location.

It was in the middle of a market in a side street, crowded and tumultuous. Victor, having never been good with large groups of people, laboriously picked his way through with many an apology, keeping his head down to avoid accidental eye contact. Surrounded by the smell of raw meat, even Victor—a dedicated meat eater—tried not to breathe too deeply. Purchasing pre-packaged frozen meat in a supermarket was entirely different. This, he was quite certain, had been mooing or bleating only hours ago. Some of it still was, in point of fact, which was evidenced when he had to dodge around a herd of small goats ambling along the thoroughfare.

197

Victor paused to stare at them, vaguely worried. He was not an animal person, but they were… well, cute. Then again, he was hardly going to lead a one-man liberation of the future milk providers and dinner cuts of the market; so, with a faint smile as the last one scurried off, tail wagging, Victor continued on.

The butcher, when Victor found him, was a large, jolly man wielding a meat cleaver with gleeful purpose, cutting and separating meat as he sold it. He greeted Victor in a fast lilt of Arabic, and though Victor was fluent, it took him a few seconds to switch his brain over to interpret the words. Being used to doing such odd things as buying pints of cow blood, Victor ordered it without faltering. His only regret was that it was from an animal, which he had on good authority tasted fairly foul to vampires. Then again, he was hardly going to find a reputable source of human blood here. Nor would he want to try—that was more than likely a fast way to draw the wrong sort of attention.

"For foreigner, Arabic very good," the butcher praised him in unpracticed English as he handed over a paper bag, containers of blood sloshing around inside.

Victor gave him what almost felt like a genuine smile. He thanked the butcher, paid him a little extra, and set off to pick his way through the mass of people to exit the market again.

Now that he'd grounded himself in reality somewhat, the walk back to the hotel soothed him. The ebb and flow of people distracted him, taking his mind off the visions he'd seen before. The street was no longer a minefield of memories to trigger.

Jed and Redford were still out by the time Victor got home, half an hour later. He hadn't been expecting them back so soon, anyway, and he'd admit he was grateful for the continued peace.

After he tucked the bags of blood away in the mini-fridge in his and David's bedroom, Victor glanced briefly at David. The man had rolled onto his front, the fingers on one hand clenching and loosening in his sleep. Concerned, Victor stepped closer to the bed, frowning as he saw that David's fangs had slipped down, curving over his bottom lip.

A nightmare, most likely. Not surprising, considering what David had been told, what the past day had been like. It wasn't often that Victor had seen David in the throes of one. Then again, it wasn't often that David allowed himself to sleep over at Victor's apartment. Perhaps this was why.

"David," Victor murmured, gently shaking David's shoulder. The man needed sleep, but this could hardly be restful. If Victor could just wake him briefly, David could go back to sleep, bad dream hopefully derailed. "David?"

With a gasp, David sat upright. And he was gasping, mouth wide open, desperately trying to pull air into a body that was no longer designed to handle it. Eyes wide, fingers clawing at the sheets, David frantically attempted to breathe. Startled, Victor could only think of one option. Perhaps not the safest or wisest option, but it would certainly stop David from driving himself into a panic over nonfunctioning lungs.

He kissed David, cupping his jaw and drawing him into it, hard at first, then slowing down into a more gentle kiss. Victor did his best to avoid the fangs, hoping that he was sufficiently distracting enough.

For a moment, David struggled still, surprised and hands trying to push Victor away. But only for a moment. With a low groan, David sank into him, into the kiss, eyes fluttering shut and fingers curling into Victor's shirt. When they pulled away, Victor panting for air, David looked a little embarrassed. "I'm sorry," he murmured. "It was just… I'm sorry."

David had probably been dreaming about something that had happened when he was human—it explained the way he'd been trying to breathe when he woke up.

"No need for apologies," Victor replied, gently pressing his lips to David's again. He wanted to ask if David was okay, but the question would be redundant. He could see for himself. "I just wanted to wake you from your nightmare. You should get some more sleep, if you need it."

Shaking his head, David shoved his hands through his hair. "No. No, I'm awake now." Rubbing his jaw, he deliberately put more space between himself and Victor, just enough that he wasn't in easy reach. "What'd I miss? Did Jed call?" David never felt comfortable with being too close just after he woke up, knowing that his appetite would be stronger then, in the haze of recently discarded sleep.

"Not yet." Victor stepped away from the bed, busying himself with putting the paper butcher's bags in the rubbish bin. "I went out and got some blood for you. It's in the fridge."

It was obvious David was doing his best to maintain a dignified saunter over to check out the mini-fridge. Boxers half falling off, hair all sticking up and with sleep-swollen lips, he hardly appeared put together. But it was the frantic way he ripped open a container of blood, pouring it into a glass with shaking fingers, that gave away just how hungry David had been.

In deference to the knowledge that David didn't like being watched while he drank, Victor turned away. The closest thing he spotted was David's discarded clothes, so he picked them up to fold them neatly, smoothing wrinkles out of the silk. All he heard were David's desperate gulps as he drank, and although it hardly sounded pretty, it still made Victor relax somewhat. He hung David's tie up on a hook in the closet, leaving the rest of the clothes folded on top of David's suitcase.

There was the clink of glass against the table, and David walked over toward him. After feeding, even on old cow's blood, David's movements seemed even more fluid. He was like gray silk moving across smoke, feet making no noise, body's every stride pure grace. He was a predator after blood, the ultimate seducer. "Thank you," David murmured. "For the blood."

Victor was still fiddling with David's shirt, trying to decide if he should put it back in the closet or leave it to be washed. On one hand, it was hardly dirty. Vampires didn't sweat. On the other hand, it just seemed wrong to *not* wash it.

Although David's graceful walk over to him quickly brought any thoughts about laundry to a complete halt. "Oh, you're quite welcome," Victor replied, eventually putting the shirt with the other clothes. "It was the least I could do." After telling David about the vision, well, he'd wanted to do *something* nice.

It was unfair, really, how David got after he drank. He was normally incredibly handsome, and somehow became even more so when he was confident in himself, when he truly embraced what he was. It all served to make Victor's thoughts head straight to the gutter.

Before reaching out to him, though, David paused. Some of the intent hunger in his eyes was blinked away, and David shook his head, biting his lip. "No," he muttered, mostly to himself, backing up quickly. "No, this is not a good idea. Not now."

That was unusual. Victor's expression creased in confusion. Normally, he and David were practically ripping each other's clothes off by now, and he had to admit that his physical reactions had started to get a bit Pavlovian. "What's wrong?"

"Victor." David's voice was somewhere between a husky groan of need and that thready, tight tone he got when he was trying desperately to hold onto his control. "I hurt you yesterday. I lost control. Do you honestly think that this is the right thing to do? What if I try to bite you?"

Given that David had drunk from him a few days ago, Victor knew he couldn't afford to get bitten again so soon. But he still stepped closer to David, fingers trailing down David's arm. They'd never had sex without *some* form of blood involved, whether it was a serious feeding or just a few drops here and there. The latter was only able to happen after David filled himself up with animal blood.

"You know I trust you." Victor's hands found David's, squeezing briefly before dropping away. "But if you can't trust yourself right now, then we'll find something else to distract you."

"What, like the crossword?" David teased, but some of the tenseness in his face, Victor thought, did seem to ease.

"I'll have you know that I can play a very distracting crossword session." Victor sniffed. "That, or I could read my latest article to you. That always sends you right off to sleep."

Long fingers rubbed absently along David's chin, and he shook his head, eyes going distant. "No sleep. I think I've had enough of that for the moment." His hand was shaking slightly, and David curled it into a fist to hide the tremor, ignoring Victor's look and moving toward the bathroom. "Although a cold shower might not be a bad idea," David admitted, sounding faintly sheepish.

Normally, Victor wouldn't take David's words at face value. He *knew* David was hard, he *knew* he wanted nothing more than to have a good roll between the covers, but he found himself nodding vaguely to David's words instead, making his way to the main room. He pocketed his cell phone, picked up from the table as he walked past, seating himself neatly on the couch. Normally, when David was like this, when David was afraid of hurting him, Victor would spend the time to gently coax the man past his fears, reassuring him that he wouldn't be hurt.

Now he just wound up staring at the television, frustrated. If he were being honest with himself, Victor would admit that he wanted to follow David, to change that cold shower into a warm one, and distract David with touches that weren't fists and words that were anything but polite or reserved. But David sounded so adamant about not wanting something to happen this time.

Or perhaps he was just tired and reading David completely wrong.

201

Victor scrubbed a hand over his face, giving himself a mental slap for acting so petulant. Yes, he supposed he was exhausted, and concerned about David's instincts. And, if he were to be extremely truthful, a little worried about his own safety. He'd never seen David so tightly wound up before. He'd let David have his shower and ignore the fact that it was highly unusual for them not to do anything after David drank.

He let his eyes fall closed, head leaning back against the couch, listening to the sound of the shower being turned on. It probably would be cold, a horrifying thought to Victor. For a few minutes, he relaxed into the sound of water hitting tile, until—

David was definitely jerking off. In a *cold shower*. How David managed that, Victor had no clue, but the sounds he was making were beginning to be a little distracting. Victor might have been able to ignore them if he wasn't still half hard from the aborted seduction earlier. A long, ragged moan, one Victor was intimately familiar with, meant that David was now finding all those places that would make his knees weak. His head would probably be thrown back, lip caught between his teeth— Victor could picture it in stunning clarity.

A second groan utterly snapped any tenuous control Victor might have been trying to hold on to. In a flash, he was off the couch again, single-minded as he charged his way straight into the bathroom. David was even more beautiful in real life than he was in his imagination, and Victor wished he didn't sound quite so needy when he said, "David, if you don't let me touch you, I am going to go insane. Literally insane."

Startled wide eyes stared at him. David was leaning back against the wall, the shower spraying over him—not quite cold, more like lukewarm, but still definitely not up to Victor's usual standards—his cock in one hand. He was gorgeously sprawled out, legs spread, water running down his chest to drip in the grooves of his stomach, the dips of his hips. "Victor, I—" Swallowing hard, David caught his lip between his teeth. "I don't know how in control I am right now, so you'd better be sure."

Victor bit down a whimper of frustration. He hated making that noise, even if David did look especially fetching whenever he smirked about it. "I'll tie you down," he offered desperately. "I'll... I don't know, we'll find some way to make sure you don't take much blood. But in fair warning, I'm about three seconds away from stepping into that shower with you, clothes and all."

They'd had sex before where David didn't take much blood. They both knew it could be done, only it was different now. David's control was stretched so thin. His instincts, Victor knew, would be pushing him toward drinking real, live blood, no matter how much dead animal blood he'd consumed before.

One thing that they had never managed, however, was sex *without* blood play included. Victor knew why. He knew Gabriel had twisted David so tightly that he couldn't even consider sex without blood now. The need was so ingrained, and Victor was so willing to give blood, that they'd never attempted to have one without the other. Unfortunately, now was not the time to start trying.

"David. Please," Victor said again, lowly. "You won't hurt me."

When David fed, he wanted sex. No, it wasn't even a *want*. He needed it, needed the release after, or he went crazy. Victor had seen it happen, had watched how the arousal would become more and more insistent until David was willing to do anything just to find relief. Blood *was* sex for him, and masturbating in the shower was the best compromise David had found for dealing with the aftermath, even if it still left him twitchy and unfocused afterward.

It wasn't working for Victor now, though.

With a groan, David surged forward, wrapping fingers into Victor's hair and yanking him in for a kiss. It was more a battle than an embrace, a desperate clash of tongues and lips and Victor's panted breaths. "Tie me up," David begged. "Tie me up and promise you won't let me take anything. Please, Victor, please."

Although Victor would admit that he wasn't entirely comfortable with the idea of tying another person up, he'd done it with David a few times, and the results had been rather enjoyable. His clothes were beginning to get soaked through, droplets of water making it hard to see through his glasses. Victor nodded hurriedly, gently coaxing David out of the shower. "I don't know what we'll use for restraints," he mumbled, lips pressed against David's jaw, blindly trying to find the towel. After finding it and nearly dropping it, he forced himself to slow down, to be calmer, smoothing the towel over David's back and arms to dry him off.

"Ties," David managed hoarsely. His whole body was shaking, worked up, and he was greedily taking every kiss Victor would give him. "Unless you brought handcuffs."

Despite his growing need, Victor stuttered out a laugh. "No, I'm afraid I didn't think to pack any." Once David was dry enough—still slightly damp, still warmed a little from the shower—Victor curled his fingers around David's elbows, walking backward to lead him into the bedroom. "Any preference on the ties? I wouldn't want to ruin your good ones."

It was a distraction tactic, making David think about such things. Hopefully slowing him down somewhat, calming the need that was running hot through his veins.

It worked, a little. David blinked at him, dazed, hands running over Victor's body. He was unbuttoning Victor's shirt, impatiently yanking at his belt, which made him pause. "This," he decided, shoving the leather belt into Victor's hands. "Use this instead. It's stronger."

Victor had to stop for a moment, staring down at the belt, trying to figure out exactly how one would use it as a restraint. It didn't tie easily like rope did. But he nodded, giving David a nudge over to the bed. He wanted to ask if David wanted to undress him—David liked it, sometimes, said it was similar to unwrapping a present—but David looked so tense that getting him tied down as soon as possible would probably be best for him.

"On the bed?" Victor coiled the belt in his hands, running the smooth leather through his fingers. "Er. If that would be best."

Cupping Victor's face in his hands, David barely ghosted his lips across Victor's. "Don't ask," he murmured, voice low, rippling with need. "Tell. Demand. I need that."

Victor just barely suppressed an embarrassed laugh. He was *terrible* at giving orders. Many of the students in his linguistics class never did their homework, simply because Victor had never gotten the hang of telling, not asking. "On the bed with you, then," he repeated, making his voice a bit firmer, hoping that would do the trick.

Sliding back onto the bed, David raised his arms over his head, wrists together, and spread his legs. There was a sharp, eager look on his face, something predatory in the way his gaze tracked Victor's movements. "Yes, sir," he rumbled, lips curving into a smirk.

Victor did chuckle then. "Don't call me sir. It makes me feel so terribly old," he rebuked. The first order of business was leaning over the bed to wrap the belt around David's wrists. After some fumbling, and figuring out exactly what would work, Victor looped it several times, fastening the belt buckle through the posts in the headboard. He tugged at it once, frowning. "That isn't crushing your wrists, is it?" It didn't look like it would, leaving David's wrists in a bound loop several inches below the headboard, but he did want to make sure.

"It's good." The words were tight, barely controlled, and David flexed his fingers, wriggling a little in his bonds. "Please, Victor." Leaning down, Victor gently bit at David's lower lip, kissing him for a long few moments. He had to draw back to stop himself from just crawling all over David there and then.

First, he had to get rid of his drenched clothes. Victor pulled a face at the wet squelch his waistcoat made when he dropped it to the floor. He didn't feel like being neat and tidy right now, not when David was *naked* and *right there*. His shirt followed next, after Victor decided that putting the wet clothes in the bathroom would be a better idea. By the time he was pulling his boxers off, his fingers were shaking in need, and he was utterly unable to look away from David.

Finally naked, he crawled up to perch on his hands and knees above David, knees brushing against David's hips. Victor ran his fingers over the belt again. "Still okay?"

"Oh my God, stop asking me that." David's voice was desperate, thready, and he arched his neck up in an effort to touch any part of Victor he could reach. "Fuck me. Please, fuck me. I need you right now."

"I'm allowed to worry about hurting you, too," Victor murmured, ducking down to rake his teeth over David's throat. The light movement had every one of David's muscles jerking, hips arching up to meet Victor's. "Although I will agree that I'm not nearly as dangerous as you are."

"Dangerous in a different kind of way." David laughed, strangled and hoarse. "Victor, I…." David licked his lips restlessly, hands twisting in the belt. "You smell really good."

A kiss wouldn't particularly distract David from thinking about blood, but Victor tried anyway, capturing David's lips in a slow, languid kiss. David was a remarkable kisser, all passion and movement, the kind of kiss that Victor had never even dreamed of receiving before he'd met David. He could kiss the man for hours, although he knew eventually one or both of them would get incredibly impatient. Breaking away, Victor nosed in under David's ear, hands smoothing over his chest.

David's legs had come up to wrap around Victor's hips. Rocking up into him, David flashed his fangs in a smirk, head tipped back as Victor's lips traveled along his neck. The noise of Victor's breathing seemed even louder, reflected back by David's low moans, by the creak of the bed as they moved. Despite the tone of their kiss, Victor knew this wasn't a time to pick a leisurely pace.

That was just fine by him. He was feeling like he could come any second just from the feel of David's skin against his.

He gave a reluctant frown as he had to pull away slightly, reaching out for the lube they kept in the bedside table drawer. Victor smoothed it along over his fingers, kissing David again, giving a quick smirk of his own as he bit at his lip. Then, sitting up over David's hips, he kept his eyes locked on David's face—wishing briefly that he could have eye contact—tracing his fingertips down over his own chest, sliding his hand between his legs, far too slowly easing a finger inside of himself.

"Just watch," Victor murmured, his free hand roaming over David's chest, occasionally running over David's cock, grasping it teasingly and letting go again. He was being *too* teasing, perhaps, but he couldn't help it. The widening of David's eyes and the needy growl that rose to his throat was far too enjoyable. Victor wasn't exactly being gentle in getting himself ready, the slight ache of the pace only driving his arousal higher.

By the time he withdrew his fingers, kneeling up over David's cock, he *needed* so much that he was shaking with it. David's hands were twisting in the belt, a faint hint of yellow beginning to creep in around the edges of his eyes.

Victor shouldn't find it hot. He knew he shouldn't. He should be scared. He shouldn't want to have sex with a vampire that was on the verge of losing control and biting him. Playing with fire, he knew, was not something that a person should typically find enjoyable.

That didn't stop him from fitting a hand around David's cock, guiding it inside him far more slowly than he would have liked. Unfortunately, injuring himself would not be terribly arousing. Victor was biting off curses as he sank down, hands pushed flat against David's stomach, the curses turning into wordless noises of pleasure as he finally sat flush on David's hips.

There was the rattle of the headboard as David mindlessly tried to reach out for him, cursing when he couldn't. The sight of him, swollen lips parted as he moaned, body tensed and tight, the yellow of his eyes obvious even without fully meeting them, was enough to make Victor *very* happy he'd decided to interrupt David's shower. David thrust his hips upward, moving in Victor, stuttering out groans. Victor tried to stay still for a few moments, tried to give himself the time to adjust—David was not an insubstantial man—but the need took over, driving him to lift up, thighs shaking with the effort, biting his lip at the friction, and ease back down. Slowly at first, interrupted by Victor leaning down to kiss David hard, the force of it pushing David's head back against the mattress.

The shift in position had David's cock rubbing neatly over his prostate, and the kiss was promptly broken off as Victor muffled an embarrassingly loud moan against David's collarbone. "God, I've never felt anything as good as this," he managed lowly, rising up again with trembling arms.

Slow wasn't enough then. The pace was agonizing, torturous, driving Victor to push down hard next time, snapping his hips against David's, riding him in short, fast movements. David's head turned, trailing along the crook of Victor's arm, tongue teasing the veins there. "Please," he was muttering, teeth just barely scraping along the skin. "I need you." The last thing Victor wanted to do was take his arms away, but he made himself do it, shifting them out of David's reach. He was treated to a warning snarl, David's fangs flashing as he snapped at him.

If Victor had any kind of courage, he'd snarl right back—his would be substantially less feral sounding, probably a bit awkward—and maybe it would help David's instincts think he was an equal, perhaps. Instead, he just fucked down harder, hands pressed to David's stomach again. It was incredible, as it always was, each time seemingly somehow better than the last, and Victor was quickly lost to the ecstasy, head thrown back as he rode David. He scratched his nails over David's stomach, curving around his hip, finding the coordination to look back down at David again.

David, who was whimpering in frustration, expression torn between pleasure and sharp hunger. His hands were twisting more in their bonds, reaching for Victor. The leather was creaking, but it didn't look like it was going to give in and break any time soon. Victor's eyes fell closed again, arousal overwhelming him, trying desperately to hold off on his own orgasm until David was close.

Like most things in Victor's life, he didn't have much luck in doing that. A few particularly spine-shivering pushes of David's cock, seeming to go so much deeper, so much *better* than before, had him hunching over David, stuttering out a moan as orgasm washed over him. He only paused for a few seconds, though, just a short moment before he started moving again, hissing in a sharp breath at the overload of sensation.

It was addictive, and Victor didn't know why—continuing to do this after he'd come, the way his muscles would tremble and ache with exhaustion and need, the growing pleasure in David's expression. They'd done this so many times, and Victor still couldn't explain why he loved it so much. Why he loved it when David would pause for mere seconds before fucking him for a second round or using his mouth again.

This time, though, David's moans were more needy than usual. The way he was moving had a desperate edge that had normally faded by now. David wasn't coming, though he looked like he was on the brink, muscles shaking and head fallen back, fingers white-knuckling around the leather belt that tied him down. It was the lack of blood, Victor vaguely realized.

Throwing caution to the wind, he leaned down, kissing David, pushing his tongue against one wickedly sharp fang. The groan that rumbled through David was bone shaking, his hips jerking sharply upward, and he eagerly sucked on Victor's tongue, wanton and greedy for even those few drops. Fucking up into Victor harder, reducing Victor's mind to an incoherent mess, David came, biting down on Victor's tongue to take even more.

The pain was dim, once removed, although Victor was aware enough to be vaguely glad that David didn't bite a hole right through his tongue. That would have made it very difficult to talk for the next few days, and Victor did enjoy talking.

Gingerly pulling his mouth back from David's, Victor wound up slumped over him, his spine in a sharp curve as he pressed his forehead to David's shoulder. Cautiously, he moved his tongue, trying to assess the damage. It didn't seem *too* bad, and from the satisfied relaxation of David's muscles, it was worth it.

David was staring at the ceiling, still and slack in his bondage. "Did I hurt you?" he asked hoarsely. The same question he did every time.

"No." The word rolled lazily around in Victor's mouth as he smiled stupidly. "Although Jed might be disappointed that you didn't injure my tongue permanently." Languidly, he reached upward to clumsily undo the belt, his fingers slipping over the smooth leather more than a few times before he finally got David's wrists free. Victor smoothed his fingers over the reddened marks they'd caused, although he hardly needed to encourage blood flow.

"I'm sorry." David still apologized. It might have been annoying, after more than a year together, if he didn't always look so guilty afterward. David wanted to go without feeding off of people, Victor knew, but he was a vampire. There was only so much self-control could do for instincts.

Sitting up probably wasn't the wisest venture right then, given that Victor was still firmly seated on David's cock, but despite the shock of sensation, he didn't want to part just yet. "Hmm," he replied lazily, rubbing his palms over David's chest. "Just enjoy the afterglow, David. Stop apologizing." He gave David a smile, eyes half-lidded in satisfaction.

After a few moments, though, David was rolling over, gently untangling them. Victor gave a groan that sounded rather sulky. "I'm going to go watch the news," he murmured, kissing Victor's cheek absently. "You sleep. I'll wake you if anything interesting happens."

"I don't need to sleep," Victor muttered. "Give me a moment. I'll be right with you." If David wasn't going to lie around and be lazy and sated, then Victor would just do it for the both of them. He stretched out on body-warmed sheets, his normal inhibitions about lying around naked gone for the moment.

The sound of the television washed over him, just white noise for the moment. Judging by the time on the clock, it was nearing dawn. Jed and Redford should be back soon, and maybe they could all sit down together and have a conversation that didn't involve threats or shouting. When the phone rang, Victor barely reacted. He just hoped it wasn't Jed calling for bail money or the like. That might ruin his morning.

"How did you find me?" There was something in David's voice, filtering in from the next room, that cut through Victor's satisfied daze. It was strain, fear, naked and without even a hint of David's usual skill at covering such things up. "What do you want?"

Looking out into the main room, Victor saw that David had come to a complete standstill. It wasn't just that he'd stopped moving. Back held rigid, whole body one long, lean line, David gave off the distinct impression that he'd stopped *being*. Like whatever it was that held a vampire together had left him, and his body hadn't gotten around to realizing that fact. There was no life at all in his face; nothing registered in his posture.

Well, that wasn't entirely accurate. Nothing registered except for fear. Stark-raving, bone-deep terror.

"I realize this is your country." David spoke again, and Victor was treated to the sound of a vampire grinding his fangs. It was a particularly chilling noise, like someone had rubbed a chalkboard the wrong way. "If only you'd stop kidnapping innocents, I could leave you to it."

Passing his hand across his face, David shook his head. "So you keep telling me, Gabriel." Victor was torn between the desire to go to David's side, to show some sort of support, and the instinctual urge to hide. It was how David said his sire's name, the faint tones of power that came from the barely audible voice at the other end of the phone. It spoke of a hierarchy that even Victor couldn't hope to understand. Supernatural half blood or not, he would still be food in that world, and food only survived by going unnoticed.

With a low noise of frustration—and need, Victor realized, of a need so deep and so great that it didn't have words—David hurled the phone from him, eyes sparking when it hit the corner of the table and flew into pieces. Dropping to sit on the couch, burying his face in his hands, David remained, unmoving and seemingly unaware that Victor was still in the suite at all.

Victor couldn't think of anything to say. He wanted to know just how Gabriel had gotten David's number, if that meant he was close, what it meant that Gabriel was calling David.

Since throwing his phone, David still hadn't said a word. In fact, he continued to be silent, even as he stood up and grabbed the end of the coffee table, tossing it across the room. It crashed into the far wall, nearly splitting down the middle. Victor stood, useless and shocked, as the television was next, hefted up and smashed against the ground, followed by a lamp, a decorative vase, a pile of Victor's books. Everything that wasn't nailed down was hurled violently around, cracking the drywall, shattering glass, until David was standing in the middle of a circle of destruction, staring blankly.

Expression never changing, David sat on the one couch that remained untouched, trembling fingers folding in on one another, eyes fixed on some point on the floor. He was still then, surrounded by broken and fractured things.

Victor tentatively made his way over to the couch. Still bereft of anything useful to say, he sat next to David. He very carefully reached over, his hand hovering above David's knee. In a moment of indecision it was withdrawn again, folded neatly back on his own lap.

Gabriel had found David, despite their best efforts to lie low, and Victor couldn't do anything about it.

So they sat. Silent. David's fingers were still shaking, and every once in a while Victor opened his mouth to say something and cut his own words off. There was nothing he could say that would make any of this better.

CHAPTER
10

Redford

"WHAT the *fuck* happened here?"

Jed's voice rang out into the hotel room, seemingly bouncing off the shattered television and broken shards of lamp. Victor, on his hands and knees sweeping up some fragments of glass, looked up guiltily. "It's taken care of," Victor hastened to explain. "David gave the hotel his credit card to pay off the damages."

Redford inched his way into the room from behind Jed, his gaze sweeping over everything in shock. It looked like they'd been attacked, but there was no scent of fresh blood in the air. David was sitting on the couch, staring at the opposite wall. He'd barely reacted when Jed had spoken.

"David got a call from Gabriel," Victor continued. "Needless to say, he wasn't entirely happy about it." He sat back on his haunches, eyeing the shards of glass in the carpet with annoyance.

"Well, shit, princess." Jed was frowning at the room, taking stock. "Aren't you just the queen of understatements." Carefully picking his way over the shattered vase by the door, Jed snapped his fingers in front of David's face. "Earth to bloodsuckers."

"If you don't get that hand out of my face, I will bite it off." David's eyes flicked up to Jed's face, narrowed in annoyance. Redford thought that if anybody other than Jed had done that, they wouldn't have gotten the warning.

"He lives!" Jed crowed sarcastically as he flopped down onto the couch. "Well. In a manner of speaking."

Redford followed Jed, though he didn't sit. Instead, he nudged the remains of a broken lamp with the toe of his shoe, watching the way it crumpled further on contact. With a sigh, he borrowed the dustpan from Victor and crouched down, sweeping up the broken ceramic. "What did Gabriel say?" He lifted his head to look at David, curious.

There was the snap of fangs, a low irritated noise, and David stalked off into the kitchen. Obviously that was not a welcome topic of conversation. Jed, though, apparently was not picking up on those subtle clues. Or, more likely, he just didn't care. He followed David, arms folded and eyebrows arched inquisitively.

"That's the million dollar question, Davie," he prodded. "What'd your leather daddy have to say?" The smirk broadened on Jed's face, a look in his eyes like he just couldn't resist. "Have you been a bad boy? Did he call to give you a spanking?"

"Jed—" Victor started to warn. He looked furious for a moment, an expression that Redford had never seen the man wear. Though he obviously wanted to say more, he cut himself off, leaving David and Jed to it.

David's fist shot out, but Jed dodged it. Since David was a vampire and Jed was not, Redford had to conclude that David wasn't actually intending on landing anything. Jed might be very good, but he was only human. That didn't stop Jed from crowing, though, grinning wickedly at David and doing a little dance from toe to toe, like a boxer in a ring. "Oh, come on. I've been up all night, I've had ten cups of fucking *tea*, I'm ready. Either tell me what daddy dearest said or punch my lights out, either way—"

Before another word got out of Jed's mouth, the punch to his jaw sent him crumpling to the floor. Impassive, David stepped over his prone form and shook his sleeves out, fastidiously buttoning the cuffs. "If you insist," he murmured mildly.

Surprise delayed Redford's actions, but in a flash he was up and in David's face, grabbing the vampire's shirt and slamming him back into the wall. Since anything he could say would basically be meaningless threats, he just growled instead, showing his displeasure.

It hadn't been a very hard punch, and Jed would probably be coming around any second now. And maybe he'd sort of asked for it. David's hands lifted, not in aggression, but to shrug off Redford's hold on him with a quiet snort. "Please, puppy," he bit out, showing his fangs. "I might be a half-starved cow eater, but you are hardly going to do anything but embarrass yourself. He'll wake up in a minute and annoy us all further. Now"—something dangerous flashed in David's eyes—"back away."

Redford went still, although the baring of David's fangs had him wanting to rip the vampire's throat out. Jed would have a bruise but not much more, that was true enough. He knew he should just walk away.

His knee came up sharply, hitting David right where it "hurt like a bitch." That action had been Jed's First Lesson of Fighting.

He finally backed down as David curled over himself, snarling in pain, cursing loudly. Redford allowed himself a small amused smile. "You're not allowed to hurt Jed," he murmured to David.

From over in the kitchen, Jed piped up. "That's my man." The pride was evident, even as he was holding a hand to his jaw, muffling his voice. "Now let me rephrase my question." Redford helped Jed to his feet, and Jed clomped over, looking pissed and vaguely amused all at once. "Why don't you just tell me what the fuck is going on. No punching out required."

David grimaced as he straightened up. There was something that approached grudging respect in his eyes as he gave Redford a once over, and he seemed to have gathered a bit of control over himself. "Fine. But you're insufferable."

"And you're an asshole," Jed replied cheerily. "Now hurry it up, I'm fucking tired."

Redford turned away to raid the fridge, gathering some ice and a cloth, wrapping them up. Once he was at Jed's side again, he carefully pressed the makeshift icepack to Jed's jaw, concerned at the way he kept clutching it. There was a faint huff of a laugh from Jed, but the man's arm went around his waist, holding him tightly in what Redford decided was wordless thanks.

Leaning against the wall, David stared around at the broken table, the glass, the way Victor was trying to clean up enough that no one impaled themselves on the destruction. For a moment, the vampire looked vaguely sheepish, rubbing the back of his neck. "Come on, Vickie," he coaxed quietly. "They have maids, and I'm a good tipper. Leave it for now."

Victor simply arched an eyebrow in return. "If the three of you are left alone in this room long enough, I assume that *one* of you will find a way to accidentally injure yourselves. I'm just cleaning the major things."

Redford frowned. He guessed he was supposed to be insulted by that. David and Jed just glanced at each other and shrugged, accepting the premise of the argument without fuss. David perched on the edge of the couch and uselessly swiped the broom at some of the glass in an effort to be useful. "It wasn't much of anything," he finally answered, glancing over at Jed and Redford. "Gabriel enjoys… playing. He called to taunt me, to gauge my response. He invited me to come home." The last word had David's lips twisting a little, though Redford thought it wasn't just disgust on David's face. He'd honed the expression carefully, yes, but behind it was an almost palpable sense of longing.

"You're not going, are you?" Redford figured he had to ask the question. With Victor's vision, he couldn't be sure. He didn't want to have to rescue these victims while fighting against David.

"Of course he's not going," Victor answered, a sharp bite in his words. "David is stronger than that pathetic, manipulative son of a bitch."

David reached out to pat Victor on the back, appearing vaguely surprised. "Good show," he murmured in a very gentle teasing of Victor's overly proper accent. "No, I'm not going back. Whatever games Gabriel is playing, I have no desire to participate."

Stretching, arms over his head, shirt rising up as he arched his back and yawned, Jed ruffled his hands through his hair. "Fantastic," he announced. "Now, Red and I are going to catch some shut-eye before we go back out."

"Did you find anything?" David asked, leaning forward.

Jed shrugged. "Nosed around that goddamn warehouse some more. Or at least what's left of it. Fido sniffed, I strutted, and we came out clean. Pretty sure it was a temporary flop house. Red says he didn't smell more than three non-vampires in the place. Two which we rescued, one was moved. Which means our other victim either is being held elsewhere or already dead." There was no doubt which one Jed thought was more likely. He'd told Redford the same thing in a flat, unemotional voice. Jed didn't tend to get caught up in recriminations and guilt. He said they made him sloppy, which meant more people might die. Namely him.

"The authorities think the explosion was caused by some kids playing with matches," Redford offered.

"So there's two victims still out there." Victor sighed. Redford noticed that his gaze went to the broken glasses that were sitting on the kitchen counter. "I know our previous estimate was four or five weeks, but I'm not sure how much we can count on that. Even if they have the time, I doubt we want to leave them in Gabriel's hands any longer than necessary."

"We're going back out," Jed agreed. "Two hours to recharge and give the shops time to open, and then we're going back to the bookstore. There's got to be something there, something we're missing."

In their maps, the bookstore had been at the center of all the kidnapping sites. It meant that there was *something* there. There had to be some clue or some person that knew something. On the drive back from the warehouse, Jed had ranted at length about how he didn't see the connection between the kidnappings. They'd stopped the car on the side of the road, studying the maps under the weak roof light.

If there was nothing at that bookstore, Redford honestly had no clue where they'd go next.

THREE hours later, Redford and Jed were out in the city again. The brief nap had barely taken the edge off his exhaustion, but Jed had touted his cure all—a good morning blow job, a blisteringly cold shower, and two cups of the strongest coffee Jed could sweet talk out of the hotel kitchen. Redford had the sneaking suspicion that the blow job itself was not entirely necessary, though he'd admit, he did feel much better afterward.

He'd only been able to down one of the big mugs of coffee, though. That much caffeine had him feeling jittery and strung out rather than strictly awake, so despite Jed's coaxing and the copious amounts of milk and sugar, Redford had cut himself off. Jed, though, had finished off the pot and stared mournfully at the bottom of his empty cup until Redford had dragged him out the door.

"Fucking tea drinkers." Jed sighed, looping his arm around Redford's waist as they wandered down the street. Despite the noise and the press of people, Redford was glad Jed had agreed to walk. The smells were so *new*, were almost overwhelming, but with his shoulder budged neatly against Jed's it was more fascinating than frightening.

Stopping at a cart that seemed to be attracting every local as they walked past, Jed smiled and nodded at the man working behind it, cooking up a storm. It smelled like beans and spices and rice, something delicious stewed together and served up with a huge slice of still warm bread.

Holding up two fingers, Jed passed over a few notes, and barely five minutes later, he and Redford were leaning against a wall, shoveling in huge steaming bites of the delicious food.

"This is amazing," Redford told him, eyes wide as he took in a huge sniff of the bowl. For something completely lacking in meat, it was surprisingly filling.

Jed grinned around his mouthful of bread, swiping up some of the rich broth left behind. "Worker's food, but goddamn, I could eat it every morning. Way better than cold cereal."

When they finished, they headed back out into the throng, the morning sun having burned away the last wisps of coolness. It was starting to get hot, and Redford was glad he'd shivered through the dawn in short sleeves. They wandered, seemingly aimlessly, down one side street, through an alley, to pop into another main thoroughfare lined with brightly colored shops and people flitting about like butterflies, an intricate dance of pedestrians and vehicles of all types and sizes. Redford gaped around him, eyes round as saucers as he drank it all in.

Before he knew it, they were standing in front of the bookstore where the latest kidnapping victim had been last seen. It was this bookstore that all Redford's careful mapping showed at the center of each person's probable disappearance site. Jed paused in front of the store, looking in the huge windows that lined each wall. Turning on his heel, he stared around at the street opposite, the corner across the way, two dark alleys, all easily seen from the bookstore.

"What do you see?" Jed asked, voice a low rumble, expression giving nothing away.

Biting his lip, Redford made the same motion, feeling awkward where Jed had looked so fluid and in control. But he looked, as Jed had asked him to, turning to try and *see* whatever it was that caught Jed's eye. It was a busy street, the bookstore sitting on a bend in the road. There was a cafe directly opposite with outdoor seating, a bus stop with a bench, a few homeless men crouched in an alley out of the sun. Tourists and native city dwellers alike flitted in and out of the nearby shops, the bakery, the cafe, filling the streets with movement.

"People?" Redford ventured, hesitant. He felt Jed's hands come to rest on his shoulders, Jed's chin settling in close so he could whisper in Redford's ear.

"Good," Jed murmured. "Now think. What else might you see, if you watched long enough?"

Worrying his lip between his teeth, Redford squinted, staring. After a moment, Jed reached up to cover his eyes. Sputtering a protest, Redford sighed when he felt Jed elbow him lightly, a wordless urge to focus. So he did.

Redford had a wolf's eyesight, true. It was better when he was shifted, but even as he was, he could see better than Jed. Looking wasn't *seeing*, though, as Jed so often told him, and that had nothing to do with the quality of his vision. Redford was looking like a normal person, not seeing what was important. But with his eyes covered, everything fell to his nose, and for a moment Redford was overwhelmed.

Slowly, he began to pick through things. Scents were like streaks of colors against a canvas. Some were light, barely there before they were gone again, leaving only a trace behind. But others lingered. They were stronger, bolder strokes, and Redford's face creased in concentration as he focused on those.

The stench of garbage, rotting in the dumpster twenty feet away.

Food, old and new, creased into the street from years of cooking and eating.

Exhaust from vehicles, the acrid stink of rubber, of heated metal.

And under all of that were the people. Each had their individual scent, each drop shimmering on its own before being lost into the whole. It was the swell of humanity underscored by unique notes, and Redford found that he could breathe deep enough to sink into those while ignoring the distractions that surrounded them. The faint brushstrokes he dismissed—travelers, only briefly there, window-shopping or simply passing through. But the others, the bold sweeping swaths of color, they were people who'd lingered. Or those who'd come back, day after day. The staff of the stores and cafe, the regular patrons, the—

"There," Redford breathed.

"What?" Jed's voice was so low Redford barely heard him.

"Two... no, three, three scents I've smelled before. At the warehouse. There's more, but they're harder to catch. Vampires, old blood, they don't stand out like the others."

Jed's hand fell from his eyes, and Redford blinked rapidly in the bright sun. "Someone watched for them. They were here a long time or often. The place reeks of them once you look for it."

A look of pride crossed Jed's face, and he grinned widely at Redford, a beaming smile that lit up his whole face and sent Redford's stomach into a wild lurch. Redford couldn't help his return smile, shyer, a little hesitant until he felt Jed's hand tighten on his, curling their fingers together. "Exactly," he murmured. "Someone was using this place to stalk victims."

Jed leaned in closer, nosing in behind Redford's ear. "You're amazing," Jed told him, sounding completely awed. "That was so cool."

When Jed pulled away, Redford missed the warmth of him at his back. Then again, he supposed they couldn't just curl up and cuddle right in the middle of a bustling Cairo street, no matter how much the urge had stricken him. Instead, Redford ducked his head to hide his pleased flush, reaching out to take Jed's hand again. "Let's go in," Redford suggested. "I think I'll be able to smell vampire on someone if they've been around them a lot." They'd stink like Victor did, like some odd mix of an extinguished candle and clotted blood, underneath their own scent. It wasn't easy to pick out, especially if they'd washed recently to try and hide it, but the warmth settling in his gut made him think he could handle the difficulty.

The bookstore was deceptively small on the outside, tucked into a corner away from tourist eyes, sandwiched between two run-down shops. Inside, it was somehow even more shabby, dust lying thick on the shelves and getting up Redford's nose, making him sneeze a few times. With the bookstore being suspect at the center of all these kidnappings, Redford wasn't entirely confident about going inside. If something here gave them a clue, though, or an answer, it would be worth it.

With Jed at his side, Redford made a sharp left, hiding behind a tall bookshelf before anybody could see them. He felt a little ridiculous doing so. He took a deep breath in through his nose.

There. A human. A human with the stink of vampire all over him.

Like Jed had taught him, Redford put a very casual expression on his face. Vaguely interested, but mostly bored, like he was just here to browse for books and wasn't even terribly invested in it. As they came out from behind the shelf, Redford tried to nod nonchalantly at the shopkeeper.

Beside him, Jed made an odd strangled noise, a cough that sounded suspiciously like a laugh.

"Tone it down there, Mr. Bond," Jed murmured, reaching down to thread his fingers with Redford's. "You don't need to oversell it. Why don't you pick out something you'd like to read? Come on, it's been weeks since you've bought a new book. I bet you're dying."

Redford glanced wistfully at the rows of books. It had indeed been a few weeks since he'd bought something new to read; they'd just been so busy. Undoubtedly Jed had some Egyptian pounds on him, so Redford smiled happily at him and moved over to peruse the titles and dusty covers. He could also work on his "relaxed" face, which seriously needed some practice.

His gaze caught on a small book, titled *Egyptian Myths Through the Ages*. "Jed, look," Redford enthused, holding the book up for Jed to see. The excitement of finding the book had nearly distracted him from the fact that they were in a bookstore with someone involved with a vampire. With the *kidnappings*. "It's got all of the legends!"

With a soft laugh, Jed reached out to take the book, flipping through it. "Not nearly enough pictures for me," he teased. "But perfect for that big brain of yours. Maybe I'll make you read it to me and explain what the hell is going on." He handed it back, smiling, looking relaxed, like they really were just out for a day of sightseeing. "Get it," he urged. "Can't have too many books, right, Fido?"

Redford took a step toward the counter and paused. The man who reeked of vampire was counting the cash, his eyes cast downward. He wanted to ask Jed what they should say, how to go about gathering information, but it was so quiet in the bookstore, and hiding again might seem a little weird. Jed, having more courage and know-how than him, had already closed the gap to the counter, talking to the man behind it.

"That is a *beautiful* bracelet you're wearing."

Redford spun on his heel, jumping at the sound of the voice. He'd been so absorbed in the man behind the counter that he hadn't been keeping watch for anybody else. Just behind him stood a portly man with a friendly face, gold-rimmed glasses tugged down his nose to peer properly at the bracelet.

"Oh. Um." Redford lifted his hand to look at the bracelet. "Thank you?" His hand was caught, the man using both of his hands to fold over Redford's.

"A scarab, I believe?" The man's voice was like velvet, so smooth and rich, and he was smiling beautifully at Redford in a way that made him feel like maybe they knew each other. Or at least that was the impression the man wanted to give him. Redford nodded dumbly, completely unsure what to make of this. The man continued, "Yes, and lapis lazuli. The scarab, the ancient Egyptians believed, was a very powerful form of protection. And the stone was seen to be fit for kings."

"Yes, my, uh… Jed bought it for me," Redford stammered. Was this man flirting with him? He couldn't be sure, but the holding of his hand seemed to be a very big clue. Even when he tried to tug his away, the man just gripped tighter, and now Redford could see that the interest in the bracelet was not the main focus of the man's attention.

The man followed Redford's gaze, sizing up Jed, who was standing at the counter. Redford relaxed then, because everybody who mistakenly looked at him wound up getting far more interested in Jed.

This time, though, Jed was apparently dismissed. The man looked back at Redford, smiling. "Well, I can say one thing for 'your Jed'. He has good taste."

"I know. I really like this bracelet," Redford replied.

"His taste in *men*, dear boy." The man looked like he was smothering a laugh. Redford tried to fight down a flush. "Although the bracelet is very nice, yes."

"It also stands for faithfulness and truth." From over the larger man's shoulder, Redford saw Jed's smile. It wasn't the soft one he was giving Redford earlier. Jed's whole expression was brittle, manic, just begging to get to punch someone. Deliberately, he reached out and pulled Redford's hands out of the man's grasp and stepped into the curve of Redford's arm. "Pretty much the Egyptian equivalent of *back off, he's taken*, am I right?"

The friendly smile on the man's face faded somewhat, turning vaguely disappointed. Before Redford could react, his hand had been brought up again, his knuckles kissed with a featherlight touch. "The good ones are always taken." The man sighed. "But it's nice to see that you have such a dedicated boyfriend."

221

With that, he turned to look at a shelf of books on the other side of the store, leaving Redford vaguely stunned. As far as he was aware, people didn't flirt with *him*. They flirted with Jed. Or Jed flirted with them first. Redford would admit, deep down inside it was a little gratifying to see the stormy way Jed was glowering at the back of the man who'd complimented him, to feel how firmly Jed had shoved himself into Redford's side, as if wanting to be claimed as belonging.

"He seemed nice," Redford said.

"He was fat and stupid and he smelled," Jed growled. The murderous expression fell a little into something more agonized, and Jed asked, worrying his lower lip, "You thought he was *nice*?" It was an uncharacteristically unsure moment from Jed, and Redford had to take pity on him, letting his arm curve around Jed's waist, fingers resting lightly on his hip.

"He made me nervous," Redford murmured. "But it was sort of nice. I'm glad I'm not so weird looking that people's eyes pass right over me."

When the man had exited the store, Redford leaned up, pressing a kiss to Jed's cheek. "And it makes me extra glad that I have you."

Jed looked faintly shocked, though he melted easily into Redford, warm and solid against his side. "What on earth makes you think someone wouldn't look at you?" he murmured. "You're the most gorgeous man I've ever seen. People would have to be half blind and stupid not to fall in love with you in a heartbeat." He paused, eyes narrowing. "And I will set something on fire if they do. Fuckers."

Redford muffled a laugh against Jed's shoulder. He didn't know why, but he really liked it when Jed got possessive. "I know you. You'd set *them* on fire." Nudging his lips closer to Jed's ear, he continued lowly, "Did you find anything out from the shopkeeper?"

As always, when Redford's mouth strayed too close to Jed's ear, little shivers worked their way down Jed's spine. Redford could feel them under his hand, resting on the small of Jed's back, and he heard Jed bite back a sigh. "A little. I was just warming him up when fatty decided to get all handsy. Come on, we can go double-team him."

Redford started to say something about how the man had been, physically, the exact same type that Jed would get flirty with. Instead, he just smiled a bit and nudged his shoulder against Jed's. They walked back to the counter, where Redford finally handed over the book he wanted to buy.

The man behind the counter, now that Redford saw him up close, was pale and thin. A name tag, crookedly pinned on his shirt, read "Ismail." He was wearing a scarf, unusual in this heat, and Redford wondered if it was to cover up bite marks. He *did* reek of vampire.

"Hello," Redford greeted tentatively. He wasn't sure where Jed had left off his conversation with the man, so he looked at Jed.

"As I was saying, sweetcheeks—" Jed smirked, leaning his elbows on the counter. "—I couldn't help but notice the view. And that you're overdressed." With one flick of Jed's wrist, he'd grabbed the end of the long scarf and tugged it away from Ismail's neck. Sure enough, there were small constellations of bruises and faint white scars. The man's hands flew up to his throat, trying to cover the marks, and Jed's knowing grin just grew wider. "What do you say we take a little stroll to the back? I think us three have some wonderful things to discuss."

"Not with a *werewolf*," Ismail said, his nose wrinkling in distaste. "I do not have the nose, but it is very clear."

Without losing an inch of his smile, Jed's expression somehow got dark as thunder clouds. "I will shoot your head off right here and now, darlin'," he drawled lowly. "And I'm thinking *you* won't come back from it like your friends do. Two rules." Jed held up two fingers, ticking them off. "One, you don't ever talk about Redford again. And B, we stop playing games like you actually have a bite behind that bark. We all know you're just a tasty snack that can play fetch in the sunlight."

A sour scent of nervousness began to rise from Ismail, his face growing even paler. Redford stared him down, trying to look as menacing as Jed did. He'd studied Jed's expression, but apparently he didn't do it as well, given that Ismail's gaze just passed over him on its way to Jed.

Or maybe it was the werewolf thing. Redford was beginning to suspect that vampires—and anybody that associated with them—viewed werewolves as utterly beneath them, not even worthy of being cautious about.

"Yes, yes," Ismail bit out. "What do you want to know?"

"Well—" Jed purposefully raised his voice, looking around with that same shit-eating grin. "—I was really wanting to talk about the vampires—"

He didn't get any further before a nervous Ismail grabbed Jed's arm and, darting glances around them, shushing Jed, dragged them to the back storeroom.

Slouching down onto a wooden crate, Jed leaned back. "Much better," he agreed. "Privacy is a good thing."

"I am not permitted to tell you anything," Ismail stammered, his eyes darting back and forth.

"Well, *duh*," Jed drawled, poking one finger into the man's forehead, once, twice, three times, his smirk growing in direct proportion to Ismail's apparent irritation. "If you were supposed to tell us, well, then, what'd be the fun in that?"

It looked like Ismail was struggling to keep his mouth closed, until he burst out with, "They are called the Usire clan. The vampires that are doing the kidnappings."

Jed's face crumpled, very slowly, into disappointment. "Aw, come on. You're supposed to let me threaten you more before you start talking. The Ursine clan?"

"Usire. It's the native name for the ancient god that the Greeks named Osiris," Redford murmured. "He was a god of vegetation, of living things, until he was killed and resurrected and became the god of the underworld. Remember, David mentioned vampires identified with him as a god figure."

Jed let out an amused snort. "Right. It does sound a lot like the blood suckers." He paused, thoughtful. "Or Jesus." His stare instantly turned menacing again as he looked back at Ismail. "So what the fuck do they want? Attention? Fast food? What? And where does Gabriel come into this?"

At the mere mention of Gabriel's name, Ismail shrank back slightly. "He is not involved—"

"Yeah, that's what we keep getting told, but we've got someone in our camp that's pretty damned sure he *is*. And although he's an asshole, I trust his word more than yours."

Redford carefully kept silent. He knew Jed didn't actually believe that Gabriel was at the head of this, but he supposed Jed was saying that as an interrogation technique. Jed had one hand clenched in Ismail's shirt, keeping him shoved against the wall and getting into his personal space. "So. This Urine clan—"

"Usire." Ismail scowled.

"Whatever," Jed dismissed. "The Umpire people." Jed was just doing it on purpose now, Redford thought. "They're not led by Gabriel?"

"Usire is the father of those who walk in shadows," Ismail said cryptically. Jed's face fell into a confused frown. "His balance is the path we follow."

"What the fuck are you talk—"

A loud shout came from just outside the store. It was startling enough that Jed's grip loosened, and before either he or Redford could do anything, Ismail was darting away. The shouts outside turned into laughter, just before Ismail shoved open the front door, running away.

Jed started forward, taking only one step before he stopped again. "Shit," he growled. "We can't chase the fucker in broad daylight."

"At least we have something to go on," Redford murmured. "The Usire clan. That's more than we had this morning, right?" He smiled a little, hopefully, trying to think back to all the legends that Victor had been telling him about.

Jed was still scowling at the door. He gave a frustrated little grunt. "All sounds like bullshit to me, Fido. The Usire vamps, Gabriel, moving the victims, doing all this shit in broad daylight. It'd be nice if *someone* could fucking tell me what was going on." They began walking out of the shop, ducking around a gaggle of tourists to try and get out of the store. Redford was leading the way and actually got onto the street, blinking in the sun, before he realized Jed was no longer behind him.

Turning back, Redford found Jed staring at a statue on the counter of the shop, frowning slightly as he poked the dark carved wood. "This look familiar to you, babe?" Jed asked as Redford rejoined him. "Swear to fuck I've seen this ugly ass bastard before. Just can't place him."

Redford carefully picked up the statue, examining it. "This is Set," he realized, recognizing the appearance from the pictures in Victor's books. "Wait, I can show you." Redford pulled the mythology text from under his arm and flipped through the pages to find an entry on the gods of ancient Egypt. "See? Set, brother of Osiris, god of chaos. Also storms and foreigners."

Peering over his shoulder, Jed grunted a bit. "That looks like him," he agreed. "Fuck, where did I...." He stopped, eyes going a little wider. "The factory," Jed breathed, and he gritted his teeth in a flash of frustration. "There was one of these in the goddamn blow-it-out-your-ass factory."

"Are you sure?" Redford asked hesitantly. "Victor told me that to the untrained eye, Set and Anubis are often confused for one another."

"I'm sure." Jed had progressed to full-on frowning. "I thought it was just shitty decoration to go along with the shitty bastards inside."

A quick look around the bookstore confirmed that this was the only statue in the place. Redford turned his gaze back to it, running his finger down the finely crafted tail. Set was an odd-looking deity. A sleek, strong human body with an animal head, like the majority of the Egyptian deities. Victor had said that what made Set unusual, though, was that even academics couldn't agree on what animal Set's head was supposed to be. The ears of a donkey or a jackal, a face somewhere between a canine and an aardvark, a forked tail, bright red skin—it all added up to an appropriately chaotic looking deity.

"This has to mean something," Redford said, setting the statue back down.

"Yeah. Haven't got the faintest clue on *what*, though," Jed replied. There was a frustration under his words, but he smiled and nudged Redford's shoulder. "Hey, you get a free book, though. I don't think Ismail's gonna get on your case if you take it. Not unless he wants two black eyes and a gun up his ass."

AN HOUR and a call to David later, Redford found himself staring at a camel.

It stared back.

"*Camel rides*, Red," Jed exclaimed gleefully, pointing at the sign. "Fucking camel rides! We are doing this. I don't care how much money I have to fork over. I always wanted to do this. Once I woke up and a camel was pissing next to my head, but I never got to *ride* one. Hey, excuse me! Guy in the hat? Yeah, how much?"

While Jed was apparently trying to haggle for the price of a camel ride, Redford stared curiously into the animal's dark eyes. It chewed placidly, completely unconcerned.

"Jed, I thought we had work to do," Redford said. "We can't just ride around on camels and ignore the—" He glanced at the man in charge of the camels. "The *business*."

"All the *business* we have right now is resting on David trying to figure out what the deeper meaning behind some old as fuck dead god is." Jed handed over some money, all but bouncing his way back to Redford's side, grinning widely. "So while David attempts to use his brain for the first time in his life, we, Red, are gonna ride some goddamn camels."

Redford turned his head back to look at the camel. It lifted its head to look at him again. It opened its mouth, and with a horrible groaning sound, puffed out what looked like a spit-covered bag of flesh.

The man in charge started laughing uproariously as Redford stumbled backward with a yelp and as Jed cried, "What the *fuck*?"

"That is *altzawj ald'ewh*. His shout for females," the man said, his voice heavy with amusement. "The skin of the mouth comes out."

"Jesus fucking Christ, I thought it was spitting up its own balls." Jed gave a dramatic shudder, which only made the camel owner laugh harder.

Though Redford wasn't entirely sure he wanted to get on the back of an animal that played its own mouth lining like bagpipes, he nonetheless climbed carefully up the steps next to the animal, slinging his leg over its back. The saddle was decorated with cloth in a riot of color and patterns, brushing warmly against his legs. A moment later, Jed was seated behind him, his arms clasped around Redford's waist.

"I'm fucking traumatized, Fido," Jed muttered against his back, to which Redford just laughed. "It's not funny." Grumbling, Jed poked Redford's sides, though Redford could feel the beginning curve of Jed's smile against the nape of his neck.

The sun was high overhead as they set off, the camel's walking a smooth rolling motion underneath them. The guide, on a camel ahead of them, called back with plans for the trip, how they'd go along the Nile for a bit and then cross over to the Great Pyramids. Behind him, Redford felt Jed digging through his bag, muttering to himself. A hat was promptly tugged onto Redford's head. "You're gonna get so sunburned, babe," Jed remarked. "Should'a gotten some of that lotion shit back in town."

Redford rolled his eyes upward to look at the brim of the hat. It looked like something bought at a tourist store, wide-brimmed and a little silly looking, but he just smiled and wore it anyway. "I hope you have one too," he replied, twisting his head to look at Jed.

"Me?" Jed snorted, resting his chin on Redford's shoulder. "Nah. I look stupid in hats."

Redford resigned himself to having to deal with Jed getting sunburned and complaining about it later. He'd heard aloe vera was really good for spreading on burned skin, so he supposed he'd pick some of that up. Either that or hear Jed moan and groan every time his shirt touched his neck. Although perhaps he'd walk around naked. That might be a very good compromise.

Their trip to the pyramids took just over an hour. Redford wished he'd brought along a camera to capture the flock of ibis they saw, the grazing animals, the gentle waves of the dunes that emerged once they got farther away from the city. The pyramids seemed to grow as they'd approached, rising from the sand like relics of ancient time.

"The Giza Pyramids," their guide said, clearly enjoying their looks of awe. Even Jed looked stunned, his mouth dropped open slightly as he took in the sight. "The three pyramids of Khufu, Khafre, and Mankaure. And to their left, the Sphinx."

"They're amazing," Redford murmured.

"The Stinks dude has no nose," Jed said. His head was tilted to the side, eyes squinted as he studied it. The lack of a nose seemed to bother him greatly. "He's seriously putting out an MJ post-surgery vibe."

"The nose was destroyed by invading Turks, we think," the guide replied. Where there had been a previously sunny grin, his expression soured. Turning his head, he spat with fervor; apparently that was all that needed to be said about his opinions on the matter.

"It's a shame," Redford agreed. The Sphinx was still nonetheless impressive, even noseless and apparently channeling the surgery advice of dearly departed pop stars. Redford liked that his nose was missing. It was like the Sphinx had battle scars but was still standing proud and tall and would continue to do so more for many more thousands of years. Redford reached a hand up and absently touched his thumb to one of the scars on his own face, rubbing along the edge on his cheek.

"Can we go climb on this shit, or what?" Jed, not surprisingly, wasn't as interested in the history lessons as he was wanting the chance to run around. Bouncing a little on the back of the camel, Jed shot their guide a sunny grin. "It's not like we're going to break it, right?"

"No, you cannot go 'climb on that shit'," the guide said witheringly. "You may go inside the pyramids, however."

"Sweet!" Clambering down from the camel, Jed held out his hand for Redford. "Treasure hunters, ahoy!" Sitting for more than twenty minutes, for Jed, sometimes seemed like torture. Redford had learned that any extended period of time was dealt with by sleeping or getting increasingly jittery. Now, able to stretch his legs, Jed laced his fingers with Redford's as they headed through the warm sand toward the nearest pyramid. The guide sat with some others who had made the same trip, watching their respective groups explore the area, the camels lazily sunning themselves.

There was a gaggle of tourists gathered just outside the pyramid. Redford's gaze went past them to the small entrance, barely big enough to allow one person through. When he looked up, the pyramid appeared colossal in size. He had seen skyscrapers at a height that took his breath away, but this seemed *more*, somehow, maybe because it was so old. The ancient Egyptians hadn't had cranes or motors or electricity—everything relied upon now for construction—that they were capable of building something so perfectly formed was awe-inspiring to Redford.

One of his grandmother's books had been about the pyramids. When he first read it, Redford had never imagined that he'd have the chance to see one in person, let alone actually go inside. The inner sanctum of a pyramid seemed like such a mysterious thing, so old and impossible to comprehend.

And now he was getting to see one for himself.

The descending corridor just inside the entrance was hot and stifling. Blowing out a breath, Redford took off his hat to fan himself, eyes wide as he looked at the small sandstone hallway around them. "We're inside a pyramid, Jed," he said lowly, awed.

Jed moved closer to the wall, prodded it with one finger as he glanced around. "Yeah," he replied, staring up at the perfect lines of the walls and ceiling, the precision with which the corridor was formed. "Fucking nuts."

The group of tourists shuffled its way into a corridor that abruptly turned on an incline. Redford and Jed hung back from the group slightly, getting away from the noise. Redford preferred it that way—it was like just he and Jed were exploring the pyramid alone.

"Look at that, Red." Jed's stunned voice echoed around them, even when he spoke in a whisper. His arm looped around Redford's waist, and he pointed up at the hieroglyphs that were etched into the walls. They were fenced off to prevent curious tourists touching them, preserving their beauty from erosion. "Wonder what they mean?"

Mystified, Redford shook his head. Victor would probably be able to tell them. "To me, it just looks like… bird, a man holding something, another bird. A plant? And then a sun. Or a circle."

"So they had a chicken, the guy came out and killed the chicken, they made a fire, and that was their day," Jed decided with a nod. "It's a cookbook. Fried poultry, Egyptian-style. Now we have to find the bit about grits, and it'll be just like back home."

Redford laughed and didn't correct Jed. Victor had told him that the language didn't work that way, but it was amusing to try to puzzle out the hieroglyphs as if they were a picture book. There were more carvings as they kept walking upward, including one sequence that Jed claimed was a very athletic sex position. How he got that from two people symbols and what looked like a reed, Redford would never know, though Jed did volunteer to demonstrate.

As they continued walking, Redford kept his neck craned to stare at the hieroglyphs. He wondered how old they were, who had carved them, how long it had taken the artist. The work was so precise, lovingly etched into the stone. He knew that their meanings would be religious, probably speaking of the pharaoh entombed there.

The crowd slowed down as they came to a stop in the first real room of the pyramid, the Queen's Chamber. "Look, babe," Jed announced with a huge grin, "a whole room just for us."

Up ahead, the guide was saying that the name was mistakenly given by Arab explorers, for there was never intended to be a queen in this room, which seemed to disappoint Jed. As bare as it was, Redford still thought it was amazing, his gaze roving over the walls and the pink granite flooring. There were no hieroglyphs here, which Redford thought was odd. Nobody seemed to know what this room had actually been for.

As he looked around, he tried to figure it out for himself. The room was beautiful despite its lack of decoration. Perhaps it had been for the builders, he thought, to rest as they worked on the inner hallways of the pyramid. To the north and the south, he saw what looked like small tunnels cut into the walls.

"Jed," he said excitedly, pointing them out. "I remember reading about those. Look at this." He dragged Jed closer to examine the hole cut into the stone, ducking down to peer into it. All Redford could see was the shaft descending into darkness. "People sent robots up here to find out what was inside," Redford continued. "And they discovered, two hundred feet later, two limestone doors with copper handles. And behind that, there's another door. There's some hieroglyphs in red paint, but nobody really knows what's beyond that."

"What's in the box?" Jed grinned, drawling out the last word like some kind of pronouncement. He appeared to be incredibly pleased with himself.

"No one knows," Redford explained again, patiently. "Victor was telling me all about the recent discoveries yesterday. And it's not a box, really, although the rooms are incredibly squared off."

He didn't understand why Jed looked so disappointed, though he was highly tempted to kiss away the over-exaggerated pout.

Farther on, while Redford listened intently to the tour guide, he felt Jed stiffen beside him. All the joking, the grins, they were gone, Jed's expression intent as he stared over the crowd around them. "Did you see…." Jed moved toward the passageway leading out of the room, trying to shoulder his way past all the other people milling about the chamber.

"What?" Redford had to move fast to keep up. It was like the crowd was swallowing Jed whole, closing up behind him as he moved through.

"That fucknut from the bookstore," Jed growled over his shoulder. He paused every so often, stretching up on his toes to try and peer around the people in his way. "Ismail. I could have sworn I just saw him standing there."

Redford frowned, trying to look over the crowd. "I don't see—" He inhaled deeply. Not with his eyes, he had to remember. Jed was the eyes. He could "see" far better with his nose.

The scents in the pyramid were incredible. So many thousands of years of history. Stone and wood, sand and water, ink and parchment and the faint remnants of surprisingly few people. He tried to focus in on Ismail's scent, recalling its memory. "He *is* here," Redford muttered, surprised. "Maybe he's taking a tour?"

231

"Yeah, and maybe I really am the fucking queen." Jed's expression darkened, the bright lights above them, strung on the walls of the chamber, shadowing his eyes. "Stay close."

With brute force, Jed shoved a way through the rest of the tourists. It was like a maze, darting around a school group, a family, a fat man with black socks and sandals on, until they reached the doorway that led to another corridor, one Redford recalled hearing the guide call the Grand Gallery. Jed barreled them down it, gripping Redford's hand tightly, his other hand shoved into his pocket. Redford only barely had time to notice the features of it, the slanted roof, a hole cut into it that he recalled Victor saying led to a place called the Relieving Chambers.

The Grand Gallery opened up in the very heart of the pyramid, the King's Chamber. Still following Ismail's scent, Redford tugged Jed into the room. "He's—"

Ismail wasn't there.

Jed growled in frustration as he spun around on his heel, searching. The walls were blank, mocking them in smooth granite. No other doorways were apparent, no hint as to where the vampire lackey had gone. There were once again two shafts cut into the walls, and a rectangular granite sarcophagus with one broken corner, but nothing else was in the room.

Still half in the mindset of enjoying the tour, Redford noted saw-marks across the walls, the way this room looked less polished than the previous ones. It was roughly finished, which he found strange, considering it was supposed to be the most important room in the pyramid. "Look at these shafts, Jed," Redford couldn't help but point out. "Did you know that they align with certain stairs and areas of the north and south skies? Old academics thought they were for ventilation, but Victor told me yesterday that scholars now think they have a ritualistic purpose. They're how the king's soul goes to heaven. Or... wherever the Egyptians went when they died."

"Yeah, well, unless they're vampire-lackey asskisser shaped, I don't give a shit," Jed muttered darkly, pacing around the outside edges of the room again. "That fucker disappeared into thin goddamn air."

Cursing more under his breath—with, from what Redford could hear, some extremely creative word combinations—Jed kicked something across the room. It skidded across the floor and hit the stone with a dull, metallic clang. Redford moved over to where it lay. On its back, leering up at them with its rigid, carved grin, was a small statue of Set.

"Jed," he called, bending to pick up the statue. This one was made of metal, which was different, and shorter than the others they'd seen. He had a brief moment of panic, thinking that Jed had kicked and possibly harmed some priceless artifact, but the metal smelled too new.

Joining him, Jed muttered, "Son of a bitch," reaching out to take Set. A surge of tourists, the next wave of the tour, washed into the room. Jed held up the statue to the light, squinting before he shook it.

"It's a goddamn piggy bank." Turning it over, he showed Redford the small slot cut into Set's neck. "Come on, let's go back. I have a feeling this wasn't left here for just us."

They joined the tourist group again, the pace painstakingly slow. Jed swore lowly the whole walk back, and Redford tried to forget the weight of the piggy bank in his pocket. Suddenly, he found that he couldn't enjoy the pyramid tour so much anymore, not when they'd just had a reminder that there were still two victims out there.

Exiting the pyramid was like emerging into a completely different world. Where before they had been entombed in an ancient building dedicated to a king of old, now they had reunited with the sun, and the air, which was somewhat cooler when they got back outside. Jed guided Redford back to their camel owner, who gave them a small wave when he saw them. "We're ready to go back," Redford greeted.

"Well, gentlemen, the ride back requires a tip." The camel owner smiled at them. It wasn't a nice smile, not like the ones he'd used back in town. Redford was all at once aware how far out in the desert they were, how empty the area surrounding them was. The tourists had all seemed to dissipate back to their own guides or buses, leaving them alone with this man and his two camels. Redford reached for Jed's wallet, supposing this was probably normal. Jed's fingers on his wrist stopped him.

"We already paid you," Jed pointed out in a drawl, seemingly unconcerned. Redford knew that glint in his eye, though. This was clearly not part of the arrangement.

"Yes, and now you are to tip me," the camel owner replied cheerfully. "It is very normal. Camel tours are very expensive, you see."

"Yeah," Jed gritted out, "and we *already* paid you an arm and half a fucking leg. So get Bessie movin' again, sweetheart. We don't have time

233

for this shit." Redford was just looking between them, stunned, not entirely sure what was going on.

The smile vanished from the camel owner's face. "Then you must have another ride back to the city, yes? Because you will not get a ride back with me if you do not tip."

Huffing out a long-suffering sigh, Jed pulled out his gun, cocked the hammer, and pressed it to the guide's nose before either he or Redford had time to move. "Let's try this again, darlin'," Jed said, voice hard as nails. "We're not some two-bit tourists you can ride hard and put away wet. We paid, we paid *well*, and now you are going to move the fuck over and give me those goddamn camels before I decide to see just how far that thick head of yours flies. How's that tickle your balls?"

"Jed," Redford went to protest, but he stopped at the dark look on Jed's face. A sickly smile spread over the camel owner's face, fear touching his eyes.

"Perhaps we can work something out," the man agreed.

The gun disappeared back into Jed's coat, and he moved over to the lead camel. "That's what I goddamn thought," he muttered, irritated, hooking his leg up and settling onto the camel's saddle. "Come on, baby," he urged the camel. "Let's get movin'." The camel surged to its feet with a look of utter contempt. Redford just hoped it didn't spit things out at them again. "Red, the other beauty's yours. Let's go."

"Jed, but then *he* can't get back," Redford pointed out, reaching a hand up to Jed.

Instead of answering him, Jed leveled a glare at the guide. "Your English is damn good. Makes people feel all trusting and warm-fuzzy-like, doesn't it? How many tourists do you pull that con on?"

A spluttered reply was all he got, but that seemed to be good enough for Jed. "Get on the fucking camel, Red," he muttered. "This bastard can walk. See how he likes being stranded."

"I'm not leaving him out in the desert, even if he is a scammer," Redford replied stubbornly. He folded his arms, leveling a look at Jed. "He's a person too."

"He's an *asshole*," Jed corrected. "And we don't have time to fuck around with his change of heart. *Get* on the *fucking* camel." He looked less than happy with Redford, and the camel, sensing him tensing up, moved a few steps away. Jed didn't bother to bring it back. "Come on!"

Redford just glanced at the camel owner, then back at Jed, and didn't say a word. He was not going to leave a person, no matter what they did, out in the desert. If the man tried to walk back, he could die of heat exhaustion.

"Either let me up on that camel, or I'm taking the other one *with* the owner," Redford said softly, frowning at Jed. "He's just a scammer, Jed. Not a murderer."

"You don't know that!" Voice tensing in frustration, Jed shot them both a glare. "Fine. Whatever. Enjoy your romantic camel ride with Buttface the Scam Boy." Jerking the camel's reins around, Jed let it go, the animal settling into a slow jog as it turned the corner and disappeared behind the far pyramid.

Redford let loose a long sigh, staring despondently after Jed. He supposed he may as well get on the other camel now.

He nodded at the owner and climbed onto the camel. Jed had vanished, and Redford couldn't help but feel a little irritated that he would leave someone relatively innocent out alone in the desert. "What's your name?" he asked.

"Al-Safi," the man replied. "Thank you. Thank you for not leaving me here. I have a wife and children at home—"

"No, you don't," Redford muttered. He couldn't smell any family on the man. "Come on, it's a long ride back."

"Well, I *could!*" Al-Safi insisted. "And now I will have an opportunity, thanks to you."

In the distance, Redford could see a camel making its way back. The rider wasn't sitting on it well, leaning too far forward, as if to urge the huge animal on faster. But it was the loud, long, constant string of curses that clued him in as to who it might be.

"Come the fuck on, Fido." Jed halted his camel next to them, looking pissed as hell but reaching out a hand for Redford. "Leave the bastard his goddamn camel."

Redford couldn't help the faint smile that touched his lips. He got off the camel he was on and walked the short distance to Jed, reaching up to grasp his hand. Jed swung him up behind him, settling him in, Redford's arms looped around his waist.

Al-Safi was thanking them again, reaching out for the reins of his camel. Face impassive, Jed pulled out his gun and shot him in the foot.

235

Ignoring the man's scream of pain and Redford's yelp of shock, Jed turned their camel around and urged it into the odd loping gallop that jostled them around. It was slightly faster than its normal pace, though, and they soon left the pyramids and Al-Safi behind.

Redford, not being able to think of anything to say, just rested his forehead against the back of Jed's shoulder. He thought shooting him *anywhere* was still uncalled for, but at least it wasn't a fatal wound. Jed didn't smell happy at all, and the set of his shoulders was tense. It was a long ride back to the city, Jed not saying a word the entire time.

It took Redford a long time to work up the courage to say, "Maybe we should leave the camel where he had them penned up?" He saw Jed's jaw clenching, but the man didn't argue, just swung the camel down the side street and trotted it right up to where they'd met the guide. Using the stairs, Jed and Redford climbed down, Jed stretching as soon as they reached the ground again. Making sure the camel was secure, Redford at least was certain that when Al-Safi came back to town, his herd would still be waiting for him.

"Jed," he tried, but fell silent again as they started the walk back to the hotel. This time, Jed didn't sling an arm around his shoulders or tuck his hand into his back pocket. Redford just stared at his back as they walked.

Turning abruptly on his heel, Jed was all at once facing him. Redford nearly ran into him. "What the fuck, Fido?" Jed hissed, trying to keep his voice down. "What the hell was that all about?"

"What?" Redford said defensively, shoulders hunching. "I didn't want to leave him to possibly *die*."

"He would have done it to us!" Hands moving as he gestured in irritation, Jed nearly knocked the hat off a passing woman. "Jesus, Red, you think for five seconds he wouldn't have left our asses if we'd just been some random tourists who wouldn't pay? He's a fucking lowlife, and leaving him there is the nicest thing I would have done to him."

Redford frowned. "It doesn't matter if he would have done the same. You *shot* him, and—" He broke off, frustrated, not finding the words he wanted to say. "That wasn't good, Jed."

Eyes wide, Jed blinked at him. "Are you *pissed* at me?"

"Sort of," Redford mumbled, staring down at the ground. "I just… maybe he would have left us, yeah. But if we left him that would have made us the same."

236

Opening and closing his mouth a few times, speechless, Jed finally just blew out an enormous sigh. He paced a few steps away before coming back, trying again, and winding up just shoving both hands through his hair with a low noise of frustration. "Fuck."

Reaching out, Jed hauled Redford in, wrapping his arms around him in a tight hug. "You're mad 'cause you think I'm better than some camel-ball-hocking lowlife," he muttered, nudging his face into Redford's neck. "And I shot him in the goddamn foot because it made me feel better. Do you see how that doesn't make sense?"

"You *are* better," Redford insisted, his voice muffled against Jed's shoulder. "You're the best person in the world. You took me to see the pyramids." Jed had made a wish of his come true, a wish that Redford never would have thought would be realized, not while he'd been stuck in his grandmother's house.

With a strangled-sounding laugh, incredulous and breaking around the edges, Jed pulled back enough to look into Redford's face. His expression was torn between disbelief and something else, something that made him reach out to gently cup Redford's jaw, leaning their foreheads together. "Jesus, babe," he murmured, eyes closing, jaw tight. "I'm sorry I left you there. That was a shit move. I just… I'm not used to having someone else care what I do. It won't ever happen again."

"You came back," Redford said confidently. "You always have." He tilted his head up, pressing his lips to Jed's forehead. "I know the only time you don't come back is because you *can't*."

"Won't ever happen," Jed told him softly, with a fierceness that seemed to wrap Redford up in protection, in warmth. "Don't care what happens, Redford. If my dumb ass ever gets lost, you bet everything in the bank I'll find a way back to you. No matter what."

Redford nodded. He knew. He knew because Jed had already done so—bullets and wolves and blood hadn't stopped him from getting to Redford before. Even wounds that had left behind scars, even Redford changing into something neither one of them quite understood, weren't enough to keep Jed away.

"And maybe we can work on not shooting scammers?" Redford gave Jed a coaxing look. The man huffed out a long sigh, looking plaintive, but Redford held firm.

Finally Jed nodded, trying to keep his irritated look. It was ruined by the soft, wondering little smile that had started to crease up one corner of his lips. "Fine. No shooting people who don't really deserve it, even if they piss me off." Leaning in, Jed kissed Redford very lightly, just the barest breath of a touch. "This rate, you're gonna make an honest man out of me, Red," Jed complained. It was hard to take the grumbling too seriously, though, when Jed's hand was held tightly in his again, when they were walking down the street once more shoulder to shoulder, like always.

Then after a moment, Jed said, "What about David?"

"You can shoot David," Redford acquiesced.

"FOR the last time, Journey, I *don't know* what the hell *Set* means. I don't know why some group of vampires is choosing to name itself after Usire. And no, I was not *dropped on my head* as a child, you insufferable lout."

David was snarling, standing toe to toe with Jed, who wasn't even remotely fazed. They'd been arguing back and forth for the better part of a half hour, the metal Set-shaped piggy bank set on the table between them. Apparently, the day hadn't given David any further insights into all the Set imagery, and the appearance of Ismail's latest clue wasn't helping matters along.

Redford gave a sigh and nudged a bishop forward. "It's your turn," he said to Victor, watching the man contemplate the chess board.

"Well maybe if you used that tiny dick for something other than pissing me off—"

There was the sound of a glass breaking, the fourth one of the evening, by Redford's count. Neither he nor Victor even looked up. After the first several moments of trying to get David and Jed to calm down, he and Victor had decided to let them duke it out. It wasn't like either of them were going to *listen*, anyway. "Knight to E4," Victor noted.

"Nice move," Redford approved.

David was snarling again, and Jed was back to cursing. Insults flew back and forth; Redford had lost track of who was apparently fucking goats this time, but he was pretty sure that David was losing the penis size battle. All at once, though, there was silence.

238

"Holy fuck." It was David, this time, the crude exclamation sounding almost odd in his precise tone. He was holding the metal piggy bank, only it was headless. "It twists off. There's...."

"A note," Jed said, digging out a tightly furled piece of paper. "Goddamn, now this fucker's passing notes? What are we, in grade school?"

Hearing the lack of fighting, Redford and Victor looked up from their game, peering over to the slip Jed was holding. "What does it say?" Victor asked curiously.

"It's time to come home," Jed read out loud. His face creased in confusion. "That's all it says."

With shaking hands, David grabbed the scrap of paper out of Jed's hands. Like it held much more than five words, David stared at it, reading it over and over. If Set meant nothing to him, then this message apparently held all the meaning in the world.

"David?" Victor started, but David brushed past him, heading toward the door. "David!"

"I'm ending this," the vampire growled, grabbing his jacket. "Tonight. Right now."

Victor stood, accidentally bumping the table with his hip, sending some of the chess pieces scattering. "That still doesn't explain just what you're going to do," Victor said. "Do you know where the kidnapped victims are?"

"Stop nagging!" Whirling around, Redford saw that David's eyes were rimmed in yellow, his face unusually tight and tense. "For the love of *God*, Victor, for once in your life, just leave well enough alone! I am going to end all these stupid games. That's it. That's all you need to know."

The door slammed behind him, reverberating loudly. Victor sank back down into his chair. Redford caught Jed's glance before he moved to the door, grabbing his own jacket. "I'll keep an eye on him," Jed muttered, his and Redford's fingers gently touching before Jed shrugged on his coat, checking his weapons. "Keep your phone on. I'll call when I figure out where the fuck he's going."

"Jed," Victor cautioned. He looked like he was going to warn Jed not to go, but his expression softened. "David is going to see Gabriel. I'm sure of it. Whatever you do, don't interfere. Gabriel won't kill David. That's the last thing he wants. But if it looks like David might be… losing control, try and separate them somehow."

"Don't worry, princess." Jed treated them both to a cocky smirk. "I'm good at this shit. David won't even know I'm there." He kissed Redford quickly before he disappeared out the door, leaving Victor and Redford alone.

Victor's shoulders slumped. "Bloody fantastic," he muttered, attempting to right the chess pieces. "Well. I believe it's your move."

"They'll be all right," Redford said, and he was almost sure of himself. Victor just nodded, absently, turning a pawn over in his hand. His gaze drifted to the kitchen counter, where Set's figure was placed, leering his jackal grin at them both.

"Not the most pleasant visage, is it?" Victor said wryly. "Nowadays he's equated to Satan, which academically frustrates me to no end."

Redford gave him a curious glance, his fingers resting on the top of a bishop as he considered his move. "Why is that?"

"For most of Egypt's history he wasn't a bad deity," Victor explained. "He was simply chaotic. In Egyptian philosophy, chaos in and of itself was not a bad thing. It was simply a part of nature. In several stories he was the classic antagonist figure, but he was still worshipped widely. Good, evil, it was all on the same spectrum to the people of ancient Egypt."

Redford watched him eagerly, intrigued by the story. Victor gave him a wan smile, sincere if slight, as he raised his gaze from the chessboard. It was easy to see that he wasn't used to people actually listening when he went off into his academic lectures.

"One of the more classic Set myths is a story about him and Osiris. Deities had many names. Osiris, at this point, was a god of vegetation." Warming up to the topic, Victor leaned back in his chair as he talked. "Set, they say, once held a party. Jealous of Osiris's position as pharaoh, Set conspired to trick and kill him. He made a wooden coffin, perfectly constructed to Osiris's measurements. At the party, Set invited the other deities to play a game—to see who would fit in the coffin. All of the other deities tried, though some were too big, some were too small. Nobody fit."

"This sounds a little disturbingly like some fairy tales I've read about," Redford murmured.

"Well, it was hardly a glass slipper," Victor replied with a faint laugh. "Nor beds or bowls of porridge. No, Set's coffin had a much more sinister purpose. When Osiris climbed inside and found that he fit the coffin perfectly, the lid slammed shut, sealing him inside. The deities, thinking that this was an amusing game, eventually left the party, sure that Osiris would find a way to get out of the coffin. Once they left, however, Set lined the coffin in lead and dropped it to the bottom of the Nile."

Victor pushed a rook forward. "Isis, Osiris's wife, was distraught. She thought that without a proper burial, Osiris would not be able to move on to the afterlife. So she searched for him day and night, but Set got to him first. Knowing that Isis was looking, Set dismembered the coffin—and therefore Osiris—into fourteen different pieces and scattered him across the lands."

Redford paused, considering his next move. While Victor waited, he continued, a lot less academically, "Well, and then there was a whole mishap where a fish ate Osiris's penis, so Isis had to fashion him a new one out of gold once she found all the bits of his body. The point of the story is, once Osiris was resurrected, he became the god of the underworld."

"That doesn't exactly sound like a deity that someone would worship," Redford said dubiously. "Who would follow someone that killed a fellow god?"

"In our way of thinking in this day and age, perhaps not," Victor murmured. "But things were very different back then. Set was also responsible for a great many good deeds, and he later even guarded the sun god's barque, fighting off the serpent Apep as they traveled across the sky."

Redford still looked like he didn't particularly get it. "So he was good?"

"Most certainly. Until political struggles between the north and south of the ancient Egyptian lands. When the Osiris worshipers gained power, they destroyed temples to Set and started to claim that he was an evil god to, shall we say, flex their power over those they'd come out of on top of."

"So," Redford frowned, glancing back at the statue, "What does all of that have to do with that statue or vampires?"

Victor's smile was rueful. "I have absolutely no idea. Perhaps things aren't what they seem. Perhaps Gabriel is trying to get David to remember something. Perhaps the local knickknack shop had a two for one special. It does seem a bit opaque at the moment."

Redford rose from his chair to move to the kitchen counter, carefully lifting the statue of Set. Under the harsh lights the metal shone, twisting the carved leer even further. "So Osiris and Set were complete opposites," he mused.

"Quite," Victor agreed. "Set stood for chaos, Osiris for balance."

"Right." Redford twisted the statue in his hands. So what did that mean for a clan that named themselves Usire, and the fact that Set statues had popped up three times now? Over and over Jed had coached him to see the whole picture, not just what he was looking at, to let his gaze expand beyond the obvious. Patterns and relationships between two seemingly unrelated things only really were noticed if you *looked* instead of just saw.

"It's your move," Victor prompted expectantly.

Redford's reply was less an acknowledgement and more a vague hum of noise. "Victor," he said slowly, "You remember the jug of blood David was sent? The vampires that keep telling David that Gabriel isn't behind this?"

"Yes, it's rather hard to forget being presented with a large carafe of human blood," Victor replied dryly, though his expression was curious. "What are you thinking?"

"What if this is another message from Gabriel, telling David he's not behind this?" Redford set the statue down, his mind whirling as he tried to put the pieces together. "You said that Set and Osiris were complete opposites. Isn't that just another way of saying that Gabriel wouldn't do what these vampires are doing?"

Without waiting for a confirmation from Victor, Redford rushed into the bedroom to find his phone. It was a new model that he hadn't quite gotten used to—a month ago, Jed had destroyed his old one in what Jed had termed a "controlled C4 test". Redford still didn't think that explained why Jed was setting off minor explosives in the kitchen. He found his phone and jabbed at the screen, briefly getting frustrated when the device kept chirping at him and trying to bring up a map of local pizza delivery places.

"Jed," Redford greeted excitedly when he finally managed to place the call, "I think I know what the Set statues mean."

"Am I on speaker?" Jed's voice was slightly tinny, far away, and Redford could hear the rush of voices and music in the background. He was obviously out on the streets, the blare of a horn momentarily blurring his words. "Is that on purpose or can you just not figure out how to turn it off again?"

"Both," Redford admitted, shifting a quick, sheepish glance over at Victor. "When we get home, I'm making you let me read the manual, I don't care how silly you think it is."

"Manuals are for pussies, Fido," Jed grumbled, but Redford could hear the smile in his voice. "What, you miss me already?"

"No, I really do think I know what the whole Set thing is about," Redford said, setting the phone down on the table between himself and Victor, who gave a suspicious stare at the phone. Redford slapped Victor's hand away from it as the man tried to touch a button of the screen. "Don't do that, you'll push something weird and then I'll be stuck on Urdu translations for the rest of the week." It had already happened once. Although now he did know the Urdu terms for 'home' and 'call', so it hadn't been a total loss. "Sorry, Jed. Victor keeps trying to touch my phone."

"Tell him I'm the only one who gets to push your buttons." Redford could practically see the leer he knew Jed would be wearing. "In fact, I'm on speaker. I'll tell him myself. Hey, princess, stop techno-groping my man."

"Oh, do be quiet," Victor said witheringly. "I see the mute button and I'm not afraid to use it."

"There's a mute button?" Redford wondered, leaning over to stare. He was getting off track. Shaking his head, he refocused. "*Anyway*," Redford continued. "I think the Set statues and the vampires calling themselves Usire mean something, Jed. Set and Osiris were completely different, set up to be mythological opposites, so I think the statues are another way of Gabriel telling David he's not behind these kidnappings."

There was the faint noise of the city from the speakers, the rolling lilt of Arabic as Jed passed people, the blare of traffic, the faint sound of bells from a mosque. He didn't speak for a moment and Redford frowned, wondering if he'd lost connection. "So basically, you're saying someone has to tell Crazy McSnappypants that the whole reason he's over here is a big pile of shit?" Jed's voice sounded heavy, quiet, more serious than his words would have implied.

"Of course not," Victor sighed. "We're still here to rescue the kidnapped people and make sure that we deal with who is doing it. David knows that, even if it may not be tied to Gabriel at all."

"Fantastic." Jed's voice was clipped and short. "Fido, take me off speaker a second."

Now worried at the shortness of Jed's tone, Redford picked up the phone to bring it to his ear. "Are you okay?" He frowned a little, turning his back to Victor. "Did I get something wrong?"

"No, babe, you're amazing," Jed assured him, voice still loud. Apparently simply bringing the phone to his ear didn't actually do anything to turn it off speaker. "Fucking brilliant, as always. Just... I love you. Okay?"

Redford held the phone out for a moment to find the speaker button. Once he'd located it, he said, "I know, and I love you too, but why are you talking like you're going to die or something?"

He heard Jed huffing out a quick breath and there was a faint rustling sound, the noise of Jed shaking his head, Redford realized. "Because David is not going to want to hear this," Jed muttered. "And he's walking like he wants to tear someone's throat out. I'm thinking a chat with his leather daddy isn't going to improve his mood. Just not looking forward to meeting him after the party he's walking into is all."

"You'll be okay," Redford assured. "You're Jed Walker, remember?"

"Fuck yeah I am." Jed breathed a little laugh, ragged around the edges. "Everything's fine. Never mind. You did awesome, Fido. I'll be home soon."

"Just be careful," Redford said, concerned. "And be safe. I want you back in one piece, okay?"

"No fun in that," Jed replied. "Don't worry. Talk to you later."

The line went dead. Redford stared at the screen, watching it go back to its usual menu. More than anything he wanted to call Jed again, to talk to him until that hoarse little edge went away from Jed's voice.

"Any news on David?" Victor's voice was hushed.

Redford shook his head slowly. "No, but I think... I think he maybe found what he was looking for."

CHAPTER
11

David

IT WAS dark out. Not the kind of dark related to the lack of light, not the type that could be pushed back with candles and lamps and the full flush of the moon. It was something heavier than that, a physical oppression that seemed to seep into the streets, to lurk in the alleys. David waded through it, felt it clinging to his skin, dampening everything but the smell.

Blood. Not old this time, not long since cold. Fresh and warm, still pumping, still sweet, it called to him the moment he stepped out onto the streets of Cairo.

Gabriel was preparing a feast for him.

Closing his eyes, David pulled in a long inhale, tasting the air. His feet followed the scent of blood even as he struggled to remember why he was doing this. Why the urge had taken him over so quickly. It wasn't smart, this impulsive trek. In fact, it'd be exactly what Gabriel was expecting, exactly what he wanted, exactly the first step to making Victor's vision a reality. That note had been meant to push at already fracturing pieces, to spiderweb crack the last holds of David's self-control. He should be resisting.

But he didn't want to anymore. Gabriel wasn't going to let up until David showed him that he was past all of this. That he wasn't ever coming home. So let it happen tonight.

The hunger was a living thing, walking beside him, pushing him forward. His body followed it, his mind was consumed with it, with the smell of fresh blood on the air. For so many years he'd chained that hunger down, he'd muzzled it and controlled it. Now it was awake, fully, and it *wanted*.

He was stronger than this. David *had* to be stronger than this. He was not his hunger. He was not a mindless blood drone who only lived for the next feeding. Gabriel would not turn him into that, not again.

It was easy to find where the lair of the evening was. Of course it was; Gabriel wanted to be found this time. And this time, there was no lurking on awnings or peering in windows. David walked through the front door and into the lion's den.

"Gabriel." David pulled his jacket more tightly around himself, chin up, anger making his eyes gleam. "I believe you've been trying to get my attention."

Gabriel had always had a sense for the dramatic. There was the rapping of a foot against the marble floor, and David turned to see Gabriel lounging in a plush armchair. Gabriel had never looked physically imposing. On the short side, slender, fair for an Egyptian, he seemed somehow *more* threatening because of his unmenacing appearance. Or maybe that was just because David knew Gabriel could rip him into five pieces and barely work up a sweat.

"David," Gabriel greeted, a smile curling at his lips. He looked happy, genuinely so. "It's good to see you. It's been too long."

Ignoring the way that smile still made his gut clench, still bloomed anticipatory warmth all through his chest, David pointed a finger at Gabriel. At least it was only very slightly shaking. "Cut the shit," he growled, showing his fangs. "I'm not playing your games anymore, Gabe. It's over. Leave me alone."

"What game?" Gabriel looked curious, cocking his head to the side. "All I've been doing is asking you to come home." He stood, brushing an errant wrinkle out of his silk shirt, walking closer to David. He stopped just out of arm's reach. David restrained the urge to inhale, to see if Gabriel still smelled the same. For so many decades, he'd smelled like *home*. Like belonging. Steeling himself, David took a deliberate step backward, folding his arms tight across his chest.

"This isn't home anymore, Gabriel. *You* are not home. Now tell me where they are."

Grumbling, Gabriel threw himself back into his chair like a petulant child. "You're like a teenager," he said disdainfully. "Running away from home, rebelling against the authorities. When are you going to realize your place, David?"

David fixed Gabriel with a glare, controlling himself with difficulty. "Where are the other two, Gabe? I'm not here to discuss your viewpoints on my decisions. Just tell me where they are so I can leave."

"The two other *what*? Humans? You're concerned about humans, now?" From a petulant child to a very old, very disappointed benefactor, Gabriel looked at David with concern. "You honestly think that my handiwork would be so sloppy?"

It was the same thing Jed had pointed out, what Victor had so subtly implied. It was what David had known, really, since the warehouse. It was too brutish, too messy, too out in the open. Gabriel was old. He was powerful. David had sat at his feet for centuries, had watched the man with worship at first, growing to discontent, but he knew Gabriel. This wasn't like him.

But something had drawn David in. He'd been so sure, back in the States, and he wasn't going to back down now. So Gabriel had changed. So had he. Things were different now.

"I think that you were trying to get my attention. That boy? In the bookstore? That was for me, wasn't it? To see if I was watching. Well, here I am, Gabriel. Now let them go." David frowned at Gabriel, trying to be impassive. Trying his damnedest to look strong and remote.

Gabriel's eyes—permanently yellow in his age, or more likely his lack of caring to hide—fixed on him, amusement dancing in their depths. "David," he tutted. "*I* think that you came running home on the weakest excuse to do so."

A growl rumbled in David's chest, to which Gabriel just laughed, triumphant and bright. "I came to save more people from *you*," David hissed, backing up again, needing every inch of the distance he could gain.

Gabriel, having turned to lazily studying his nails, wasn't even looking at David anymore. "You're being silly," he said casually, like he was reciting the rules, once again, to a very slow child. "Vampires don't save people. We *eat* them." Suspicious, he looked up at David once more. "Has someone brainwashed you? Or, God forbid, you haven't bonded with a human, have you?"

David just flashed his fangs in what would be a challenge to anyone but Gabe. Hell, the elder vampire would probably just be amused by the show of aggression. "No. I don't bond. But I'm not going to treat other species like blood bags, either." His fingers curled into fists, his jaw tightening as he tilted his chin back in defiance. "I'll ask one more time. Where are the other two people you took?"

Still sitting placidly in his chair, Gabriel's expression turned amused once more. David remembered the vampire's moods being as quick to change as tropic weather, impossible to follow and usually utterly incomprehensible. "Are you threatening me? That's...." Gabriel waved a hand in thought, trailing off briefly and concluding with, "Adorable. It's *adorable*. You're about as threatening as an angry fly, David."

Anger rolled just beneath the surface, itching under his skin, but David held himself back. He leaned in, eyes icy cold, hands braced on either arm of Gabriel's chair. It was the closest he'd been to the vampire in ten years. "I will find them," he murmured, holding Gabriel's eyes. "And when I do, I will kill whomever's in my way. Even if it's you."

Instead of holding his place, Gabriel closed the gap by sitting up straighter, lifting a hand to rub his knuckles along David's jaw. "You'll try," he said soothingly. "And if you do find them, you'll go back to your hell of a life. Feeding on dead blood. Never being full. All because you're too stubborn to come back to me and live at the top of the food chain like you *deserve*."

A shudder worked its way down David's spine. He had to force his eyes not to close, his body wanting to instinctively lean into his sire's touch. "And what about the people you use and throw away?" he managed to grit out. "What do they *deserve*? The world isn't trash for you to play with, Gabriel. Just because we drink blood doesn't give us the right to take whomever we wish."

"Yes, David. It *does*." Gabriel's voice turned cold and sharp, a contrast to the hand that was gently cupping David's jaw. "And the sooner you remember that, the better."

David was hungry. He was *always* hungry. It had stopped being a temporary state the day after he'd walked away from his life, from the blood and the sex, from *Gabriel*. Every moment of every day, David was fighting against the want to drink, to take, to feed. The little tastes he allowed himself, the cold gulps of cow's blood he used to sustain himself, they did little more than soothe the rough edges. He was still hungry. He still wanted. It was just that he'd been arrogant enough to think he could control it.

Now? Now he was beginning to wonder. Eyes falling half-shut, David shook his head, struggling to hold on to himself. To the independence he'd forged so painfully. "You're wrong," he whispered. "I'm not better. Neither are you. I don't want—"

Before he could say anything more, Gabriel's fingers turned tight and bruising around his jaw, and David was shoved back, tumbling awkwardly to the ground. Gabriel rose gracefully, his every movement smooth and predatory, to stand over him, disgust evident in the set of his lips. "You've had your fun, David," Gabriel said, his voice almost calm. "You ran away. You've had your little rebellion. It's time to grow up."

David glared, eyes narrowed, pushing himself up on his elbows. "I don't want this. I don't want *you*. I have grown up, Gabriel, and whatever sick, twisted game you think I'm playing? It's over." He stood then, face-to-face with the man he'd given his entire life to. When he'd left, he'd snuck out in the dark, terrified and starting at shadows. Now he refused to back down. He couldn't. If he gave even an inch, David wasn't sure if he'd have enough strength to keep standing.

"The piggy bank was for you," Gabriel said, back to vague amusement now, his mind wandering in ways that David had never been able to keep up with. "I imagine you're running low on money now. You didn't steal *that* much from me when you ran away."

Going still, face graying out, David watched Gabriel warily. This was a new tactic. He never had been good at matching wits with Gabriel. Then again, it wasn't exactly his *mind* that Gabe had wanted, all those years ago. "You knew about that?"

Gabriel laughed lightly. "Of course I knew about that. My bankers are very thorough." He prodded an elegant finger against David's chest. "I just wanted you to know how little impact your leaving had. The money you stole was fractional at best. I had a new second in command the hour after you were gone."

He shouldn't care. He *didn't* care. That his grand escape had been watched and laughed over by Gabriel didn't change the fact that David had left. There should not be an ache to think of being replaced so easily. That was what Gabriel *did*. He used people. David knew that.

"I don't know why I'm here," he muttered, blinking a few times, shaking his head. Trying to clear it. "This is pointless. You've never once told me the truth about anything. Why the hell would you start now?" David turned, moving toward the door, suddenly desperate to get out. To feel the night air on his face, something not heavy and drenched in blood and incense and *Gabriel*.

"I always told you the truth," Gabriel called after him. David didn't look back, but he knew that Gabriel would be sitting once again, in the chair surrounded by elegant furnishings, the most expensive and lavish things Gabriel could afford. "I'm not sure when you became blind to it."

"Go to hell, Ib-Se-Kem," David replied. Palming open the door, he bumped into a group of laughing vampires, the noise from the rest of the clan washing over him, smothering him. He staggered out finally, blessedly, making it to the alleyway again. It seemed a lifetime ago that he'd walked in. David sagged back against the wall, head tipped up to the sky, eyes closed and fists so tight his nails were biting into his palms.

He had no fucking clue if Gabe knew where those humans were. Then again, maybe he hadn't expected to find out. Why the hell had he gone in there?

"Davie?"

The voice came from beside him, and David instinctively jumped back, baring his fangs and reaching out to wrap his fingers around Jed's neck. Thumping the man back against the wall, David pushed in, ready to bite, only to get a mouthful of gun barrel. Blinking, gagging at the taste of the acrid metal, David immediately pulled back. "Sorry," he rasped, shaking his head. "You... surprised me."

"And hello to you too, sweetheart." Jed was tutting over his gun, carefully cleaning it off. "I take it your meet and greet went well?"

"Jed." David looked up, eyes blazing yellow, feeling the very last tendrils of his control snapping all around him. "For five minutes, can you just *not talk*?"

Surprisingly, Jed just fell in beside him, their arms every so often brushing in the dark. The two men walked back to the hotel in silence, with only Jed's occasional muttered curses about *vampire cooties* on his gun breaking the quiet. It took David the full length of the trek to come even close to calm enough to walk inside the room. Jaw tense, body wire tight, ready to snap, he brushed his way past the questions and the glances and shut himself up in the bedroom.

Only then did he let himself sink to the floor, shaking uncontrollably. He managed to get a packet of the cow blood Victor had procured for him, gulping it down desperately, spilling it down the front of him. His head thumped back against the wall, and he sat there, staring at nothing. Listening to the ghosts of his past.

GOD knew how many hours had passed. The rest of the blood was gone in a frenzied glut of eating that left David's stomach churning from the cloying taste. He hadn't eaten that much in one sitting since Gabriel. Never that much of the old blood, and he found there was a reason for that, when he was hung over the toilet in the bathroom, sick and shaking and weak.

Finally managing to drag himself into the shower, David stayed there until the water turned cold. He curled up in the corner, head on his knees. He felt numb. All the way through, inside and out, he felt like somewhere along the line he'd just *lost*. He was without now, and it scared him even more than the hunger did.

Eventually, he got himself together enough to get dressed. Running a hand through hair still damp from the shower, he made an appearance out in the main room. Jed was sitting on Redford's lap, their ever-present maps spread around them. Victor was across from them, a book open on the table in front of him as he flipped through the pages. The furniture he'd torn apart had been replaced, the glass cleaned from the floor. It was like nothing had even happened. All evidence of his rage, his brokenness, had been swept away. David went to the kitchen, hunting up a clean mug and putting the kettle on. Tea would help soothe his stomach, maybe. He seemed to remember it doing that, a long time ago.

His senses must have been dulled, because he nearly didn't hear Victor come up behind him, taking the mug from him. "Let me," Victor said lowly. "You're terrible at making tea anyway."

David tried for a smile, failing utterly but moving aside nonetheless. Leaning against the wall, David closed his eyes, feeling exhaustion in every muscle and bone. "Where are we?" he asked, voice a hoarse rasp.

"Well, we ain't swimmin' in models and beer, that's for sure." Jed sat back, stretching, settling himself more comfortably in Redford's lap. "But we think we've got a decent plan. We need to figure out where these vamps are staying. Not the flophouses they want us to find, the real McCoy." Jed trailed off, shooting Victor a glare and jerking his chin toward David. Subtle, Jed was not.

Beside him, Victor was stirring tea into the pot, his eyes darting from it to David. "Did you find anything out from Gabriel?" Victor winced as he said it, a strange combination of hesitation and stubbornness in his expression. "At this point, any information we get is immeasurably helpful."

Did he get anything from Gabe?

The cool slide of fingers across his jaw, sweetly smooth and yet so strong. Always sent a shudder down his spine, every time, knowing what that hand could do, what it would *do, never quite sure what mood would strike Gabriel that evening....*

"Nothing," David said shortly, shaking himself away from the memories.

It was quiet then, the sound of Jed shifting again, the rustle of paper. David ignored it, tipping his head back and letting his eyes fall shut once more. He wasn't picturing Gabriel's face. He refused to let his mind wander that far. "So do you still believe Gabriel responsible for the kidnappings?" Victor asked, pressing the mug of tea into David's hands.

Gritting his teeth, he had to come back to the present once more. Taking a sip of the tea, he gave Victor a quick glance. "Of course he is. Nothing's changed."

Victor looked like he was building himself up to say something, but he looked over at Jed and Redford, and then glanced toward their bedroom door. "David, may I speak with you alone?"

"Don't bother moving." Jed stood, stretching again, before holding out his hand to Redford. "We're going to go take a bath. A nice hot one with bubbles and lots of fucking. So please, don't disturb us." Flashing them both a grin, Jed gripped Victor's shoulder briefly as he led Redford to their bedroom and firmly shut the door behind them.

David took another drink, coolly watching Victor over the rim of his mug. It tasted bland, like hot water with the faintest hint of something else. Deciding he didn't want to pretend he remembered what tea tasted like any longer, he put the cup aside and arched an eyebrow. "Well?"

"You nearly lost control again, didn't you?" Victor took the discarded tea for himself, taking a sip. "Jed's been bitching about vampire saliva on his gun. I assume that means what I think it means."

"That Jed is an idiot?" David folded his arms across his chest, refusing to look at Victor. "I'd say that was a safe bet, yes."

Victor looked away again, pretending to study his mug with intensity. "David, you *know* what I saw when I looked at you." A hint of desperation made his voice tighter. "I understand that Gabriel was a valuable lead, but all you've been doing on this trip is going off alone and nearly losing control."

"If he has those people—" Cutting himself off with a low noise of frustration, David paced a few steps closer to Victor, shoulders bristling. "He *has them*. I know he does. So yes, I went to see him. What would you have suggested? I send *you* instead? With those bite marks on your neck? You'd have been someone's snack before you knew what hit you."

"I would have suggested that we work *together*, like everybody but you has been doing," Victor snapped. "I'm sorry, but everything you've done alone has gotten us nowhere. And it's gotten *you* further down the road of losing control."

Grinding his teeth, David took a deliberate step backward. If he stayed this close, feeling this angry, it wouldn't end well for either one of them. "I am fine," he said, each word bitten off sharply. "Just because you fuck a vampire, Vickie, doesn't mean you know the first damn thing about us."

"I know," Victor agreed, his expression losing some of the anger. "I won't pretend to understand what it's like for you. But I'm so worried about you that I think I'm starting to go gray. Even Jed and Redford are concerned."

Normally, he'd soften. David could feel himself *want* to, could see how closed off and wild he must look, eyes still edged in yellow, expression hard and remote. All he did, though, was turn his back on Victor, going to stand in front of the coffee table. The maps were there still, where Jed had left them. "I just want to finish this," he muttered, running a hand through his hair. "If we finish it, then everything will be back to normal."

Victor made an indiscernible noise in the back of his throat. "And you? You'll go back to starving yourself?"

Shaking his head firmly, David studied the lines Jed had drawn, radiating out from the bookstore. "I eat enough."

He heard Victor take a few steps toward him. "David, I'm not proposing that you start feeding off of humans every day. But your diet is like a vegetarian that eats *crisps* six days a week. It's little wonder your control is so off-kilter."

It was a familiar fight. One they'd had before, though never this bluntly. Usually Victor would sigh and give significant glances while David pointedly ignored his input. Until, that is, Victor's throat was bared, until David was begging himself not to bite even as Victor teased him past the point of lucidity. Then Victor's *input* was very much desired, was craved, even. That little taste of blood sustained David more than even the other man knew.

"What would you have me do?" he asked lowly, eyes flicking up to Victor's face. "Give in? Do you have any idea what that would look like?"

He moved forward then, the graceful, sudden movements that were far too fast for a half blood to keep up with. One hand braced against the wall next to Victor's head, and David leaned in, a sharp hunger shadowing his face. "Feeding turns me on. But you know that." His voice was a low croon in Victor's ear, a soft purr, as David nuzzled his nose in just above that beautiful pounding pulse point. "Drinking, *all* drinking, even that disgusting swill I force down once or twice a week, makes me crave more. *This*."

Barely, just barely, his lips teased along Victor's skin, leaving a wake of goose bumps. David could feel the shiver working its way along Victor's spine, knew that fear would be tempered with something far better.

That familiar heat started rolling, low in his stomach, and David closed his eyes. His whole body pressed in tight to Victor's, stealing his warmth, feeling each throb of his heart with every inch of himself. "I don't want to just taste you, little medusa," he murmured against the soft flush of Victor's neck. "I want to *devour* you. I would drain you dry and still want more. I'd leave you behind, nothing left but your sweet shell, and I wouldn't even notice when you'd stopped gasping in pleasure, in pain. It all sounds the same to me."

He laughed then, when Victor shoved him away with trembling hands. It wasn't nearly strong enough to *make* him back away, but he had enough control left to go along with the push, to sprawl against the counter and *laugh*, wildly, brokenly, at Victor's stern look. "Do you think you could stop me?" David asked, voice cracking, that manic grin almost desperate. "If I fed, if I actually slaked the hunger, what do you think I'd turn into?"

He knew. He'd been that monster for far too long, until he'd run. Until the blood and the glazed-over eyes and the destruction were too much, even for him. David hadn't left Gabriel because he was strong. No, he'd run because he was weak, far too weak to do anything but try to save his sorry soul. Feeding was a necessary evil, was what he did only enough to keep his sanity. How could he feel full, satisfied, when that would mean someone else's death?

"Yes, and *starving* yourself is working *brilliantly*." Victor's eyes were snapping behind his glasses, his body all drawn up in proper English indignation. If David wasn't so very close to losing it, he'd be tempted to try and make the fire in Victor burn with something other than anger. Now, though, he just let his fangs slip out, showing in a sign of defiance. "Do you honestly think you're proving anything by existing like this? You are a living being, David, and just like every other living being, you must *eat*. Pushing yourself to your limits every day—you will break, and it won't be because you're a vampire. It will be because you're a bloody idiot."

The same thing Gabriel had told him, really. Different words, different intentions, even, but the same message. His instincts would out. Eventually, the control David lived by, existed within, would break down, leaving nothing but the monster.

"Is… everything all right?" The tentative voice shattered the tension between David and Victor. Both men slumped back, David rubbing a trembling hand over his face and turning away. Redford was standing in the doorway of his and Jed's bedroom, hair mussed and still damp, feet bare. His eyes, though, flashed dangerously, a warning. The room must stink of vampire, David thought absently.

"Fine," David gritted out, squeezing his eyes shut, wishing away the ache that was pounding at his temples. "I thought you and the horny beast were taking a bath?"

A soft snort escaped Redford, and he shrugged, half smiling. "Jed passed out as soon as he got in the hot water." The tender expression on Redford's face was almost painful to look at. David turned away as he continued, "Had to drag him into bed. I'm letting him sleep. He forgets to take care of himself when he's on a job."

David busied himself washing out the mug that held the now-cold tea. He just needed something to do with his hands, some other task to focus on. The silence behind him seemed ominous, though. Glancing over, David found Redford and Victor engaged in short little glances, a nonverbal argument of sorts that ended when Redford reached out to lightly push Victor forward with a muttered, "So *tell* him already."

Huffing out a disgruntled sigh, removing his glasses to clean them—David recognized the gesture for what it was, a stalling tactic—Victor said in a lofty tone, "We have a plan."

255

"A plan," David repeated slowly, eyebrow arching sharply. "Let me guess. Journey is going to blow something up."

Redford looked back at the door, behind which, no doubt, Jed was snoring inelegantly. He seemed the type. "Don't call him Journey." Redford's lips were curved up in a wolfish grin of sorts, a silent laugh. "And that might factor into it. It worked."

Rolling his eyes, David dismissed him with a wave of his hand. "Not against Gabriel."

"David," Victor said, quietly pleading. The anger had faded, leaving only weary concern, the emotion lining his face, heavy on his shoulders. "No one but you thinks this is the work of Gabriel. And honestly, I don't think *you* believe that any longer. None of what we've found points to him."

God, David wanted to fight that. To rage loud enough that they'd *hear* him. It had to be Gabe. David had seen the pattern when no one else had, when the human authorities still saw no connection. He'd come halfway around the world, a moth to the flame, to end this. To finally stand up where he'd run away before. He was going to confront Gabriel, show the vampire that he no longer owned any part of David. Instead, what had he found? A gang of disorganized, sloppy vampires, their fangs barely cut, wreaking havoc. Nothing at all like Gabriel. Why, then, had David seen him in every step?

"Who else, then?" he managed thickly, face drawn and cold.

Redford glanced over at Victor again, waiting. Apparently Victor had drawn the short straw. It must not be fun, dealing with a cranky, starving vampire. "An unrelated nest of vampires. They call themselves the Usire clan," Victor answered. "Still a menace, David. They're hurting people. You can help us stop them."

It wouldn't be Gabe. That was what Victor had been elected to tell him. All this way, all these demons David had confronted, and the evil wasn't Gabriel at all. Just some stupid vamps who were making a bid for the town's streets, who were getting careless with their hunting.

"We think," Victor said tentatively, "that the appearances of Set statues are another message from Gabriel that he's not behind this, David. You remember the mythology of Set and Osiris?"

"I don't fucking care about *mythology*." The words were a crash, a desperate plea. David needed this to be Gabriel. He needed his *Ib-Se-Kem* to be cut out of his heart, his mind, and this was how he was going to do it.

256

"What does it matter if there are statues of Set or some vampires are claiming a god who's been forgotten for thousands of years? Who *cares*, Victor? It's Gabriel. He has to be stopped. This isn't one of your goddamn lectures."

"Fido?" Jed's voice was loud, crashing down on them, and the man himself burst out of the bedroom. His hair was all in disarray, eyes wide and bloodshot with sleep, his boxers half falling off. "Red? Where—"

Spotting Redford, Jed's entire body sagged in relief. "Jesus's bouncing balls, Red." Jed sighed loudly, scrubbing his face with both hands. "I woke up and you weren't there and…." Trailing off, he shook his head sharply, obviously still half-asleep. Redford was wrapped up tightly in an embrace, Jed burying his face against the werewolf's chest. "I couldn't find you," David heard Jed mumble, sounding for all the world, for all his guns and cocky smirks and love of explosives, like a lost little boy.

Surprised for only a moment, Redford held onto Jed tightly. "I'm right here," he murmured, smoothing his hand up and down Jed's back. "See? I'm fine."

It only took a minute for Jed to wake up fully, to get himself back under control with a curse and a hand rubbed through his hair. "Yeah, okay," Jed sighed, closing his eyes briefly. "Just… weird dream." Just like that, the façade was back up, Jed smirking widely at them all. "So, what'd I miss?"

"Your trousers?" Victor pointed out, sounding insulted by the very idea of Jed walking around less than clothed. Jed, however, just glanced down and grinned.

"Oh, right. Huh." For all he seemed completely back in his cocksure, smug self, David saw the way he was holding Redford's hand, their fingers trailing apart like it hurt to separate when Jed ducked back into the bedroom to finish dressing.

"Regardless," Victor continued, looking relieved that Jed had gone to cover himself up. "The Usire clan is out there, and we must get those victims back, and we must deal with them." His lips tightened briefly, darting a look at David. "Although I don't think Gabriel is behind this, *if* he has some part in this, we will handle him too." Then he muttered, "I'm tempted to do something about him regardless, just for making certain people lose themselves."

"Are you going to scold him to death?" Jed pointed out, zipping up his jeans as he wandered back into the room. Again, he pressed in close to

Redford, almost like he couldn't bear to be too far away. "Death by British nagging, I can see it now."

David just shook his head, pulling away from the group to go and sit on the couch. The whole room stank of old tea and gun cleaner. The sooner they finished this mess, the sooner David could be home, in his clean apartment, in solitude. "So what's this brilliant plan?"

The tangle of arms and legs that was Jed and Redford settled onto the couch, Jed winding up in Redford's lap and looking quite content to stay there, grinning at David. "We're using the best nose in town," Jed said. "Oh, yeah, and you too, Davie. You and Fido are going to sniff them out. None of this temporary shit. We've got to find where they're actually based out of. Then you come back here and lounge in luxury while the three people who *don't* burst into flames in sunlight do a little dawn raid."

"And how exactly are we going to sniff them out?" David arched an eyebrow, unconvinced. "The trail was too muddled at the factory."

"I, uh." Redford vanished briefly into the bedroom and came out holding a shirt. "I may have broken into Randall Lewis' student accommodation and stolen his shirt while you were talking to Gabriel," he mumbled. "I didn't pick up his scent before because it was too weak, but he's… a werewolf."

Frowning, David took the shirt from Redford. "I cannot believe I'm doing this," he muttered, giving Jed a dark look. "Who do you think I am, *Lassie*?" But he inhaled anyway, deliberately sniffing the collar of the shirt. "Ah. Not werewolf. Just wolf. Interesting. I wasn't aware they strayed that far from their packs."

"He smells like Filtiarn did," Redford remarked.

"Yes, like a *true* wolf." Victor looked inexplicably excited. "Exactly like Filtiarn. A *cano*, they're called, from the Old Gaelic, and—"

"Okay," Jed interrupted with an overly perky grin. "Someone shove a sock in the professor's mouth or we'll be here all day." Turning to Redford, his smile turned much more genuine. "Score one for the wolf-burglar. Nice thinking, babe. So, we take the shirt, we go hunting, and we see what we can scare up. Soon as the sun goes down, we're gone. Two teams, moving counterclockwise away from the bookstore. Red and Victor marked out a likely area, so we need to cover that before dawn."

Leaning forward, Jed tugged the appropriate map out of the pile and pointed to two locations, one on each side of the street where the bookstore stood.

"Red, you'll go with Victor," Jed said, glancing up at David in what was probably meant to be a casual way. "Davie, you and me. Everyone got it?"

"All clear, captain," Victor said dryly, though he was obviously approving of the plan. Redford, in agreement, just budged his shoulder against Jed's.

David shrugged, scowling down at the floor. He understood the reasoning behind Jed's little teams. Keep the big bad vampire with the guy who carried heavy artillery. For some reason, though, it just rubbed him the wrong way, even as he knew it was the right call. "Let's just go," he muttered, rubbing a hand through his hair and pushing away from the wall he'd been leaning on. "We're wasting the night."

Redford had paused just outside of the bedroom before he cast a look at Jed. "I'll go wolf," he decided. "Better nose."

Going over to him, Jed fussed with Redford's shirt, looking like he wanted to protest. Instead, he kissed said nose lightly, nudging their foreheads together. "Okay," he agreed quietly. Reaching out, Jed gently unhooked a chain from around Redford's neck. Dog tags and a silver whistle clanked together quietly as he looped them over his own head, tucking them under his T-shirt. "For luck," he smiled, holding Redford's eyes. David let his own gaze drop. Sometimes, watching Redford and Jed was more disturbing than anything else—the way they looked at each other, how *tender* Jed would get… it was unsettling, somehow.

"Well." Victor looked unsure at suddenly being included in the action plan, but he straightened his shoulders, trying to stand tall. "Let's head out, then."

IT WAS four hours away from dawn by the time they got to the bookstore, the night air crisp and clean. Only the occasional passerby interrupted the silence.

Redford had used an alleyway to change, giving Jed a backpack full of his clothes. The werewolf had spent a long moment just *looking* at Jed, with Jed looking back, seemingly having some private, unspoken conversation, before he'd trotted off with Victor to the opposite side of the bookstore.

"Did you have a nice moment?" David muttered, rolling his eyes.

259

"I agreed not to shoot you in the face for being a pompous twat," Jed rejoined cheerfully, chambering a round into the shotgun he then tucked into a holster on his back, shrugging his jacket on over it. "So yeah, good chat." Whistling sharply, he jerked his head toward the street. "Come on, Lassie. Mush."

Deciding that the time he'd spend explaining to Redford and Victor *why* it'd suddenly become necessary to rip Jed's head off his shoulders was not worth the satisfaction it'd give him, David just smothered an irritated noise and started walking. Unlike Redford, who had trotted off with his nose to the ground, David didn't appear to be doing anything but taking a nice stroll. Then again, wolves were far from subtle creatures. David could smell the Lewis boy through the stench of the everyday, picking up the subtle spice of his blood, the tang of his sweat, and walked quickly away from the bookstore.

Perhaps he should have realized it wasn't going to be that easy. He was so focused on that one scent that he missed five others, the sharp smell of vampires only hitting him when it was too late. Turning quickly, hissing a warning, David went down to a fist across his jaw.

There were two sharp repeats, the deafening noise of a gun going off, and David looked up to see Jed's head snap back from a vampire's strike. Struggling to his feet, David bared his fangs, leaping onto the back of the nearest attacker.

"Son of a fucking bitchhole donkey fucker!" Jed's eloquence was never more underscored than when he'd been surprise attacked. Whirling around, Jed jammed the butt of his sawed-off shotgun into a vampire's gut, using the momentum to slam the vampire back into the rough brick of the building opposite. "What the hell?"

"You attack us, human?" Apparently they were going to get the villain monologue. "See how you like it."

"Yes, yes, drink his blood, I get it." David sneered. "Try to stay focused, here." Grabbing the vampire by the throat, David twisted his neck, feeling it pop underneath his hands. He knelt on the vampire's back to give himself leverage and, with a heave, ripped his head off his body.

Staring, wide-eyed, Jed looked like he might be sick. "Holy fucking fuck," he whispered. "That was…. You just…."

Luckily, David was saved from additional commentary by another vampire kicking Jed in the balls. That would effectively shut him up for a moment.

"Fucking Urine clan!"

Or maybe not.

While Jed writhed on the ground and fired ineffective shots from yet another gun he'd had stored somewhere, David grabbed a broken piece of wood from the ground, tossing it back and forth in his hands as he advanced on the remaining four vampires. One of them, the tallest one, salt-and-pepper hair completely betrayed by the lithe way he moved, swung for David. David ducked, rolling under the punch to use the board to take a hard swing at the tall one's kneecaps. They gave way with a pop.

Jed was up again, using his shotgun as a blunt weapon, beating a dark-haired vampire over the head repeatedly and driving him back. Dimly, David could hear sounds of a scuffle happening a street over, thudding footsteps and the snarling of a werewolf, but his focus was here.

Then, above the noise of Jed's cursing and the vampire's snarling, rose a bloodcurdling howl. Perhaps evolution had demanded that the sound of it freeze prey and predators alike. Even the vampires paused, looking around them before returning to the fray.

"Red." Jed, however, was barreling through the bodies like they were bowling pins. He fired wildly now, shooting over and over, just to make a bloody path. Hands grasped him, hauling him back, but Jed just turned around and started swinging. "Red!" he shouted, a desperate bellow, kicking one vampire back, stomping his head over and over with a heavy boot until he could drag himself free. "Fucking *Urine*. Red!"

A sharp yip came echoing back, a signal that Redford was alive and fighting his way toward them. The noise of paws on pavement came thudding closer, until David could see a blur of fur leaping at the vampire closest to Jed, Victor trailing behind him with a crude stake in his hands, though it clearly hadn't been used from the lack of blood on it. That, and Victor was holding it backward.

Jed reached out and grabbed it from Victor's hand, shoving the man back behind him as he bodily pushed off a vampire. "Jesus, Fido, don't *do* shit like that." As if it was something Redford could have prevented, being separated. The relief in Jed's voice, though, was palpable, and he immediately moved to Redford's side, fighting hip to wolf shoulder, using Victor's stake like an unwieldy knife.

Everybody fighting winced when Redford bit one of the vampires in the groin.

With two more vampires down through another removed head and a stake to the heart, they were left looking at one remaining vampire, who suddenly seemed to realize that his odds of winning had been drastically changed.

"I'll just go, shall I?" The vampire put on a bright grin, beginning to edge backward.

Jed very calmly shot out both of his kneecaps. "Yeah," he drawled, tucking the gun away and kicking the vampire over, the squeals of pain ignored. "That's not going to work for me."

David was drenched in blood. It was old blood, though, stolen blood, that he'd spilled and painted the ground with. Eyes glazed over, fingers shaking from the rush of adrenaline, he hauled the vampire up by the throat, holding him over his head and pinning him roughly to the wall. "Talk," he bit out thunderously. "Or I'll tie you to the ground and wait for dawn."

"Fuck you," the vampire hissed, ineffectually squirming in David's hold. "You think you'd get away with razing the factory to the ground? All of us *know* who you assholes are, and we're taking you down."

Jed was right next to David, staring up at the vampire like he was a bug on a pin. "You know, I'm still learning about this whole vampire thing," he mused. "But I've got a pissed off werewolf here and a heck of a lot of rope in my bag. What if we trussed you up and tossed you out onto the street, hm? I wonder if that'd be a fun game?" His hand dropped to tangle his fingers in the fur at Redford's neck, and he grinned cheerfully up at the vampire. "Let's find out!"

Redford gave a helpful-sounding growl to back Jed up. The vampire's gaze tracked over to the werewolf, disdain lighting his expression, turning fearful at another growl. "All right, all right, fuck," the vampire yelped. "Just don't turn me into a doggy snack. I'll tell you where the rest of us are. It's not like you'll come out of there alive anyway."

At the pressure of werewolf jaws closing around his ankle—Redford looked amused as he gnawed a little, but the vampire couldn't see that— the vampire continued, panicked, "Just outside the city to the west, we've got a big compound out there. Used to be an old jail, just by the Nile. It's big and gray and you can't miss it."

Jed reached upward to pat the vampire's cheek, none too gently. "See, now you're being helpful," Jed remarked. "That's one step up from doggy chow. Just a step *below* roadkill, though."

Jed slammed the stake through the vampire's heart, and David dropped the body, leaving it crumpled against the wall. Redford was already scampering off, sniffing at nearby cars. David wondered just what the hell he thought he was doing, until Redford gave a bark, and Jed grinned widely. "That one's good for stealing. Come on, ladies and gentlemen." He glanced at David and Victor and amended, "Just ladies."

CHAPTER
12

Jed

THEY were limping, sore, and bruised. Jed was pretty sure he'd gotten blood in places that blood was not supposed to go, Redford was favoring his right paw, and David, well, David looked like he'd gone all Carrie at the prom. The vampire was *bathed* in blood and gore, and he stank like a goddamn sewer.

Crammed into the car Jed had hotwired, they broke just about every traffic law and common-sense practice in existence, racing the sun to the edge of town. Two hours until dawn, they slid to a screeching halt just down the block from the gray-toned building. There was a rusted and half-crumbling fence around the property, boards on the windows, and a sign that Jed assumed was some kind of *Do Not Trespass* hanging crookedly from the dilapidated entrance. Well, that or it was offering free kittens and hugs. Jed's Arabic wasn't good enough to tell the difference.

He was going to assume the latter. Made his life easier.

"David, you take the rear," Jed barked, loading up his guns again. They might be wholly ineffective long term, but it was a comfort thing. He'd rather have the option to lay down some kind of cover fire, even if it only slowed the bastards down. "Red, you're on me. Princess?" Jed smirked and tossed the keys over to Victor. "Keep the motor running, sweetheart. We won't be long."

Sputtering, Victor bobbled the keys, nearly dropping them before drawing himself up to his full height in indignation. "I *can* be useful, you realize." He sniffed imperiously. "One of us should go after the victims directly, before the commotion alerts the entire nest and they're moved again."

Pausing, Jed considered the suggestion. Frankly, he had his doubts that Victor wouldn't just keel over like a Victorian woman who realized her ankles were showing the second there was trouble, but he had managed to stay upright and alive during the last scuffle. Maybe he wasn't entirely a waste of air. Finally Jed jerked a nod and threw Victor his stake back. "Fido, change of plans. You keep with the good professor, cover his exit. Then you get your furry behind right back to me, got it?"

He met Redford's eyes, waiting until the large wolf nodded, sneezing his opinion of Jed's overprotectiveness. Lolling tongue and all, he gave Jed a wolfy grin, nudging his head into Jed's arm. "Yeah, yeah, I know," Jed muttered, scratching behind Redford's ears. "You're big and bad. I still want you close, got it? And you bark like hell if you need me. Clear?"

With a soft chuff of agreement, Redford went to stand next to Victor, giving the man a reassuring tail wag. David was just standing, staring at the building, eerily still. His pupils were blown wide, rimmed in a sickly yellow, his fingers the only part of him that moved at all. They were shaking so bad Jed expected to hear his bones rattle.

"Okay, we've got ten minutes." Jed moved them into position, chambering a round in his shotgun. "Then I'm blowing this place so high that God's going to feel a draft." He checked everyone, meeting Redford's eyes one last time, making sure Victor hadn't fainted, snapping his fingers in front of David, only to have the vampire growl at him, expression one of pure rage. Not at Jed, though, surprisingly. His eyes kept sliding back to the building beyond them, as if he could sense the vampires just waiting to be ripped apart.

Jed took point, nodding them all forward. It made it easier to kick the door in and start blasting indiscriminately. There were victims here, so Jed kept the gun aimed high, using the surprise and the noise to scatter half-asleep and bloated vampires around the room.

Then David walked in.

Fangs bared, blood drying on his face, coat billowing around his thighs, he looked like every stereotypical horror-movie vampire come true. David grabbed the first attacker, a big brutish guy with a crew cut, and grasped him with one hand cupping each ear. Spinning their bodies around, David slammed Meathead against the wall, while Chuckles, the second vampire, jumped onto David's back from behind. It didn't seem to faze David, though. He just snarled, kneeing Meathead hard enough to make the vampire sag down in pain. Reaching back, he grabbed Chuckles by the hair and slammed him into the wall.

Out of the corner of his eye, Jed saw Victor and Redford slink in, hugging the walls, darting around the vampires who were gunning for him and David to get through the back door. They disappeared, and Jed did his best not to worry. Redford could handle himself well enough. Besides, he had his own problems. Three more vampires had decided to join the party, and Jed's gunfire wasn't holding them back anymore. Wounds closing up right in front of his freaking eyes, they advanced, grabbing Jed by the shoulder and yanking him close.

"Sorry, sweetcheeks." Jed grinned manically, reaching into his coat and pulling out a knife. "You aren't my type. I prefer my guys with a little more pulse." Repeatedly stabbing vampires in the neck did not, Jed found, actually *kill* them. It did slow them down, though.

Sweetcheeks himself seemed to be particularly enthralled with Jed. Not that Jed minded. "Come on then, baby," he crooned, ducking a punch, swinging his shoulder forward to knock the vampire back. "You wanna take me for a ride? Let's go."

Beside him, David was creepily quiet. There was the sound of flesh meeting flesh, the dull thuds of impact, the harsh growls of pain, but that was it. No witty repartee from David, no sir. He was blank, ripping out a vampire's throat like it was a meat piñata before moving on to the next.

Whatever. Jed had enough to worry about at the moment, with Sweetcheeks Junior joining in the fun. He'd think about David's apparent transformation into a zombie pain machine later. What was important was they were holding back the vampires, and, so far, no one had seemed to notice that this was a rescue operation.

Jed roared in pain when one vampire bit into his upper arm. Twisting away, ripping himself out of the vampire's fangs, Jed unloaded an entire clip from one handgun into the vampire out of reflex. Sweetcheeks just leered at him, Jed's own blood painting his chin ruby red. "Very nice, human," he mused, licking his lips. "I can almost see why the little *weres* bothers with you. You must make a nice snack."

The *little were*, though, with impeccable timing, chose that moment to crash his full weight onto the vampire's back, sending them both howling to the floor in a snap of teeth and fur. Jed staggered back, out of the way, face pale. For a moment, one very scary, very disturbing moment, he'd been *food*. Something had fucking taken a bite and *eaten* a part of him. "Son of a bitch," he whispered unevenly, raising his shaking arm to fire

266

again and again, until the hammer clicked dry, until he was just pulling an empty trigger over and over.

It was the feel of the entire weight of Redford's body pressing against his legs that brought Jed back to himself. Still shaking, a cold, sick sweat making his T-shirt cling to his back, Jed stared blankly for a moment before he managed to bring himself out of the shock. Redford was at his feet, growling murderously, a puddle of what Jed had to assume were former vampire parts spread out around them. Snapping a sharp bark at Jed, Redford gripped the knee of his jeans in his teeth and tugged him away.

David was still fighting, but it was clear he wasn't going to win. Six vampires now, beating on him without mercy, David snarling and ripping and tearing, using teeth and nails with as much grace as one might expect him to wield a sword. Reaching into his jacket, Jed came out with a handful of knives. With calm efficiency, he started throwing as he and Redford moved toward the door. He got one chick through the eyes, downing her, leaving her screaming as Jed took another vampire through the throat. Temporary, always temporary with these motherfuckers. Just long enough of a break to grab the back of David's jacket and drag him to the door.

Shoving David out, Jed ordered Redford in a bellow, "Go!" He didn't have to wait to make sure Redford had started running. Behind him, he heard the sound of Red growling, barking, nipping at David's heels to herd him toward the car. In front of him was a wall of vampires, bloodied and angry as all hell.

"Hey, darlins," Jed called, pulling out his last three grenades. "You showed me yours. Now I think it's my turn." A wide, raucous grin split his lips as Jed pulled the pins.

Throwing the hand grenades into the advancing run of vampires, Jed didn't bother trying to make it to the car. It was too far away. Instead he tucked and rolled behind a tree, plastering his back to the trunk and ducking his head between his knees. The blast ripped through the night behind him, sending howling flames up to the sky, licking at his heels, shuddering through the ground.

Car alarms started blaring in the distance, and Jed blinked a few times, deafened. Groaning as he unrolled himself, Jed flopped down onto the ground amidst a shower of burning debris, covered in grime and sweat and drying blood. "Fuck," he murmured. His voice sounded weird in his own ears, echoing and muffled. There was the press of paws against his chest, then hands, then Redford's face swimming in front of his eyes. No sound made it in yet, just the harsh buzz of his own breathing, but Jed could see Redford's lips move.

"You have pretty lips." Jed smiled loopily, reaching his fingers out to touch them. His hand missed, though, but that was okay, because now there were *two* Redfords hovering above him. "Mmm, threesome," he slurred before even that lovely sight was gone, faded out into a rush of white, and then nothing.

The world was painfully loud when Jed came to. Wincing, he turned his head, burying his face in what turned out to be Redford's thigh. He was half-sprawled on the man's lap, Redford's hand protectively threaded into his hair, conversation flying above him. Dimly, Jed could make out two other bodies pressed tight into the backseat of the car. An unconscious woman was half slumped against the door. Randall Lewis, Jed recognized from his photo, was staring around him with wide, solemn eyes. He kept blinking, as if trying to get everything in focus, shrinking back against the door of the cab when he saw Jed's eyes on him.

Yeah. Jed figured he must look a little crazed.

David was up front. Victor was driving, apparently, cutting corners with a lot more speed than Jed would have given him credit for. "Slow down there, princess," Jed rasped, rubbing a hand over his face and managing to leverage himself into a half-sitting position. He was still draped over Redford's lap, but this time he got to lean back against the other man, letting out a slow breath when Redford nudged his forehead against Jed's temple.

"He lives," Victor responded dryly, but Jed noticed his shoulders dropping slightly, the smallest edge of his tension easing away.

"Can't get rid of me that easy," Jed mumbled, letting himself be held by Redford. Truth be told, he wouldn't have wanted to move away from him, even if the option had been given. "Just a little shock from the explosion. Ain't the first time." He smiled a little at Redford, their hands lacing together as Redford held on tightly. "Worst part is the ringing in my ears. Sounds like I'm rimming a church bell."

Wordlessly, Redford's fingers touched the red bite mark on Jed's arm. It was almost all scabbed over already. The wonders of vampire cooties, apparently. Jed jerked away from the touch, eyes dropping immediately.

"It's fine," Jed muttered. Redford's bag was between their feet, empty of the clothes Redford had stashed. His jacket was in there, though. Redford had apparently taken it off to check him for more serious injuries. Jed grabbed it and shrugged it on, covering up the mark.

"You got bit," Redford pointed out, a low, dangerous rumble underneath his words. "That *vampire* bit you."

"Yeah, I was there," Jed muttered, scrubbing his face with both hands. "Let's talk about something else. Like our new friends." He gave Lewis, the only one awake, a wide, overly bright grin. "Hi, new friends."

"And thank you *so* much for checking to make sure we were out before you blew the whole place to kingdom come," Victor grumbled, shifting in his seat, making a quick left turn. Jed could see the lights of the hospital up ahead.

"Red was with me," Jed explained slowly, wondering if he should start bringing flash cards along to explain shit to Victor. If the guy wasn't a brainy genius, Jed would have sworn he was a few fries short. "He wouldn't have come back if you guys weren't out and safe."

Redford gave Jed a little smile, just the barest hint at the edge of his lips, in the corners of his eyes. "We're a team, right?" His arms curved more tightly around Jed's waist. "That's what teammates do."

"Damn straight." In the field, trusting someone to that extent was necessary. If you couldn't, if for even a moment you hesitated, wondering if the other guy was going to take care of his own shit, everyone died. Admittedly, not since the forced camaraderie of the service had Jed even remotely considered having anybody that close again. It was too scary, too many variables. Better to work alone.

And yet, here he was with this wide-eyed, beautiful man, and Jed hadn't even thought twice about it. Redford had appeared at his side, and Jed had known, without a doubt, that everyone was out. That Redford had done his end of things and he could move on to the next.

Ducking his head, Jed took off the chain holding his dog tags and the whistle. They were draped back around Redford's neck, and Jed wondered a little at the tightness in his throat as he did so. "You and me, babe," he murmured.

The car jerked to a halt, and Victor got out quickly. "You all stay here," Victor said, nervously glancing around. "None of you are exactly presentable. I don't want to elicit more questions than would be prudent at the moment."

Lewis was still the only one mobile, even though he looked like hell itself. Very carefully, he got out of the car, helping shoulder the load of the unconscious woman. Victor managed to drape the woman's arm over his shoulders, and they dragged her a few feet toward the entrance, where they laid her carefully down. Lewis looked about ready to fall over or puke—possibly both—but he stumbled to the door, pushing it open and calling in a hoarse voice. "Help. Please, help us."

Jed saw Lewis look back at Victor's retreating form, watching him run back to the car. Then he was engulfed in a sea of scrubs, medical personnel rushing out toward him, vanishing him from view. Victor got into the car, breathing hard, and quickly started up the engine. "We'd best go, before anyone thinks to wonder where two people appeared from."

"Good thinking," Jed agreed. The backseat was much less crowded now, but Jed didn't relinquish his place on Redford's lap. "Last thing we want is my gorgeous mug in the paper tomorrow. No one would ever live up to it."

Victor snorted loudly, and Jed just grinned absently, eyes falling shut. It was settling in now, that nice after-burn of adrenaline, the hyped-up buzz of a job completed. Hell, no one had even died. Well, other than the bloodsuckers, but that just made it better, in Jed's opinion.

Speaking of their resident Dracula, Jed cracked an eyelid open to check out David. The guy hadn't said a word the whole trip, which, frankly, was kind of weird. He'd been too busy thinking about other things to really care what bug was up Davie's ass, but now that they were headed back, Jed craned his neck to try and see what he was doing.

Staring. That was what was occupying all of David's attention. He was staring straight ahead, almost blankly, fingers knotted in his lap like a little boy who was trying his best not to touch anything. David's eyes were fixed on the road ahead of them, his shoulders so tense and tight Jed half expected to see them snap.

"What's up with him?" Jed grunted, resisting, barely, the urge to prod David in the back of the neck to try and get a reaction.

"He's fine." Victor's whole body was rigid, lips thinning out. "Just needs to wash the blood off."

Sure. Jed believed that. Also, he totally still left milk and cookies out for the fat guy who squeezed his way down Jed's nonexistent fireplace.

Then again, Victor did know David better. He was sleeping with the dude, for fuck's sake. If Victor was willing to be in close quarters with David, then who was Jed to argue? Jed was also too tired to worry about anything else that evening. They'd won. The kidnapped people were getting medical attention, the vampires were dead, and Jed had earned his fee. He was officially off the clock. David's issues could just take a hike, unless he was willing to pay for another round.

When they arrived at the hotel, David was the first one out of the car. He made his way to the room like a freaking homing pigeon, disappearing into his bedroom. Jed could hear the sound of the shower, water hitting the tile wall. Maybe Victor had been right. Also, it wasn't a bad idea. Jed felt unpleasantly sticky in a way that was not the fun kind.

"Come on, Fido." He stretched, yawning, before tugging Redford with him toward their own room. "I'm gonna hose the vampire goo off of me. Want to join in?" He waggled his eyebrows suggestively, grinning at Redford's laugh.

Redford followed him, budging his shoulder playfully against Jed's as they made their way to the shower. "I think you have a shower kink," he said fondly, fussing about the bathroom, making sure there were towels, turning the water on.

Jed shrugged off his shirt and glanced over at the mirror, pausing as his eyes met his reflection. "Yeah, well," he murmured absently. "Think how easy the cleanup is." The bite mark was standing out against his sun-darkened skin, angry red but healing quickly. Fingertips touching it, Jed shuddered and dropped his head, focusing on his belt with a frown.

Redford took over the job for him, gently unbuckling Jed's belt and helping him out of his pants. His eyes kept straying to the bite too, frowning every time he saw it. "I should have gotten there quicker," Redford muttered to himself, sounding angry. When he pulled back, he went to work getting rid of his own clothes, his movements jerky, unfocused.

"It doesn't matter," Jed said. He still felt sick when he looked at it, when he *thought* about it. The fucker had eaten him. Without too much trouble, Jed could recall perfectly what it'd felt like, teeth sliding through skin and muscle, the sharp pull of him drinking....

Shaking his head sharply, Jed frowned. "It doesn't matter," he repeated in a mumble, turning as if to hide that arm from Redford. Getting into the shower, he tipped his head back, eyes closing, letting the pounding spray sluice away the dirt and blood. Redford stepped in next to him, his eyes wide and earnest again, gently cupping a hand over the mark.

"It *doesn't* matter," Redford agreed. "It was just some stupid vampire." He took his hand away from the mark, lightly brushing his fingers down Jed's arm. "Are you okay?"

Lips quirking upward into a broken parody of his usual smirks, Jed shrugged. "Aren't I supposed to be asking you that?"

Redford just gave him a look. "No. You're not the only one here that can get protective."

Jed ran one hand through his wet hair, throat tight against his heavy swallow. "I was scared," he admitted, voice cracking at the end, eyes dropped down somewhere along their feet. He watched the rust-colored water swirl past their toes, dragging the leftovers of the day down the drain. "Jesus, Red, for a minute, I was so fucking scared."

The hands cupping his jaw gently tilted his face back up to look at Redford. "It's okay to be scared," Redford said lowly. "I know you don't think you're allowed to be. But that's what I'm for, right? I can look out for you when you're afraid." As if he wasn't sure what he was saying was right, Redford gave him a tentative, hopeful smile. There was still blood drying in his hair, on his face, patches of his skin where he hadn't thought yet to clean them off.

It was odd to see Redford—shy, sweet, earnest Redford—looking so fierce by turns. Not that Jed hadn't seen him rip the fuck out of some vamps a few hours ago. But wolf form and regular Redford had a nice disconnect in his brain. It was hard to reconcile them together.

"He *ate* me," Jed said suddenly, frowning. "Fucker bit in and chowed down. And now I'm gonna have a goddamn *bite scar*, like some goth wearing emo shit." Fuck. "Goddamn bloodsucking asswipe."

Redford lifted Jed's arm again, pressing a featherlight kiss to the mark. "I like your scars," he said, sweeping his hands up Jed's arm. "They mean that you're still alive." His fingers moved to cover the knot of a scar in Jed's left shoulder, the remnants of a bullet wound. "It means you came back for me."

Jed leaned forward with a quiet snort, nudging his forehead against Redford's. "Always." Closing his eyes, he relaxed into the hot water, into Redford's gentle touches. "But I still hate the fang marks."

"So do I," Redford admitted. "They're… they mean—" He frowned, trying to figure out how to explain himself. "They're not *my* marks."

"Trust me, sweetheart," Jed rumbled, lazily squeezing out some shampoo and threading his fingers through Redford's hair, "I would much rather you bite me. You're a lot more fun." Also, Redford didn't *eat people*, goddamn. Fucking vampires. Fucking eating people. "You jealous of fang boy, Fido?"

Redford made an expression somewhere between a scowl and a pout. "I don't want to *eat* you," he replied.

"Well, that's good to know." Scrubbing his own hair, Jed ducked under the spray to rinse off. "Unless you mean no to the fun kind of eating. Then I'm sad."

Redford's laugh was a quiet huff of air. He moved around to get the soap, lathering up his hands and sweeping them over Jed's back, careful and methodical. Silent, he moved his way over Jed's body, fingers digging into tense muscles and helping loosen the knots of stress that Jed could feel had firmly settled into his shoulders. Occasionally, Redford would just press himself close and hook his chin over Jed's shoulder, like he was reassuring himself that Jed was still whole and alive.

By the time he was clean, Jed was practically boneless, leaning back against Redford. He rocked his hips back slowly, languid movements that sent little jolts of heat tripping up his spine. "Why don't you just take me to bed and make me all yours?" he suggested, head tipped back, nudging his nose in under Redford's ear. "Please, baby. I need you to make me yours."

Redford smiled against Jed's jaw. "You're always mine," he murmured. "Some leech doesn't change that." Clearly reluctant to move away, he pulled back to rinse the shampoo out of his own hair, pushing it back from his face.

"I am," Jed said lowly. "Just remind me, okay?" He leaned against the wall and watched as Redford washed himself quickly, those beautiful hands smoothing soap all over his body.

"You're such a voyeur," Redford teased. Jed flashed him a wolfish little smile, reaching out to draw him in. He bit lightly at the curve of

273

Redford's shoulder, a playful snap of his teeth, smirking at the shiver that ran across Redford's skin.

"You're too good to look at," he complained, kissing the slope of his neck. "I can't help it."

As soon as he'd gotten all the soap washed off his body, Redford reached out to turn the shower off. He gently nudged Jed out and grabbed a towel, draping it over Jed's head to dry his hair. His movements were still light, careful, and thorough, as if toweling Jed off was suddenly the most important thing he could do.

"Hey," Jed whispered, catching Redford's hands. "I'm okay." Tugging Redford in, Jed kissed him, more desperate than normal, with an edge he didn't normally let out. "See? I'm right here." This wasn't the worst job Jed had ever done. Hell, it wasn't even the most bloody. So why the fuck were his hands still shaking? Why was he turning his arm away from Redford, hiding that fucking ugly scar?

Every time he did, though, Redford caught him, turning him back so that he wasn't hiding it anymore. "I just worry," Redford admitted. "And stop hiding. The mark doesn't make me angry."

"It makes me sick," Jed muttered hoarsely. "I was fucking weak, and there wasn't anything I could do. And now I get to carry the damn thing around with me and—" Breaking off, wrapping his fingers around the back of Redford's head, Jed hauled him in for a hard, bruising kiss. "Make it yours," he begged against Redford's lips, pressing in tight to him, so much that it seemed his skin was warmed with Redford's heartbeat. "Please, I want it to be yours instead."

Redford gave him a soft smile. He bent his head, lips pressed to the round scar on Jed's shoulder. "I was going to do that anyway," he murmured, moving to a nearly invisible line on Jed's ribs. When he got to the bite mark, sitting high on Jed's bicep, the kiss he gave it was even lighter, mindful of the still healing wound. Then, quickly, he moved up half an inch and bit down, making his own mark, a faint rumble of a growl sounding deep in his chest.

Hissing in a breath, head falling back, Jed gripped Redford's arms for balance. "God," he managed, voice thick. "Redford."

Redford jerked back, looking apologetic. "Did I hurt you?" He looked at the reddening mark, eyes wide. Then, he looked downward, to the evidence that said that Jed wasn't feeling *pain* right then. "Oh. Okay, good." His expression softened again. "Bed?"

Frowning at Redford, Jed gave his own bite to the sweet dip of Redford's neck. He didn't temper himself, catching his skin between his teeth, soothing the sting with a sucking kiss, with long swipes of his tongue. "I am not," he grumbled, making a twin mark on the opposite side of Redford's throat, "made of fucking glass."

Bed indeed. Jed made it there without leaving off sucking his way across Redford's chest with heated, open-mouthed kisses. When they tumbled onto the blankets, Jed nipped lightly at Redford's nipple before sprawling back, offering his body up for Redford's perusal. "So stop acting like you're gonna hurt me." He leveled a look at Redford. "You and the wolf and whatever else you've got going on in there—I want it. All of it. No more holding back."

Redford just looked at him for a moment, stunned, as if he was going to protest. Jed liked the actual response he gave much better—which was to lean down and bite Jed's thigh, *definitely* no holding back. "Even the shedding?" Redford gave him a smile.

"That's why we got the Dustbuster." Jed moaned loudly, squirming a little under Redford's assault. His legs spread wider, teeth catching his lip. "*Fuck.*"

Looking rather pleased with himself, Redford moved upward, taking the lip Jed was biting and soothing it with a kiss. "I love you," he murmured, kissing Jed properly, resting a hand over his heart.

Jed's fingers went up to lace with Redford's. "I know." He buried his words into another kiss, drawing Redford in closer. Their tongues were tangled together, their breaths panting in time, bodies fitting like that was what they'd been made for. "I love you too, Red. Forever."

Redford's necklace was a cool counterpoint to the heat that was rising under Jed's skin, the metal resting on his own chest, dragging whenever Redford moved. Jed had given Redford the whistle to help him feel safe, to make sure Redford always knew that Jed would be there whenever he called. Now Jed found himself taking the same comfort from it, the knowledge that Redford would always be there too. Redford was a pleasantly heavy weight draped across his limbs, slim lines and sharp curves of bone. Jed wrapped his arms around the man, maybe a little too tightly, burying his face into Redford's neck.

275

"I'm here," he heard Redford whisper, lips nudged against Jed's ear. "Do you want to know what I'm thinking?"

Confused at the turn of topic, Jed pulled his head back to look at Redford, who was wearing a rare, mischievous smile. "I'm thinking," Redford said slowly, "that you should find that lube, because it feels like it's been too long since I've had you inside me."

A slow grin curved its way across Jed's lips. "Your wish is my command," he replied, chasing Redford's smile with kisses until he couldn't remember what it was like to breathe apart from him. His hand went out to their nightstand, slapping around a few times before his fumbling fingers found the drawer. The tube of lube was inside, never too far away, and Jed pulled it out eagerly.

Rubbing his hand down Redford's back, Jed slid his palm along the curve of his ass, loving the way Redford would arch into him. Jed's lips trailed along Redford's neck, the slope of his jaw, the little dip just below his ear that he loved so much. He flicked open the tube, slicking up one finger and using it to make slow circles against Redford's hole. Redford rumbled a pleased noise against Jed's jaw, ducking down to nip at his collarbone.

With a slightly clumsy movement, Redford rolled them, laughing at the way his leg awkwardly got trapped under Jed's for a moment—the sound of Redford laughing during something like this still startled Jed, he'd admit. He'd never been with anyone who felt free enough, comfortable enough, to *laugh* in the middle of sex. But there Redford was, sprawled out on his back now, hair curling in damp tangles across the pillow, the scar over his face softened in this light, which cast the eyes that smiled up at him more toward gray than blue.

Impatient, Redford grasped Jed's hip, arching up to kiss him. Pulled out of his contemplation of Redford by the press of lips, the slight nip of playful teeth, Jed smiled at Redford's eagerness. Ducking his head to suck lightly at the curve of Red's throat, Jed eased one finger inside of him. He had to bite back a moan at how tight Redford was, how hot, how his whole body seemed to pull him in. Redford's legs wrapped around his hips, and he gave the most amazing whimpering groan, rocking into Jed's hand.

"God, you're beautiful," Jed told him in awe. He was always in awe. Always so goddamn *amazed* at how every time Redford touched him, it was better.

A second finger then, scissoring in and out of Redford, Jed bracing himself over Redford's body with one arm. Watching him eagerly, Jed's eyes never left Redford's face. He wanted to memorize every moment, how a flush would start high on Redford's cheeks and curl down his neck, how his pupils would dilate, his eyes turning dark with need. How his lips would part, panting in air, exhaling moans and pleas for more. How Redford's entire world would become *them*.

Redford's hands came up to tangle in his hair, dragging Jed into a kiss that was mostly gentle bites and pants of air. "Jed, come *on*." Jed smothered a smirk, hooking his fingers up and watching eagerly as Redford arched up again with a moan. He could practically time Redford now. He knew exactly when Redford would start to twist and squirm underneath his hands, wanting more, wanting it faster than the pace Jed insisted on when getting him ready.

"Savoring the moment, Red." Jed chuckled, placing a kiss on Redford's chin. "You take your sweet time when you do this too."

"Yeah, but...." Whatever retort Redford was going for didn't make it into actual words, a frown meaning that he conceded the point. Redford, Jed would swear, was an even worse tease than he was. Not that he minded. All that serious contemplation would turn to him. The light in Redford's eyes would be tied up in Jed's pleasure. Never once before, never in his life, had he ever felt *more* than when he was here, like this, with Redford.

Kissing away the frown, Jed added a third finger, rubbing against Redford's prostate with every other thrust. He loved the way Red's body would tighten around him, how he'd roll his hips back, *needing* more contact. Nipping his throat, his jaw, the curve of his shoulder, Jed pulled back. Red was sprawled out against the sheets, pale skin and dark hair and eyes burning with arousal, so fucking gorgeous it hurt. Hovering over him, Jed soothed away his protests with featherlight touches of his lips, teasing his tongue along overheated skin, tasting how much Redford wanted him.

Finally, he settled between Redford's legs, running his hands down Red's sides to hook under his hips, lifting him up. Easing inside of him, Jed caught the long groan, biting his lip. Redford's legs tightened around his hips, gripping him hard, spine arched in a sharp curve as he pressed against him. Jed pressed his forehead against Redford's collarbone as he waited for Redford to adjust, panting against flushed skin. Fuck, it was *torture* to have to wait even a few seconds, but it was worth it.

Jed lifted his head, watching as Redford's expression shifted, settling into the overwhelmed look he always got when he had Jed deep inside of him—like he couldn't quite believe how good it was. Redford shifted his hips a fraction, making Jed groan at even the slight friction.

Redford nodded shakily then, running a hand over Jed's back, moving his hips up again. "Jed," Redford murmured, the word catching on a moan as he moved at a good angle, pushing Jed's cock over Redford's prostate. It felt like every muscle in their bodies was held tense and tight, waiting, trembling in need which only grew stronger when Jed started to move.

It was like magic. Jed hadn't ever believed in fairy tales, in happy endings, in any of that crap. This, though, this was every good thing in the world, this was *perfection,* and it was enough to push a little hope of fairy godmothers and prince charmings. Jed buried his face into Redford's neck, muffling long groans that seemed to shake him down to his core.

"So good," he managed in a pant, raising his head to kiss Redford. It really was more of a messy grasp, a desperate need to be closer, but Jed couldn't ever bear to let even the smallest bit of distance get between them. Especially not now.

Redford was the first person he'd ever done this with. Oh, he'd had a lot of sex in his life, with a lot of different men. Honestly, when he'd met Red, he'd pretty much assumed nothing could surprise him anymore. But *this,* sinking himself into Redford, feeling his body move in response, it was something absolutely incredible. Red was his first, his only, the only one he'd ever want. "I'm yours," he mumbled, catching Redford again in a hard kiss, hips moving faster now. Friction was sending little dazing pops of heat all along his body, and Jed was desperate for more.

Redford's arms were around his shoulders, his legs around Jed's hips, holding on tight as their movements grew harder, need driving them faster, pushing them inches along the mattress until Redford had to throw an arm out to brace against the headboard with a breathless laugh. "Mine," he agreed roughly, arousal making it impossible to form more than one word at a time. "Yours."

The whistle was probably digging an indent into Jed's chest, but he didn't care—all that was important was moving deeper into Redford, feeling Redford's body shake around him with every thrust. Soon, like he always did, Redford's every exhalation was ended with a whimpered moan, a whisper of Jed's name, a plea for more. For someone who was so quiet and hesitant, Redford was *loud* in bed, and every time it started it

278

made Jed grin with utter determination to make Red reach new auditory heights.

Snapping his hips upward, Jed grinned widely at the long howl of need he drew out of Redford. With a growl, Redford bit his neck, sucking hard enough that Jed knew he'd be sporting a huge bruise later. It didn't matter, though. The pain of it shot straight through him, mingling with the overwhelming jolts of pleasure, making Jed almost dizzy with how *good* it all was.

With both of them so keyed up on adrenaline, it didn't surprise Jed when he spotted the signs of Redford's orgasm approaching. Then again, maybe he was just that damn good. Smirking as he nudged their foreheads together, Jed hitched Redford's legs up over his shoulders, his ears getting bumped with Red's knees with every thrust. "Come on, baby," he groaned, angling the next thrust deeper, bracing himself against the mattress. "Jesus, Red, you're so fucking good. Come for me, sweetheart. I want to watch you."

Redford had occasionally mentioned that just hearing Jed's voice was enough to tip him over—now his fingers dug bruises into Jed's shoulders as he came, panting heavily, gripping him tighter. Jed could hear his own name on Redford's lips, pleas mixed with moans. Drawing it out, Jed's thrusts turned slower, deeper, Redford's almost silent whimpers driving him absolutely crazy. There was nothing sexier in this world than Redford like this, his skin all flushed and slick with sweat, his hair in disarray, lips swollen and parted as he gasped in short, scattered breaths. God, he wanted to see this every day for the rest of his goddamn life.

It started as a tight coil in his stomach, as a shake in his legs. He felt it in every muscle, like he was wound up tight, like he was pressed further and further until he was almost mindless with the need. Face tucked into Redford's neck, Jed moaned loudly, hips rocking forward, desperate for just a little more—for the heated friction, for the way Redford's body was holding him close. Coming with a gasp, Jed shook from the wave of pleasure, from the way it picked him up and spun him around until all he knew was the blaze of it. Sagging down, heaving in long breaths, Jed managed to shift himself so he was only half crushing Redford. "Fucking hell."

Redford seemed reluctant to let him go, arms and legs still wrapped around him. "Uh-huh. Fucking hell," Redford agreed fuzzily, pushing his face against Jed's chest. Jed's fingers combed the hair out of Redford's eyes, and he found he couldn't resist kissing him, slow and gentle, smiling so hard his cheeks ached.

"You are perfect," he murmured, absently tucking Red's hair behind his ears. "God, I want to spend every day just like this."

Redford lifted his head to smile at Jed, eyes half-closed in pleasurable exhaustion. "I like that idea," he replied, nudging his nose against Jed's.

"Then it's a deal." Jed stretched, rolling them over, Redford sprawled out on top of him. "You and me. And sex. Every day. Promise?"

"Promise." Redford rubbed his cheek against Jed's chest with a contented little sigh. He curled up on top of Jed, seeking as much contact as he could get. "What about our jobs? If we are going to have sex every day we might have to work less."

Every ache and pain of the day was settling in now, underneath the after-burn of really fucking good sex. Yawning so hard his jaw cracked, Jed just soothed it all away with the warmth of Redford's body, trailing his fingers absently up and down the other man's spine. "Good. We'll work less. All work and no deep dicking makes Jed a very dull boy."

Laughing quietly, Redford just arched an eyebrow at him. "You could never be dull."

"That's because your cock is big enough to go really deep," Jed returned with a wide grin, ducking when Redford playfully batted at his head. Catching his hand, Jed brought his fingertips up for a kiss, trailing his lips against each one. "And because you make me that way." A more somber tone worked its way into Jed's voice. He held Redford's eyes, their hands resting over his heart, the cool metal of Redford's necklace caught between them. "Seriously, Red. You make me."

"You too," Redford replied softly, leaning down to press a kiss to the back of Jed's hand. "I wasn't a real person until you found me."

A smile teased up one corner of Jed's mouth. "You're my blue fairy."

Redford, once again, just looked utterly perplexed. "I'm a werewolf. And not blue."

Rolling his eyes, Jed arched his neck up to kiss away the furrows in Redford's forehead. "Nah, I mean like that story, about the boy with a wood problem and the old guy. You know, the whale and the lying and the little bug?" Redford looked even more confused. Jed sighed heavily. "Anyway, the blue fairy, she came and made the guy real. He was just, you know, *nothing* until she got all sparkly and magic shit happened. You're like my non-sparkly, non-blue blue fairy."

"Oh." Slowly, the confused look vanished, to be replaced with a pleased little smile. "That wasn't in the encyclopedias my grandmother kept around. I like that story."

As always, any mention of Redford's dearly departed bitch of a grandmother made Jed wish for the ability to raise the dead, just so he'd have the pleasure of killing her again. The simple smile on Redford's face, though, made it difficult to wallow. Jed just shook his head, wrapping his arms around Redford and hauling him in even closer, resting his forehead against Redford's shoulder. "Yeah, well, stick around, Fido," he mumbled. "I think the happily ever after shit happens next, and I hear it's the best part."

"Good. I like the sound of that." Shifting to one side, Redford settled into the curve of Jed's side, one arm thrown over his waist. They curled up together, warm and content and yeah, he'd say it. Happy. He was fucking *happy*.

281

CHAPTER
13

David

IT WASN'T that David was unfamiliar with violence. Sometimes it felt like that was everything he was anymore, as if the metamorphosis that had transformed him from merely human into something so much more had also steeped him in blood so deep he could never quite be free of it. A particularly morbid line of thought, really, and one he didn't usually indulge himself in. But that night, feeling the sun's rays creep ever upward, stealing the gray sanctuary of darkness from the streets, David *felt* it. Deep in his bones he felt it, in every inch of his skin. He'd been born out of violence—the final cry, the death rattle, the last blood—and maybe, really, he couldn't ever escape it.

The water from the shower had long since turned cold. It hardly mattered. David stood under it, the spray beating against the dried blood on his skin, too caught up in his own mind to bother actively washing it away. Every snap of bone, every rip and bite and tear, every churning moment played itself out again and again. David felt like he was coiled too tight, a string stretched taut and quivering.

For the first time in a decade, he'd lost himself. It had only been for an hour, two at most, but David had been gone.

Violence was the first part of the hunt, the very tip of the bite. He'd been taught that almost from the moment Gabriel had turned him. Pain meant pleasure, fight meant food, and blood was sweetest when it was taken. When it was won.

Shuddering, David finally turned off the shower. His skin had been beaten clean, a rust red ring around the drain the only remaining evidence of what he'd come home with. But he felt lost. *Cold.* He remembered this from before, waking up dazed, trying to piece together what he'd done.

Gabriel called it the Vampire's Haze, the sweet spot wherein the only thing that mattered was violence and blood. He'd loved waking David up from it in bed, until David hardly knew what to do with himself when he was left alone instead of finding Gabriel over him, watching for that first burst of lust and recognition in David's eyes.

He shook off the memories, stoically drying himself off. Gabriel wasn't going to reach him. Not here, not now. After all this time, David had to be more than that blood whore, begging for his next bite. He *was* more.

"David?" Victor's voice came from the doorway of the bathroom. The other man was leaning there, arms folded, watching David carefully. Such a serious little thing was Victor, all furrowed brow and proper clothes and hair just a bit out of place.

"I'm fine." Turning away from Victor, David slung the towel around his hips, wiping the condensation off the mirror and fussing around with his toothbrush. "Did we get everyone out?"

"You don't remember?" Victor moved forward, reaching out. David ducked his shoulder away from Victor's hand, dropping the toothpaste in his haste.

Slowly, he dared to glance over at Victor. "It's kind of a blur," he mumbled, scrubbing his face with both hands. He felt a featherlight touch then, fingers sliding up his arms, the warm exhale of Victor's breath against his skin. Groaning, David shook his head. "It's a bad idea, Vickie. I can't—"

"It's okay," Victor murmured. David shivered as he felt the soft brush of lips along the curve of his shoulder. "You know I trust you. We don't have to have this conversation every time."

It was different this time. David could feel it under his skin, boiling in the back of his mind. It wasn't just hunger now. Every instinct in him was awake and trying desperately to shake off the leash.

But *God*, Victor smelled good. And he was warm and sweet and there, willing. David leaned forward even as he murmured, "I think we shouldn't do this."

"I think you need to feel something other than Gabriel," Victor responded lowly.

Jerking away at the mention of his sire, David scowled and shook his head. "Don't—"

283

"We can end him." Victor followed David out into the bedroom, a stubborn set to his jaw. "David, we're here now. We have the opportunity. We should take it."

"I thought you said Gabe wasn't behind the kidnappings," David retorted, grabbing some pants and pulling them on, movements jerky, fingers trembling.

They were stilled by Victor's hand covering his own. "Maybe not these." Victor moved in front of David, a resolute hardness in his usually soft face. "But he has before. I dare say he will again. If my visions are to be averted, the best chance you have is to take Gabe out now."

David didn't want to figure out why the thought of killing Gabe made him feel sick, why he had to restrain the urge to shake Victor's hand off and run to protect his sire. It was just some leftover twisted mind games shit, just a ghost in the machine. He had nothing to do with Gabriel now. He never wanted to be part of that world ever again.

"Why the sudden change of heart?"

Victor hesitated, standing and going over to their closet. He pulled out a blue shirt and handed it to David silently. "All those people we rescued had dark hair. Dark eyes. They resembled you, David."

David turned away to pull on the shirt, concealing a faint shudder with the movement. He had to concentrate on the buttons, on making sure everything was on straight.

"That was you, once." Victor's hands were on his shoulders, smoothing down his back. "I think we'd be remiss not to take out the second threat while we're here."

A sharp nod was the only response David could give. He closed his eyes, struggling against the tightness in his throat, the way he felt like he was drowning, piece by piece. To live in a world where Gabriel didn't exist—how could he even begin to fathom it? Gabe had been *everything* for so long that David couldn't even remember who he'd been before. Even now, in the midst of his rebellion, Gabriel colored his thoughts, dogged his actions. The struggle to be apart seemed to make the man even more of a fixture in his mind.

"How?" he finally asked, turning to look at Victor.

"I have a plan."

"PRINCESS, that is the stupidest goddamn plan I've ever heard in my life."

They'd gathered in the living space, calling Jed and Redford from whatever hedonistic celebration Jed had cooked up. Neither one looked particularly happy about it, although Redford had gotten a strangely intent look when Victor had mentioned going after Gabriel. Even Jed hadn't argued too much. Although, apparently, he did not agree with Victor's ideas.

David was sitting on the couch, hands tightly folded, fingers laced together like it was holding him together. There was a weird disconnect in his brain, buzzing there. If he didn't sit very still, if he didn't try his damnedest not to notice how Victor's pulse picked up when all eyes were on him, or how Jed smelled like he'd go down fighting, blood sweet with anger and fear, David would fly apart at the seams.

"I suppose *you* have a better plan, then?" Victor said archly, arms folded across his chest. "Running in blindly and exploding something won't work here, Jed. Gabriel is nothing like those two-bit vampires you killed earlier. Gabriel's *clan* is nothing like them."

"I bet they'd be just as dead, though," Jed grumbled, folding his arms. One of his legs was hooked over Redford's, their shoulders budged tightly together. David didn't like the smell of Redford right then; his scent was too wild, was too *wolfish*. Too much effort.

Jed glanced over toward Redford. "What do you think, Fido?"

"I think walking right up to Gabriel is kind of crazy," Redford admitted. "But it could work."

"Gabriel is so arrogant that he'd *let* us walk right into his house," Victor explained. "We know where he is. We have a rough estimate of how many vampires he has with him. We corner him, alone, in a private room, and we deal with him."

Jed tipped his head back and frowned at the ceiling, drumming his fingers against Redford's knee. It was his "thinking face." David was just amazed he didn't see smoke. "So Red and I go bust up the bloodsuckers' party and kill David's leather daddy?" A slow smirk crossed Jed's face. "Fine. But it'll cost ya."

David stood up abruptly, walking away from the group. From the whole goddamn conversation. They were bantering about killing Gabriel like it was *nothing*. As if he was just another job, just some trash to be cleaned up on their way out of town.

Victor gave Jed a withering look. "I'll pay you. But take note that I am a new professor in a middle-of-the-road college. How much do you really think I could offer you as a fee?"

"Don't care. It'll cost you twice as much." Jed grinned. "Two of us means double the fee. We're a team." With a snort, his smile turned positively Cheshire. "Besides, you drink tea that doesn't come from the grocery store, and your suits are tailored—nothing that ugly comes off the rack. Don't pretend you're in abject poverty, here."

"Jed, we don't need—" Redford tried to protest.

"Fine." Victor looked like he wished his eyes could kill. "Do you want it now, or later?"

"Standard methods." Jed shrugged. "Half now, half when it's done."

David couldn't listen to this anymore. He stalked out of the room, slamming the bedroom door behind him. Pacing back and forth, each step only building up the tense knot in his gut, David crossed his arms tightly across his chest. Gabe dying was a good thing; he knew that. *Intellectually* he understood that it was necessary. All he could think of, though, was the first time he'd seen Gabriel, the man picking him out of a crowd, smiling at him like David was actually something special.

You're going to become something extraordinary, my sweet boy. Just you wait and see.

The first time they'd kissed, a hot tangle of tongues and lips and the sharp catch of Gabriel's fang. How David had felt *alive* for the first time. He'd walked home in a dream. He'd barely recognized the streets he'd grown up on, the people he'd known all his life. Nothing had compared to the magic and wonder that Gabriel had opened him up to.

He barely heard Jed's scandalized tones from the next room, exclaiming, "Just how fucking rich *are you*?" It trailed off into cursing, and the door opened with a soft click, closing behind Victor.

"David?" Victor didn't try to touch him this time. He just tracked David's pacing. "I apologize. Framing everything like a business transaction, I think, is the only way Jed will do anything."

The first time Gabriel had bitten him, David had cried afterward. It wasn't the pain. It was that the bite had ended. All David had been able to think, while Gabe held him close, while those beautiful fangs were so deep in his throat, was that he didn't ever want it to stop. Just for those few moments, Gabe had needed *him*. He had been the only thing in the world for the older vampire.

"I know." Swallowing hard, David came to a halt in the middle of the room. He looked helpless, on edge, rubbing his fingertips along the two whitened scars on the side of his neck. "I know."

When he'd been turned, Gabriel had sat by his side. He'd held his hand. When David woke up, when he'd been reborn, that had been the first thing he'd felt—strong fingers gripping his own, guiding him back to life.

Victor moved forward, his own hands fluttering uselessly. "David, if you *truly* don't want Gabriel dead, then we'll call this whole thing off," he admitted. "He's dangerous, but you're my primary concern in this."

Shaking his head, David found he was gnawing on the inside of his cheek. Christ, he hadn't done that since—

Stand up straight, darling boy, and for God's sake, what are you doing? None of this, no biting your cheek, no hiding in the back. You are a glory, my David, you are a star. Never let anyone tell you different. Would I bother with you if you were anything less?

"No, it's good," he muttered hoarsely, closing his eyes. It was good. Gabriel was only going to keep going. He'd draw other people in. He'd do to them what he'd done to David. He should be stopped.

He caught Victor's nod out of the corner of his eye. Not usually one to remain so quiet, Victor sat silently on the edge of the bed, not saying anything else. His goal, presumably, was to provide David with company that didn't insist upon talking about his feelings.

David didn't want that. He wanted to bite. He wanted to feel blood, *real* blood, coursing through him. He wanted what Gabriel offered him, what his body still craved, even after all this time. With a frustrated noise, David walked away, bound by the faint sunlight sparkling against the rug, seeping in under the curtains. He couldn't leave. He *really* should leave.

The next time he stalked past the bed, Victor caught the edge of his sleeve, fingertips lightly pressed against the inside of David's wrist. "Can I do anything to help?"

Yes, David thought. So much.

See them struggle, David? Watch how much they want it, even as they try to get away. The fear makes them sweeter. Now drink. Take. It is your right.

Staring down at Victor's hand, David gritted his teeth. He was out of cow's blood. Although it probably wouldn't have helped.

"You should go," David told him, pulling away. It was harder than it should be, to step back, to not seduce and enthrall and take. His hands were shaking. David stared at them, like they weren't even a part of his own body, while he mumbled, "Go. Leave me alone."

"I'm not going to leave you alone, David," Victor replied quietly. "If I do, you'll just sit and think about Gabriel too much."

"If you stay," David half laughed, the sound breaking and shattering around him like glass, "I'm going to stop resisting."

"David." Victor stood, walking closer again, reaching out to take David's hand and holding tight. Every beat of his heart was like a siren's call, the soft, pale skin David had tasted so many times almost impossible to withstand. "It's okay. Maybe you *need* to stop resisting and channel that want into something positive." He smiled faintly, bemused at his own words. "I know that sounds rather New Age."

Snorting quietly, David did manage a quick smile in return, the expression barely touching the corners of his lips. "Positive, huh?" He could do that. He could drown out Gabe's voice in his head, the backslide into absolute violence. Steeling himself, he reached out, gentling his hand down Victor's cheek. "No blood," he murmured, a frown creasing his forehead. He'd never had sex without blood. But maybe he could try. Maybe it was time to start.

"I'm not expecting it to be easy for you," Victor replied. "But... if we kill Gabriel, you could start moving on." He reached up to clasp David's hand, holding it against his cheek.

Making a decision, David moved forward, lightly pressing Victor backward until they hit the wall. "I don't want to talk about Gabriel," he said lowly, ducking his head to catch Victor's lips in a hard kiss. He could focus on this. On Victor. There didn't have to be blood or the ghosts of his past. Surely, if he was as separate as he claimed to be, he could stop acting like Gabriel had taught him to.

Like always, Victor met him happily in the kiss, giving as good as he got. Victor kissed with his whole body, moving close, gripping David's shoulders to pull them tighter together. "Just try to take that want for blood and translate it into something else," Victor whispered.

Nodding, David pressed his forehead against Victor's, resting it there for a moment. All that hunger that was so insistent, all the noise in his head, he tried to find someplace else to put it. Some other way to sate it. His hands ran down Victor's body, gripping under his thighs and pulling him close, lifting him to turn them around. In a few steps, he had landed them on the bed, with David hovering over Victor. Desperate kisses trailed from his lips, down his chin, and David ripped open Victor's shirt in his haste to get to even more skin. Any protest the man might have given about his shirt was discarded when Victor decided that kissing was the much more favorable option.

"You are *far* too clothed," Victor complained, trying to deal with the buttons of David's shirt. When he managed to undo them, Victor sat up, eagerly hooking his fingers around David's belt, gently closing his teeth over David's collarbone.

The bite made him arch upward, his whole body responding. David had to muffle the moan, had to hold himself back from returning in kind. No biting. *God*, no biting, he wasn't an animal. He could do this.

Shucking off his pants, David went for Victor's. His fingers fumbled through getting them off, finally managing and shoving them down Victor's hips. His mouth was restless, moving over every inch of Victor's skin, David trying to get his fill by the taste of him, the way he'd shiver under each kiss. There was almost none of his usual grace in his movements, none of the fluidity that had made this always feel like a dance. Now David stumbled, he clumsily kissed, he rolled them over and nearly fell off the bed. All his concentration was on refusing his instincts, on being, for once, more than what he'd been made.

Victor looked like he was tempering a smile at the clumsiness. With light touches, he eased David back into it, guided him into focusing on the physical. He ran a hand down David's chest, fingertips brushing lightly over his cock, back up again. Closing his eyes, David tried to center himself. He concentrated on the way Victor's fingers felt, the cool strokes against overheated skin. With a quiet moan he arched up into the light touches, seeking more.

As Victor kissed his way down David's chest, David realized that Victor was talking lowly—some ancient, dead language that he didn't recognize right away, but it was another anchor. Something else that he could force his senses to focus on, touch and sound attempting to overcome the gnawing hunger in the pit of his stomach.

His hands went to rest on Victor's shoulders, painting a trail down his arms and back up again. If he could just forget everything but Victor's warmth, but the way his lips and tongue were moving along his chest, then maybe it would be okay. "More," David murmured restlessly, a flicker of a frown creasing his forehead. He could feel Victor's heartbeat speed up at the demand, and David tried to drown it out with another kiss.

Breaking away, Victor watched David for a moment—perhaps gauging where his state of mind was at—before ducking down, pressing his lips to the base of David's cock. In any other situation he'd be going fast, but now he took his time, each movement of his lips and tongue designed to draw David's attention away from blood. He settled himself in between David's legs, getting comfortable, looking rather content as he gently drew the tip of David's cock between his lips, sucking lightly, one hand roaming over David's hips.

Glancing down at him, all smugness and mussed hair, and those brilliant blue eyes so focused on his task, David just gripped the sheets and struggled to not insistently move. "Horrible tease," he muttered, head falling back, biting his lip. Yes, this was good. This wasn't about blood or feeding or pain. The rush of arousal was drowning out Gabriel's voice in his head. He could do this.

His plan not to be insistent was put to the test when Victor grasped his hips, lifting them slightly, coaxing him to move. Though Victor wasn't meeting his eyes, he was looking upward at David's face, a smile dawning at the edge of his expression. He broke away from David's cock to say, "Move, David. I want you to," before ducking down again, tongue trailing over David's cock again and taking him in.

The heat of Victor's mouth, the soft play of his tongue, the way his cheeks would hollow out as David rolled his hips upward, all of it was *perfect*. One hand made its way into Victor's hair as David moaned, the noise rumbling in his chest, caught between his lips. His whole body was one long curved bow, trembling there, hovering in some wild state of pleasure.

If he could taste Victor, even a little, that would make this so much better. It would be the last thing he needed, the final wave of pleasure to push him over. David whimpered, needy and hungry, toes curling into the mattress. "Please," he begged, almost a sob of sound. "God, *please*."

Victor's gaze flicked up at him again, but instead of moving to bare his neck, he stayed right where he was. Dimly, David could recognize that

Victor was pulling out all the tricks he knew, all the knowledge of what David liked after getting so familiar with his body. He was going right for that spot just beneath the head of David's cock, rubbing his tongue against it, moving a hand downward to brush his thumb, far too lightly, over David's hole. It was instinctive to spread his legs wider for Victor, words lost in a rush of moaning pleas.

The hunger retreated again under the new sensations. It was a delicate balance he was toying with, wavering between pleasure and instincts. Every touch made him want blood more, made it something he *needed*. But the desire Victor was drawing out of him was overlapping the want to bite, until David felt strung out on both, barely aware of anything but Victor's touch, but the way he smelled, the thrum of his pulse under pale skin.

He heard the sound of a bottle of lube being opened. Then, hazily, some minutes later, after tongue and lips vanished, Victor was rising up, and David's world narrowed down to the sensation of Victor sinking down on him. Victor braced his hands on David's chest, lip pulled between his teeth as he slowly settled on David's hips.

Staring up at him, David just gripped Victor's legs, holding them both still. Victor was so tight it was almost impossible for David to think about anything else, to even notice the way the vein in his neck, the one under two round scars, throbbed with every moan.

Immediately slamming his eyes shut, David gritted his teeth and tried to focus. Victor. He was with Victor. Hunger didn't matter, instincts didn't matter, because he was better than that. Please, God, let him be better.

Victor started moving, slow rocks of his hips, just back and forward at first, one of his hands sweeping up David's chest to cup his jaw. "Open your eyes," he coaxed, his voice rough with need. "Sight is another sense. It will help."

Grasping Victor's hand, David obeyed. Victor's body was flushed, beautiful as he rode David. So completely unlike the tweed suits and stuffy books he hid himself behind. Jaw tight, he watched as Victor moved, rolling upward to meet him, every jolt of pleasure grounding them together.

He could feel the blood rushing, though, in the veins of Victor's wrist. They were pressed against his cheek, so close he could smell the arousal in every heartbeat. David's fingers tightened, his eyes flashing yellow as he turned his head, as he traced his tongue around the soft dip of Victor's wrist. Christ, he was so sweet.

The hand was slowly drawn away, going back to David's chest, and David tried to curb the displeased growl that wanted to make its way past his lips. Again, he tried to force his focus back to the arousal, to the way that Victor was riding him harder now, faster, gripping him tight. But at the end of every thought, his eyes went back to the pulse beating in Victor's throat, the rush of blood quickened in need.

He'd never been able to come without blood. To feel any kind of satisfaction without feeding. Every push of arousal only made him *want* so much more. "Victor," he moaned, reaching up for him, gripping his hand, his arm. David didn't know if he wanted to pull him closer or push him away. He wound up caught in some horrible in-between, almost sobbing with how much he needed it, how much he hated himself for being so weak. All he wanted was to sink into Victor, to forget everything else, but Gabriel's voice was still in his ear, all those lessons still drove him. "I can't," he groaned, eyes falling shut again. "God, I can't."

He was addicted. He *needed* blood—and until that moment, he hadn't realized how much Victor was addicted too.

Victor's hands were on his shoulders, prompting David to sit up. Settled on David's lap, still so tight around him, Victor made a despairing noise. "David, just—" His voice broke off, warring with himself. Then, so slowly, Victor tilted his head forward, pressing his forehead against David's temple. "I can't finish *without* you taking blood." Victor gave a weak laugh, his hand wrapping around the back of David's neck, encouraging him. "Just… try to take less than usual, perhaps. Try to focus on the arousal still."

Licking his lips nervously, David glanced at Victor's face, half hidden in the shadows of the room. He'd never thought about Victor's side of things. Vampires could make the act of feeding extremely pleasurable, even without bonding. He'd always wanted Victor to feel good, even when he was giving in to his weaker side. "I'm sorry," he murmured. Apparently this was what happened.

David's eyes dropped to the tempting curve of Victor's neck. Arms wrapping around Victor, fingers digging into the muscles of his back, David braced himself. He wouldn't take much. Just a sip. That was all he wanted—a taste.

With a low growl of need, he lunged forward, fangs sinking deeply into Victor's throat.

They moved together, every pull echoing in the thrust of David's hips, in the gasps and moans that Victor was spilling out. All it'd taken was a drop on David's tongue, a sweet bloom of blood that coursed through him, and he was gone. It raced through his body, each mouthful filling him up, making him *live*. How had he gone this long without this? Gabriel was right. He'd always been right. Denying himself was only making him weak.

They wound up with Victor on his back, David sprawled over him, pinning him down as he drank deeper. There was nothing else, nothing in the world except the spicy, intoxicating taste of him, the way the warmth was pooling in David's gut, spreading through him, tingling just under his skin. God, he needed this. He *craved* it. Victor was moving a hand over his back, gripping his shoulder, still encouraging him. His grip turned tighter, briefly, like he was thinking about shoving David away, but it relaxed again, urging David on further.

It wasn't about sex. Maybe it never had been, not with Gabriel, not any time since. It was about *this*. Victor giving himself to David, David filling himself up with all the life and warmth that had once been Victor's. David sank his fangs in deeper still. He knew, in some distant part of his brain, that he was taking more than he ever had before. With Victor he'd always been so goddamn careful.

Victor was supposed to be his redemption. He was the opposite of everything David had come from, and he was supposed to save him.

And Victor wasn't stopping him.

It had been a decade since David had drunk so much, had felt so awake and aware. This was what it meant to be a vampire, what it was to be *himself*. No slinking around, begging from butchers, no cold dead blood that he hadn't felt pull from the body itself. He was strong like this, with blood streaking down his chin, pooling in the dip of Victor's collarbones. Bracing himself, David gripped a hand through Victor's hair, tilting his head further to the side so he could get more, could take as much as he was given.

Out of the corner of his eye, he could see Victor's expression change. He looked so peaceful, so content—then, suddenly, his eyes flew open. "David," he tried, his voice barely even a whisper. "David, we need to stop." But he still wasn't pushing David away. His grasp was still encouraging, still smoothing over David's back as he said the words.

Very slowly, like he was having to force himself to do it, Victor's hand moved underneath the pillow. David didn't take notice of it.

Not until the holy water splashed into his eyes.

David jerked back with a hiss, blood smeared around his lips, eyes wild and blazing. That was when the full force of a hundred pound wolf smashed through the door and barreled into his chest. David was knocked to the floor, struggling against Redford's jaws clamped around his shoulder. His whole face felt like it was burning, and he howled in agony as he was dragged away from the bed, away from his prey, *his* blood.

Away from Victor.

Blinking, feeling like he was forcing his head above the water again, David looked around him, dazed. "Victor?" Oh, God, what had he done? What just happened? "Where—is he all right?"

Redford snarled at him, thumping two huge paws into his back to keep David on the ground. Victor's voice floated from the bedroom. "I'm quite all right. I'm so sorry about the holy water." He sounded hazy, not quite there. Fading fast. The smell of far too much blood was thick in the air.

Face pressed to the carpet, David didn't try to struggle anymore. He could feel how much he'd taken. He could smell it, just as well as Redford could. He'd drained Victor almost dry. After everything, after all that misplaced trust, after *trying*, it hadn't mattered. He'd still turned into the monster. At the end of the day, that really was all he could be.

David watched Jed wrap Victor in a blanket and heft the man up, barking orders at Redford. The words didn't matter. David was too busy watching the swing of a limp hand from the bundle in Jed's arms, Victor's watch glinting in the dim light. Then they were gone, leaving David on the floor with a werewolf, staring at the closed door.

The heavy weight on his back lifted, and a cold nose was shoved against his shoulder. David was hardly an expert on werewolf expressions, but he could almost swear that Redford looked concerned for him too. "I didn't mean—" David choked off the words, shaking his head and closing his eyes. "Please, just go make sure he's okay."

Redford retreated, though he never turned his back to David, backing carefully away from him. Who would have thought that the innocent werewolf would figure things out faster than Victor? Better to treat David like a dangerous animal; apparently, he couldn't be anything else. Redford vanished and within the minute came out of the bedroom again, human and fully clothed, giving David a glance before he went out the door.

The sun was blazing in, faint curls of it showing under the heavy drapes. Curling himself into a ball in the corner of the room, David watched the light move. He'd told Gabriel he didn't belong to him anymore. For ten years, he'd pretended it was true.

All it had taken was a single week of stress and confronting his past for that to break.

CHAPTER
14

Redford

THE waiting room of a hospital, Redford discovered, smelled *terrible*.

Since neither he nor Jed were Victor's family, they resigned themselves to waiting. There were small children, injured adults, sick people, dying people. Redford seriously began to think about waiting outside. At least then he'd only have to deal with the pack of smokers loitering outside, and cigarette smoke was surely better than the scents of chemicals and sickness.

Jed's boot was beating a rapid pace against the floor. There was still some dried blood on his shirt, but he seemed not to notice it in favor of casting longing glances toward the exit.

"How do you think he is?" Redford glanced down at Jed's foot, knocking his own against it to stop the tapping. "He lost a lot of blood."

The last he'd seen of Victor was the man being wheeled into the corridor beyond the waiting room. He'd been strangely euphoric. When Victor had broken into laughter over something, Redford had been vaguely disturbed. He hadn't thought that nearly dying would be anything approaching amusing.

"Beats me," Jed grunted in reply. He'd moved on to tapping his fingers against the plastic chair arm. "What was David doing when you left?"

Redford gave a vague shrug, a small shift of one shoulder. "I don't know," he admitted. "He seemed upset, I think. He wanted me to check that Victor was okay."

Redford didn't really want to know what had happened in that bedroom. He could take a guess, and that guess wasn't something he wanted to linger on for very long.

Jed's second replying grunt wasn't very informative, so Redford fell silent, going back to watching the doors. There was no way he'd be able to see Victor through them, but he kept looking nonetheless. Just in case.

There was a clock on the wall, but Redford studiously avoided looking at it. Time already felt like it was traveling slowly; he didn't want to have hard evidence of it. It felt like a few hours when a doctor came out, informing them that Victor was getting transfusions, but other than that he was in fine shape. Jed talked circles around the doctor in order to avoid getting questioned about the "animal bite," and with the knowledge that Victor would be able to leave the hospital in half a day, Jed and Redford left.

SIX hours, four stacks of pancakes, and countless beers later, they caught a taxi back to the hospital, where they collected Victor.

Victor, Redford thought, did not look good. To help him out of the hospital, they were allowed into his room, one shared with three other people. Redford was just trying not to breathe through his nose.

"Christ Almighty, *finally*," Victor grumbled, pushing the blankets off of him. He shot Jed a glower before Jed could even think about commenting on the hospital gown. "Where are my clothes? I need to get out of this hospital as quickly as possible. I abhor hospitals."

Jed, however, was not on board with the plan of letting Victor get his pants back. Leering quite openly, Jed cocked his head and watched as Victor flounced around the room, his eyes very obviously below the waist. The hospital gown was open in the back, and Victor had been naked under the sweats Jed had pulled on him on the way out the door. It was a view that Jed was obviously appreciating.

"Oh, no," Jed drawled, lips curving up into a smirk, "I seem to have dropped my pen onto the floor." He tossed a pen out of his pocket in front of Victor. "Vickie, be a sweetheart, bend over and get that for me?"

Victor wasn't amused. "Jed," he seethed, "Give me my trousers."

Pouting, Jed gave a long-suffering sigh. "Oh, come on, have a heart. What about my pen?"

"You can bloody well pick it up yourself." Victor scowled, turning his back on Jed. He apparently forgot, temporarily, that the gown was backless. Jed had not, as evidenced by the large grin that spread across his face.

He did pick up the pen, though. He also very gently used the tip of it to pull up the hem of Victor's gown and peer under it, laughing when he was batted away. "I think David sucked all the fun out of you too, Vickie." Sprawling out on the bed, Jed bounced a few times, testing it. "Oh, babe, come check this shit out. It *reclines*." Waggling his eyebrows at Redford, Jed patted the mattress next to him. "What say we give the good professor a demonstration?"

Redford sighed faintly. Jed was obviously going over the top to avoid talking about what had happened. Victor seemed fine with it, though. Maybe he didn't want to talk about it either.

"The sooner you give me my trousers, the sooner I can get out of here." Victor snatched the sweats out of Jed's hands, giving him a glower for good measure as he tugged them on. "Did anything happen while I was gone?"

"I found the only spot in Cairo that sells both pancakes *and* beer at ten in the fucking morning." Jed grinned. "Who needs maple syrup when you have half-flat, warm piss beer?"

"Who indeed," Victor replied dryly. He gratefully took the jacket that Redford handed to him, seemingly not noticing that he was now dressed in sweats and a tweed jacket, a bandage with bloody spots on it wrapped around his neck. "Now, can we get out of here, please?"

Out of the corner of his eye, Redford could see the manic grin slip a little from Jed's face. It wasn't too difficult for him to guess why. *Getting out of here* translated to *going back to the hotel*. The hotel where David was, where the room still stank of blood and sex and Victor's fear. David's despair. No, Redford wasn't looking forward to walking back into that again either, especially not with Victor in tow. The man still looked so pale, dark circles underscoring his eyes, the bandage a vivid reminder of what had taken place, even if Victor seemed to be pretending that nothing worrisome had happened.

But Jed didn't vocalize any of his worries. He just took the opportunity to grope Redford's ass as he walked past—and Victor's too, though he winked at Redford as he did so, smirking at Victor's indignant squawk— and hustled them all out the door. "Come on. We'll get a cab back."

Redford was glad to be getting out of the hospital too. He breathed through his mouth again as they navigated their way through the myriad hallways, each more confusing than the last. Relying on Jed to get them through the maze, he paused when a new scent hit his nose, right about the same time that Victor stopped in front of the open door of a room.

"Jed, hold on a second," Victor murmured, an odd look on his face as he withdrew the battered glasses from his jacket pocket. "Recognize him? That's Randall Lewis."

Peering inside the room, Redford looked at the man lying on the bed. He looked like he was trying to sleep but not having very much luck with it. Even with the strong smell of antiseptic and sickness, Redford could still pick out the scent of wolf on the man. Except instead of the jarring scent of werewolf, it was closer to what Filtiarn had smelled like, a more pure, earthy tone.

"I'm just, er, I'm going to say hello," Victor said, fidgeting with the glasses. "From everything we know, the poor man has no family here. He probably needs a friendly face." He glanced at Jed, as if asking for permission.

Huffing out an amused-sounding breath, Jed shrugged. "Fine. Go have happy hand-holding time. I'll check in with the nicely buxom nurses to find out if you need suppositories every hour or whatever the shit and meet you out front." Glancing at Redford, Jed nodded toward Victor. "You watch him, Fido. Make sure he doesn't pass out, 'cause I ain't hauling his pert little ass anywhere."

Victor just shook his head in bemusement as Jed left, and he and Redford walked into the room as quietly as they could. Redford stayed near the doorway, just in case—in case of *what*, he didn't know, but with everything that had happened lately, he was feeling more than a little on edge.

"Mr. Lewis?" Victor spoke softly. "Are you awake?"

"'Mr. Lewis' makes me sound old." The voice that spoke up was soft and worn, sounding exhausted and hoarse. "Call me Randall." The man's face was pale, drawn, but the eyes that looked out from under messy brown hair seemed kind. "I'm sorry, are you with the hospital? Your accent...."

"Er, no," Victor stuttered. He looked around the room to make sure there were no nurses present before whispering, "My associates were the ones that rescued you. I, er, I found your glasses outside. I wanted to return them to you." Victor carefully set the battered glasses down on the table next to Randall's bed.

Slowly, Randall reached out for them. His fingers were trembling as he took them, fumbling them open to slide them onto his face. Though Randall's head bowed as if to hide it, Redford caught the wetness on his cheeks. "You found me?" Randall asked in a very quiet whisper. Clearing his throat, he managed, "Thank you."

Victor attempted a reassuring smile. Redford didn't think he was very good at it. It mostly came out as a pained grimace, the half smile making him rub over the bandage at his throat. "Yes, well, you mostly owe your rescue to my associates. I am glad that we managed to get you all out, though."

Redford shifted, tilting his head to peer out the door into the hallway. There was a nurse coming, maybe not even headed for this room, but this entire place was making Redford feel antsy and a little paranoid. He also didn't like the idea of leaving Jed alone with David. "We should get back," he urged Victor lowly.

Victor looked back at Redford, blinking slowly. "Yes, quite," he replied in a murmur. "Mr. Lewis, is there any way I can help you further? Do you have any family here in Cairo?"

Randall shook his head, forehead creasing as he looked down at his hands, knotted together on top of the pristine white blanket. "No. No, I was here on a research trip for my studies. My brothers…." He took a deep breath and looked up at Victor, reaching out to very lightly grasp his arm before he let his fingers fall away. "You have done more than enough, thank you. I don't want to keep you." Another pause, Randall's hand going up to rub at the bandage around his own neck, a twin to Victor's, keen eyes studying him from under the scratched and slightly bent glasses. "If there's ever anything I can do for you, though, I hope you'll let me. I don't have much, but for what you did, what you saved me from, I won't ever be able to repay you."

"No repayment needed," Victor replied, and Redford definitely detected a smile this time.

"Please," Redford urged. Now he couldn't get his mind off of the idea that Jed could get impatient and go back to the hotel, alone with David. If they didn't hurry, he'd just leave, Redford was *sure* of it, and then God only knew what would happen.

Victor glanced back at him again. "Yes, yes," he sighed, not looking all too happy about the prospect of going back. "Well, I hope to see you again, Mr. Lewis," he said. "It was very nice meeting you."

Much to Redford's relief, Victor turned to leave then, and the hallway was blessedly deserted. No one was staring at them or acting as if they were coming to get them. He really was getting overly paranoid, but after the past few days, Redford figured it was better to err on the side of caution.

"Wait," Randall called after them, and he and Victor turned to see him reaching out, sitting up in his bed. "I don't even know your name."

Victor paused, clearly flustered. "Oh, er." He tugged his glasses off of his nose, cleaning them on the edge of his jacket. It was, Redford recognized, a nervous tic. "Perhaps it'd be safer if you just considered me a concerned citizen."

Hesitating, Randall nodded, a very small smile curling up the edges of his lips. "All right. Well, thank you, whoever you are." Redford grabbed Victor's sleeve and forcibly dragged him out of the room, ignoring Victor's protests. He continued hauling Victor through the seemingly endless hallways of the hospital, aiming for the exit. From there, Redford knew, they'd have to take a taxi to get back to the hotel. He just hoped Jed was still there.

He all but burst through the double doors of the exit, relaxing when the scent of pine and gunpowder hit his nose. Redford led Victor through the people outside, making his way toward Jed and the taxi Jed was holding up. "You're still here," Redford said gratefully.

"Keep your fucking panties on. Jesus Christ, I'm paying you to wait!" Jed pulled his head out of the taxi where he'd been having a very loud discussion with the driver and cocked a grin at Redford. "What? Yeah, of course I am. Where the hell else would I be?"

Redford opened his mouth to explain his worry that Jed might have gotten impatient and gone back, but withheld the words. He nudged his shoulder against Jed's, smiling at him. "Thank you. And sorry we took a while."

Despite having blood transfusions, Victor still looked alarmingly pale in the sunlight. "Can we all get into the taxi now? I need a sit down. My legs feel quite odd."

Hustling them all into the cab, Jed elected to press into the backseat next to Redford, wrapping an arm around his waist and hauling him in close. After they'd pulled out into traffic, Jed nudged a kiss against Redford's ear and whispered, "I'm always going to be waiting for you, babe. Don't you know that yet?"

"I'm beginning to realize that." Redford's smile grew as he leaned into Jed. He stayed that way as the chaotic drive through Cairo's main roads started. Victor, seated on Jed's other side, gradually listed more and more to the left until he was leaning on Jed too. To no one's surprise, Jed seemed perfectly all right with the arrangement.

"So, this Randall kid, he going to be trouble?" Jed asked lowly, shooting a glance up at the driver. "I mean, is he gonna be on Oprah talking about the muscle-bound hero and his giant wolf sidekick who saved them from the bloodsuckers? 'Cause I imagine that might cause some problems."

Victor shook his head tiredly. "I doubt it. If he outs us, he outs himself. He's clearly a wolf of some variation."

Jed issued a long-suffering sigh as he glanced between Redford and Victor. His other arm had gone around Victor as well, to steady the man as they made a sharp right turn. "Wolves, werewolves, bloodsuckers, snake people.... Has my life become a freak convention, or what?" He paused, nose wrinkling. "Does that strike anyone else as odd? I mean, David barely comes near Red, 'specially around full moons. Why would suckers want a furry to munch on?"

"If your life is a freak show, it's because *you* are the star, Jed," Victor replied blandly. With a broad grin, Jed actually laughed at that, pressing a loud, over-the-top kiss to the top of his head and ruffling Victor's hair when the man recoiled violently.

"Very well played, princess, but seriously, anyone else notice an overabundance of the weird and paranormal lately?"

Victor nodded vaguely, looking like he was using all of his energy just to keep his eyes open. "There may be many variations of supernatural creatures, but it is rare that you see vampires and wolves, of any sort, in the same place. Most vampires think of wolves the way we think of domesticated dogs. As in, a little stupid and not on the same level."

A low, irritated growl rumbled in Jed's throat, and he hooked Redford just a little closer in. Redford went gladly. He didn't particularly feel offended by Victor's comment—he'd seen evidence of that school of vampire thought in David. "Well, they're a bunch of panty-sniffing pretty boy suckers, so what the fuck do they know?" Jed scowled.

Victor made a sound that might have been a laugh. "Try telling that to their faces." He paused, seeming to consider Jed and his penchant for overly violent explosions. "On second thought, don't. I think we've had enough bloodshed for today."

By the time they arrived at the hotel, Victor had all but nodded off against Jed's shoulder. With a long-suffering expression, but with a great deal of gentleness, Jed hooked his arms under Victor's body and carried the man up to their room. He paused outside the door, shifting Victor into Redford's arms and pulling out his gun. Tapping lightly on the doorway with the barrel, Jed eased in, holding up a hand to keep Redford outside. "David? You here, buddy? Come out with your fangs in the air."

"Very funny, Jed." The dry voice made Redford jump. David walked out of the bedroom, dressed and put together and looking like nothing had happened. "It's perfectly safe. Tell Redford to stop lurking outside and come in."

Redford didn't consider waiting warily to be "lurking," but he went inside, passing David to carefully lay Victor down on the couch. Victor shifted but didn't appear to wake up. At the sight of him, David went very still, fingers twitching for a moment before he rested them very deliberately on the back of a chair. A chair which he was keeping between himself and the rest of the room.

"Are you okay?" Redford gave David a look, a little concerned.

"Yes, perfectly," David answered airily, waving off the question. "Now, I think—"

Jed plowed him straight into the wall, arm pressed against David's throat, the loud click of his gun being cocked echoing around the room. Pushing the barrel of the gun against David's temple, Jed gave him a frankly terrifying smile. "You almost drained the princess dry, Davie. Look, I like you. We've worked together, and you've only screwed me the normal amount over the years. So I'm trying real hard to give you the benefit of the doubt. But I need to know with a fucking quickness if you've got your shit together enough for you to be here with Redford, because I swear to all the fat little babies in the world, David, I will *end you* if you so much as breathe at him." He paused and then shrugged. "Metaphorically speaking."

Irritated, David shrugged Jed away, smoothing out the front of his shirt. Redford noticed, though, the way his fingers shook before he curled them back against his palms, the way his shoulders sat, tense and wary. "I know," David spat out, that control slipping, just for a moment, the pleasant facade he'd been wearing cracking all around the edges. Softer then, he repeated, "God, I know. I... I didn't mean for it to happen. I slipped."

"You going to do it again?" Jed demanded, expression hard.

David shook his head, looking sick. "No. I swear, I won't."

After a long moment, Jed lowered his gun, reaching out to grasp David's shoulder. "He's gonna be fine," Jed said, moving back toward Victor and carefully taking the man up in his arms again. "But you're sleeping on the goddamn couch, David."

With that, Jed stomped into the bedroom and laid Victor on the bed, gathering David's things and bringing them out into the common room. "I am getting too old for this bullshit," he muttered, stomping his way back across the room and heading to his and Redford's bedroom, where he kicked the bathroom door shut behind him with, "I'm gonna take a shower. I stink like hospital people."

Which left Redford and David alone in the room. Redford shifted awkwardly, trying to decide between checking on Victor or going with Jed. David didn't seem to have anything to say, and he definitely didn't look inclined to go bother Victor, so Redford escaped to his and Jed's bedroom.

The first order of business was getting changed out of his clothes into something that didn't carry the vague scent of blood and sickness. Jed had shut the bathroom door, oddly, so Redford didn't attempt to join him. Instead, he sat himself in a chair next to the bed, looking out the window to the streets outside.

His gaze kept going back to the closed bathroom door. It was highly unusual of Jed to have shut it. In fact, Redford was sure that this was the first time he'd ever seen Jed close a bathroom door. Jed said that he liked to keep it open so he could see out when he showered—just in case someone tried to attack him in his own home, Redford assumed. It was also a permanent invitation for Redford to join him, which Redford took quite frequently.

To have closed the door, Jed must not want to see what was outside. Redford could take a guess as to what it was that Jed wanted to avoid. He'd worked with David for much longer than he'd known Redford. By the time Redford came along, Jed already had dozens of stories about working with the vampire, and recently, some of Jed's opinions about David must have been turned on their head.

Jed was scared.

So Redford took up sentinel outside the bathroom door. He'd make sure that he kept an eye on everything.

He could time Jed's showers down to the minute, usually, but Jed took longer than usual. Redford was just about to knock on the door in concern when Jed came out in a billow of steam and condensation. "You took a while," Redford noted. "I was about to knock and ask if you were okay."

Jed just shrugged, looking a little startled to find Redford so close to the door, tightening the towel around his waist and heading over to the closet. Redford was somewhat shocked that Jed wasn't just walking around naked. "Just, you know. Washing. Had that pesky shampoo in the eyes scenario, but I lived through it." That was a lie, Redford knew. When Jed got shampoo in his eyes, the entire street heard about it.

Jed gave Redford a smile, but it was flat and distracted. Turning back to the dresser, Jed fiddled through the drawer, seemingly unable to make a decision about what he wanted. It wasn't until he pulled the whole drawer *out*, flinging it across the room with a hoarse noise, that it became totally clear that nothing he was looking for actually resided in his haphazardly folded clothing. Redford's quick step to the side barely saved him from being hit in the face with a pair of jeans.

"Jed?" Redford's voice was tentative. "Are you...." It was useless to ask if Jed was *okay* when he clearly wasn't. Instead, Redford stepped closer, putting his hand on Jed's back. "What's wrong?"

"There was this guy, like, three or four years ago, I don't know." Jed seemingly hadn't heard Redford's question, though he could feel Jed's muscles jump under his touch, skin still warm and damp from the shower. "Anyway, some snack, some fling or whatever, that's hanging all over

David when I stop by to bring him some info. Cute kid, little button nose, freckles, maybe all of twenty-three. Not my type but, you know. Cute."

Jed turned around then, rubbing his face with his hands. He looked tired. "Whole thing lasted about a week. That was pretty typical for David, you know. Went through them like a crack whore goes through condoms. Never thought anything about it." Eyes going distant, Jed just frowned. "Mark was his name, I think. Mark or Sean or something. Jesus, I can't remember."

Redford rubbed his hand over Jed's back. "What happened to him?"

"I call them snacks, you know? Even the princess, though he's been around the longest. 'Cause they're just what David has before he gets bored. Like the other day when you ate half a bag of those shitty cookies." He smiled a little at Redford, expression never reaching his eyes. "You just... eat it, you know, 'cause it's there? That's David. He doesn't have boyfriends or whatever the hell, he has *snacks*." Shaking his head, Jed closed his eyes, complexion gray, like he was fighting back being sick. "And all I can think, Red, is that Sean kid... all I can do is ask myself if David ate him too."

Redford grimaced at the idea, though he didn't stop rubbing Jed's back. He knew nothing of David's history. He didn't know if David really had killed people he'd gone out with. It seemed likely, though. All too likely.

"Maybe," he said honestly. "But he seems like he's trying to *not* do that now."

Sucking in a slow breath, Jed just shook his head and pulled away from Redford, moving to stare out the window at the street below. People were walking around, cars were driving, the noise of the city faint and once-removed from them up here. "I know him, Red," Jed said hoarsely. "I *trust* him. Trusted him. I just... everything's so different now. I wish I could go back."

Though Redford smiled at the comment, he had to point out, "Nothing would change if you went back. He'd still be a vampire. You just wouldn't know it. At least now you know?"

"Maybe it's better not to know." Jed scrubbed a hand through his hair and glanced over at Redford, the corner of his mouth pulling upward sadly. "This is a whole river of shit we've wandered into, Fido. And I think I left my paddles at home."

Redford gave a faint huff of laughter, walking across the room to join Jed at the window. Together, they watched the traffic fade into the distance, bright red and white lights blurring together. "I sort of understand David," he offered hesitantly. "Not the eating people part. But he's so worried about hurting the people around him because he can't control his instincts."

Nudging his shoulder against Redford's, Jed turned to watch him instead of the world below them. "You afraid, Red?" he asked quietly.

"Of my instincts?" Redford nodded. "Yes. All the time."

His forehead creasing in obvious concern, Jed reached out to him, cupping his cheek. "I'm not," he told Redford honestly, meeting his eyes. "I love your instincts. I love *you*. You couldn't ever hurt me."

"Maybe Victor thought the same of David," Redford murmured. He leaned into Jed's touch, continuing, "Maybe Victor thought that David would never drain him like that."

"Victor didn't love David," Jed protested. "And he's a dumbass. They're not us, sweetheart."

It was such a simple statement, but Redford found himself relaxing. His instincts had never wanted to hurt Jed—protect him, claim him, fight for him, yes, but never *hurt*. He had to assume that David was different, that maybe every person was potentially food.

"You're right," Redford replied. He smiled at Jed, rubbing a hand over his arm. "And I do love you." After a moment, he added, "Are we still going through with Victor's plan?"

Rumbling out a short laugh, Jed shook his head. "Fuck if I know. We'll ask him when he wakes up." Tipping his chin up slightly, Jed kissed Redford softly, taking his time. "I just want you right now, okay? Let's have something good for a little while."

IT TOOK them two hours to get around to talking to Victor.

When they got to Victor's bedroom, they found the man sitting up in bed, paging through an old, thick book. "Yes, I still want you to go through with killing Gabriel," he said, gaze still fixed on the book. "You have a *look* about you."

Redford took a look at Jed's face. He did indeed have a *look*—a hesitant look that Jed very rarely wore. "Nobody's gonna think less of you if you want to call that off," Jed ventured, cutting a glance over at Redford. "This ain't a Very Special Episode of *90210* or whatever. Billy really *doesn't* beat you to show you he cares."

Victor rolled his eyes. "Just go ahead with the plan, Jed. I'll give you more money, if it means anything."

"Oh, no, that's not necessary—" Redford started, only to be cut off by Jed, grinning hugely.

"Means a hell of a lot to me! All systems go, captain."

"Excellent," Victor replied dryly. He still looked pale and exhausted, but there was a gleam in his eyes. "Same plan as discussed, then?"

"Yup." Jed lounged back onto the desk just opposite the bed, fiddling with an ornamental ball from the arrangement placed there. "Now, in order to pull this off, we're going to need a few things." Tossing the ball to Redford, Jed ticked off on his fingers, "Two suits, some cash to flash around, a cane, and a top hat." Pausing, he added with a charming smirk, "Oh, and a nice car. None of the rust heaps we've been renting. Something with some flash."

While Redford was trying to figure out exactly why Jed wanted a cane and a top hat, Rathbone sighed wearily and leaned over to retrieve his wallet from the bedside table. He took a credit card from it and held it out to Jed. "I'm hardly in a position to procure suits and cars and tawdry accessories. Take my credit card, and you get whatever you need."

"I assume there's a limit to how much we can spend?" Redford said cautiously, watching Jed study the credit card.

Victor smiled. "Not particularly."

Eyes lighting up, Jed tucked the card away. Redford would bet a great deal that he was already trying to figure out how *not* to give it back to Victor. Or order jet skis. He was a little obsessed with them. He kept claiming they were a *business essential*. Redford just thought that Jed wanted to be like those movies Jed had shown him once—something with an "international man of mystery."

"Thank you," Redford said, because Jed's mind had clearly gone off to other, more cash-related places. "We'll do our best to see this through."

Victor set his book down on his lap, nudging his glasses further up his nose. "Good. I hired you both for a reason."

"You probably don't *know* any other mercenaries," Jed pointed out, apparently coming back down to earth, slinging his arm around Redford's waist and pulling him in, resting his chin on Redford's shoulder. Victor just gave a soft, short laugh, tilted his head in agreement, and looked back down at his book. "Not that it matters. We're pretty much the best damn thing you're gonna find outside of your grandma's panties."

Redford took a moment to think the plan through, leaning against Jed. It was a good one, he thought. Except for one part that didn't quite make sense. "Jed, why do you need a cane and a top hat?"

Jed explained slowly, as if totally baffled that Redford hadn't instantly understood. "We're going to be undercover as two rich playboys."

"Yes, we know," Victor agreed. "But is there any particular *reason* you feel the need to do a Mr. Peanut impersonation as well?"

Jed just scowled at him, looking offended. "Um, because that's how rich people dress. Get with it, sweater vest."

Victor made a noise that was somewhere between a snort and a laugh. "People with money do not dress like that, Jed. People with *new* money do, if you want to be treated like that."

"Oh, for fuck's sake," Jed groaned. "What, are you now the expert on *that* too? Pretty hoity-whatever for a professor." Jed waggled Victor's credit card and smirked. "Just let the experts handle this, princess. You stay there and don't worry your pretty little head about it."

SOME time later, Redford was tugging uncomfortably at his bow tie. He was fairly sure that it was much too tight around his neck, but Jed had assured him that it was perfect.

The rumbling of the car engine quieted and stopped as they pulled up outside a building on the outskirts of the city. Redford leaned over to peer out the window. On the surface, the building didn't look like much. Redford's nose, however, picked up a large concentration of the smell of dead blood—much like how David smelled.

Jed, sitting next to him, was similarly dressed to Redford, with the addition of a top hat sitting jauntily on his head. Redford took another moment to admire how good he looked in the suit. His staring must have been rather blatant, because when Jed caught him, he gave a quick smirk. "Offer still stands, babe," he murmured, though it was pointless to pretend David couldn't hear just as well. "I'm more than happy to help you break in that monkey suit."

"Do I really have to listen to this?" David bit out, gritting his teeth and keeping his eyes locked out the window, as if he was afraid to let himself look anywhere else. Those were the first words Redford had heard the man speak since they'd sent him to the couch to sleep. David looked worn, cheeks hollow and eyes sunken in.

"Hey, it's not my fault my boyfriend looks positively edible in that suit," Jed said, holding up his hands with his best innocent look. "I'm as much a victim as you are."

Rubbing his forehead, David gave an irritated growl. "Just get on with it," he muttered.

"Yeah, yeah." Jed rifled around in his bag and pulled out a juice box, which he then offered to David with an overexaggerated expression of concern. "Now, they were out of the Blood-Soaked Professor flavor, so I got the Red Fruity Punch instead. This is the *only sucking* allowed. Got it, fangs?"

David bared said fangs at Jed, slapping the juice aside. It hit the window with a dull *squelch*. David's warning look did nothing to dim Jed's smirk, though. "Try to behave," Jed called, waggling his fingers at him and ducking out of the car. Holding open Redford's door, Jed extended a hand for him to take. "Shall we, sweetheart?"

Redford took Jed's hand and, still tugging at his bowtie, took a deep breath. "There's a lot of vampires in there," he murmured, staring up at the building. Even the smell of them triggered a wary growling in the back of his mind.

"Yeah, well, isn't it their bad luck that there's a lot of us out here." Jed brushed his hands over his sides, the small of his back, checking the weapons carefully concealed under his suit. He'd taken a lot of pains to make sure there weren't visible bulges under his suit to give them away.

"There's only two of us, Jed," Redford pointed out. He could feel the heavy weight of a gun at his own hip, even though he still wasn't sure how he felt about using it. Given that his best weapons were his fangs and his claws, carrying a gun just seemed unnatural. "And dozens of them."

"That's what makes it fun." Flashing Redford a grin, eyes lit up in anticipation, Jed swaggered up to the door and threw it wide open.

As Redford quickly followed, Jed announced, "I hear this is the place to go to get my freak on!"

Redford could almost hear the exasperated growl David would have given. It was matched by the vampire standing at the door, looking at them with eyebrows raised incredulously. Beyond the vampire, further into the room, Redford could see plush carpet, gilded decorations, everything gold, black, and red. There were people—no, more vampires—lounging over every available piece of furniture, dressed in expensive suits and dresses, sipping out of crystal glasses.

"We, er," Redford started. "We're here to... get bled? We heard that this is the place to go for that." At least, Redford supposed, his nervousness wasn't "out of character."

"And a little fucking wouldn't be amiss," Jed added with a leer toward... well, everyone in the room. "How about you, darlin'? You look like you're just itchin' to give me a good deep thrust." Though Redford knew it was an act, he had to bite down on his tongue to keep from growling.

The vampire just uttered a sigh of vague amusement and turned aside to let them step inside. "You only get bled if someone wants to bite you," he rumbled. "We get enough people in here begging for a bite." He eyed their suits and Jed's cane. "Just came into some money, did you?"

The charming grin faded quickly into an irritated scowl, and Jed glanced over his shoulder, back toward the entrance, muttering something about *know-it-all, tight-ass sweater vests*. "Yeah, sure," he sighed. "Just knocked over a bank. You know how it is, we're Scrooge McDucking it all over the place now. Looking for a little action." Jed looked the vampire up and down, the leer returning. "You interested? We play real nice with others."

"You'll find action if you're good enough," the vampire dismissed, tilting his chin over at the room and its vampires. "You pay, and then you hope someone feels like a snack. We're not that desperate."

Redford searched his pockets, finding the bundle of cash they'd withdrawn. He hesitantly handed it over to the vampire, whose eyes lit up when he saw the amount.

The vampire gave a low whistle, flicking through the bundle before pocketing it. "For that, I think Gabriel might want to meet you. He's interested in return clients."

"Good." Redford gave a decisive nod. Out of the corner of his eye, he could see some of the closer vampires wrinkling their noses, staring at him. "We like what we've heard about your clan. We'd like to repeat this experience if we find it satisfactory." His gaze cut over to Jed, silently checking that he was saying the right things.

Apparently he was, because Jed squeezed his ass, continuing to play the part of, well, *himself*, only slightly more blood-sex crazy. "Before we go, tell me," he said seriously, arm around the vampire, expression one of deep contemplation. "Exactly how hung is this Gabe fellow? Because, frankly, I don't want to waste my time with the lesser of the vampires, if you catch my drift."

The vampire gave a booming laugh and shrugged Jed's arm off his shoulders, giving them a little push in the direction of a hallway. "Gabriel won't fuck you," he said, deeply amused. "A human and a *werewolf?*"

Redford clenched his hand into a fist to restrain a visible show of panic. They knew what he was, but at least they weren't attacking.

"No, Gabriel just plays in business transactions with you lot," the vampire continued. "And take my advice: be polite. Be *really* fucking polite."

Jed patted the vampire's cheek. "Sweetheart," he murmured, smirking, "you ain't got one thing to worry about. Me and my associate here, we're practically Miss fucking Manners. Lead the way."

They were led down a hallway—the vampire was muttering under his breath to himself, and Redford could pick up words like *fucking dog* and *Gabe will be amused*. It was another example of how vampires didn't think too highly of werewolves. Redford was surprised they were letting him in here at all.

"Here we are." The vampire stopped outside the door at the end of the hallway. He gave a disdainful look at Redford. "Don't piss on the carpet or anything."

And just like that, in one motion so smooth and quick Redford had barely seen it happen, the vampire was up against the wall, Jed's arm pressed across his throat, Jed's knee jammed unceremoniously between his legs, pinning his balls to the drywall. "Hey," Jed said, grin sliding into something a bit more manic and hard, "how about you never say shit like that again. Or I'll see just how far I can squeeze a pair of dried-up family jewels until they pop. How's that for a fun game?"

The vampire gave him a rather disgruntled—and pained—look. "Fine." He appeared as if he wanted to say more, but he cut himself off. "Don't get yourself killed or anything. We like humans with money around here. It'd be a shame to lose you."

Releasing the vampire, Jed patted him on the shoulder and turned to Redford. "Fucking bloodsuckers," he muttered, straightening Redford's bow tie and brushing a strand of his hair back. "Okay, babe. Let's meet the big guy."

The office they were guided into was, if possible, even more lavish than the rooms they'd walked through to get there. Jed's shoulder brushed against Redford's as they walked deeper into the space, a solid, reassuring bump. A quick glance over showed that Jed's gaze was darting around, memorizing the layout, the possible exits, what he could use as a weapon. He looked relaxed, but Redford could almost smell his tension.

Gabriel walked out of a side room, wiping his hands on a small towel, leaving streaks of red over white cotton. He appeared to be unconcerned about their presence at first, moving gracefully to a large desk instead, a faint frown tugging at the edge of his lips. Unlike everything that Redford had imagined about the man, he wasn't big, or mean looking, or flashing his fangs everywhere. Gabriel was on the shorter side, dark hair hanging loose around narrow shoulders, which were accentuated by his finely cut suit.

"Oh, yes, you two," Gabriel murmured, glancing up at them like he'd just noticed they were there, like they were little more than flies on the wall. "Are you here for any particular reason?" He sniffed, wrinkling his nose.

Redford waited for the insult about dog smell, or something similar, but it never came.

"We're looking to become regular customers," Redford offered. He looked at Jed, wondering if continuing the lie was even necessary at this point. They were, after all, right in the belly of the beast.

"Oh?" Gabriel smiled. It wasn't a pleasant expression—too wide around the edges. "Well, I can't smell a lie, but I *can* smell that neither of you have ever been bitten properly."

"What?" Jed smirked, taking a step closer. His eyes were hard, glittering in the candlelight that Gabriel seemed to favor. "You don't cater to virgins? Come on now, sweetheart, you can't tell me none of your little bloodsuckers wouldn't be interested in all this untouched real estate?" He tipped his head to the side, exposing the long slope of his neck. "Just because we haven't before don't mean we're not interested now. Always a first time, right?"

Where any other vampire would have been staring at Jed's neck like it was the last steak on earth, Gabriel just gave a dismissive sniff and shuffled some papers on his desk. "Far too messy for my liking," he replied. "All that whimpering and screaming. It gets old after a few thousand years."

"You rejecting me?" Jed laughed, brittle and dangerous. Another step forward for him, getting close enough that Redford started to get nervous. He knew the way Jed was moving, that little glint in his eye. Such things usually heralded some kind of violence. "I'm hurt, sweetcheeks, really, I am. But I never said you had to do the bitin'. We just wanted to see who was in charge of the joint before we laid out our cash. I find it best to talk to the madam before you start spreading legs, if you know what I mean."

Gabriel, now seated languidly in the chair behind the desk, just sniffed again. "Oh! Look at that." He laughed, "I think I *can* smell a lie." Redford tensed up, expecting either Gabriel or Jed to strike. "And you, my friend, are a terrible liar. Why don't you get to why you're really here?"

Looking genuinely insulted, Jed just pulled a hurt face. "Me? I am not a—" Turning, he pointed at Redford. "Red! Tell this ugly man that I am *not* a bad liar." Whirling back to Gabriel, he crossed his arms, glaring. "Also, your hair is really terrible. I mean, seriously, who are you? Fabio? Get a fucking haircut, Jesus."

Gabriel just threw his head back and laughed. "You're *adorable*." Impossibly graceful, he stood, rounding the desk to come nose-to-nose with Jed. "And where is David?"

"Not here," Redford cut in, taking a few steps forward. He went to put himself between Gabriel and Jed, but before he could shove the vampire aside, Gabriel had taken two quick steps back.

BLOOD IN THE SAND

"Pity." Gabriel sighed, his gaze going over to the windows. "Another lie, but I suppose I'll just wait for him to gather his balls and show up."

"You'll be waiting a hell of a long time. Why don't us grownups just have a chat?" Jed flashed his teeth in a dangerous little grin. "So. I'm here to kill you. How's that tickle your dick?"

Gabriel just gave Jed an inscrutable look. "May I ask why, before we get into the fighting?"

Jed just smirked. "Got paid to." After a beat, he moved forward, not nearly as liquid fast as Gabriel had, but fast enough to all at once be close enough to Gabriel to reach out and straighten the lapel on his jacket. "But a sick, twisted fucker like you? Oh, I'd do this one just for the boner I'm gonna get making sure you're dust in the goddamn wind."

"Ah." Gabriel's reply held no particular emotion in it. "As I expected. This isn't about the kidnappings, then?"

Redford frowned sharply. "You weren't *part* of the kidnappings."

The sound that Gabriel made wasn't so much a laugh as it was the creepiest giggle that Redford had ever heard. And Jed had made him watch several movies where dolls came to life and ate people. "Wrong," Gabriel chirped, sitting himself on the edge of his desk, watching them eagerly. "Now, enough of all that boring talk. How about I introduce you to someone of interest, werewolf?"

"It was the Usire clan," Redford insisted, reaching out to grab the back of Jed's jacket, just in case he decided to attack in the middle of the conversation. If they were getting answers, Redford wanted to hear them.

"No interest in who I'd introduce you to?" Gabriel looked upset, his moods shifting as quickly as the wind. "Fine. Bring David in here and I'll tell you *all* about it."

"What? Fuck you, we're doing this now." Jed shook off Redford's hand, taking a step forward. His hand went in his jacket for a weapon.

Now, Jed was good at his job. Redford had seen him in a hundred different fights, usually against more than one person, oftentimes against people bigger or stronger or better armed than him. And he always walked away. Jed lived for this, trained for it, had been taught how to be the most effective, ruthless fighter possible. His arrogance in the matter, in Redford's eyes, was not entirely unfounded.

315

But his face met the floor before Redford even had time to bark out a warning. Gabriel just smirked down at him, pinning Jed to the ground with nothing but his bare hands, ignoring his curses and struggles. "No? Not going to go and get my dear boy? Fine, I'll send for him myself."

Redford started forward, his gaze narrowing in on the weak spots that Jed had taught him. "Garrett!" Gabriel called.

Before Redford could move, he smelled ash and burnt fur, blood and dirt. A massive weight crashed into his side, sending him toppling to the ground. A huge paw pushed down on his chest, a black-furred muzzle looming above him. The low growl the wolf made vibrated through him.

"This is my puppy," Gabriel crooned. "He's a good boy, aren't you, Garrett? Yes, you *are*. Hold the nasty werewolf still while David gets here."

Redford twisted his head to look at Jed. He was pinned on his front, arms twisted behind his back, one of Gabriel's knees planted on his lower back. He looked okay for the moment, despite the anger twisting his face. He turned back to look at the werewolf—Garrett—who didn't seem inclined to let him up any time soon. If he shifted, he could maybe—

"Don't even think about trying to go wolf," Gabriel snapped. "You'll spoil the picture. *Wait* until David gets here, for goodness' sake."

As if summoned, two vampires strong-armed a struggling David through the door, throwing him inside. The door slammed shut behind him.

"David!" Gabriel sounded cheerful, though he didn't loosen his grip on Jed. "I thought I smelled you lurking around outside. Now, I believe that I taught you that loitering is rude." There wasn't a sound from David, not a movement other than a faintly trembling hand smoothing down the front of his shirt. David's eyes were fixed on the ground, as if he barely noticed his surroundings.

Gabriel stood, releasing Jed, and snapped his fingers to signal Garrett to step away too. The massive wolf gave a grumble and trotted to Gabriel's side, lying at his feet with a baleful glare in David's direction. Bouncing up like a spring released, Jed spat curses in Gabriel's direction but, instead of charging him, went to Redford's side. "You okay, Fido?" Jed muttered, shooting murderous glances up toward Gabriel.

"He'd be better if he had a friend," Gabriel cut in, tangling his fingers in the thick fur along Garrett's nape. "You, werewolf, how would you like—"

"No," Redford replied. He was starting to get a little sick of Gabriel's ramblings. It didn't help that there was a werewolf at his feet with barely any humanity in his eyes, intelligence replaced by a crazed, blank expression. "Just get to the point."

Gabriel frowned, cocking his head. "You'd like to know about the kidnappings. Very well, I have some time, and you lot are mildly entertaining. We may as well talk." His gaze went to David. "Do you have anything to say for yourself?"

Again, David's hand slid down the front of his shirt, as if by erasing any invisible wrinkles he could control the whole situation. After a moment, he managed, very quietly, "Go to hell, Gabe."

"Predictable," Gabriel huffed. "You *should* have something to say for yourself. Never mind the rabble you're keeping company with. The kidnappings are your fault, after all."

Head jerking up, David's eyes went wide for a moment. He looked lost, like some scared little boy who'd just been told he'd be punished later. It was a strange expression on his face, one Redford hadn't ever seen before. David always looked so in control, so confident. Now he was shaken, skin pale, shoulders rounded and hunched in. "You're lying," he whispered after a moment, gaze narrowing. "I had nothing to do with them. I came to *save* them."

"David." Gabriel sounded like he was on the edge of reprimanding him. "*David*. Honestly. You have *everything* to do with them."

Redford's gaze went back to David, confused. He was sure David couldn't have set any of this up. David had fought alongside them, hadn't even been in Egypt when the kidnappings had started.

Gabriel slunk closer to David, an eager smile lighting up his features. "It was the only way to get you to come back home, David. All those bleeding victims were for *you*. So you could feed and be strong again. You were looking for it, weren't you? Some scrap of your old life?" A long finger traced down David's cheek; the vampire shuddered but didn't move, eyes wide and locked on Gabriel's face. "All the way across the ocean, all those years, and you never stopped looking for me. I knew all I had to do was come back here, to Cairo, to where I found you the first time, and you'd come running home."

Muttering "Son of a bitch," Jed moved a step closer to them, hand straying to his jacket pocket again. David didn't seem to notice. His whole body had gone still, completely immobile, guilt etching years into his face.

"No," he said quietly. Redford didn't think David believed his own protests. "No, Jesus, I... I came to *save* them."

"Did you?" Gabriel murmured. "My *nefer*, didn't you see that they were your coffin? I lured you inside with my little rag-tag vampire clan, so eager for destruction. It was such a perfect fit for you. And you hoped it was me behind it all, didn't you?" His hand traced the same path down David's shirt that David had been trailing earlier. "I do get so bored, David. And what better than some rabble of untrained, stupid vampires killing indiscriminately to bring you back here? They did make such a noise."

"I thought it was you," David admitted, voice breaking. For a moment the two vampires stood, Gabriel pressing forward, David curled in on himself and unsure. A dynamic that was older than Redford, older than this room, that was part of David's very bones. But a beat passed, and then another, and David repeated, "I thought it was you."

Raising his head, jaw tightening, David stepped forward. "I *knew* it was you. I was right. You sorry, disgusting son of a bitch, I smelled you halfway around the world." Another step then, David so close, eyes searching Gabriel's face. "But why *Set*? Why the statues, the clues? Why some ancient god? Just tell me that, Ib-Se-Kem. He was your god, not mine."

All of the irreverent cheer, all of the disdain for the company of the human and a werewolf, all of it vanished. Gabriel looked *hurt*. "Because you're my Osiris," he murmured gently, raising a beseeching gaze to David. "Don't you know that?"

David's eyes narrowed as he jerked back, fangs flashing in a snarl. "I'm not your *anything*. Never again. And I'm going to end you."

"Are you?" Gabriel sounded bored with that notion. "I—"

With a roar and a shout, with a flurry of motion, Jed pushed forward. Fists flew, Jed striking Gabriel right across the jaw, taking advantage of the momentary surprise to kick the werewolf aside. "You talk too damn much," he grunted, leveling another swing at Gabriel.

"For goodness' sake," Gabriel growled, moving out of the way of the next punch. "Stop making a fool of yourself."

Pulling out his gun, Jed pressed it into Gabriel's forehead, eyes cold. "I'm not the one about to eat metal, sweetheart."

Gabriel's lips parted in an amused grin, baring his fangs. "And how long do you think a bullet to my head will stop me? Haven't you tried that before?"

Gunshots were always louder in real life than one might expect. This one rang through the room, a deep brass tone that shuddered through Redford, leaving his ears throbbing. Not hesitating, Jed unloaded a second shot into Gabriel's heart as the vampire's body fell gracelessly to the ground, then a third. "I dunno," he muttered, a disgusted look on his face. "Let's find out."

Redford breathed out, his gaze fixing on Gabriel's body. Garrett let loose a mournful howl, and instead of attacking like expected, the wolf draped himself over Gabriel's chest—only to be shoved off as Gabriel rose, still grinning despite the hole in his head.

"*Humans.*" Gabriel sniffed disdainfully. Blood was leaking over his eyes and mouth, turning his face into a hollow-eyed mask.

"Jed." David spoke up, finally moving forward, his skin gray and eyes locked somewhere over Gabriel's shoulder. "You said you had a plan." Tone more than a little desperate, David's shoulders rounded forward, tensed, ready for a fight even though he looked on the verge of being sick.

Flipping a knife out of his pocket, Jed grasped Gabriel by the hair and, before the vampire had time to mock him further, plunged the blade deep into his chest. With a smirk, he kicked Gabriel back, appearing supremely satisfied as Gabriel fell once more to the ground.

"That's what we call an ace in the hole," Jed crowed.

David didn't look nearly as thrilled. "What the fuck was that?"

"My magic knife," Jed explained very slowly, as if he were speaking to a small child. "Duh. It's what killed that bastard, Fil. I packed it in my checked bag, in my shaving kit. Suck on that one, Fabio."

319

Blinking, David's eyes went wide. "*That* was your plan?" Grabbing Redford's jacket, David shoved him toward the door, quickly following behind, leaving Jed looking bewildered.

"Uh, *yeah*. It's a magic knife."

Redford shot a wary glance toward Gabriel. The vampire was still on the floor, the silver knife sticking out of his chest. Garrett, once again, had retreated to snuffling around Gabriel's neck, making quiet noises that Redford could only identify as upset whimpers.

"Jed, you giant, blind, *human* idiot." The door was locked. David beat on it uselessly for a moment, growling in frustration. "*There's no such thing as magic.*"

"Says the vampire," Jed shot back, eyes narrowing.

"Excuse me," Redford offered quietly. "Don't you think it would best if we stopped arguing and—"

"That's different!" David shouted in frustration. "That knife worked on Fil because it was pure silver, coated in blood, and that's how you kill a goddamn wolf. You know what it does to vampires?"

"Tickles a little." The smooth, patiently amused voice wrapped around them like iron, velvet sweet and sour as death. Gabriel rose, his movements like a marionette being awkwardly pulled from the floor by its strings, jerky and unnatural. "A magic knife? Really?"

"Okay, then," Jed said hastily, pulling out two larger guns. "How do you kill a vampire?"

"*Now* you're asking?" David was pressed up against the door, all but shaking, trying desperately to look stoic. "I'm telling Victor to only pay you half."

"*David*," Gabriel singsonged, but Redford wasn't listening. He reached to his hip, jerking out the gun that Jed insisted he always carry, and shot at the locked door. One shot and the handle broke, a second broke the lock, and Redford shoved his shoulder at the door, forcing it open.

He grabbed the back of Jed's jacket. "We can't kill him," Redford snapped. "Now *run*."

David didn't move. It was like a rabbit in the gaze of a snake. He'd frozen, eyes locked on Gabe, a soft whimper of fear working out of his throat. Hesitating, Jed muttered a curse, firing both of the guns in his hand at Gabriel, peppering him with bullets until the vampire fell.

"Move it, fang boy!" Jed shouted, kicking David to make him stumble forward, nudging him with his shoulder until David broke into a run of his own.

Reaching into his pocket as they raced through the main room, Jed pulled out two grenades. He pulled the pins with his teeth, tossing them behind him as he shoved Redford and David out the door. They fell to the ground outside, Jed blanketing on top of Redford, a solid weight while the building erupted behind them.

This felt entirely too familiar. Even as debris was flying, even as the heat of the explosion washed over them, Redford took a moment to ponder the fact that Jed had most likely blown up every single building they'd been in so far. Except for the hotel, though Redford wouldn't be surprised if that ended up a pile of rubble too.

As the explosion died down and Jed rolled off of him, Redford picked himself up. The building was burning now, and he could hear screams from inside.

"Maybe *that's* how you kill a vampire," he supposed.

CHAPTER
15

David

SOME people said the smell of a fire was comforting. Something about the burning wood, the lingering smoke, it was supposed to evoke feelings of *home*, of *rest*. To David, it just seemed to hang in his throat. The smell of it was acrid and too strong, covering up everything else. Vampire noses were better than most, but here he couldn't seem to catch a hint of the incense and sweet copper that always seemed to follow Gabriel.

He'd been right there. Standing right where David was now, and he couldn't smell him.

The day had been too long. David had been convinced that Gabriel was still alive. Surely hundreds of years of history, all of that pain and torment and obsession, surely it wasn't just *over*. So they'd come back, as soon as night had fallen again, and now David was standing in the middle of the burned remains of the building, searching for a sign.

"I'm telling you, there's nothing here." Jed was grumpy. He'd been paid, the job was over, and he just wanted to go home. Picking his way through the rubble, the man followed behind a dark, shaggy wolf as Redford nosed along, looking for a hint of the vampires who'd been there. "The police have come and gone, and the news said no bodies. The place was listed as abandoned. We're not going to find anything, David."

"Just keep looking." Lips tight, David turned away, walking through what once was a wall to the sidewalk outside. Victor was leaning against their car, wrapped in two sweaters and a jacket that was far too large. He looked *small*. Vulnerable. Completely unreachable behind glasses and a stoic expression.

David couldn't blame him. What was there to say, really?

"You didn't have to come," he murmured after a moment, eyes dropping. "I could have taken you to the airport first."

"I'm the one that paid for Jed to do this. I wanted to see that he did a satisfactory job," Victor replied. The words were entirely businesslike, bland, and Victor wasn't even trying to look at him. David refused to acknowledge the jolt of pain that came from the man's dismissal. It was better this way. This day had been coming, and perhaps David should have ended this months ago. How could he honestly have expected anything different?

He was a vampire. He fed on humans. That equation wasn't going to change so long as David allowed himself even a drop of blood. What he'd had with Victor had only been postponing the inevitable.

"Fang boy!" Jed certainly liked his new nickname. Jaw tightening, David briefly closed his eyes before turning around and arching an eyebrow at the man.

"Yes?"

"Get over here. Fido found something you might be interested in."

Glancing over at Victor, David straightened his jacket and gracefully climbed his way back over to where Redford and Jed were standing. With a whine, Redford plopped himself down next to Jed, leaning against his leg and panting, looking worried. He turned his head, pointing his muzzle toward a glint of metal partially hidden by some rubble.

Hesitating, David stooped down, digging carefully through the ashes and soot-blackened boards. Underneath the pile was a trap door. It had been bent by the fallen ceiling, but David could see the dim outline of a path beyond it.

An escape route. Hadn't Gabe always told him to have one? Of course the man wouldn't have left anything to chance. If he cared to look, he wouldn't doubt he'd find several throughout various parts of the building. Not a single vampire had died here, unless he missed his guess. It'd all been for show.

But why?

Standing, expression tight, David started to move away. He was stopped by a soft chuff. Redford nudged his head into David's hand before trotting a few steps to their left. There, sitting on the raised platform where Gabriel had received them, was a small pendant. It was clean, shining gently in the moonlight. Obviously left there after the fire.

It was looped on a thin silver chain, and David let it twist in front of his eyes as he examined the pendant. The head of an Egyptian deity—but a strange one, not like any animal that existed. A long, slightly bent snout

323

like an aardvark, ears like a jackal, eyes rimmed in black. The metal itself was slightly tinged with red. It was Set, smiling maliciously back at him.

As he closed his hand around the pendant, David would swear it burned.

"So, what, the fucker's just gone?" Jed wasn't going to let this go. He didn't miss a target, ever, and now Gabriel had messed with Jed's professional pride. David wearily shrugged, rubbing a thumb along the image of Set, regarding it quietly.

"Perhaps," David murmured after a long moment. "He's old, Jed. Older than anything you've come across. Older than even I know. I'm not sure anything could have killed him. Certainly not a messy explosion."

Redford whacked his tail against David's leg, looking insulted on Jed's behalf. Jed's eyes flashed in irritation, squaring his shoulders. "That was a damn good explosion, Davie, and you fucking well know it. It's not my fault some vampires are apparently kaboom-proof. Besides, it's not like you were exactly Mr. Helpful on this trip."

And here they went. David had wondered how long it would take Jed to get to the recriminations. Folding his arms tightly across his chest, David gritted his teeth, trying to bite back the urge to attack. Tempers wouldn't help the situation, and David was too exhausted to fight, even with Jed. "I suppose you think that if I'd just stood aside and let you wander around half-cocked that Gabriel would be dead right now."

"First off," Jed said, holding up one finger and dropping his other hand down to cup himself lewdly, "there ain't nothing half about this. I am twelve inches of summer lovin', and don't you forget it."

Redford made a noise that sounded suspiciously like a snort. When Jed's finger swiveled from pointing at David down to poke Redford lightly on the nose, Redford huffed out a sigh and flopped to lie on the ground, putting his paws over his muzzle.

"Don't make me do show and tell, Fido," Jed warned, but his anger softened a bit and he nudged his foot up against Redford's side.

The mood didn't last, though. Turning back to David, Jed went on, words brittle around the edges, "And yeah, actually. You were holding back every step of the way, and yeah, Davie. That's what I'm saying. I'm saying you didn't help. I'm saying if you'd have told me up front what was going on, Gabriel would be a big pile of vamp dust right now and we'd be popping corks on the way home. That"—Jed had moved forward with every step, until he was standing nose to nose with David—"is exactly what I'm saying."

"I think you're full of shit," David hissed. "And blaming me for your mistakes—"

"My mistakes?" Now Jed was shouting at him, ears turning red in anger, blood pounding under thin skin, a tempting bass drum underscore to his words. "Fuck you, David. You did exactly what we bitch about these fat-ass clients doing."

"Yeah?" David bit out. "And what is that?"

"You hired me for a job you didn't want done." The words hung there, accusing and loud, shattering the air between them. David stared at Jed for a long moment, unmoving, expressionless. Jed blinked and took a deep breath, a flicker of pity on his face before it was hidden behind a scowl. "You hired me, and then you stopped me from doing what I do, Davie. The sick part is, you know it. I think you just wanted me here so when it all went south, you had someone here who gave a shit."

The Set pendant was digging into the palm of David's hand, he was gripping it so hard. David's gaze fell, going to that half-hidden escape route.

Gabriel was alive. He was free and walking around only God knew where, and that thought did not fill David with dread. The only thing that could have terrified him more than news that Gabriel had survived was proof that he was dead.

And that, as Jed would probably so elegantly put it, was why he was so goddamn fucked up.

"What did he mean?" David looked back to Jed when the man spoke again, a grudging question David realized he must have been holding on to all night. "He called you his Osiris. What was the bastard talking about?"

With an aborted, strangled laugh, David paced a few steps away. He ran his hand across his face helplessly and kicked a burned piece of wood. It crumbled to ash under his boot. "I'm his balance, I think," he answered slowly. "I'm his other half. Osiris and Set, they're two sides to the same coin, and Gabriel was...." He wished he could breathe. He wished, strangely, desperately, that there was a way to pull oxygen into old, dead lungs, to wash out the scent of Gabriel with a huge breath of the Cairo evening air. "Gabriel was claiming me again." Shaking his head, David waved his hand, dismissing it. "I don't know, Jed. Does it really matter to you what an insane vampire thinks?"

After a beat, Jed grinned at him, forced and slightly too brittle, a bit too manic. "Nope," he agreed, overly cheerful. "You want anything else off this crapheap?"

David just jerked his head toward the car. "That's it. Let's go." For once, Jed kept his mouth shut. They trooped back to where Victor was waiting with the car, looking rather morose. David said nothing as he slid behind the wheel, pulling out into traffic.

"Just drop me and Red off at the hotel," Jed told him. He was sprawled in the backseat, idly scratching behind Redford's ears. The wolf looked perfectly content to stay as he was—he was still apparently too shy to change in front of everyone. "We have to finish packing. Our flight's not until later, anyway."

"I can't believe I gave you all that money, and you couldn't even kill him," Victor muttered. "You need to read a book every once in a while, Jed."

Snorting quietly, Jed rolled his eyes. "I blew up the goddamn building. What more do you want?" David cut a glance back at him, and Jed sighed, reaching into his pocket and counting off several bills from the stack. "Fine. Here. Half the money back."

He shoved it into Victor's hand and sagged back on the seat, obviously upset. Not about the money, though, David thought. Jed had failed a job. They'd known each other for years, and David wasn't sure he ever remembered that happening.

"So, how *do* you kill a fucking vampire?" Jed spoke up after a few minutes.

David could see, out of the corner of his eye, Victor giving him a look. The man's face was unreadable, but he thought he could detect a hint of apology in there. "I did try to tell you." Victor, remarkably, refrained from further recrimination, which was nearly as remarkable as Jed actually listening to the man. Small victories, perhaps, but David thought they should take what they could get. "You destroy the head, Jed. Not just a few bullets. You have to chop it right off and sever the spinal cord," Victor murmured. "Or use a wooden stake, straight through the heart, though that has a higher risk of failure if you miss. Anything else just means an angry vampire. I thought you would have figured that out, watching David fight them."

"Nah, I just assumed he was really into it. And I've stabbed people with way weirder shit than some toothpicks. Thought it was the only thing you could find at the moment." Considering that, Jed stared out the window for a moment. "So that must be where the zombie stuff comes from," he mused. "Red"—he poked the wolf, a smile working its way across his face—"we need to go machete shopping when we get home." The grumble Redford gave sounded rather unenthusiastic.

"You're not going to sleep for a week when you get home?" Victor shifted, stretching his arms in front of him. "I am. That's my only plan for the foreseeable future."

"We're going to have as much sex as humanly possible when we get home," Jed returned with a grin. Redford thumped his tail against the seat in agreement. "After we spring Knievel from the kennel. And then we're going *fishing*. Nothing but a beach and beer, and my guy and my girl. It'll be heaven."

"That sounds...." Victor trailed off. He glanced again at David. "Nice," he finished haltingly.

Yes. Nice. David didn't remove his eyes from the road. The moon was gently brushing strands of silver against the hint of sand beyond the city, the desert thick with history and age and the thousand miles that lay between its borders. David wished he was out in it, with nothing but the ground and the sky. Maybe he could remember how to breathe out there, just for a moment. He certainly wouldn't be magically pulling any air in here, with tension taking up all of the oxygen.

"No one wants to hear it, Walker," David growled, jerking the wheel over and pulling up in front of the hotel. "Don't miss your flight, and for God's sake, don't break any more furniture. That room is already going to cost me a fortune."

Victor gave a slight huff and twisted in his seat, reaching back to hand the money over to Jed again. "He can pay for it," he said to David. "It's not like he doesn't have the money now."

Glancing briefly over at Victor, then back at Jed, David said stiffly, "The room was part of the contract. I keep my word."

Jed, looking between the two of them, very carefully handed the stack of bills back to Victor and urged Redford out of the cab. Before he climbed out, Redford shoved a wet nose against the back of David's neck, giving him a huff. "Uh. Yeah. Well, good stuff. We'll see you guys stateside," Jed said. Then they were gone, the door creaking shut behind them, cutting off the noise of the street beyond. Now it was just Victor and himself. Alone.

327

David awkwardly shifted in his seat, caught for a moment in the strange state of having absolutely no idea what to do. Eventually he started the car up again, fingers wrapping tightly around the wheel as if to hold it all together with that simple grip. Clearing his throat, David let his eyes slide over to Victor and then quickly away again.

This was always going to end. He had known that from the start, from the first moment he'd laid eyes on those ridiculous clothes and the glasses and the way Victor had been so intently studying the melon selection. He'd gone to the store to test himself, perhaps, to prove that he could be among humans and not break. And there had been Victor—beautiful and studious, serious and so unlike Gabriel. So unlike everything in that world he'd run from. After ten years without Gabriel, after two years of denying himself, he kept finding himself in the exact same situation.

Blood ruled him. Perhaps it always had. But with Victor, he'd hoped to find a new way to exist. For a little while, he wasn't a monster. For a few beats, a handful of moments, he had believed he really could change.

That was all over now.

They didn't speak for a long time. Then Victor said quietly, "I'm sorry."

David looked over at him, startled as much by the words as by Victor breaking their silence. Brown eyes widened, wordlessly questioning, before he managed to get himself together enough to whisper, "Don't."

A few more beats of Victor's heart, tasted and heard, throbbing through David just as strongly, and he shook his head in frustration. "It's me, Victor. It always has been. I can't be… human. I don't even remember what that would be like. Why are you apologizing for what I did?"

"If I'd *expected* you to be human, then I'd be very stupid indeed." Victor smiled thinly. David only caught the edge of it, as Victor turned to watch the scenery passing by. "You're not the only one at fault here, David."

No, he wasn't human. But who in their right mind would be involved with a *vampire* if they actually understood what that would mean? Victor might understand the nuances of the race, might have studied them, but on some level, surely he'd expected David to be like him. Just like David had clung to the idea of what Victor meant for him, Victor had needed David to be his own release.

"I'm the one that bit you," David stated bluntly. "Nothing else matters. I hurt you, and…." Worrying his lower lip, David shrugged, refusing to look over into Victor's face, the one he'd memorized. The one he wouldn't be seeing again. "I cared about you, Victor. I do care. So let me say I'm sorry. I owe you at least that much."

There was no immediate reply from Victor. The man didn't move, but he had a line between his eyebrows that David knew meant Victor was thinking heavily.

After a few minutes of silence, Victor spoke up again.

"Before I met you, my life was... boring." He smiled again, faintly. "I know that's probably obvious. But it was. It was dusty and dry, all of my academic peers were two decades older than I, and we were all expected to sit down at noon and drink tea, discussing the latest, equally dry, academic journal article. My house was too big and too old. I can't look into my own eyes, but I could see my future as clear as day."

In a nervous gesture so unlike him, Victor clasped his hands on his lap, his knuckles turning white. "You *weren't* boring. You were...." Victor struggled for the right word. "You were dangerous, David. I knew exactly what I was getting into when I started a relationship with a vampire. I wanted that." He turned in his seat, shifting to fully face David. "And I encouraged everything that you were trying to stop being. So I am sorry."

They stopped in front of the airport. David didn't move, listening to the soft pings of the cooling engine, the footsteps of people outside, the rush of a plane overhead. Finally, gathering up all his courage, he turned to face Victor. The man really was beautiful, hidden behind glasses and sweaters and proper English manners. And David had cared about him, perhaps more than he'd cared about anything since Gabriel. He *did* care about him. That might not go away.

But they weren't good for each other.

Reaching out, his fingertips very lightly traced along Victor's cheek. "When I left Gabriel," he said lowly, voice barely loud enough to be counted as spoken, "I spent years trying to deny who I was. But I broke every time. When I walked into that market I was two years without human blood. And I was desperate for something, *anything* to help me move on. You were so different from Gabriel, from the patterns I kept falling into. I really did think I could do it. That I could have sex without blood, that I could be close to someone without hurting them. It was easy to pretend, back home. To have my nice little routine, to think that a few mouthfuls from you were hardly enough to fall off the wagon. Then I came back here, heard Gabriel's voice again, and all that façade of normalcy seemed to crumble around me."

Letting his hand drop away, David gave Victor a half-formed, bitter smile. "I wanted something other than what Gabriel gave me. Now look. I'm right back where I started. Somewhere, the bastard is laughing his ass off."

Victor took David's hand back, curling it around his own and raising their joined hands to press a kiss to the back of David's knuckles. "I am sorry that I couldn't help you do what you wanted," he murmured. "I'm fairly sure I only made things worse."

"No." David shook his head, cupping Victor's cheek. "No, you were...." Kissing his forehead, David closed his eyes, regret sour at the back of his throat. "You know I gave you everything I could, don't you? This isn't your fault, Vickie. I just can't be the sort of person you need. Or any kind of *person* at all. Maybe I never will be. But what we had, it meant something to me. Please tell me you realize that."

"I know," Victor replied softly. "Of course I know. And I'm terribly fond of you as well." He brushed some of David's hair back behind his ear, stroking his thumb over his cheekbone. "We were exactly what each other needed, at the start. I wish it could remain that way."

Forcing a smile, David nodded. "Me too." God, he did. How much simpler everything would be if he and Victor would just *work*. But whatever they could be for each other was gone now. David had killed it with flashing fangs and blood. Right then, the kindest thing, the best thing, was to move on.

Gently, he pulled back. "You'll miss the check-in for your flight," he murmured, touching Victor's cheek again. A farewell, he supposed, letting his hand slip down to rest above Victor's heart.

Victor gave a laugh that almost sounded like a sob. "I wish there *was* no damn flight," he muttered, but he reached over to open his door. "Help me get my bags out of the trunk?"

Nodding, David moved smoothly out of the car, easily carrying both heavy bags up behind Victor. They made their way to the counter, and David remained quiet as Victor showed his ticket and passport and got checked in. The bags were gone then, the noise of the airport bringing them back to crushing reality.

David shifted, glancing around before turning to Victor. "I can't go any further without a ticket," he murmured, smoothing his hands down the front of his coat, an uncharacteristically nervous gesture. "So I... this is goodbye, then."

"I suppose it's back to dusty old windbags and tea at noon for me," Victor said dryly. He absently straightened David's collar, an odd little smile coming to his expression. "You're wrong, though. You will, someday, be just the kind of person that someone needs."

Choking out a laugh, David pulled Victor into a hug, resting his cheek on the top of his head. "Oh, my sweet, innocent professor," he mumbled into Victor's hair, as Victor grabbed him just as tightly in return. "What am I going to do without you?" A kiss to his cheek and David released him, turning quickly and walking away before the other man could see his forced calm break.

Turning, though, at the last minute, he called out, "And you *like* tea at noon, you stuffy old Brit."

Victor pulled a face that was somewhere between sad fondness and irritation. "He'll be blond," he called back. When David gave him a startled look, Victor's lips settled into a bittersweet little smile. "I've seen it in your eyes. You always did have a thing for blonds."

David moved to leave. He was going to leave, going to bundle up all the choked back sorrow and scoring regret that was knotted inside of him and forget it. But something pulled him back. Lurking at the edges of the room, he kept out of sight, stalking along behind Victor, just to be sure. Gabriel was probably halfway around the world by now, but David wanted to be certain Victor got on his flight.

The security checkpoint area paralleled where David was able to walk freely. On the other side of a glass corridor now, Victor looked around, surrounded by people, looking so much more tired than he had before. Eventually he decided on an out of the way table, settling in and pulling out a book to read. David felt a faint, fond smile touch his lips. Soon, he'd be able to think of such things without pain. For now, though, that fondness was chased with a sick, tight ache.

Someone bumped against Victor's table, knocking into the man, and David moved forward, alarmed. After a moment, though, and hearing the copious amounts of apologizing the young man was doing, David relaxed marginally. It didn't seem to be a threat. More just a lanky, nervous boy, shoving his glasses up on his face and repeatedly murmuring his apologies. With a little effort, David could hear them over the din of the quiet airport.

331

"I really am so sorry," the man said again, before letting his eyes fully rise for the first time to Victor's face. He didn't hide his surprise well. "You... I know you, don't I? You were at the—" Cutting himself off, he raised his hands to the bandages just barely visible under his shirt collar. "I mean to say, I've seen you before."

"Yes. Hello again, Mr. Lewis." The smile Victor gave was forced, weary, and too thin. "My colleagues were the ones responsible for your rescue."

"Yes, of course." Lewis—Randall, David thought his name had been. In his mind he'd simply referred to them as the victims, never quite stopping to give them names and faces and lives beyond his own need to save them—seemed to realize that Victor wasn't quite in the mood to chat. The boy smiled, very faintly, looking rather awkward in his too-large clothes and shaggy hair. "I never did get your name. I've simply been referring to you as my Beatrice."

"Victor Rathbone," came the reply. The thin smile turned into something more genuine. "Wouldn't Virgil be more appropriate?"

"No." Lewis's own smile seemed to grow rather in proportion to Victor's. "Beatrice guided him through Heaven. Hell was there, but being saved, having another chance at everything, how could that be anything but Heaven?"

"I suppose that's true," Victor murmured. "Sit if you like, Mr. Lewis. I've got a little time until my flight."

"I do as well." Lewis gratefully took the chair offered, a kind of ease in his limbs now that he was relaxing, a power there hid under a waistcoat and loosened tie. A bookish wolf. Not the stereotype, David supposed, but there had to be one somewhere. "And please, I'm Randall. Mr. Lewis makes me feel old and with slightly less hair."

Lewis hesitated before he offered, hopefully, "I owe you, at the very least, some tea. Victor." He paused on Victor's name and smiled again, slowly. "I was just going to fortify myself with some. I'm trying to get back on the right time zone, and I'll need the help. Please, let me get you a cup?"

Victor glanced at his watch. The choked laugh was only very faint to David's ears. "It's nearly noon, where I'll be going." He rubbed a hand over his face, clearly fortifying himself. "I suppose I *will* need some tea, then."

It seemed vulgar to watch any more. Victor was safe, he was on his way home, and there was nothing more he could do for him now. David saw Lewis leap up, happily eager to please. The soft noise of their talking he let fade into the slush of voices from everywhere, the sights and sounds of people milling about the airport. Turning, David nodded quietly to himself. "Goodbye," he murmured, perhaps to Victor, who couldn't hear him, perhaps to no one at all.

And he left the airport, to disappear onto the streets of Cairo.

EPILOGUE

Jed

THE flight had been long, some snot-nosed kid had gotten literal, like, *snot* all over the seat in front of them, and Redford had refused any and all efforts to make him a part of the mile high club. Jed had still fucking hated every second of it, choosing to drown his jitters in alcohol, shouting at said kid, and then glowering murderously at everyone around them.

Good times.

It was fucking *fantastic* to be home, though. The first stop, before the apartment or showering off the plane smell, had been at the kennel. Jed had practically run through the doors, pounding on the counter until a woman had come out, looking less than amused at the way Jed had *demanded* his cat immediately. Bitch. He'd been gone for *ages,* and his baby had been locked in a cage. He didn't care how nice the facilities were or that Knievel had apparently bitten three workers.

Finally, though, Knievel was brought out, and Jed grinned enthusiastically, picking her up out of her carrier. "Hey, honey," he crooned, scratching under her chin. "Did you miss me? Huh? Did you— *Ow!* Shitting hermit son of a goat fucking *bitch!*"

Knievel had apparently not missed him so much as wanted to murder him. With a yowl and a flurry of claws, she bit and scratched her way down, snubbing Jed to wind her way around Redford's ankles. Looking far too smug as Jed assessed his wounds, she meowed ever so politely at Redford until he consented to pick her up. He did so with an expression of patient amusement and a little bit of affection, as he allowed the cat to rub her face all over his.

"She'll come around," he consoled Jed. "She's just angry."

Pouting openly, Jed just growled, "Yeah, whatever," and ushered them both to the door, hand on the small of Redford's back. "It's not my fault, you know." This was directed at Knievel with a mournful little look. "I was on a job! I called and everything!"

Redford just gave him a bemused look, cradling Knievel closer to his chest as she purred and happily kneaded holes into his shirt. "I'm surprised they even let you back into the building after that call."

Jed just smirked, arching an eyebrow. "Please. I'm a man who loves my cat. Ain't nothin' wrong with that at all." Sauntering out to the car, Jed opened the door for Redford and Knievel, kissing Red's cheek as he went and patting his ass, just for good measure. Getting behind the wheel, he started them toward home.

"You're going to have to forgive me, you know," he told the cat archly. "You know why?" Knievel yawned through his dramatic pause, but that didn't deter Jed. "Because I know where the good cat food is hidden. And because you can't operate the can opener."

Purring out a meow, Knievel wiggled her way out of Redford's arms and plopped herself in the middle of Jed's lap, chirping happily at him. Jed laughed, scratching behind her ear. "I knew that'd get you," he said, perfectly content in that moment. Redford's hand had stolen over to take his, and they were heading home, bruised and weary but richer than when they'd left. The job was over, everyone lived, they'd gotten paid. It was a good day.

The first thing Redford did when they got into the apartment was head straight for the kitchen, the familiar sounds of the coffee machine whirring to life. As Jed threw their bags into the bedroom and got Knievel settled, he heard Redford ask, "Do you think David and Victor will be okay?"

Flopping on the couch, Jed sprawled out gratefully. Nothing was better than his own couch. It was like a happy ending, only with all his clothes on. "Nah." He shrugged, wondering if he could summon a beer to appear by sheer will power. "But that's life. Most of the time, shit doesn't work. And David and Victor, they... it was just too hard, you know? Too much stuff was stacked against them. Even if it wasn't, the majority of the time, everything's going to come tumbling down anyway, for one reason or another."

Sometimes he forgot that Redford was still so innocent about the ways of humanity, that he'd formed most of his assumptions about how life worked by reading old storybooks in his isolated youth. Redford looked uncertain, his hands hovering over two mugs he'd been about to pick up. "Does that mean we won't work?"

Jed looked over at him, startled. "What? Jesus, Red, where the hell did you get that idea?"

"You said... the majority of the time, everything stops working," Redford replied quietly. "Is that why you flirt with other people?"

Mouth dropped open, Jed stared for a long moment, at a total loss for words. Gathering himself, he stood, crossing the apartment to Redford and resting his hands lightly on his upper arms. "That really what you think, Red?" he asked, concerned, searching his eyes. "Flirting is... shit, it's just something I do. Is it really bad?"

A faint hint of red flushed over Redford's cheeks. "It makes me jealous," he admitted. "And possessive. Because I want you all to myself."

Cupping his jaw, Jed shook his head. "You have me. I'm yours. I'm... shit, Red, I'm so sorry. Nobody else even means anything, you got that? Even if I'm an idiot and do whatever it is I do, it's not because I want anyone but you. You're it for me."

Redford smiled, lighting up with the expression. "Good. Because I want us not to be the majority. I want us to work for the rest of our lives."

Jed leaned in and kissed him softly, almost chastely. "We're not the majority," he agreed, wrapping his arm easily around Redford's waist. "You and me, babe." Touching his fingers to the slight bump of his dog tags and the whistle under Redford's shirt, he smiled, nudging his forehead against Redford's. "See? I'm right here. Always."

And really, wasn't that the point? Fuck if Jed knew why he flirted the way he did—all the shrinks in the world hadn't been able to figure it out, so he knew he sure as hell wouldn't be able to. But none of that mattered. He wanted to be with Redford, he wanted to come home to him every night. Wouldn't matter who flirted back, really, because the only person he really *needed* was right here.

"I love you," Jed whispered, kissing Redford's nose, his forehead, the sweet curve of his cheeks. "I love that you chase squirrels and get all growly, I love that sometimes I don't understand you at all, and I love that you're here, with me. That's all I really want, Red. Okay? I know I'm a shit a lot, I know you don't want to tell me stuff, but I'm here. I promise you that I'm always going to be here."

Redford got that face, that kind of squinted, pursed expression that he usually got when he was thinking about something that really mattered. He reached out and took Jed's hands, carefully tangling their fingers together. "I want to always be here too," he replied softly, meeting Jed's eyes. "So maybe I should talk about what Dr. Alona and I talked about in our sessions. About what's going on with my instincts. Because I was kind of not talking about it before." He squeezed Jed's hands apologetically.

For a moment, Jed just froze. It wasn't that he didn't want to hear. Fuck, he'd kind of been letting Redford do his own thing, playing the whole supportive-partner-whatever role and hoping against hope it was the right call. So yeah, he wanted to hear. Whatever was going on in that huge brain of Redford's, he wanted to be a part of it. But Jed didn't really do this: the conversations, the emotional bonding, the sharing and caring—that wasn't him. He ran away from shit like this. He hid behind lewd jokes and guns and he was pretty happy in that state.

But here was Redford with his big eyes, looking all trusting and vulnerable and like he really might have something important to say. So Jed didn't run away this time. He didn't change the subject. Taking a deep breath, he nodded, steeling himself. "Okay," he said, gripping Redford's hands in return. "So, what's up with the paper chewing?"

"I...." Redford looked down at their hands, clearly gathering his strength to say what he wanted to. He'd never had a problem with talking about emotional matters—it was just that, Jed knew, he'd never had much of an opportunity before. Anytime he'd wanted to talk and get a load off his shoulders, only the basement walls of his grandmother's house had been listening. "I'm really scared," Redford admitted.

And just like that, Jed's heart broke.

Hauling Redford in close, wrapping his arms around him, Jed shook his head. "Don't be," he said gruffly, scowling, as if by sheer willpower he could chase off anything that made Redford sound like that. "'Cause I'm here, you got that? I'm right here and there's not anything that's going to change that. So whatever's going on, we'll handle it. Promise me, okay? Don't go someplace I can't follow you."

"I don't want to," Redford mumbled, his chin tucked against Jed's shoulder. "But what if I do? I know I'm not just crazy, I know this stuff is happening because of what Filtiarn tried to do, but what if it doesn't stop? What if it just gets worse?" He drew in a deep breath and said very quietly, "What if it's not squirrels I kill next? What if it's you?"

In all his life, Jed hadn't loved one damn thing the way he loved Redford. It filled him up, it ached for how big the emotion was. How bone deep it'd burrowed. Jed didn't know how it was possible for one person to feel as much as he did, but Redford almost demanded it. He deserved a hell of a lot more than what one broken guy could offer him, but Jed tried, he did. He wanted to give Redford the whole damn world.

Pulling back, he studied Redford's face. Rubbing a thumb along the scars that etched across his cheeks, chasing the freckles hidden in his skin, Jed just shrugged. "Then you do," he murmured hoarsely. "And I die loving you."

That probably wasn't the answer that Redford wanted to hear. Redford got up off the couch, heading towards the bedroom. There was a rustle through their bags, and he came back with the silver knife in hand, a very determined look in his eyes. "I don't want to be the thing that kills you," Redford said firmly. "So you're going to carry this on you at all times. And if I attack you, you defend yourself."

There were a lot of things that scared Jed. Sharks were fucking terrifying. Seaweed, especially when it got all tangled up in his legs. He wasn't a huge fan of flying, and he didn't care what anyone told him, Tom Cruise was definitely a lizard person in disguise. Things that got normal people all shaky and afraid were normal to him—explosions, guns, blood. Death. That was just part of life. But this, right here, it was scarier than the idea of old Tommy riding a shark flying through a cloud of seaweed. Redford, his beautiful, innocent, amazing Redford, was holding a knife. And he was telling Jed to use it on him.

He couldn't get rid of the damn thing fast enough. Grabbing it, Jed walked straight over to the window, yanked the pane open and threw the knife as far as he could. Shaking, jaw tight, he stalked back over to Redford, eyes hard. "Do not," he said in short little staccato bursts of sound, pointing a trembling finger at him, "ever, *ever* do that again. You hear me? Weapons are not used on you. Sharp things do not go near you. And don't—" Cutting himself off, he grabbed Redford by the arms, hauling the man in for a desperate, bone-grinding hug. "Listen to me," Jed said urgently. "Please, please, listen to me. You can't say shit like that. I can't lose you. Not ever. Okay?"

He felt Redford's shoulders slump in defeat. If Jed could see his face, he knew Redford would probably be doing that bad dog expression he hated so much.

"But I'm allowed to lose you?"

Swallowing back that sour drop of fear, Jed closed his eyes, hanging on tighter than he'd thought possible. Just for a minute more he clung, still shaking, still so scared. Still wishing he could erase the image of Redford asking him to use that fucking knife.

"Everything I do is a risk, Fido," he managed, trying to hold his voice together. He let Redford go, just far enough that they could meet each other's eyes. "I run into places everyone else is getting the hell away from. I keep C4 in the fucking bathroom sink. That's my life. I've been half expecting death for so long I wouldn't know what it was like to stop planning my goddamn funeral."

Jed ran his fingers along Redford's cheek, a desperate plea in his gaze. "You are the one risk, the one thing I need. If you told me tomorrow I had to give up everything else, I would, if it meant I got you. Do you understand that?"

Redford nodded, although he still didn't look especially happy about the subject of Jed's eventual death. "I understand," he said softly. "But I also don't want you to just accept death if I wind up attacking you."

A quick frown crossed Jed's face. "I can't hurt you," he whispered. "Even if it means you hurt me. Please, don't ask me to do that."

"But you'd do everything you could to get away, right?" Redford looked so hopeful that the answer would be yes.

It wasn't something Jed wanted to think about. Leaving Redford to deal with his instincts alone was like giving up. It was walking away. Fuck, Jed hated this. If he could find Filtiarn and kill that bastard one more time for good measure, he would.

"Yeah," Jed sighed, giving in. "If I think I can't handle it, I'll run." The words were given painfully, his voice little more than a grudging mutter. Redford's eyes grew wide, probably at the fact that Jed had just admitted there might possibly be a point in his life where he wasn't completely in control. Jed's chin dropped, shoulders rounding defensively. "I'm not saying that will ever happen," he amended. "Just that I like my ass unchewed, so yeah, I'll haul it out of there if it comes to that. Which it won't."

Very slowly, a smile dawned over Redford's expression. He reached out, cupping Jed's cheek with his hand, lifting Jed's face to look at him. "Thank you," Redford said. "It... you don't know how much better it makes me feel to hear that."

Letting out a soft breath, Jed leaned his forehead against Redford's. "I'm not afraid of you," he murmured. "Wolfy you, bitey you, squirrel chasing you—I don't care. And even if I do have to run, Red, I'm always coming back."

"You like it when I get bitey," Redford replied, his smile growing into something a little more mischievous. "If I recall correctly."

Jed gave a loud snort, and his somber look was replaced with a wide, leering grin. "Fuck yes I do." Fingers slid up Redford's sides before, without warning, Jed dug in to tickle him. "Now I believe I'm going to take you to bed. High time for a proper homecoming, don't you think?"

He knew Redford's weak points by now—and that spot on his sides, just below his ribs, was the best place to make him howl in protesting laughter, shaking that serious, sad look off his face. "Jed! Don't you dare, you know how this ended last time." But instead of the guilt Redford had worn about biting Jed's hand and giving him a new scar, this time there was an amused light in his eyes.

"Yeah?" Jed smirked. "So why don't you catch me, Fido?" He took off running, darting around a yowling Knievel to hide behind the couch, laughing loudly when Redford vaulted over the furniture to give chase.

It was fucking good to be home.

BOOK ONE

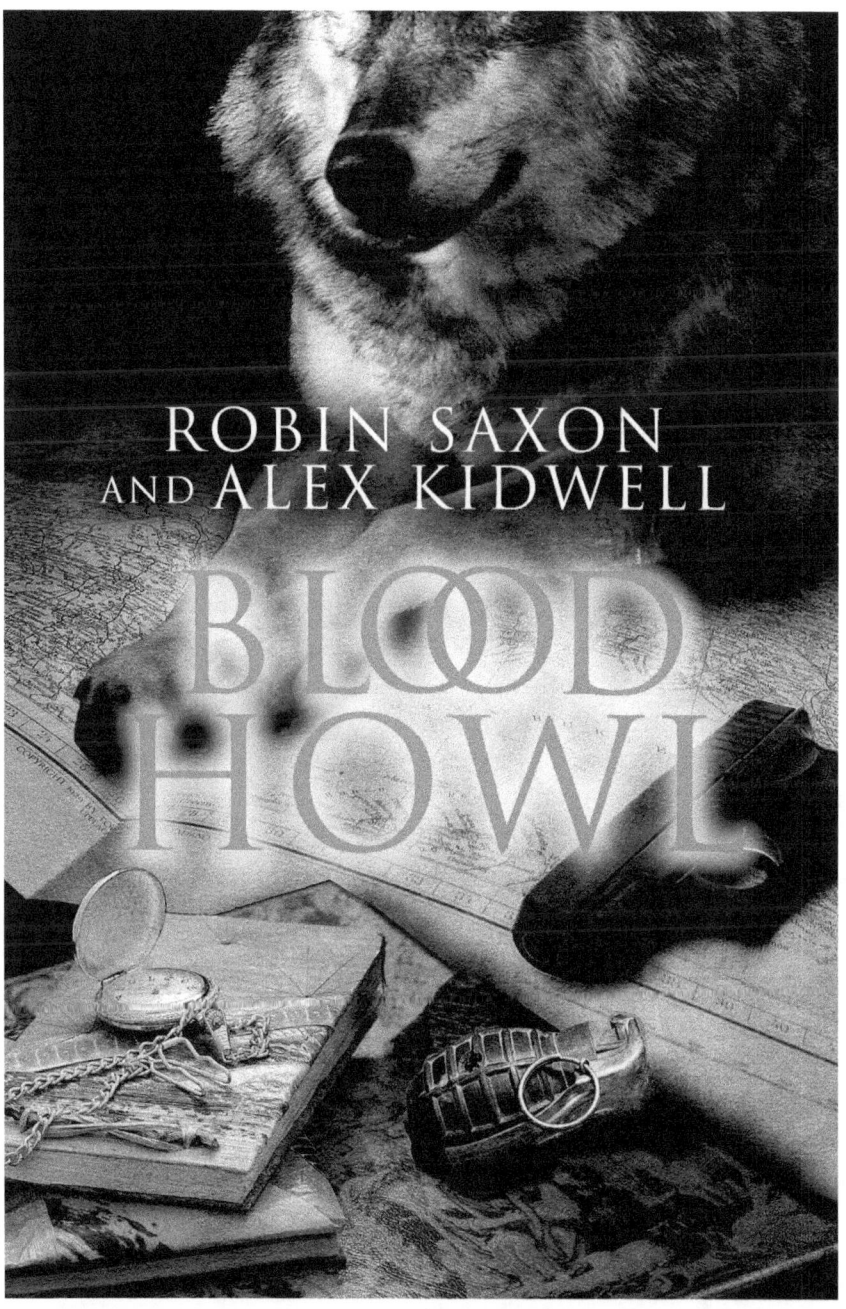

ROBIN SAXON
AND ALEX KIDWELL

BLOOD
HOWL

http://www.dreamspinnerpress.com

ROBIN SAXON, born and bred in New Zealand, lives in the Midwest with partner Alex Kidwell. When not writing or daydreaming about ideas for more stories, Robin is usually found playing MMOs like *World of Warcraft*, reading, drawing, and fussing over their cats, Starsky and Hutch.

In the rare times when she is not being pestered by their cats, Robin also listens to heavy metal music and enjoys everything from classics like Chaucer to urban fiction, as well as cooking vegetarian meals and inflicting them on Alex.

Visit Robin's blog, http://saxonkidwell.blogspot.com/, and Facebook, http://www.facebook.com/profile.php?id=100002277559369, or e-mail Robin at robin_saxon@yahoo.com.

ALEX KIDWELL, confirmed geek and bibliophile, lives in the Midwest with partner Robin Saxon. Alex relaxes by slaying dragons in MMOs, listening to music that can be sung along with in the shower, and enjoying BBC programming.

Other than writing, Alex enjoys knitting and is currently attempting to learn how to knit in the round. There are plans for a future of cat hats, which Alex is certain will go over well with household-running felines, Starsky and Hutch. Alex also indulges in too many cooking shows while only owning one pan.

Visit Alex's blog, http://saxonkidwell.blogspot.com/, and Facebook, http://www.facebook.com/profile.php?id=100002270719608, or e-mail Alex at alex.kidwell@yahoo.com.

Paranormal Romance from DREAMSPINNER PRESS

www.ingramcontent.com/pod-product-compliance
Lightning Source LLC
Chambersburg PA
CBHW050032030726

47506CB00001B/238